A League
of
Warriors

GARY ALBYN

In exercising his authorial right to express certain interpretive views on historical events, some inexactitudes or omissions may have occurred. While unintentional, the reader is reminded that *A League of Warriors* remains, essentially, a work of fiction. Although the story's protagonist and his nemesis are entirely fictional, the names of several supporting characters are indeed real: in many instances they have been authentically portrayed. The author is grateful for being given permission to incorporate them in the plot. Beyond that cast, any likenesses—be they names, characterizations, incidents or events—are entirely coincidental and the product of the author's imagination.

DEDICATION

For my wife, Cathy

CONTENTS

PROLOGUE

With age and looking at what has become of this country, I can say the whole war effort was not worth it. I personally regret the incidents. In hindsight, I realize that I should not have been involved in these acts in the first place ... acts that resulted in more than 100 innocent people losing their lives, but that is what war is like, young people are used to do stupid things ... I was young and I was used, when I look at what we were fighting, I realized that this is not it. It makes me very sad.

Nkululeko Norman Mabhena

Extracted from an article appearing in the February 2017 issue of *Zimbotoday.com*, Mabhena expresses regret over his role in the shooting down of two civilian passenger aircraft in Rhodesia in 1978 and 1979. The article coincided with the commemoration of the downing of the Viscount Umniati in 1979, the second of two such atrocities.

Mabhena was a former member of the Zimbabwe People's Revolutionary Army (ZIPRA).

GARY ALBYN

A LEAGUE OF WARRIORS

1

GREEN LEADER

Leaving a sinister clue to its skyward track, a wisp of gray vapor spiraled from the missile's glowing exhaust. Twenty two pounds is all it weighed—its lethal warhead much less. Astride the rocket, the reaper urged his mount toward its final rendezvous. It scorched through clear skies at over a thousand miles an hour.

It had a plane to catch.

Jinking like a cheetah after its quarry, the rocket hunted down its prey. *Target Acquired.* Unerringly guided by its infrared homing device, the Soviet-made surface-to-air missile slammed into the starboard wing of flight RH825. The Russians thought it amusing to refer to it as a revenge weapon.

Minutes before, the elegant silver-blue Vickers Viscount had lifted off from the Kariba runway. The four-engine civilian aircraft was named *Hunyani* after one of Rhodesia's large rivers. She was heading to Salisbury on the last leg of a triangular route that included Victoria Falls; one of the country's other popular tourist destinations. *Hunyani* hadn't been airborne for much longer than five minutes when she was struck by the Strela-2 missile.

Billy Mbudzi had chosen the name Stix as his war moniker. Early in his training, his Russian commissars had been impressed with his martial aptitude. Honoring the extra effort they put into his development, Stix didn't disappoint: moving quickly through the ranks, he was eventually promoted to platoon leader. While Stix had been groomed to shoulder greater responsibility, he had also been taught how to shoulder-fire the Russian-made Strela-2 missile.

After striking the plane, the small band of terrorists jubilantly gathered around their leader. He'd bagged a fine trophy. They had all seen the oily belch trailing behind the plummeting object: judging from its path, they estimated that they were close enough to the crash site to go and inspect their handiwork. Stix urged his men into a slow jog. He led them toward where he'd seen the plane disappear behind a range of distant hills.

Wrestling with his controls, the captain had no choice but to attempt a forced landing. He aimed his crippled plane for an open field. If it wasn't for a deep ditch halfway down the rutted cotton field, there may have been more survivors.

Initially, that is.

The *Hunyani* cart-wheeled and disintegrated as it struck the unseen ditch. Thirty eight passengers died instantly. Eighteen managed to survive the horrific impact. Dazed by the crash, they staggered around the wreckage. Organizing themselves according to their injuries, a small group of able-bodied survivors struck eastwards in search of help: they were to be spared the unfolding horror that awaited their fellow passengers.

Of the survivors that remained, most were incapable of putting much distance between themselves and the smoldering plane wreck. A few, fortunately, had managed to crawl to safety in the nearby bush. When Stix's band of thugs arrived to exalt over their trophy, those remaining survivors were exposed and vulnerable. Cowering in the nearby bush, the others were to remain hidden until help eventually arrived.

Ten hapless survivors weren't so blessed. They were callously gunned down by the gang of smirking degenerates.

The following day, on September 4, 1978, Joshua Nkomo gloated in front of the world's press. As the Marxist-backed commander of the ZIPRA army, he rejoiced over his cadres' role in the downing of the Air Rhodesia Vickers Viscount.

Commemorating the victims a few days after the tragedy, the Very Reverend JR Da Costa delivered an arching sermon in Salisbury's Anglican Cathedral. The pews were crammed with mourners.

Barely a minute into his homily, the reverend started shaming the reticent, the hypocrites and the close-mouthed leaders of the free world. "But are we deafened with the voice of protest from nations which call themselves 'civilized?' We are not! Like men in the story of the Good Samaritan, they 'pass by on the other side.' One listens for loud condemnation by Dr. David Owen, himself a medical doctor, trained to extend mercy and help to all in need. One listens, and the silence is deafening."

In measured tones, the Reverend's voice permeated the hallowed sanctuary. "One listens for loud condemnation by the President of the United States, himself a man from the Bible Baptist belt and again, the silence is deafening. One listens for loud condemnation by the Pope, by the Chief Rabbi, by the Archbishop of Canterbury, by all who love the name of God. Again, the silence is deafening."

While revenge was the furthest thought from the reverend's mind, it was uppermost in the minds of Rhodesia's military hierarchy.

Operation *Gatling*, launched forty-six days later, would avenge the despicable act.

The ageing fleet of Rhodesian Air Force Canberra bombers was getting tired. Like another gray hair on an old man's head, every stress-inducing maneuver was a reminder that they were slipping beyond their prime. After each sortie, aircraft technicians would scrutinize the 'G' forces recorded on each precious airframe. To a man, the squadron's pilots nursed their bombers in flight; they knew that even a single, hard 'G' pull-up after a bombing run could knock a dozen hours off the airframe's life.

Strapped in the pilot's seat, Squadron Leader Chris Dixon was flying northbound in the lead Canberra. The echelon of jets had left New Sarum Air Base less than an hour earlier and were heading toward Zambia. With the exception of a handful of planners back in Rhodesia, the only other people who knew their objective that day were those who were currently airborne.

At several predetermined markers, Mike Ronne called for minor adjustments to his commander's track; he was Dixon's navigator. A Sony cassette recorder had been wired into the Canberra's radio set. For the sake of posterity, it was to record the events of that momentous day.

Squadron Leader Dixon's call-sign for the mission was *Green Leader*. It was October 19, 1978 and Dixon was commanding the retaliatory raid into Zambia. Avenging the downing of the Viscount *Hunyani*, the mission was code-named *Operation Gatling*.

"Oh shit! I hope the fucking wings don't fall off!" It was a scorching day over Zambia and the heat exacerbated the turbulence during their low level flight. The medium-sized twin-engine bomber was being brutalized by the air pockets. Dixon was genuinely concerned.

Later that day, as dozens of elated pilots, navigators and airmen gathered around the cassette recorder back at New Sarum, they clearly detected the jolting effect of the turbulence on the aircrew's recorded voices.

"What's your speed?" asked the navigator.

"275—which is the 15 you wanted off. Do you want me to get down?" asked Dixon.

"Yes. You can go down a bit," the navigator paused for a moment. "Okay, we're on track, on time."

"Dead right—it's about a minute and a half before the Hunters leave us." The almost imperceptible change in the pitch of Dixon's voice was betraying his adrenaline response.

The air force's Hawker Hunter jets represented the country's primary strike capability. On Dixon's mark, they would peel off from the formation, streak toward their target and unleash their deadly arsenal.

Chris Dixon was heading up the first of three external raids planned for that day. The three concisely-coordinated attacks involved dozens of air force aircraft and helicopters, as well as hand-picked, specialized airborne units of the Rhodesian Army. Each one was timed so that waves of returning aircraft could refuel and rearm, then sortie back into battle. With its small air force, the Rhodesians had no choice but to plan it this way.

"There's not a peep out of tower so that's going to be superb." Dixon had been monitoring the Lusaka tower frequency and, at that stage, there had been no radio traffic from the Zambian controller; he was blissfully unaware that his nation's airspace had just been violated.

Earlier, while crossing the Zambezi River, the Rhodesian aircraft had dropped down low over in order to evade radar detection. "We won't have to talk to him," Dixon averred.

It was almost time for the Hunters to break formation and accelerate toward their own targets. "The Hunters will be going in about 50 seconds," said Ronne.

"Roger," replied Dixon.

"Go right another two degrees," instructed Ronne.

"Three zero eight?"

"*Ja.*" Rhodesians spoke a unique brand of slang. To outsiders, the patois could be both colorful and unintelligible. In this case, the navigator had affirmed his instruction in Afrikaans.

Just then, a new voice crackled over the net. The Zambian air traffic controller in Lusaka tower had just broadcast a message to an incoming Kenya Airways flight.

"That's the bloody tower," Dixon cursed. He knew he'd have to make contact with Lusaka tower at some stage of the operation.

Westlands had once been a bountiful farm. It was located a mere ten miles north-east of Lusaka, the capital of Zambia. Sympathetic to the cause, the Front Line States bordering Rhodesia had openly backed the liberation efforts of the communist-inspired ZIPRA and ZANLA armies. The so-called 'freedom fighters' of both armies were engaged in a vicious war against Rhodesia.

ZIPRA had been gifted Westlands Farm by their Zambian hosts and had transformed it into their main headquarters and training base. They had named it Freedom Camp. Cozying up to their hosts proved to be strategically beneficial for the ZIPRA command. Ultimately, it would be instrumental in the war's final outcome. But ZIPRA's leaders, lulled by their proximity to the city of Lusaka, believed the Rhodesians would never be so brazen as to strike on the outskirts of a sovereign nation's capital.

On this occasion, they badly underestimated the resolve of their foes.

The Rhodesians' surprise assault not only targeted Westlands Farm, but two other camps in Zambia: Mkushi Camp, about an hour's flight due north of the Rhodesian border, and CGT—Central Guerrilla Training Camp—at Chikumbi, about fifteen minutes' flying time into Zambia. The three raids were to be carried out in quick succession.

Striking deep into the heart of enemy territory was a bold endeavor for the Rhodesians. Up to that point the country's military hierarchy preferred to limit their cross-border raids to targets located close to the international boundary.

Like his pilot, Mike Ronne was an expert at his craft. His navigational skills were amongst the best. Lying prostrate in the nose of the aircraft, Ronne noted both their time and their ground position. Toggling his intercom switch, he called out to Dixon, "Okay. Go Hunters. Go!"

"Blue Section Go. Blue Section Go," responded Dixon. Flying in tight formation off the Canberra's wings, the three

Hunters broke away on *Green Leader's* orders.

"Okay, they were spot on time," said the navigator.

"That's okay. Roger—270 knots. You uh got it now. Shit, they only accelerated bloody quickly," Dixon marveled at the speed at which the Hunters had accelerated away from their formation.

It was just before 08h30 local time and the ZIPRA troops were about to muster on the parade ground.

Two hundred kilometers south of Lusaka, a number of Rhodesian military personnel clustered around the radio set in the Joint-Operations Command tent at the Kariba Forward Air Field. JK, as he was known to his friends, was one of them. He'd already donned his flying suit: if a Rhodesian plane was shot down over Zambian territory, he was to immediately board his twin-engine Lynx aircraft and initiate a search and rescue. To a man, everyone prayed that he wouldn't be called upon to fulfill that role.

Somewhere near the Zambian capital the sleek Hunters were prowling overhead. They were making their final preparations before swooping down on the camp.

After parting company with the Hunters, Dixon altered course so as to be able to approach his target with the sun behind him. His palms were clammy inside his chamois flying gloves.

"Little dam coming up. We're drifting port. Go to the right. Two-eight-three. Two-eight-four." Ronne gave his pilot the necessary corrections.

"Two-eight-four? Or two-eight-five?" asked Dixon.

"D'you want to do a kink, sir, to get it spot on?" Even in the adrenaline-fueled environment of a combat bombing mission, the navigator deferred to Dixon's seniority.

"Tell me when to roll out," said the pilot.

"Go left. Two-eight-two."

"Roger, coming up to two minutes to run. Two-eight-two. Got two minutes to run. Perfect." As the tension grew Dixon's voice rose an octave.

"Go left a bit. Steady."

"Two-seven-eight?" asked the pilot.

"Two-eight-two!" By this stage their pulses had reached 140 and their breathing rates sharp and shallow. Their dialogue was also leaner.

"A school coming up—acceleration point. Two-eight-two is the heading," Dixon called out.

"Okay. We should start accelerating now," advised Ronne.

"Roger. Shall I go?"

"Just leave it in case they are going to be a bit late—to the minute." The navigator had advised his pilot to delay their acceleration fractionally in case the Hunters weren't on target at the allocated time. As it turned out, the Hunters' timing had been perfect.

"Okay," said Dixon.

Ronne counted down in his head. "Accelerate!"

With Squadron Leader Chris Dixon at the controls and Mike Ronne navigating, the Canberra bomber unleashed its fiery payload upon the terrorist training camp at Westlands Farm.

After the breathless lead-in and the euphoria created by the bombing run, the crew's attention now turned to the next task at hand.

Altering course slightly, Dixon pointed his nose toward the nearby Lusaka airport. "Just check the tape recorder while you're there. Otherwise just leave it." The pilot wanted to make sure that the ensuing exchange would be captured for a subsequent time.

"Okay. Still turning," said the navigator.

"Roger. Okay. Let me try and get this spiel off," said Dixon.

"Lusaka Tower, this is *Green Leader*. How do you read?" Dixon's first attempt at contact went unanswered. "Lusaka Tower, this is *Green Leader*." Dixon's insistence was more apparent on his second attempt.

"Station calling tower?" The controller enquired apprehensively.

"Lusaka Tower this is *Green Leader*. This is a message for the station commander at Mumbwa from the Rhodesian Air Force. We are attacking the terrorist base at Westlands Farm. This attack is against Rhodesian dissidents and not against Zambia. Rhodesia has no quarrel, repeat, no quarrel with Zambia or her security forces. We therefore ask you not to intervene or oppose our attack. However, we are orbiting your airfield now and are under orders to shoot down any Zambian Air Force aircraft which does not comply with this request and attempts to take off. Did you copy all that?" Dixon had read from a prepared script.

"Copied," answered tower.

For a brief period that Thursday morning, Zambia was at the complete mercy of a very determined foe. Meanwhile, civilian air traffic had started to build-up, both on the ground and in the air.

"Rhodesian Air Force, 118.1," ventured the controller.

"Go ahead," answered Dixon, still circling above the airport.

"Can you confirm we can let our civil aircraft take-off from here? You have no objection?" pleaded the tower controller.

"Roger. We have no objection there, but I advise you for the moment to stand-by on that. I request that you hang on for a short while—half an hour or so," instructed Dixon.

"I copy. Can you please keep a listening watch on this frequency so we can ask you what we want to ask?" pleaded the controller clumsily.

"Roger will do," said Dixon.

"What do I call you?" By this stage the tower controller was undeniably affable.

"Green Leader!"

Within a few hours the Rhodesian planes had been turned around and were heading right back into battle. There were still two more bases to destroy. Being located so far from their enemy's border, ZIPRA's high command at Mkushi had reasoned that they were less vulnerable to an air assault from

Rhodesia, and had chosen to install fewer anti-aircraft guns than their more southerly-located comrades. Based on this intelligence, the Rhodesian Air Force planners had decided to deploy their slightly slower Lynxes in an ancillary role.

During the Mkushi raid, JK held a wide circuit over the battlefield. The fighting was intense as he watched wave-after-wave of heli-borne troops inserted into position.

Mission accomplished, he turned his Lynx onto a southerly bearing and headed back to Rhodesia. En route, he noticed a suspicious-looking encampment located off his port wing. He knew that the third and final attack on CGT Chikumbi was imminent, but wasn't aware that such a formidable-looking camp existed in this part of the country. Re-checking his position, JK made sure that he wasn't perhaps mistaking this new camp for CGT Chikumbi.

As the Rhodesians were soon to discover, this particular camp had materialized out of nowhere: it had never been mentioned in any of the pilots' mission briefings.

Unbeknownst to the Rhodesians, they had a traitor in their midst. After being tipped off about the imminent raid, the guerrillas had hastily relocated their camp; and JK had unwittingly identified their new location.

As soon as he landed back at Kariba, JK notified his air force superior of this fortuitous discovery. The news was quickly conveyed to the Commander of Rhodesia's Combined Operations, Lieutenant General Peter Walls. The general was never far from the action; he was there to oversee *Operation Gatling* from the command tent based at Kariba airport. He listened intently while JK described the new camp he'd just discovered.

Less than an hour later, as the third and final assault was launched on CGT Chikumbi camp, the pilots circling overhead reported that the camp was deserted.

2

SIX SQUADRON

Attacking his large blackboard, the math teacher ignored the knock at his classroom door. A light sprinkling of chalk-powder covered his hand and forearm. The students were undoubtedly in awe of Mr. Ferreira's prodigious intellect, but they sure did welcome the possibility of an interruption to his brain-warping lesson. Furtively glancing toward the open door, they willed their teacher to acknowledge his guest.

Billowing resplendent in one of her customary marocain dresses, the colorful bursar was quaintly oblivious to her advancing years. She wasn't quite yet ready to risk a second knock. Instead, she waited patiently for Mr. Ferreira to finish his impressive exposition.

Triumphantly underscoring his opus with four bold lines, the teacher scrawled the letters QED in the bottom corner of the blackboard. A puzzlement of formulae adorned the vast board.

"Yes Mrs. Norton, how can I help you today?" Mrs. Norton hovered self-consciously at the door. With a cupped hand held close to her bosom, she gestured pleadingly for Mr. Ferreira to come outside to speak to her privately. "Keep the noise down," ordered the teacher as he strode toward the door.

Dax Hunter was a scholar at Prince Edward High School in Salisbury. He had only just turned sixteen. Being summoned to the headmaster's office was never good. Being summoned during a lesson didn't bode well at all. His mind raced as he turned the corner and headed down the long corridor toward the main admin block. Dax had no idea what awaited him. He wasn't aware of any recent misdemeanor or tomfoolery that might have invited the headmaster's wrath. Steeling himself, Dax knocked on the door and waited. Ordinarily the boys would hear the disciplinarian's booming voice ordering them inside. Instead, Dax heard the scrape of a chair followed by the sound of muffled footsteps. *Must be a mistake,* he thought.

The headmaster's usual stern appearance—the only one familiar to the boys—had been replaced by a look of desolation. From the man's demeanor, Dax knew that the news was grave.

Dead ... both of them.

His mother and father had been blown up by a landmine buried on one of the dirt roads that connected their farm with the small rural town of Karoi. The devastating news heralded the end of Dax's prelapsarian youth.

What had started as a series of intermittent farm attacks by insurgents a decade earlier had now escalated into a full-blown war. Unshakable in the early part of the war, the resolve of the Rhodesian forces was slowly being undermined by the ever-swelling numbers of their adversaries. Appeasement politicians across the globe were also artfully plotting the country's demise. Despite the odds—and with a resilience reminiscent of their forebears—the Rhodesians continued to fight like lions.

Dax Hunter's roots ran deep in this warrior league. A product of pioneer stock, his recent ancestors hailed from South Africa. His great-grandparents had settled in the farming community near Tengwe and had hewn a productive tobacco farm from the virgin bush. In succession, Dax's grandparents, and later his own parents, had further developed the farm.

Reminiscent of the era, the Hunter's had run their farm—in particular their labor force—with an embracing style of paternalism. The Hunter's laborers were unfalteringly loyal. Despite great personal danger, it wasn't uncommon for trusty farm laborers to secretly update 'Boss' Hunter about activity in the rural community: communist insurgents were forever trying to indoctrinate the locals. Spreading their Marxist ideologies was a crucial step toward charming the local inhabitants.

It was his forebears' legacy—and Dax's birthright—that one day he too would inherit the farm. But never under these circumstances.

Over seven hundred people attended the Hunters' funeral service. Many of the mourners were from the farm's loyal workforce. Dax's rage burned deep. With tears burning his eyes, he made a graveside oath: he promised that he'd avenge his parents' deaths.

With an ever-increasing number of insurgents pouring across Rhodesia's borders, the conflict was intensifying on a daily basis. The demands of war were taking their toll, not just on the soldiers, but also the wider civilian population. The duration of compulsory military service was forever being extended and the regular call-up of auxiliaries was becoming more frequent.

Naturally, the strain was also starting to take its toll on the country's economy. Not even the nation's farmers—vital to the robust, agri-centric economy—were exempt.

Like every other farmer, Dax's late father had also been eager to contribute to the war effort. Being a keen private pilot, he'd dutifully volunteered to fly for the Police Reserve Air Wing: this motley bunch of patriotic flyers was affectionately known as the PRAWs.

'Boss' Hunter had been an infectiously sociable man. With his gregarious nature—and a slew of new aviator friends—it wasn't long before the front lawn of his farm had become an impromptu landing pad for the helicopter gunships of the Rhodesian Air Force. Dax's mother always seemed to have a freshly-baked cake available for her unscheduled guests. For the visiting crew and passengers it was a brief, even genteel respite from the harsh realities of the Rhodesian Bush War. For Dax, it had been the perfect introduction to the intoxicating allure of helicopter flight.

He was never sure whether the air force hierarchy back in Salisbury knew of these unauthorized stops or not, but he suspected they weren't altogether sanctioned.

With their parents gone, the Hunter boys' halcyon days were over.

'Boss' Hunter was himself a product of Prince Edward Boys' High School in Salisbury. As far back as he could remember, Dax had been preparing for his chance to go to this acclaimed school.

One could never tell with Prince Edward boys if they were blissfully unaware of their school's soaring reputation; whether they were endearingly modest about it; or just downright smug. Either way, for a brief time, this renowned school probably produced more sporting world champions, leading academics and international business leaders than any other on the planet.

Such talismanic influences must surely have rubbed off on the boys. Through its heady blend of reputation and ethos, PE's scholars could be justifiably proud of their school's legacy.

Dax Hunter, like so many of the boys who'd passed through its hallowed corridors, was a cut-above. He struck an imposing figure; even before his sixteenth year he'd reached six feet. 'Boss' Hunter had been a dedicated farmer and hard task-master: he insisted that Dax and his two younger brothers do their fair share of work around the farm. Naturally, the long days and demanding nature of the work contributed to Dax's overall physical development. He was no slouch in the classroom either. His academic results were well above average and he excelled at math and the sciences.

The eldest Hunter boy bore the loss of his parents with a worrying stoicism. After the funeral everyone expected him to fulminate; instead, he appeared to suppress his grief. It took several months before his circle of concerned friends noticed the return of his indomitable spirit.

Hunter found his escape on the sports field. Whatever the game, he was driven to win. His warrior spirit was best assuaged when the sport was confrontational: rugby was his favorite. Through a combination of his grueling farm work and his participation in a variety of sports, the blond haired boy developed a rangy, yet useful physique. He was also a natural leader: whatever the team sport, Dax was invariably made captain. In his second-last year at high school Dax was selected to play at flank for the Rhodesian Schools rugby side. He made the position his own and was re-selected in his final year. He was also appointed as the school's Deputy Head Boy in that same year.

With compulsory military service awaiting every school leaver, a fair degree of deliberation went into choosing which branch each boy would apply for. Unsurprisingly, Dax's heart was set on becoming a military pilot. But he'd first have to make it through the intensive selection procedure. Typically, the air force's annual pilot training program would attract as many as three thousand applicants, but there was only ever room for eighteen cadets on each intake. It was indeed a tough course to get onto. Everyone except Dax knew he was a shoo-in for the next intake. In the two weeks after his final interview, Dax waited anxiously for the news that he hoped would shape his future.

After successfully completing his final 'A' Level exams at Prince Edward School, Dax learned that he'd been accepted onto the air force's exacting pilot training program.

Standing around and waiting in the open car park of the Salisbury railway station, the candidates for the new pilot training course were starting to reacquaint themselves. Many friendships had already been forged during the rigorous selection phase that had taken place over the preceding four months. So this was it: if this group of young men could navigate the punishing eighteen month course, they'd earn the right to wear the air force's coveted wings. A handful amongst this group had opted to train as air traffic controllers—for the first six months of the course they would undergo exactly the same training and preparation as the aspirant pilots.

There was no sign of any air force personnel around the car park. Dax struck-up a conversation with his old friend Holloway. He'd attended a rival school close to Prince Edward and was a worthy opponent on the rugby field. The two friends were bantering on the pavement when a loudly-barked order interrupted their conversation. A neatly dressed corporal had materialized from nowhere and started berating the gaggle of young men. With unmistakable authority he ordered the group to form two rows of twelve and then stand to attention. Trying to count the number in each row, the men jostled clumsily. The fiery-eyed corporal belittled the cadets' pathetic efforts. "From this time forward, you shit-gobbling bunch of retards belong to *me,*" the corporal's stamp of ownership was emphatic. He seemed oblivious to the hundreds of gaping commuters that crisscrossed the car park. Clearly offended, a few stern-faced mothers quickly hustled their sons and daughters out of earshot. "I am your mother, father, priest and god and I am here to turn you into something that resembles real men. Drop and give me twenty." His voice boomed out across Manica Avenue in downtown Salisbury.

Twenty-four bewildered men, most still in their teens, knew the drill. Down on the blistering pavement, the suited-and-booted group attempted to do their push-ups. Some fared better than others. Their uncoordinated efforts did not impress their new drill instructor. "You are shark shits, every last one of you. No, you are lower than shark shit ... you are shark shit shadow. Now, get back down and on my count, one-a, two-a, three-a ..."

And so the notion of a revered, cravat-wearing fighter pilot was forever dashed by Mad Max; the pilot course's new drill instructor. The man made an immediate and forceful impression on the cadets: it was obvious to all that he was someone you wouldn't trifle with. The muscles in his forearms were like knotted hemp. Like an old dock fighter, his shoulders sloped down from a pugnacious head. His knuckles were grotesquely disfigured and his eyes—glinting like polished flint—bore through each cadet with malevolent intent. In private, the recruits later joked that Jim Croce must surely have been writing about Mad Max when he penned the lyrics to his hit song, *Leroy Brown*.

The next eighteen months of Dax's life were the most demanding he'd ever experienced. His squadron's motto— *Aspire to Achieve*—couldn't have been more apt as the dedicated corps of instructors attempted to forge skilled airmen out of clumsy novices. Every day offered a new challenge; and every day the cadets' flying skills improved bit-by-bit.

The air force's prestigious Sword of Honor was an accolade reserved for the most deserving of the pilot cadets. Only the most gifted amongst them was capable of consistently maintaining high scores in both the theory and practical components of the program. While every pilot training course produced a top student, not every top student received the coveted sword. In order to convince the specially-convened merits board, the recipient's performance had to be exemplary throughout the course. Bestowing the venerated sword was no trivial decision.

In August 1978, eighteen months after commencing their course, the cadets of Dax's intake stood to attention on the parade square at Thornhill Air Base: they were about to be presented with their wings. Crisply turned-out in his Number Ones, Dax saluted the Rhodesian Prime Minister, Mr. Ian Douglas Smith. Along with his coveted wings, he'd just been presented with the Sword of Honor. *This is for you, mom and dad.*

Two months later, on October 19, New Sarum Air Base was abuzz. Over at the last hangar, the aspiring 7 Squadron helicopter pilots knew something was brewing. Although they weren't privy to the details, it was obvious to them that a big external raid was underway. Since a number of their own helicopter instructors had been sequestered to fly in the raid, flight training had been temporarily suspended without explanation. But the young pilot officers knew why.

The formulae and technical diagrams in Dax's text book swam before his eyes. Mastering the theory of autorotative flight would just have to wait. Dax's mind was wholly preoccupied. Knowing that a dangerous external raid was underway right at that moment was proving to be too distracting. Throughout the course of the morning, and into the early part of the afternoon, he'd been listening-out for the returning bombers of 5 Squadron. Having counted their departures and arrivals, it was only after the last aircraft touched down that he was eventually able to relax.

"Come lads, we've been invited over to the 5 Squadron hangar." Barrel was in a jovial mood. He was Dax's boss and the senior helicopter instructor at 7 Squadron.

Unsurprisingly, spirits were high inside the 5 Squadron crew room. Small clusters of airmen gathered around each of the Canberra pilots to hear their personal account of the external raid into Zambia. Peter, the senior officer in the room, clapped his hands to get everyone's attention. "Okay everybody, gather around. We've got Chris' cassette wired up and ready to roll. I think you're all going to like this." Barely hours before, Chris Dixon had led the early morning raid on Westlands Farm outside Lusaka.

Everyone leaned forward, straining to hear the dialogue between the Lusaka air traffic controller and mission leader, Chris Dixon.

In response to the controller's question: 'what do I call you?' the room erupted when they heard Chris' curt reply, *'Green Leader!'*

For a short time that morning—forever immortalized as *Green Leader*—Dixon and his band of intrepid Rhodesians had owned the skies above Zambia. Along with every other person in the crew room that day, Dax was proud to be a Rhodesian.

3

THE BUCHAREST AFFAIR

Anton Morozov had always idolized Lenin. His wife, ever wary of antagonizing him, nodded meekly as he returned from the registry office bearing the birth certificate of their first-born. She knew what it said, but she held her tongue. She knew better.

> NAMES: *Vladimir Ilyich Ulyanov* SURNAME: *Morozov*
> SEX: *male* PLACE OF BIRTH: *Sverdlovsk, USSR.*
> DOB: *5th January, 1959*

Her son was to bear Lenin's name for the rest of his life. Anastasia was appalled.

Anton clumped his boots noisily on the wooden floor. "That toothless bitch at the registry office smiled when I showed her my son's name. 'Comrade,'" he affected the old crone's reedy voice, "'you name your boy after the Motherland's hero, huh? And your family name, Morozov, it means *bitter frost*, no?'" He dropped the pathetic imitation. "That fucking bitch knows a good name when she sees one." Anastasia pretended to listen, but continued busying herself at the faux wood countertop of their sparse kitchen. She hoped Anton hadn't seen her trembling hands as she fumbled with the lid of her East German powdered milk tin.

Vladimir Morozov, or simply Vlad to his father, grew up sullen and friendless. God knew she tried, but Anastasia just couldn't bond with her son. Though she performed her maternal duties well enough, there remained a perpetual disconnect between mother and child. Even at a young age she could tell that the boy was superficial and manipulative.

Like her mother before her, Anastasia was a battered wife. Five years earlier, naïve and pregnant, the seventeen year old had readily accepted Anton's chivalrous proposal. She believed it was the fairytale escape from her own domestic hell. But, just like her long-suffering mother, she too began to bear the brunt of her husband's labyrinthine complexes. She had miscarried twice before going full term with Vlad.

By the time he was six years old, Anastasia was convinced that Vlad was possessed. Embodied in her son, she recognized all his father's disturbing pathologies. At the age of eight, Vladimir had started delighting in his mother's frequent beatings. By age ten—already physically stronger than any of his peers—the boy began assaulting his own mother. Caught in a desperate cycle between the two men in her life, Anastasia found it impossible to appeal to either.

In late 1969, a few months before his eleventh birthday, Vlad's father was summoned to his son's school. One of the teachers had brought a caged canary to class to show the children. In that hard-bitten environment, the notion of keeping a small bird as a pet was inconceivable to most of the children. Vladimir had found it most disagreeable: during his lunch break he'd amputated the bird's legs with a pair of scissors.

It was the last straw. Without exception, every one of the boy's teachers had witnessed some-or-other display of aberrant behavior. With the authority vested in him by the tightly-run state education system, the senior teacher advised Anton Morozov that his son was to be transferred to one of the so-called auxiliary schools outside Sverdlovsk.

Cowed but surviving—and largely bereft of emotion—

Anastasia had been elated.

Two troublesome years passed. Bogdan, the head of the auxiliary school to which Vladimir had been sent, was first-and-foremost a disciplinarian. But even he had to acknowledge that he couldn't contain the boy's mulishness. Vladimir's worrisome characteristics troubled the teacher. His behavior was inscrutable. His mannerisms, or those that he chose to display, were unsympathetic. The boy glowered perpetually.

Bogdan's patience eventually ran out. Having endured two years of the boy's remorseless behavior, it was time to be rid of him.

Feigning an interest in Vladimir's formative development, he called upon Stanislaw, an old teaching friend. Rising through the state system, Stanislaw had been promoted to Head of Recruitment at the famed Suvorov Military School of Sverdlovsk. Renowned for the grooming of future army officers, the Suvorov Military Schools had developed a fine reputation since their inception during World War Two. With an emphasis on discipline and military subjects, it was the ideal boarding school to send the troubled teenager. Bogdan had pleaded with his old friend to enroll Vladimir.

But Bogdan was also shrewd. He'd spared Stanislaw much of the detail surrounding the boy's delinquencies. When the small bus from Suvorov arrived to fetch Vladimir from the auxiliary school, Bogdan was there to bid him farewell. The teacher wished him luck as he climbed aboard the drab colored bus. Although Bogdan had been sure to paint a rosy picture of Vlad's prospects, he remained fearful of the boy's penchant for retribution. He felt uneasy as the bus pulled away.

During his last two years at the Suvorov academy, Morozov became the school's light heavyweight boxing champion. He was also a feared enforcer on the ice rink. At six foot three, and supremely strong, he could've excelled at either, or both. But Morozov's personality was better-suited to the brutality of the ring: *let the golubye play hockey*, he goaded his fellow cadets.

Vladimir's old boxing coach had gone to his grave with a well-kept secret. He'd quickly figured out that his protégé had the skill and aggression to drop any opponent in the first round. But instead of delivering the knock-out blow, Morozov used to toy with his opponents. In small measures, he'd inflict just enough punishment to ensure that his opponent was capable of staggering out for another grueling round. It didn't take long before Morozov's coach had identified the perversion for what it was. Although he'd figured it out, the coach never told anyone: he feared as much for his own safety as that of Morozov's opponents.

Ample food—coupled with compulsory gymnasium during his four year stay—had added sixty pounds of useful muscle to Morozov's frame. Approaching his eighteenth birthday, the boy had excelled at the military academy. Given his overall results, plus his martial traits, the teenager had earned the right to apply for the military unit of his choosing.

After graduating, Morozov was given an opportunity to try out for the respected *Devyatki*—the Ninth Chief Directorate of the KGB. They were responsible for providing bodyguards for the leaders and families of the CPSU—the Communist Party of the Soviet Union. Other duties included asset and site protection of some of the USSR's most secret installations: nuclear launch sites; the highly-classified Moscow VIP subway system; as well as the secret underground town known as Ramenki 43.

Morozov excelled in the *Devyatki* and quickly cemented a reputation as being a skilled professional. Once word of his prowess had filtered through to the KGB hierarchy, the agent was offered a dream posting. Who could refuse an opportunity to join the Personal Protection Branch for Soviet Dignitaries?

Whilst on assignment to the USSR embassy in Bucharest, Morozov was tasked with guarding the wife of the Commissar of Russian Antiquities. Somewhat younger than her husband, the attractive woman had been invited to join her spouse as an official envoy: with the soul of a debutante, she enlivened many a boring state banquet.

Apart from Morozov, the small entourage included a handmaid for the commissar's wife, the commissar's own personal bodyguard, as well as his personal *aide de camp*—a retired major in the Soviet Army.

After the second day of official duties, the commissar's wife dispatched her handmaid on a prolonged shopping errand. On the pretext of not feeling well, she then sent her husband to the opening of the new State Opera House with just his own bodyguard in tow.

Presuming Morozov's discretion, she called him to her hotel door. "Comrade, my husband's *aide de camp* will be coming up shortly. He will be assisting me with some pressing administrative duties."

Pressing indeed. The implacable guard nodded once.

Despite the heavy doors, the sound of their lustful symphonies was unmistakable. Morozov thought their behavior was contemptible: instead of concentrating on his duties, he began to engage his scheming mind.

Over the following two days, Morozov initiated a series of conversations with the major. By the third day he believed he'd won the man's confidence. It was time to start laying the trap. "Comrade, forgive me, but I need to applaud you."

"Applaud me?" asked the *aide de camp*. He was sufficiently self-centered to seek out further affirmation. "Applaud me for what, comrade?"

"Your dalliance with the commissar's wife. I'm sorry comrade, but the two of you aren't exactly being discreet." Morozov nudged the major's arm and winked. "You must've known that I was aware of your tryst?" he whispered conspiratorially. "You are a stallion, comrade. I am proud of you. Rest assured, your secret is safe."

Morozov was nobody's friend, but he sensed the major was starting to think of him that way. His plan was working. Each day, as opportunity presented, he continued playing the conceited major. Falsifying his own allegiance, he told the *aide de camp* that he was actually a disaffected communist, more inclined to listen to evil western rock music than defend Marx's convoluted ideologies. The more Morozov shared, the more voluble the major became.

Knowing that even lowly hotel cleaners could be Romanian spies, Morozov had instructed the major to hold his tongue whenever they were present. "Our private conversations must remain exactly that, comrade." It all added to the major's trust in his new friend. Any time a hotel staff member appeared in the corridor, the two men feigned a conspiratorial silence. *He's bonding. He's falling for my ruse.* Morozov was wholly satisfied with his plan.

"You know comrade, you and me, we are very similar in so many ways," said the major. "I too feel no love for Mother Russia. I am a Cossack on my mother's side. She told me after my father died in the Battle of Stalingrad. She had lied to him their entire time together—he never knew of her real roots. My mother's people, you know, they were systematically repressed, and often eliminated during the Soviet's policy of Decossackization. My mother's family lost everything … her two brothers even disappeared mysteriously and their bodies never discovered." The major fell silent for a moment.

Morozov seethed with xenophobic hatred. *A fucking Cossack!* Despite his revulsion, he encouraged the major to continue.

"The pogroms, the warped efforts at social engineering, the genocide and elimination of undesirable social groups: it's fucked up, comrade. It's all fucked up," lamented the major.

The intricately-carved doors of the presidential suite swung open. The cuckold smiled genially at the two men standing in the corridor and bade them good morning. Standing behind her husband, the woman risked a flirtatious peek in the direction of the major. Morozov clenched his jaw in anger.

Later that afternoon, while attending to private matters involving the repatriation of gothic artifacts to the State Russian Museum in Leningrad, the commissar left his wife in the capable care of her bodyguard and his own *aide de camp*.

Like a Queen's Guard outside Buckingham Palace, Morozov stood rigidly outside his client's room. A short distance away the elevator bell chimed as the doors swished open. Striding out confidently, the *aide de camp* approached the suite. He winked at Morozov and knocked discreetly. Cracking the door open no more than an inch, the Commissar's wife peered out into the corridor. She hurriedly ushered the major inside.

Beyond the closed doors, Morozov detected a muffled exchange between the two lovers. Not for the first time, the major reassured the woman that her bodyguard's discretion was guaranteed.

Since commencing this detail, Morozov had paid close attention to the room cleaners' schedule. He checked his watch. Apart from the improbable arrival of room service, no one else was expected to visit the presidential suite for at least an hour.

Morozov knew he had to time his entry to perfection. If he left it too late, the lovers would have both been caught *inflagrante delicto*: that would have been awkward for him to explain.

Beyond the closed doors, all had fallen silent. Morozov steeled himself. He'd have to act quickly. The bodyguard knew the door was locked. Bracing his shoulder, he crashed through the woodwork like a wrecking ball. Splinters flew as the lock succumbed to the force of his entry.

Still down on her knees, the diplomat's wife let out a shrill scream. The major sat up and blinked disbelievingly. He fumbled with his fly.

Morozov strode over to the wife and silenced her scream with a stinging slap. She was about to unleash an inglorious rebuke when she saw the look in his eyes. His cold stare was enough to silence any further protest.

Gathering his wits, the major sprung forward to defend the woman. With the four fingers of his right hand held together and his thumb extended at a right angle, Morozov's hand shot out toward the major's throat. He drove the web into the major's Adam's apple. His victim convulsed. He tried to scream but his thyroid cartilage had disintegrated under the force of the blow. Limp from the pain, incapable of breathing, and certainly unable to defend himself, the major offered no resistance. Morozov spun him around. Across the room, the major saw his own reflection in the mirror. He gasped grotesquely. The terrified wife was helpless. Morozov reached around his victim's neck with his left arm. Gripping the Cossack's right shoulder, he pressed down tightly on the man's chest. Bringing his right arm up, he used his forearm and bicep to envelop the lower part of the major's face and jaw. Morozov took hold of the top of his victim's head with his right hand, then rapidly twisted the major's shoulder forward with the other. Using a counter-rotating movement, he wrenched the major's head with his right arm. The man's neck snapped like dry kindling. Morozov pushed the limp body away from him. The major collapsed face down on the floor. He looked over toward the woman. A scream had snagged in her throat

Fourteen seconds since crashing through the door. Morozov didn't have much time to spare.

Among his many aberrations, Morozov was an avowed misogynist. He felt nothing but revulsion for the commissar's wife. He would've gladly dispensed with his ward but knew there would be too many questions. Besides, her death would've reflected poorly on his record. Morozov took two threatening paces toward her. The woman cowered; her feet rooted to the floor. The bodyguard seized her throat. He wanted to exert just enough pressure to distress her, but not enough to choke her completely: her undivided attention couldn't be guaranteed if her overriding instinct was to fight for her survival. "Listen carefully, you philandering bitch." He waited for her eyes to refocus. "You understand I can kill you right now, just like I killed that fucking Cossack?" She nodded frantically. Her earlier defiance had been replaced by terror. "I am about to leave some unpleasant but superficial welts on your throat. When my superiors arrive, you will tell them that your husband's *aide de camp* had attacked you violently after you rejected his amorous advances." Morozov shifted his weight and kicked a porcelain lamp off the bedside table. "A short scuffle ensued and you screamed for help. That is when I came in and took care of matters."

Twenty seven seconds since coming through the door: I must finish this quickly.

During periods of extreme stress a massive surge of adrenaline is released into the bloodstream. It has both a psychological as well as physiological affect on the body. As the hormone fires into action, blood to the brain's cognitive center, as well as certain non-essential organs, is redirected to the larger muscles. Audio exclusion and tachypsychia are two of the other consequences associated with this state of heightened preparedness. Intrusive loud noises, like gunshots, sound muffled. The neurological condition known as tachypsychia alters the brain's perception of elapsed time.

Due to the heightened state of anxiety over her immediate safety, the commissar's wife would later describe her ordeal as having lasted several minutes—a typical consequence of the condition. Morozov, on the other hand, had been trained to control the affects of adrenaline. Without the need to consult a wristwatch, the KGB man was capable of accurately judging elapsed time. His estimate was as accurate as any rational human could make under stress-free conditions.

"If you deviate from this story, and I am compromised in any way, I have many dangerous friends who won't just leak evidence of your indiscretions, but will hunt you down and exact revenge on my behalf."

With only the second-hand confessions of a dead man, Morozov knew he had no such evidence of her dalliance. He was merely extorting her compliance through fear. Besides, how was she to know he didn't have any friends?

"Are we perfectly clear?" Morozov's grip tightened on her throat. He eased up. "Are we perfectly clear?"

"Yes," she rasped, "please, Vladimir, you are hurting me."

Quick. Forty four seconds. Someone will be here shortly.

"When I let you go, your state of shock must be utterly convincing. Someone from the hotel will soon be here." Morozov stared at her contemptuously before shoving her away.

Fifty eight seconds. This is good. Morozov had calculated that he had no more than one minute before the noise of the crashing door would be relayed to the front desk by a concerned member of staff or hotel guest.

A minute earlier, while descending between floors, a room cleaner in the service elevator had heard a mighty crash, accompanied by a woman's scream. She believed it had come from the floor above. Infuriatingly, the antiquated elevator stopped automatically on each floor. The maid was frantic by the time it reached the lobby. Trying to keep her composure, she hastened across the marbled floor in search of the duty manager. He was just cradling the phone as she rushed up to report the incident. A concerned guest had also just called to advise him of a commotion on the fifth floor.

Beckoning for his concierge to join him, the two men sprinted up the stairs.

Morozov heard their pounding steps as they ran up the corridor. Upon entering the room, the first thing they noticed was the bodyguard offering the commissar's wife a glass of water. He also appeared to be consoling her. With a protective arm around her shoulder, he led her toward one of the cabriole lounge chairs in the far corner. The woman followed meekly.

Morozov could tell that the two men had already drawn their own conclusions. Their body language also suggested that they were relieved. Both staff members knew that Morozov was the envoy's bodyguard. They were also well-aware that a dead client would invite all manner of uncomfortable investigations by the Romanian Securitate, let alone the KGB, given that the guests were Russian.

Here, clearly, the bodyguard had saved the day. While the hotel would not be entirely exonerated, it was a relief for them to know that the investigation would take place at an altogether different level.

"Comrades, this is a matter of state. It is a Russian affair. Please, one of you must call my embassy and get them to send somebody. Explain who my client is, and tell them she is safe." Morozov knew it was best to keep at least one of them in the room. He would not only be a useful witness, but his presence would prevent the commissar's wife from trying to engage with her bodyguard. Morozov needed the woman to think carefully about her story.

The duty manager—used to giving rather than taking orders—succumbed to Morozov's authority. He picked up the phone and dialed the switchboard. "Connect me with the Russian embassy … it's urgent."

Eternally thankful for Morozov's timely intervention, the commissar's wife lobbied her husband. He, in turn, petitioned the KGB hierarchy to reward their man for his decisive action: after all, hadn't he just saved the life of dignitary's wife?

The hastily-concluded verdict was that the disaffected Cossack had been subdued and eliminated before he could unleash his pent-up revenge on one of the Motherland's more comely daughters.

Morozov had taken his first human life: it aroused him deeply and he knew he wanted more.

4

OPERATION PIGGY-BANK

Sylvia Sneddon clutched her newborn against her bosom. With his pink face puckered in indignation, the tiny bundle tested his brand-new lungs. She loved him immensely, but had already decided he'd be an only child.

"Nurse, can you write down the following for me please. February 11, 1932 ... let's record the time of birth as 09:15 local time." It was Akron General Hospital's second birth that day.

"Sure doctor," said the nurse, turning to fuss over the new mother. "We've gone to fetch your husband Mrs. Sneddon. Have you decided on a name for him yet?" asked the midwife.

"We sure have," purred the proud Ohioan. "Akron Wilberforce."

Her husband was an encyclopedia salesman, born and raised in Akron, Ohio. Sylvia was a music teacher who hailed from the small town of Wilberforce, Ohio.

Exactly two years later, two thousand two hundred miles due south of Akron, Ohio, Ricaurte anxiously paced the length of the sterile corridor. He was at the Panama City General Hospital. Beyond the heavy swing doors a large overhead fan stirred lazily inside the delivery room. It did little more than rearrange the humid air currents. Outside, the temperature had already reached a sultry 100°F. Reaching across with her right hand, one of the nurses dabbed her patient's brow with a damp facecloth. Ricaurte's wife, Maria Feliz Moreno, held the nurse's other hand in a fierce grip. The expectant mother grimaced as she bore down on the shiny stirrups. Probing with his bloodied fingers, the doctor encouraged the woman to push again. "*Empuje ... si, si, empuje.*"

Despite the heavy doors that separated the ward, the expectant father could still hear Maria's anguished cries. He continued his fretful pacing.

Maria was utterly spent. Ignoring the nurses' encouragement, she started keening softly; it was as much in pain as in defeat. Just at that moment, she experienced a powerful spasm. Maria launched into a tirade of ghetto obscenities. The doctor suppressed a smile: more so in relief at seeing the baby's purplish crown appear between her legs. Working frantically, he massaged the slick newborn from its mother's swollen pudendum. He was concerned by the bruised coloration of the baby's emerging pate. With a slippery gush, the squirming mass collapsed into his waiting hands. He handed it over to the midwife. While she cleared the infant's mucus, the doctor clamped the umbilical cord. Glancing up at the wall clock, he called out. "Nurse, please record the birth time as 9:15 AM."

Outside the delivery room, Ricaurte gnawed at his thumb. He heard the squeak of a hinge. Using his backside to push through the swing doors, the doctor appeared in the corridor. With arms bent, he held his bloodied hands up at chest height. Had they been hanging limply at his side, it would have signified defeat. However, with his messianic pose, the doctor exuded his profession's universal sign of surgical mastery. Ricaurte exhaled in relief and smiled broadly; he didn't need the doctor to say anything.

"Congratulations Ricaurte. You have a son," said the exhausted doctor. "What will you name him, *amigo*?"

"Thank you Doctor Antonio, thank you!" A sheen of perspiration reflected off Ricaurte's beaming face. "I will name him after the doctor who delivered him. He will be Manuel Antonio Noriega Moreno," pronounced the proud father.

Akron's early years were mercifully untainted by the kind of teasing that usually stalks badly-named kids. He was a quiet and studious boy. By the age of nine he'd come to resent his name; he thought it sounded pretentious. It hadn't helped that his parents insisted on combining both names when addressing him. Upon reaching the momentous age of ten—his personal coming of age—the precocious boy chose to introduce himself only as Sneddon. He'd called for a formal meeting with his parents and had advised them of his wishes. They knew he was being dead serious. The family agreement was solemnized over the sharing of milk and cookies.

Although quiet by nature, Sneddon was no shrinking violet. If provoked, he wasn't afraid to roll up his sleeves. But he preferred to argue his battles with his sharp mind. The boy was a voracious learner. He enjoyed flexing his intellect but seldom used it to belittle anyone. Instead of being marginalized, the likeable class nerd managed to attract a mixed group of friends. He wore the pens in his pocket like the jocks wore their letterman's jackets.

The Saturday after payday was always a treat for the two Sneddon men. In fact, it had become their tradition. "Let's go and see us a good 'ol western, Sneddon." Akron's dad affected a bad Texas drawl. With much reminding, he'd eventually come around to the idea of calling his son by their surname. Although he'd never admit it to his wife, he quite liked it.

Pretending to be older than his twelve years, the young Sneddon rose up on his toes as he and his father approached the ticket lady's booth. The movie was different but the banter between the two adults was now getting stale. "Twenty six cents?" bemoaned Sneddon Senior. "It was a quarter last year!" Still up on his toes, Akron surreptitiously spied the ticket lady's ample bosom; he enjoyed that as much as seeing Roy Rogers ride across the silver screen.

Although Rogers was a legend, it was Gene Autry who was his all-time favorite. *Hopefully he'll be back to make more movies if he survives World War II ... what am I thinking? He'll survive—he's Gene Autry.* Akron worshiped Gene Autry: his admiration for the singing cowboy had been cemented when the actor had volunteered to fight the Nazis. Like Autry, Akron vowed he'd one day serve his country.

Clutching a large box of buttered popcorn, father and son rushed inside the mildewed movie house. The younger Sneddon hadn't wanted to miss the seven minute propaganda newsreel covering events in Paton's Europe, Monty's North Africa or MacArthur's Pacific.

Barely able to tear his eyes off the screen, Akron fumbled for a handful of popcorn. Scattered around him, adults were already drawing deeply on their cigarettes: a fresh infusion to add to the stale fug that already tainted the air.

Expectation grew as the lights were dimmed. A murmur of excitement was quickly hushed by a few of the more seasoned patrons. Akron's anticipation was visceral.

From the secret booth somewhere up behind them, the projector's first images probed the darkness. Immediately, flickering ghosts evanesced in the smoky veil above their heads. Barely capable of containing his excitement, Akron's fists shook with anticipation as the grainy numerals counted down from ten. He simply couldn't understand why the other kids in the audience insisted on counting down in unison. *How childish.* First the music: a flourish of trumpets to herald the paragons. Heroic it might be, but the volume was far too loud. Somewhere up behind him, Akron heard the scrape of a chair as the projectionist dived for the volume knob. In the gloom, the boy risked a quick glance at his father; he needed to check that he was equally enraptured.

Materializing on the screen, a phalanx of brave men stormed a Nazi stronghold. Gripped by the images, the audience erupted in applause. While scenes of American heroism were spliced between edits of surrendering Germans, the narrator's booming voice filled the theater. *'Through Europe's weak underbelly, the Allies' advance on Germany continues unabated.'* Waxing authoritative with his fashionable Mid-

Atlantic Accent, the commentator's voice rumbled over the clatter of the 35mm projector. *'The latest Axis stronghold to fall is Monte Casino in Central Italy,'* continued the commentator. Akron's imagination took flight. *With little regard for his own safety, it was the enormously brave act of one young American, Private A.W. Sneddon, who hoisted the last grenade that blew open the heavily defended ramparts of Monte Casino. Low on ammunition, and only armed with his M1 Garrand, Private Akron single-handedly slew the last fifteen Huns that defended the abbey.*

Try as they might, Sneddon's parents couldn't change their son's mind. With grades good enough to qualify for most Ivy League universities, Akron was adamant about the path he was going to follow. He was going to fight the communists in Korea. With a vocabulary influenced by the old newsreel presenters, Akron argued that the encroachment of the evil communists needed to be arrested. Confidently quoting from Churchill's speech—delivered four years earlier at Westminster College in Fulton, Missouri—the stubborn eighteen year-old presented a compelling argument for the need to conquer communism. "Remember what Winston Churchill said?" Poised on the edge of their overstuffed sofa, Akron's parents sat dutifully through their son's history lesson. "'From Stettin in the Baltic to Trieste in the Adriatic, an iron curtain has descended across the continent.' Mom, dad, the Cold War has begun in earnest. In four short years, Churchill's allusion to the Soviets' impenetrable cloak has already become cemented in the modern lexicon."

"Yes, but …" Sneddon's mom tried to reason with him.

"Wait mom. He also said that there is nothing which the Soviets admire so much as strength, and there is nothing for which they have less respect than for military weakness." Sneddon delivered the line with a passable Churchillian impersonation. "Besides, as he delivered those very words, Churchill drew an appreciative nod from President Truman. Mom, our *own* president agreed with him. Churchill's not just a statesman, he's an astute visionary. In his speech he argued for even closer relations between us and Great Britain. I hate to say this, but his words have proven to be prophetic in the past. He's warned us that the Soviets' policies in Europe can only be contained by the great powers of the English speaking world. That's us, mom … dad." Akron paused for effect. "The buck stops here."

Sneddon's parents looked at each other. Who could argue with a phrase coined by their own president?

Although Ricaurte Noriega managed to hold down his job as an accountant, the family struggled financially. At age five, Manuel was informally adopted by his aunt, Mama Luisa. Some family members were of the belief that it had less to do with Ricaurte's financial situation than the embarrassment caused by his son's aberrant behavior. Worrying signs had started to emerge, even at the tender age of five. Despite the hardships, Manuel Noriega received a good education at the Instituto Nacional in Panama City. While his heart was set on studying psychiatry, a combination of inadequate grades and poor finances kept him out of medical school. Noriega eventually won a scholarship to attend the prestigious Chorrillos Military School in the Peruvian capital of Lima.

In Akron's mind it had already been ordained that his bravery would best be witnessed on the battlefield. But the US Marine Corps clearly hadn't received his heroically-crafted script. Before his induction had even started in earnest, Sneddon faced an ignominious rejection. An undiagnosed affliction— descending arches in both feet—was about to put-paid to his boyhood dream. Assuring him that there'd be no injury to his patriotism, the Marines' recruitment officer was adamant that Akron be shown the door: but the young man stubbornly refused the free pass. Out-arguing a slew of junior officers, Sneddon was unrelenting. An exasperated major eventually arranged for him to speak to his uncle, a commissioned army veteran of the Battle of Normandy.

The crusty colonel—a wise campaigner who understood the

value of military intelligence—saw before him an agile-minded youngster. "Akron, you might just possess the aptitude to succeed in this crucial role. The Central Intelligence Agency coordinates the nation's intelligence activities as well as correlating, evaluating and disseminating every bit of intelligence that affects our national security." It took some convincing but Akron eventually came around. The idea that he might be of great value to the United States of America in an intelligence role was especially appealing; more so now given the intensification of the Cold War. It wasn't Quantico, he rationalized, but at least he'd be in the same state. Calling in a few favors, the colonel arranged for Akron to meet with an old colleague who had recently transferred to the newly-formed Central Intelligence Agency.

Overlooking Sneddon's physical impediment, an exception was eventually made and three weeks later he received an official invitation to join the CIA trainee program.

Akron was the youngest recruit in the intake of fifty-three men. Initially dismissed as being a bit light-weight, he soon won the others' respect with a combination of results and dependability. Sneddon and his fellow recruits had joined the program under the specter of the Korean War. The Communist-backed North Koreans had invaded South Korea mere months before.

From the sanctuary of their classrooms and training grounds, the batch of new CIA recruits watched anxiously as politicians and sections of the press continued to malign their fledgling agency. North Korea's surge across the 38th parallel in June that year had caught everyone by surprise: Truman's Administration; Gen. Douglas A. MacArthur's Far Eastern Command and, most embarrassingly, the newly-formed CIA. They were accused of failing to warn the president of the imminent danger—a failure of the highest magnitude.

Back in the classroom, Akron's teachers emphasized the importance of diligent record keeping. Refuting the accusations, the lecturers produced reams of documents proving that the CIA analysts had indeed submitted numerous reports on the situation in Korea. If an accusatory finger was to be pointed, perhaps it was at the manner in which the danger had been framed. Given the perceived global threat posed by the Soviets, the analysts could be forgiven for describing the menace not in a Korean context, but rather against the backdrop of a larger Kremlin threat. With the USSR sponsoring proxy wars on many fronts, events in Korea were seen as nothing more than another interrelated, Soviet-backed Cold War hot-spot. Although the situation had been escalating, the analysts genuinely believed that the regional mischief-making was evidence of another Kremlin-backed tactic aimed at testing America's response.

Sneddon graduated a credible eighth in his class. Lecturers and peers alike were impressed by the youngster's ability; he had a natural flair for analyzing intelligence material. His diligence paid off. Along with twelve other graduates, he was transferred to Seoul, South Korea, toward the end of 1952. It was in the hurly-burly of an international crisis that Sneddon really impressed his supervisor at the Directorate of Intelligence. Within six months of arriving, Sneddon landed himself one of the most sought-after jobs. He was selected to join the team that was tasked with compiling the US president's daily brief. The responsibility wasn't lost on the bright young man: never before had he been so aware of the importance of word choice.

During his stint in Korea, Sneddon had cemented his reputation as a natural intelligence analyst. After seeing out the last ten months of the Korean War, he was transferred to West Germany. Through hard work and some good old fashioned luck, Sneddon managed to work his way up through the ranks of the CIA. In early 1959 he was promoted to Chief Special Agent and reassigned to the CIA's Central Hub in Panama City. In the context of the Soviet threat, the CIA considered the territories around the Gulf of Mexico and the Caribbean as being strategically sensitive. During this time, only the Soviet menace in Europe was regarded as a higher priority.

It was from Panama City that the CIA monitored the entire region. Although their overarching reason for being there was to monitor Cuba, there was also a strategic imperative to keep an eye on the immensely important Panama Canal.

Traversing the narrow Isthmus of Panama, the canal represented one of the USA's most strategic geopolitical assets. Built and funded by the Americans, the 48 mile Panama Canal had been completed in 1914. From the moment it was opened to maritime traffic, the canal—along with a strategic buffer zone around it—had been administered by the USA as a sovereign territory.

The canal represented a time-saving alternative to the treacherous and costly voyage around the Cape Horn route. Given the Soviets' sinister agenda, maintaining political stability in the region was supremely important to the USA. But it wasn't an easy task. Following Castro and Che Guevara's revolutionary example, an endless string of postulants yearned to pilfer their own Central American fiefdoms. Even the stable, pro-western democracies in the region were vulnerable to these strutting egomaniacs.

Sneddon's team had been tasked with identifying all of Latin America's military strongmen—or the upstarts with the makings of strongmen—with a view to methodically luring them into America's pocket. In order to protect the USA's regional interests, so the logic went, the CIA needed to know that they could count on their Latin American stooges to keep the evil red tide at bay.

Harnessing the minds of their top psychologists, the CIA commissioned an investigation into the practicality of such an audacious project. After much deliberation, the psychologists produced a lengthy report in which they emphasized two important caveats to the procedure. The first point stressed that the grooming process would have to be undertaken with a great deal of patience. As the report explained, the unsuspecting subjects of the CIA's recruitment program were likely to be both devoid of scruples and wholly self-serving. In contrast, their CIA recruiters would have to build and maintain their subjects' trust over a long period of time. The second point, linked to the first, warned of an ominous consequence. Wittingly or unwittingly, any candidate brought on board in such a manner would eventually be inclined to seek equally rewarding deals elsewhere. The report warned that it was a hallmark of their make-up. From memory, Sneddon could quote from the report's concluding paragraph. 'Given the typical profile of the men to be recruited, it would be prudent to remember that double-dealing is part of their DNA.'

The CIA was perched on the horns of a dilemma. After careful deliberation, the wise heads opted to implement the program, arguing that the alternative—having *no* allies in Latin America—would undermine America's regional interests. Under a veil of secrecy, the recruitment of a select band of Central America's military strongmen was given the green light. It was code-named *Operation Piggy-Bank*.

Soon after arriving in Panama, Sneddon was sent on assignment to the Chorrillos Military School in Lima, the capital of Peru. The prestigious academy had cemented its reputation as a fine nursery for Central and South American army officers, and not a few military dictators.

On the first day of his assignment, a lost-looking Sneddon was pointed in the direction of the school's main office. Knowing that the brigade general in charge of the academy was a busy man, Sneddon had mentally prepared himself for a lengthy wait. He was surprised therefore when the impressively-bedecked commander came out to greet him at the allotted time.

The American followed his host into his spacious office. A large sepia photograph hung above the general's desk. Two uniformed men posed proudly for the camera. Inscrutable behind their large sunglasses, the men affected a menacing look. Sneddon seized the opportunity to show his grasp of Peruvian history. "Ah, Brigade General, am I correct in saying that the other man in the photograph with you is General

Manuel A. Odria?"

"Yes, that is correct Mr. Wilberforce." Sneddon had required an alias for his new task in Peru. While it wasn't exactly a pseudonym, it worked well enough. He'd had business cards printed which simply gave his name as 'A Wilberforce – Military Analyst.' "That photograph was taken in the hours after I helped orchestrate the military coup that saw my friend Manuel Odria assume the presidency of our beloved Peru."

"If I'm not mistaken, he graduated top of his class at this very academy. Then went on to become a hero of the Ecuadorian-Peruvian War of 1941," added Sneddon.

"You honor our history by being so well-informed, Mr. Wilberforce," said the general, smiling. Over a punishingly strong coffee, he gave Sneddon a brief chronicle of the academy's history, then explained what he wanted from the American. "As you have seen from my previous correspondence Mr. Wilberforce, I am of the opinion that my academy's entire curriculum on matters related to clandestine operations and intelligence gathering is woefully outdated. We look forward to your contribution and wish to thank you and your government in advance for coming to help us revise our syllabus."

Painted in eggshell green, the academy's impressive buildings formed a quadrangle around a vast grassed area. An effigy dominated the center of the quad. Holding a pistol in one hand, and with feet planted firmly on a large plinth, the bronze statue depicts a patriot brandishing his country's flag. The pedestal bears the soldierly inscription: '*We have sacred duties to fulfill and we will fulfill them until the last bullet is fired.*'

It would be here, at the Chorrillos Military School, that Sneddon would discharge his role as a specialist guest lecturer. It was a simple ruse that would give him the chance to identify and win over the cooperation of Latin America's future military leaders. He had been given three months in which to achieve his objective.

Chairs scraped as the class of cadets rose in unison. With Sneddon in tow, the brigade general strode into the lecture room. He got straight to the point. "In a welcome show of diplomatic cooperation, the USA has agreed to send us a visiting lecturer to cover this term's topic of Intelligence and Analysis. Cadets, please welcome Mr. A Wilberforce."

Scanning the room, Sneddon picked out Noriega in the second row. He was one of a handful of cadets that the agency had already identified as being a strong candidate for grooming. The general stepped aside and indicated for Sneddon to say a few words.

The American stood and faced the class. "Brigade General, thank you for the introduction. Cadets, it is indeed my pleasure to be given the opportunity to lecture you over the following months on a topic that is dear to my heart." Although the texture of his Spanish was more Mexican than Peruvian, his diction was nonetheless superb. "You will be relieved to hear that this will be the last time you will hear me butcher your beautiful language. The Brigade General has assured me that the development of your English language skills far surpasses my own selfish desire to improve my Spanish while in your beautiful country." Hesitating but a moment, the cadets checked to see that the general had also found the quip amusing. After seeing his hearty guffaw, they politely applauded. It had been an ideal ice-breaker.

The CIA's background report on Noriega had said that he could be somewhat surly. From his position in front of the class, Sneddon saw that even he was laughing. The American had studied the black and white photographs of each of the cadets before leaving Panama. While Noriega's picture had shown evidence of some acne disfigurement, Sneddon was shocked to see how bad his affliction really was. A vengeful adolescence had left the Panamanian's skin cratered and disfigured. It reminded Sneddon of 'No-Man's Land' between opposing sets of First World War trenches.

Over the following three months, Sneddon handled his lecturing role with panache. Showing both patience and insight, he was a natural teacher. His superiors couldn't have been more pleased with his progress. Beyond the four soldiers he had been tasked to groom, Sneddon had also succeeded in securing the trust of several other cadets.

Closely adhering to the guidelines laid out by the CIA psychologists, Sneddon had methodically lured each one of his subjects into his net. Although the template for *Operation Piggy-Bank* was based on a broad-brush strategy, each recruit's development had been plotted in accordance with their unique personalities. Sneddon had been encouraged to record each one of his subjects' quirks and nuances. Via the US embassy's daily diplomatic pouch, Sneddon dispatched his latest notes and observations to his CIA colleagues on the outside. In return he received updated guidelines—usually within forty eight hours—from the shrinks back at headquarters. Through the psychologists' evaluations he'd been able to pluck the strings that best resonated with each of his subjects.

Over-and-above his obsession with the occult, the psychologists had been particularly interested in Noriega's fascination with Hitler. The accuracy of the Panamanian's profile improved as each newly-discovered quirk was revealed. Within six weeks of initiating the program, the CIA psychologists warned that Noriega displayed most of the characteristics associated with psychopathy. More chillingly, they predicted that he possessed the potential to indulge in recreational murderer.

Although they'd discovered the common ground that satisfied each other's agenda, neither Noriega nor Sneddon considered the other as a friend. As Sneddon reported in his final submission from Chorrillos, he saw their relationship as being inharmoniously symbiotic. Despite Sneddon's reservations about the man, there was a compelling reason why his superiors had insisted on keeping Noriega in the program. Hugely charismatic, he'd been identified as a genuine contender for a leading role in his country's future. If Noriega ever rose to such a position, his anti-communist tendencies would be a useful foil against the Soviets' regional ambitions.

Noriega graduated from the Chorrillos Military School in 1962 and returned to Panama. He immediately joined the Panama National Guard. The newly-commissioned sub-lieutenant soon gained the respect of his fellow officers but, more importantly, the eye of military leader Omar Torrijos. Noriega quickly became enamored with Torrijos' fiery brand of nationalism. He went on to serve loyally in Torrijos' court and vigorously helped recruit and cultivate a crop of like-minded junior officers.

Throughout this period, Noriega gloried in the attention lavished on him by Sneddon and the CIA. He quickly became one of *Operation Piggy-Bank's* most valued assets. In 1967, Sneddon arranged for Noriega to travel to the USA; specifically, the military school at Fort Bragg in North Carolina. While there, Noriega received specialized training in psychological operations. Soon after his return from Fort Bragg, Sneddon arranged for a further round of specialized training, this time at the SOA—School of the Americas—located at Fort Gulick in the Panama Canal Zone.

Established in 1946, the SOA had already trained thousands of Latin American soldiers in an array of advanced military skills. But the SOA wasn't short of detractors. Furthering the ambitions of whichever junta they supported, SOA graduates were routinely accused of using torture, rape, assassination—even genocide—to enforce their paymaster's ideologies.

Noriega thrived at the SOA. Some of his classmates even swore it was he who coined the name 'School of the Assassins.'

Created under the aegis of the US Department of Defense, the SOA had been established with one specific purpose in mind: to provide anti-communist counterinsurgency training for government personnel in Latin American nations allied to the United States. Not only was the CIA aware of the SOA's murky reputation, they acted as the school's marketing department. It was the CIA who was responsible for sending a steady stream of recruits to the school—among them, handpicked men like Noriega.

A mere seven hundred miles to the north, Cuba's Castro still inspired revolutionary sentiments across much of Central and South America. The CIA—and America by extension—believed they needed to do everything in their power to prevent another communist regime from gaining a foothold in the region. It needed ruthless men like Noriega to face down the communist threat, and if that meant sending them to the SOA, then so be it.

Equipped with his new-found skills, Noriega became even more beneficial to his mentor, Torrijos. Along with a cabal of co-conspirators, Torrijos led a coup d'état in 1968. The thrice-elected Panamanian president, Arnulfo Arias, was summarily ousted from power. His third and final tenure had lasted a mere eleven days. Although Torrijos was never to assume the official title of president, he nonetheless became Panama's de facto leader. He preferred instead to be known as the 'Maximum Leader of the Panamanian Revolution.' He counted Noriega amongst his phalanx of trusty aides.

Having inserted himself at the helm, Torrijos challenged the status quo and quickly wrested control from the country's social and political elite. The poor, Spanish-speaking majority warmed to their new leader and proclaimed him to be a true representative of the masses. But Torrijos' ambitions went beyond reforming social and political imbalances. His idée fixe was to secure the sovereignty of the Panama Canal.

The waterway had been under US administration since 1903. Navigating a series of delicate negotiations, Torrijos eventually managed to secure the USA's relinquishment of the Panama Canal. Signed in 1977 by himself and US President Jimmy Carter, the final accords became known as the Torrijos-Carter Treaties. Under the terms of withdrawal, there was to be a staggered hand-over of control over the following twenty two years. On the last day of the twentieth century the United

States would eventually renounce all claims to ownership of the Panama Canal.

But the signing of the treaties triggered concerns in some quarters. Although the USA retained the right to defend and maintain the operability of the canal, the ultimate surrender of such an important geopolitical asset didn't sit well with many strategists. Now, more than ever, the USA needed to maintain political stability in Panama. Cozying-up to strongmen like Noriega had never been more important to the CIA.

Despite reports of deviant behavior, rumors of political liquidations, evidence of drug abuse and signs that he practiced witchcraft, Noriega continued to be of great value to the CIA. Cooperating with the Americans on their domestic war on drugs, he'd not only promised to staunch the flow of Colombian drugs through his own country, but had also reported on known cartel shipments to the American market.

But Sneddon had started picking up worrisome reports about some of Noriega's strange and unsavory bedfellows. Colombian drug lord Pablo Escobar—head of the Medellín Cartel—had started featuring prominently on the radar of a number of US intelligence agencies. Operating deep undercover, a few CIA agents in Colombia had reported seeing the two together in Medellín.

5

ALFA TEAM

After the incident in the Romanian capital, Vladimir Morozov had been granted a few days leave. He had nowhere special to go, so decided he'd pay his father a surprise visit. Although he knew he would have to conceal his exciting news, he desperately wanted to tell his father about Bucharest. He reasoned that if anyone would understand, it would be Anton Morozov. But Vladimir's unannounced arrival, and subsequent stay in Sverdlovsk, lasted only two hours.

Snaking westward through the Urals on the overnight train, Morozov plotted and schemed his next move.

Directorate 'A' of the FSB Special Purpose Center is a stand-alone sub-unit of the Russian Special Forces. Known as Alfa— or the Alpha Group as the CIA preferred to call them—this crack unit of elite soldiers only attracted, and rejected, the highest caliber candidates. Morozov had only recently discovered the unit's existence; not surprising since they'd only formed four years prior. Their reputation, however, had already taken root within military circles.

With their mobilization orders coming directly from Russia's top political leadership, Alfa troops were tasked with defending key strategic installations. More recently, their ambit had been extended to include police and paramilitary duties as well as covert operations both domestically and abroad.

On his return to Moscow, Morozov submitted a hastily-drawn request for a transfer to Alfa. He needed to get away.

Far away.

Even Vladimir was surprised by the speed with which his application had been processed. He wondered if the system might've had him marked for special privilege: *killing a man while on official duty must've oiled my application process.*

Four days later, Morozov was ushered into the interview room. "For the record, can you state your name." Morozov was seated in front of a three-man panel. It was the KGB colonel who'd just spoken.

Morozov knew it wasn't a request: it was more an order. "Vladimir Ilyich Ulyanov Morozov." Dressed in a dowdy brown uniform, her back arrow straight, the middle-aged secretary worked the stenograph on her desk. She was positioned a short distance off to Vladimir's left.

Vladimir had an agile mind. Even while engaged in conversation he was capable of managing several of his own inner dialogues. *Father, how were you supposed to defend yourself with so much vodka in your veins? Don't worry. I dealt with that evil bitch after she sunk a meat cleaver into your chest. I know you would've been proud of me.*

Chenko, the psychiatrist on the three-man panel, had been watching Morozov closely. He'd just made a mental note of Vladimir's small eye tic. It had occurred at the same moment at which the interviewee appeared to be lost in his own thoughts.

Morozov knew of Chenko by reputation, but didn't know the other two; they'd made no effort to introduce themselves. The psychiatrist had been an intern during the early part of Leonid Brezhnev's reign and had participated in the Soviet-sanctioned practice of abusing psychiatry for political ends. Diagnosing political opposition as a psychiatric condition, thousands of non-conformists had been labeled as having psychopathological mechanisms of dissent. For those that opposed the official dogma, or disagreed with the teachings of the Founding Fathers, their mental disorder was described as being as a result of philosophical intoxication. In severe cases, many patients were introduced to the gulag system in order to hasten their recovery.

The uniformed man was proud and arrogant, a perfect KGB colonel. The third man, like Chenko, was also dressed in a cheap suit. Bespectacled and balding, he possessed the air of an intelligence officer, and probably came from a strong academic background. From his crisp enunciation, Morozov put him as a graduate of either Moscow State or The Peoples' Friendship University, located just south of Moscow city center.

"So Comrade Morozov," said the academic, "as you may well know, my department at the Peoples' Friendship University, in conjunction with the politburo, is offering higher education and professional training to our comrades in Asia, Africa and South America." Morozov applauded himself for pinpointing the academic's origins. "Your application says you seek a position in Alfa Group, KGB Spetsgruppa 'A.' We are keen to understand why you have a specific interest in a foreign posting?" Morozov let the question hang, unsure if the academic *knew* of his reasons for requesting a transfer.

Unable to comprehend—let alone recognize—the full spectrum of human emotions, Morozov mulled over the inference that now hung in the air. *They don't know I threw her out the window. I made it look like a suicide after her murderous attack on my father. It's probably best that I leave the country for a while … especially if they start investigating the connection.*

"Comrade Morozov, you would be interested in a foreign posting?" The academic persisted.

"Yes, comrade. I would," said Morozov, his eye tic reappearing.

The academic continued speaking. "Well comrade, working in tandem with the Political Science department at my university, the Alfa group aim to extend," he paused in search of the right phrase, "let's call it 'new philosophies,' to our comrades in central Africa."

Thin tendrils of smoke rose languidly from the panelists' cheap cigarettes. The stenographer's fingers remained poised as a long silence draped itself over the group. A chair creaked uneasily. "We can arrange an internal transfer for you," the colonel broke the awkward silence. "You served with distinction in the Ninth Directorate. You proved to be a very capable bodyguard in the Bucharest incident. Your captain penned an impressive testimonial. If you have no further questions…" The colonel drew the interview to a close.

Morozov was about to stand up when a knock at the door kept him in his seat. "Enter," the colonel ordered.

Clutching a thin folder, a junior orderly hastened toward the colonel. He nervously proffered the document. Morozov was about to excuse himself but decided, instead, to wait until being dismissed. The colonel's brow began to furrow as he read, then re-read the missive. He eventually passed it across to his two colleagues. With his elbows on the desk, the colonel cradled his fingers and looked directly at Morozov. "Comrade Morozov, it pains me to tell you this, but I have just received news from the militsiya in Sverdlovsk. Your parents. I am sorry. They are dead."

Morozov quickly formulated two possible scenarios. The militsiya had solved the crime and already figured out that he had killed his mother. Or, they'd discovered his mother's broken body in the street, then found her husband: a victim, perhaps, of a scorned woman's jealous rage. They may have figured that she'd ended her own life as the enormity of her crime had sunk in. If he was to be arrested, so be it; if he was merely being given bad news however, it was important that he behave accordingly. But Morozov didn't know how to react to such grievous news. He affected a look of disbelief.

Chenko, ever the inquisitive psychiatrist, observed the grieving son closely. "The report says it appears that your father had been drinking heavily when your mother attacked him with a knife." Chenko watched as Morozov stared ahead impassively. "After comprehending the magnitude of her wrongdoing, she took her own life by throwing herself out the window." Chenko noticed Morozov's eye tic again.

The colonel's head was stooped as he studied the other

document that lay open in front of him. "The militsiya report says that the deaths happened on Saturday night, four days ago," said the colonel. "Comrade, this entry in your personnel file," he jabbed his index finger on the interview document opened in front of him, "it was made over a year ago. It says you have no next-of-kin. Why didn't you name your parents when you enrolled in the KGB? Why does your file say 'no next-of-kin'?" Morozov wasn't in the clear yet.

"Comrade Colonel," Morozov feigned the first signs of shock, "as you see from my record, I was sent to juvenile auxiliary school at the age of eleven. At fourteen, I was sent to the Suvorov Military School, and at eighteen I joined the *Devyatki*. My parents gave me up and sent me away when I was eleven. I lost them when I was a boy." With utmost mastery, Morozov allowed his voice to taper off. It was infused with a sense of deep regret. The acclaimed psychiatrist later ascribed it to a repressed melancholia.

"Comrade, we are sorry to be the bearers of this bad news. Give yourself time to deal with your parents' personal matters, then grieve, as you must." The colonel was uncomfortable in an empathetic role. He paused before continuing. "We await your return to Moscow, when you are ready, of course. We will then process your transfer to the Alfa team. In the meantime, the militsiya report offers a reason as to why it took so long to trace you. Neighbors in your parents' apartment block hadn't seen you in over nine years. They thought you had died a long time ago."

The colonel reached over and drew a small tin box toward him. He flipped open the lid. After rolling his stamp on the moist pad, he slammed it down onto the application form in front of him.

ACCEPTED

Vladimir Morozov boarded the Ilyushin Il-76 at the secret military air base known as Vnukovo-2, located just outside Moscow. The four-engine strategic airlifter was filled with an assortment of intelligence officers, political commissars and specialist instructors.

Their first stop was the Socotra Archipelago, specifically the covert Soviet military base on the main island. Located one hundred and fifty miles off the horn of Africa, it is best described as the most alien looking place on earth. A third of Socotra's plant life is found nowhere else on the planet.

Through its carefully-orchestrated process of geopolitical expansion, one of the USSR's most prized global assets during the Cold War was the Socotra Archipelago. Located south of Yemen and east of the horn of Africa, it is in close proximity to the Suez Canal, the Red Sea and the Gulf of Aden. With such a foothold in the Arab Gulf Region, the Soviets' strategic advantage was inestimable. If provoked, the Soviets could influence the flow of seventy percent of the world's crude oil shipped through the Suez Canal. With a fixed base, they were also perfectly positioned to extend their authority into the Indian Ocean and its bordering territories. In comparison, the United States could only project their power in the region via the deployment and positioning of their mighty aircraft carriers.

The Yemen, ideologically and politically divided as it was, had formed two independent states in the 1960s: the Yemen Arab Republic and its communist-aligned half-sister, the People's Democratic Republic of Yemen. In return for a variety of economic favors, the USSR—one of the PDRY's closest sponsors—extracted the right to establish a formidable base on the Socotra Archipelago. But the USSR's geopolitical ambitions were far more Machiavellian than just controlling the busiest—and most strategic—waterway in the world. After all, the Port of Aden in South Yemen had once been the world's second busiest after the Port of New York. No, the Soviet Union's ultimate prize was Africa. If they controlled Africa, they would obviously derive enormous benefit from the continent's natural blessings: its largely untapped arable lands; access to pelagic protein; and, of course, its vast mineral wealth. Gold and diamonds in South Africa, manganese in Rhodesia, copper in Zambia—the list of the continent's diverse mineral wealth was almost incomprehensible. But the grand prize was the Republic of Zaire: probably one of the world's most blessed nations in terms of its natural resources. It was out of the Zairean mines that plutonium—used for the atomic bombs of America's Manhattan Project—was extracted.

But Russia's ambitions were even more strategic than merely having access to nuclear fuel and natural resources. If the Soviets were able to control the vital east-west shipping lanes through the Suez Canal—which, conceivably, was well within their ambit in the 70s—it would force the West to divert its maritime traffic around Africa's Cape of Good Hope. If the USSR held dominion over Africa, or, in particular, southern Africa, they could achieve strategic control of the bulk flow of goods around the world.

Checkmate.

Morozov was part of a cadre of Eastern Bloc experts that was to spearhead the USSR's efforts to snag the African prize. The Soviets knew it was a process that involved a lot more than just providing the matériels of war. Theirs was to be a calculated process of indoctrination that included winning the hearts and minds of the populace.

In his speech delivered to the South African parliament in 1960, Britain's Prime Minister Harold Macmillan warned of the 'wind of change' sweeping across Africa. As predicted, nationalistic fervor peaked as dozens of former European colonies were granted independence. Withdrawing to the sanctuary of their gilded castles, the colonial masters were disinclined to oversee an orderly transfer of power to their former minions. Transitions were haphazard and left power vacuums that became fertile grounds for misguided autocrats; and not a few megalomaniacs. Across the continent, millions of Africans were buoyed by nationalistic fervor as their former colonizers withdrew back to Europe. The newly-acquired taste for political power was proving to be intoxicating to Africa's new breed of tin-pot leaders: it was they who the USSR was eager to court.

Morozov had been given his orders shortly before leaving Moscow. *Vladimir Ilyich Ulyanov Morozov, you are being transferred to Lusaka, Zambia.*

After disgorging a small number of its passengers at the military base on Socotra, the refueled Ilyushin Il-76 lumbered to the end of the runway. "Comrades, this is Captain Popov. Our flight time to Mogadishu is ninety minutes. After your third vodka at the Secondo Lido Beach bar in Old Mogadishu, I highly recommend a sight-seeing trip along the Corso Somalia. East Africa's finest ladies are always eager to meet a real Russian." Peals of laughter rippled through the cavernous belly of the plane as the captain finished his announcement.

Due to a delay to their departure time in Moscow the previous night, Morozov knew that he'd miss his scheduled connection to Nairobi by at least two hours. After landing, he walked to the Somali Airlines counter to enquire about the next available flight. The ocher-skinned Somali attendant flashed a welcoming smile. "Mr. Morozov, you are in luck. Your flight to Nairobi was delayed and will be boarding shortly. Proceed through Gate 1 and wait in the passenger lounge. We will call the passengers shortly." Hanging from the ceiling, two pathetic fans idled ineffectually in the passengers' lounge. Fetid air filled Vladimir's lungs. The place was punishingly hot. That vodka sounded like a good idea.

The Boeing 707-300 of Somalia Airlines had seen better days. Walking across the concourse, Morozov could see why the plane had been delayed for two hours. A phalanx of grubby technicians was still tinkering inside an open panel on the underside of the fuselage. Despite its mechanical woes, the plane eventually made it to Jomo Kenyatta Airport in Nairobi.

After clearing through Kenyan Customs and Immigration, Morozov took a taxi to his hotel off Ngong road. The cab smelt of stale sweat and salted fish. He was exhausted. He hadn't been able to sleep on any of the three flights he'd just taken. His taxi driver promised to come and fetch him at 04:30 the following morning. Morozov's Kenya Airways flight to Lusaka was due to depart from Jomo Kenyatta Airport at 05:50 the next day.

Although the Kenya Airways captain had already instructed the crew to prepare for landing, his voice crackled over the intercom again a few minutes later. "Ladies and gentlemen, this is your captain speaking. I wish to advise that we have been instructed by Zambian Air Traffic Control to enter a holding pattern. We will not be landing in ten minutes as I previously stated. Please remain seated with your seatbelts fastened." Morozov thought it odd, but wasn't alarmed. He carried on staring out the window at the scenery below.

Something in the distance caught his eye. Off near the horizon, a bright orange fireball had flared momentarily.

As a child, Morozov recalled seeing a similar glow at the state steel works in Sverdlovsk. Still viscous at 1300°F, the slag would flare up angrily as it was tipped out of the crucibles onto the giant waste heaps. He remembered it being particularly vivid at night. Morozov wondered if it might be from just such a mill. *But how does it glow so brightly on such a clear morning?* Just as he was about to consider another possibility, a second plume blossomed in a fiery hue. But it wasn't in the same spot as the first. Wisps of black smoke were now visible from the spot where the first glow had appeared. Suddenly there was a third … then a fourth. Just at that moment, the Kenya Airways jet started banking. Morozov twisted around in his seat and focused intently on the scene, eager to get one last glimpse.

Peering out, he immediately saw what was causing the series of small infernos. Like angry wasps, he made out several black dots circling the area. In orderly procession, they each appeared to wait their turn before swooping down onto their targets. Each dive was accompanied, seconds later, by another fireball. As the Kenya Airways plane banked further, Morozov lost sight of the apparent carnage.

His mind was racing. *It is inconceivable that the Zambian Air*

Force has a practice bombing range so close to the city's capital. Morozov knew that the Rhodesians had recently escalated the frequency of their cross-border raids into Zambia and Mozambique. *Could it be the Rhodesians attacking a guerrilla camp?* Not inclined to register emotion, Morozov immediately became stimulated by the possibility. He hoped that the airline pilot would hold his pattern and take the plane around at least one more time.

"Ladies and gentlemen, your captain again. I regret to advise that we have been instructed to remain aloft for at least a further fifteen minutes." On cue, a large number of passengers started grumbling. "The runway is temporarily inaccessible but I assure you that it will be opening again shortly," he offered in placation.

Morozov sensed that the pilot was about to complete one loop of his oblong holding pattern. Considering his latest announcement, it was obvious that the captain had been instructed by tower to hold for a second circuit. *But why?* Anticipating the unfolding view from his tiny porthole, Morozov waited for the telltale smoke on the horizon. *There it is.* The Russian noticed that this time, however, the black dots had disappeared. Gone too were the deadly orange blossoms. Instead, in their place, tendrils of greasy smoke pointed accusingly at the sky. Nothing in the cabin suggested that anyone, besides him, had noticed the distant palls of black smoke. Nor, for that matter, the flaring fireballs that he'd witnessed on their earlier circuit. Morozov's mind worked furiously. Along with the event he'd just witnessed, the pilot's instruction to remain aloft in a prolonged holding pattern must surely have been connected. *Could it be because of a preemptive raid by the Rhodesians?*

Prior to his departure, Morozov had been handed a large bound document with the words TOP SECRET embossed across the cover. He'd read and re-read the weighty digest. It covered every aspect of the state of affairs in southern Africa, along with the USSR's long-term strategy in the region. It was impressively thorough. He was left in no doubt about Russia's strategic imperative to first subdue the Rhodesians, then turn their focus toward South Africa.

Unable to identify with his emotions, Morozov was insensitive to the feelings, thoughts or attitudes of others. His condition allowed him to effectively detach from the consequences of his actions; more specifically, the affect that his actions might have on others. But that morning, two thousand feet above Lusaka, he began to experience a new excitement: an infatuation with the thought that he, Vladimir Morozov, was at the vanguard of the USSR's objective to crush the Rhodesians.

A local KGB operative was waiting at the Lusaka Airport to collect Morozov. In the immediate aftermath of the attack, as many as two hundred Zambian officials and military personnel had descended upon the airport. In the general mêlée, it was relatively simple for the KGB man to eavesdrop on their feverish conversations.

Only after the two Russians had cleared through the chaos and confusion did Morozov's KGB colleague discuss what he'd overheard.

Morozov was right—the Rhodesians had just attacked at the outskirts of Lusaka.

6

ZAMBEZI

Like implacable behemoths, the two presiding escarpments have for eons fixed each other with a sullen glare. Between them—the jewel they so jealously guard—the languid Zambezi River runs her seductive course. Along this section of the valley the brooding monoliths are aligned in an east-west direction. The opposing cliffs appear to act like some elongated interstellar beacon, ushering the sun's pitiless arc to the very heart of the geological cleavage.

Accompanied by the vexing shrill of the cicadas—not to mention the cloying humidity—the Zambezi Valley simmered like one of Dante's furnaces. And worse was to come, for it was only mid morning.

The gang had made the treacherous river crossing the previous night. They'd boarded their fiberglass boat a little way up the Kafue River, still well within the sanctuary of Zambia. A short distance downstream, the greasy green waters of the Kafue merged with the great Zambezi—Africa's fourth largest river. It was this river that divided Zambia from its southern neighbor; but neighborly they were not. It was Morozov who had insisted on leading this mission into the territory of their sworn enemy: Rhodesia.

Billy 'Stix' Mbudzi's face glistened in the heat. He was used to it, but it was the tortuous climb, along with his heavy pack, that had him sweating. His gang had chosen a relatively new path up through the Zambezi escarpment: the Rhodesians, wise to the location of the terrorists' preferred access routes, had recently sprung several successful ambushes along their various paths. Dozens of communist-trained comrades had been eliminated. Stix was bringing up the rear. There were nine of them in total, and the mad Russian, Morozov, had been setting a brutal pace.

Stix found it hard to believe that Morozov had already been in Zambia for five months; the Russian had arrived on the same day that the Rhodesians had attacked Westlands Farm. Morozov had assumed control of the camp in the immediate aftermath of the attack. Apart from revising the camp's overall defense response, he also immersed himself in the task of improving their soldiering skills. In four short months he'd transformed them with his brutal training regimen. Since taking over their schooling and development, the days had become torturous. Starting with a 5:00 AM reveille, the recruits' day began with a series of punishing physical exercises. After breakfast they attended compulsory 'realignment' classes: a highly propagandized introduction to the philosophies of Marx and Lenin. Their afternoon training was no less intense as the guerrillas spent endless hours learning about the various weapons systems supplied to them by their Russian masters. Their blistered fingertips soon developed hard calluses.

Stix adjusted the load on his back. Steeling himself, he forced his legs to try and catch up to the back of the file. Not only was the gang alert to the possibility of an ambush, but there was always the real threat of spooking a dangerous animal. Up here, on the rough slopes of the escarpment, elephants were often encountered as they made their way up or down the well-trodden paths. Despite the potential threats, the gang had made good progress. Since crossing into Rhodesia the night before, they'd already covered at least fourteen miles. They were now deep in enemy territory and on schedule to make their intended destination.

Homing in on his exposed neck, a pesky tsetse fly had made

several attempts to sink its needle-like proboscis into Stix's flesh. With his hands largely occupied trying to steady his cumbersome load, Stix could only manage the odd jerk to dissuade the irritating fly. When the bite came, it was intensely painful. All he could hope for was that this particular fly hadn't infected him with the dreaded sleeping sickness virus.

Morozov led his gang toward an impressive Kigelia tree situated a short distance off their path. It was time for a much-needed break. After propping his AK-47 assault rifle up against the trunk, Stix shrugged off the carrying straps of his Strela-2 missile. It was the same devastating weapon that he'd personally fired at a Rhodesian passenger aircraft just a little over five months earlier. With its infra-red optics and sensitive trigger mechanism, this Russian-made, man-portable surface to air missile couldn't be tossed about in the same blithe manner as the hardy AK-47 assault rifle. Stix eased the Strela-2 gingerly to the ground. The men were just breaking open some dry rations when they heard the distinctive sound of a Rhodesian Air Force helicopter passing close to their location. "Stay in the shadows and don't move," Morozov barked at his men.

With its characteristic low nose attitude, the chopper passed about five hundred yards due west of their position. It was heading in a northerly direction, straight toward the river. None of the men dared make a move. As the chopper clattered away from them, Morozov slowly raised his hand and indicated that they should remain frozen. High up on the southern slopes of the escarpment, the gang had an unobstructed view toward the river. About four minutes had elapsed since the chopper had passed them: although fading quickly, it was still just possible to make out the receding dot. From their vantage point, Morozov and his men watched as the chopper made a deliberate descending turn. It was obvious to the Russian that it was going to drop off some soldiers—soldiers intent on following him, no doubt.

Given the helicopter's ground speed, as well as the elapsed time since it had passed, Morozov estimated that the soldiers were being dropped about nine miles behind his current position. Morozov allowed himself a rare smile: *I pushed my men hard up the escarpment for just this reason. They may've found our tracks but they wouldn't have factored-in our brutal pace. Plus, the Rhodesians might not yet know of this new route we've chosen up the escarpment.* Turning south, the chopper was soon heading back toward where Morozov's gang lay secreted under the canopy of the massive Kigelia. Forced once again to hide from view, Morozov didn't care much for this loss of valuable time. Through squinched eyes, he could make out only two figures in the nimble chopper: the pilot's gunner was perched menacingly behind the barrels of his door-mounted twin machine guns and appeared to be looking directly into Morozov's black soul. As the chopper disappeared over the crest of the escarpment, the Russian called for the group to move out.

Morozov had usurped Stix's position as unit commander on this mission. From beneath the peak of his camouflage cap, Stix watched his commander closely. He could have felt resentment toward the Russian, but instead, he felt proud. The crazy Russian was an uncompromising martinet and stickler for detail. Such attributes were foreign to most of Stix's contemporaries, but he considered himself different. Being naturally ambitious, Stix knew he had both the aptitude and desire to succeed in a military role. To have been hand-picked to accompany the Russian on such a dangerous mission into Rhodesian territory was an honor. Stix believed he was one of Morozov's best disciples, and was always eager to show his command of new subjects and drills. Stix's fealty hadn't gone unnoticed by Morozov either: he was a useful adjutant who eagerly implemented the Russian's orders around the camp. "Alright comrades, let's move. We only have five hours left to make our position," said Morozov. Stix shouldered his bulky pack and cradled his AK-47.

Just as they were approaching the crest of the escarpment the gang's southward march was again interrupted. Morozov guessed it was the same chopper that had forced them to take cover less than forty minutes before. The chopper was again heading in a northerly direction, but this time with a four-mile offset. It paralleled the same path it had taken before. Morozov watched as it descended to the ground. Luckily, like the first drop, it too was way behind their present location. As it dropped out of view behind a copse of acacias, it became clear to the Russian that the chopper had inserted a second drag net to snare his group.

On foot, in this terrain, the hardy Rhodesian soldiers were at least three hours' hard march behind the insurgents. Morozov didn't have time to spare. He set a blistering pace and chided anyone who faltered.

7

WAFA WAFA

It was mid-afternoon on Monday, February 12, 1979. The Air
Rhodesia ground staff was overwhelmed by the number of
passengers that had just arrived for the two flights back to
Salisbury. There were certainly enough seats available, but the
passengers all seemed to have descend, *en masse,* at exactly the
same time.

Eventually, to ease the confusion, travelers were issued with
colored cards: red card holders would depart on the first plane,
green card holders on the second. Everyone was in a jubilant
mood. Kariba had always been a popular tourist destination
and the resorts lining the lakeside were seldom empty. Judging
from the atmosphere that day it was clear that everyone had
enjoyed a typical, fun-filled weekend under the Kariba sun.

Amongst the many passengers milling about the airport that
day, a familiar face suddenly appeared in the throng. At least a
dozen young men stood up respectfully when they recognized
their commander, Lieutenant General Peter Walls, striding
across the concourse. He too was due to fly back to Salisbury.
"Young man," he said jovially to an off-duty soldier clutching a
red card, "I think I might need to swap cards with you." He
held his up. "Mine's green. Don't you think I should be
allowed to get back sooner? After all, I do have a war to
conduct." The two men laughed.

As a result of the general confusion at the airport, the first
of the two Viscounts only got airborne at five in the afternoon.

Due to its delayed departure, coupled with the pilot's probable desire to make up for lost time, the aircraft forwent the standard procedure of first circling above the vast lake to gain altitude.

Less than six months prior, ZIPRA terrorists had shot down an Air Rhodesia passenger plane soon after its departure from Kariba. Learning from bitter experience, management at Air Rhodesia had introduced a new operating procedure. In order to mitigate the threat posed by heat seeking missiles, aircraft departing from Kariba were instructed to ascend out of harm's way by circling above the relative safety provided by the massive lake. On this day—February 12—for reasons only known to the captain, the *Umniati* chose not to head out over the lake to gain altitude.

Two days prior, while attending to some admin work in his office, Morozov heard the distinctive sound of his Teletype machine spewing out a message. He read the print-out several times; he needed to be sure. It had been sent from the offices of the Soviet Program for Agricultural Assistance. They were based in Dar es Salaam. Morozov knew that seeds and fertilizer were not the only goods they offloaded in the busy port.

The Agricultural Assistance Program was nothing more than a well-disguised front for the Africa Office of the KGB. All communiqués and orders emanating from the Dar es Salaam office employed a simple form of encryption disguised to look like agricultural speak.

> *combine harvester currently out of commission stop presently in kibara stop parts to be flown at approx 16h30 on 120279 stop due back in service in salaam at 0600 on 130279 stop immediate orders: combine harvester is to be scrapped stop*

Deciphering the message was easy for Morozov. The Russians had assigned various code names to centers of strategic importance around Rhodesia. Each Rhodesian place was named for a similar place in Tanzania, where the common denominator was their shared capital letter. Kibara, situated on Lake Victoria in Tanzania, was the code-name for Kariba in Rhodesia, also located on a lake, and also starting with the letter K. Salaam, a shortened version of Tanzania's capital, Dar es Salaam, was the code-name for Salisbury, Rhodesia's capital. The deception was that simple.

In 1977, Lieutenant General Peter Walls had been appointed as the Commander of Combined Operations in Rhodesia. The KGB had given him the code-name *Combine Harvester*. Under the protocols of this encipherment, someone described as being *'out of commission'* was merely off-duty. Morozov decoded his orders:

> *Lt. Gen Walls is currently off-duty in Kariba and will be flying back to Salisbury at approximately 16h30 on February 12, 1979, where after he resumes official duties in the capital at 06h00 the following day. Subject is to be eliminated. STOP.*

Yet again, the Russians' intelligence network had proven itself to be immensely effective. With general orders to make better use of the Soviet's Strela-2 missiles in the Rhodesian War, Morozov knew what his Dar es Salaam handler was inferring—take out Walls' plane with a heat-seeking missile. If they succeeded, it would be the second civilian aircraft that they'd have shot down. Moreover, it'd be an enormous coup if they could eliminate Rhodesia's military commander along with it.

If Morozov was to make his rendezvous with death, he needed to make haste; Walls' departure was only two days away. In the dead of night, he'd have to make it across the fast-flowing Zambezi River into Rhodesia. He then faced a hard march south to find a suitable firing position as close to the eastern shore of the lake as was practicable.

The counter-insurgency techniques mastered by Rhodesia's venerated Selous Scouts are emulated by special force units the world over. The Scouts' infamous selection process took place on an inhospitable patch of land on the eastern bank of Lake Kariba. This secret location, aptly-named *Wafa Wafa* in the local dialect, translates to *He died, He died.*

Having familiarized himself with the various units of the Rhodesian military machine, Morozov knew of the famed Selous Scouts. As a professionally-trained soldier himself, he understood the aura that surrounds such formidable units. He was well-aware of their fearsome reputation: they had a penchant for conducting covert missions deep in enemy territory. They purportedly even went so far as to disguise themselves in the uniforms of their adversaries. Once behind enemy lines, they'd ingratiate themselves and then wage their unique brand of psychological warfare from within the ranks of their avowed foe.

Detecting a strong heat signature from the departing aircraft's exhaust was vital for the missile's homing mechanism. For this reason, Morozov and his gang needed to position themselves in an area south-east of Kariba airport. It would greatly improve their chances of making a kill shot. But if they positioned themselves too close to the eastern shore of Lake Kariba, they ran the real risk of encountering a band of bearded Selous Scout operators scavenging for carrion in the hills of *Wafa Wafa*. Morozov wasn't prepared to take that chance.

Along with Stix and the rest of the gang, Morozov set course for Vuti. It was one of many remote rural settlements skirting the lake. Stix knew the region well. Prior to unleashing the fury of his first missile in September the previous year, he had scoured the area in search of suitable launch sites. Remembering the location of just such a site, Stix led Morozov and the other seven guerrillas to the spot where he planned to unleash his dreadful rocket. The site was on higher ground—which was advantageous—but was also relatively close to rural settlements.

Over a period of several years, cadres of the two terrorist armies had succeeded in coercing the country's indigenous population into a form of indifferent submission. They achieved this by unleashing a debauched brand of horror on the locals. For these rural folk, the fear of reprisals was a stark reality: especially if they refused to offer help to the transient terror groups. It was here—in and amongst the terrorized folk—that the insurgents could expect to find succor. They would need it. The Rhodesians would come after them with every means at their disposal if they succeeded in bringing down another passenger plane.

The Rhodesians were nothing if not resilient. Despite the war's harsh realities, life was good. But everyone—sons, fathers, mothers, daughters—was affected in one way or another. No Rhodesian was spared the pain of losing a loved one to the war. As the hostilities escalated, so too the viciousness of each subsequent attack. The worst possible atrocity was all-too-regularly surpassed by a further heinous act. Butchering the lips off their victim's face with a pair of pliers was sadistic; bayoneting the six month old daughter of a missionary couple was abhorrent; shooting ten helpless victims after surviving a horrific aircraft crash was murderous—the wanton carnage never appeared to stop.

With little time to grieve, Rhodesians buried their loved ones and turned to face their next challenge. This resilient tribe fought hard, but played harder. And Kariba was their preferred playground. With their rifle barrels pointing outwards, convoys of fun-seekers still drove the dangerous route between Salisbury and Kariba. Whereas some holidaymakers chose to fly to Kariba, it wasn't because they feared roadside threats: the downing of flight RH825 was still painfully fresh in the country's collective memory.

8

UMNIATI

The sun stooped like a pitiless judge over a condemned man. Conjuring sun wraiths shimmied off the tarmac; it took effort just to breathe. The occasional eddy wafted off the nearby lake but doled-out little more than a moment's relief from the suffocating heat. While an assortment of military aircraft slow-roasted on the apron outside, a handful of pilots cowered from the heat inside the command tent. In the corner, a single pathetic fan squeaked with each tired rotation. Try as it might, it only succeeded in spreading the sticky current. It was the end of a long, energy-sapping day. Although Hunter was due to stand-down at 18:00, there was no real finishing time while on bush tour. He'd already flown two small PATU sticks half-way down the valley a few hours before: the Police Anti Terrorist Unit was a crack group of bush-savvy trackers.

Earlier that day, around nine o'clock in the morning, the military controller at Kariba's Forward Air Field—better known as a FAF—had received an urgent signal. It was from one of the army's string of observation posts located along the length of the Zambezi escarpment. The look-out had notified FAF Kariba that he'd spotted a small gang of eight or nine insurgents making their way up the escarpment. Dax had been tasked to chopper in the two PATU drops in the hope that they might be able to intercept the terrorists' ascent up the escarpment.

A qualified technician was assigned to every operational chopper in the air force. Not only skilled in the arcana of wildly-spinning machinery, they also doubled-up as door gunners. Since the beginning of his operational bush tour, Dax had been paired with a guy called Beaver. The young pilot wasn't yet ready to ask him how he got his nickname.

Forged during countless contacts, they'd already developed into a formidable pair. Although neither had shared the sentiment, each of them swore they could intuit what the other was thinking. Dax considered himself fortunate to be teamed with this guy Beaver.

After dropping the second PATU stick—Blue Stick Two—halfway down the valley, Dax had sped back to their base at FAF Kariba: he had been eager to find out whether either of his two PATU drops had made contact with the insurgents.

Dax tossed his grubby *SCOPE* magazine back onto the table. "Hey Tyron, any news from either of those two PATU sticks yet?"

"Fuck off Dax. If you ask me one more time I'm gonna piss on your leg." A few of the other men chuckled approvingly. Hunter must've asked five times already. Tyron, a School of Infantry graduate, had recently received his commission. He and Dax were old rugby rivals.

Dax checked his watch. It was almost 5 PM. Barring a late call-out, it was likely that he and Beaver were done for the day. Craning his neck, Dax could see Beaver pottering around their helicopter. He went outside to see if he could help.

Dax was standing chatting to Beaver when he heard his name being called. It was Tyron. He ran back into the tent. "So I've just spoken with both PATU call-signs," said Tyron. "One of them has intersected recent tracks. But even so, their tracker reckons they're already two to three hours old. They'll keep pushing until the light fades. Both sticks are happy to rough-it tonight. I want you to collect the northernmost stick at first light. Let's leapfrog them over the other call-sign and see if we can come up on our bandits."

"So neither stick has been able to locate, let alone apprehend, the infiltrators," said Dax, stating the obvious. "That's not good. Oh well … thanks Tyron."

Flipping through the stash of old magazines, Hunter came across a copy of *SCOPE* that he *hadn't* seen before. Picking up the dog-eared copy, he was reminded of a line from an old Frank Zappa song: *Like some tacky little pamphlet in your daddy's bottom drawer.* Flopping down in one of the canvas camp chairs, he tuned out the hubbub of conversation and background radio chatter. Along with the various military frequencies being monitored, one of the controller's sets was tuned into FVKB—the Kariba tower frequency.

Barely seven minutes had passed: Hunter gave-up on the idea of relaxing—the heat in the tent was unbearable. He got up from his chair and stepped outside in the hope that he might find some shade, and perhaps harness a rare breeze coming off the lake. He made his way to a small acacia tree off to the side of the tent. While standing under its meager shadow, Dax's attention was drawn to the other side of the airfield. An aircraft had just lined-up at the runway threshold. Unfettered by the clutches of gravity, Hunter was always happiest when aloft. Watching a civilian passenger plane roll down the runway was as much a marvel to him as piloting his helicopter gunship in a fierce battle.

Across the airfield, flight RH827 was about to take off. Earlier, while sitting inside the tent, Hunter had overheard the patter between the captain and the Kariba air traffic controller. Their exchanges were being broadcast over the open channel. With fifty nine civilian passengers and crew aboard, the Air Rhodesia Vickers Viscount was preparing to depart for Salisbury, a hundred and eighty miles away.

Dax heard the pilot powering up all four engines. Even from this distance he could hear them screaming in protest. He imagined the pilot's index finger dancing across an array of analogue dials, checking his aircraft's temperatures and pressures one last time before take-off. Once satisfied that all was in order, the pilot released his brakes and concentrated on keeping his nose pointed down the centerline. Dax watched entranced as the fully-laden aircraft reached take-off speed. Nudging the controls, the pilot coaxed the nose wheel gently off the ground. Moments later the main undercarriage lifted free and released the aircraft from her earthly bonds. Dax saw the pilot tuck the landing gear inside the belly then climb away smoothly from Kariba airport.

It was early 1979 and the signs were unmissable: Rhodesia's protracted war was beginning to whittle away at the nation's morale. In the preceding twelve months the insurgents had redoubled their campaign of destabilization. Despite her valiant efforts, Rhodesia was beginning to lose the ascendancy and her enemies were starting to smell victory. Whereas a handful of politicians were exhorting the country's leadership to push for a negotiated settlement, the diehards steadfastly believed that a return to the salad days was still achievable. For them, sitting around a negotiating table was anathema. And so the carnage continued.

A few short years before, Rhodesia's military high command had revised their overall strategy. With the intention of streamlining the war effort, a decision was made to fuse the various branches of Rhodesia's military establishment into a jointly-synchronized operation. Although each arm of the defense force kept their unique identity, this convergence satisfied the objective of tackling a common enemy. Comprising members of the police, army, air force and internal affairs, these Joint Operation Commands—or simply JOCs— were set up at strategic locations across the country.

Dax had been posted to *JOC Splinter*, the code-name given to the operational area that focused on defending the territory around Lake Kariba. Although he had only been an operational pilot for three months, he was already well-salted. Along with every other active Rhodesian soldier, he had to be. This was a brutal war and they were fighting with their backs to the wall. In a fair fight, every soldier relished the chance of framing an enemy combatant in their iron gun sights. But the elusive enemy fought a different war: targeting the weak and defenseless in the dead of night, they melted away into the shadows during the day. In the eyes of Rhodesia's enemies, each and every civilian was a legitimate target.

High above the airfield, just as it began gently banking to the right, Dax offered his silent ritual to the departing Viscount: *May you always have as many safe landings as takeoffs.* With that, he turned and went back into the tent.

The command tent represented the nerve center for all joint operations around the lake and was located a short distance away from the main Kariba airport building. Including Dax, there were seven people inside the tent that afternoon. No one had claimed the canvas chair he'd vacated a short while earlier. Dax collapsed into the frayed chair and reached over for the well-thumbed magazine he'd seen earlier. He found an interesting article about the Colombian drug cartels and started to read.

A low murmur of voices filled the tent. Dax was engrossed in the story about the notorious drug lord Pablo Escobar when the radio squawked to life. As he heard it, he instantly grasped the enormity of the transmission.

9

STRELA-2

The band of terrorists heard the distinctive drone of the four-engine turbo-prop aircraft before they saw it. Morozov scanned the sky for a hint of movement but was initially looking too high: *If the Rhodesians have already suffered one hull loss, surely they'd have ordered their planes to seek the sanctuary of higher altitudes while first circling above Lake Kariba?* It therefore came as a surprise to Morozov when he detected the plane at a much lower altitude. The Russian slapped Stix on the back. "There, look there!" He pointed at the dot emerging low on the horizon. Stix squinted. The sun was low and the plane was heading toward them from a westerly direction. There was no reflection off the fuselage, but Soviet intelligence had revealed that the Rhodesians had recently painted their Viscounts' undersides with a light-absorbent matt paint. A similar technique, employed by the air force, had proven to be effective against ground-launched missile attacks similar to the one that had already downed one of their civilian planes.

Morozov smirked. *The gods of destruction smile on me today. This will be an easy shot.* "Stix," he shouted, "track the aircraft but don't fire until it is overhead. I don't want the heat seeker to be confused by the sun." The passive infrared homing system of the Strela-2 missile is designed to lock onto the strongest heat source.

"*Yebo, bwana,*" acknowledged Stix. It hadn't taken Morozov long to grasp some of the basic lingua franca.

Stix already had the green-colored launch tube up to his shoulder. Due to the plane's trajectory it appeared as if this was going to be a straight-receding target. The aircraft was fast approaching their position on the knoll.

Overhead in ten seconds.

Stix estimated it was a little over four thousand feet above him. Figuring out all the variables had been part of his training on this man-portable weapon system. He'd been taught how to use it whilst in Bulgaria in early 1978. At its current height, the Viscount was just within the missile's maximum altitude range of four thousand five hundred feet.

Stix thumbed the cylindrical thermal battery to the 'on' position and depressed half-trigger. As he tracked his target through the iron sights, Stix began mentally ticking off each of the steps in his memorized firing sequence. The seeker had been un-caged and was now tracking the doomed Viscount. At that particular angle, and with that target picture, the sun was no longer capable of confusing the sensitive seeking mechanism. The device's circuitry had already identified an infrared signature.

Lock! A small unobtrusive light was located alongside the tube's sights. In his peripheral view, Stix could see that it had started blinking. A moment later, a buzzer confirmed its lock-on. The missile's electrics and gyros were by now well stabilized.

Morozov held his breath. Although flying thousands of feet overhead, the plane's track was no more than two hundred yards to the north of their position. Stix followed its path carefully and rotated his body position in unison with the aircraft's climbing trajectory.

He waited.

With the Viscount now receding, each of its four exhaust ports presented a perfect target. The buzzer trilled insistently in his ear.

Morozov was about to shout an intervention at Stix, but decided to hold his tongue; after all, this comrade was revered throughout ZIPRA for having brought down the first

Rhodesian Viscount in September the previous year. *Clearly he must know what he is doing.* Regardless, Morozov was still anxious.

Stix depressed the trigger fully and immediately corrected with a small degree of superelevation. Since the plane was receding almost in a straight line from his own position, he didn't have to add any lead. The missile's on-board power supply was activated and the throw-out motor ignited. This, in-turn, provoked the booster.

With a powerful wooshing sound, the twenty one pound missile tore out of the canister balanced on Stix's shoulder. Immediately, the two forward-steering fins unfolded, followed quickly by the four rear-stabilizing fins. In under a second, the sustainer motor ignited. With its propulsive forces enhanced, the rocket hurtled toward its rendezvous with destruction. In seconds it had reached an inescapable thousand miles per hour. The lives of the fifty nine souls aboard the plane were in imminent danger.

Morozov and his gang applauded jubilantly as the missile struck the number two engine on the aircraft's left side. It exploded with a thunderous report. The plane rocked violently as Captain Jan Andre duPlessis fought to control the doomed aircraft. With its primary flight controls rendered ineffectual due to massive hydraulic failure, the beleaguered Viscount looked incapable of executing a forced landing. Severed lines spewed volatile liquid into the white hot core of the exploded engine and ignited it in a searing fireball. With a trail of smoke daubing the sky, the stricken craft plummeted toward the earth.

Incapable of correcting the aircraft's roll—and less so the speed of its descent—the pilot wrestled with the mushy controls but couldn't prevent his plane from slamming into the broken terrain.

The remains of the hapless occupants—fifty nine innocent civilians—lay scattered amid the dismembered wreckage of Flight 827.

10

MAYDAY!

Mayday! Mayday! Mayday!

The international signal for an aircraft or ship in distress is *never* used lightly: the effect is intended to be galvanizing. Whenever, or wherever such a call is received, a carefully-orchestrated sequence of steps is immediately activated. Search and rescue teams are put on standby, as are medical personnel, hospitals, relevant authorities. Even morgues.

Everyone in the tent had detected the urgency in the sender's voice. Before even completing the last of his three distress signals, all seven individuals dashed toward the bulky radio set. They crowded around, anxiously awaiting the rest of the caller's message. "*Umniati*, 827 … 827." There appeared to be little evidence of panic in the captain's voice. A veteran pilot of the Korean War, it would have seemed to anyone listening that it was just another day in the office for the experienced officer. "Missile hit! We're going down."

Everyone in the tent stiffened. *Fuck no! They've hit another Viscount*. Dax felt a familiar knot developing in the pit of his stomach.

"On track … descending through flight level 60. Heading 085. Attempting forced landing … copy?" But for the background static, the ageing radio set suddenly went quiet. In spite of Captain Jan Andre duPlessis' unwinnable situation, his broadcast had remained impassive.

A moment or two passed. The Kariba controller keyed his

microphone. "This is Kariba Tower, we copy your last."

Dax Hunter tilted his head back and drew a slug of tepid water from his battered cannister. His throat had constricted. It was hard to swallow. He wiped his mouth, screwed the top back down onto his water bottle and waited. Everyone waited.

Apart from its faint background hiss, the radio remained mute. Seven men crowded around the set, concern etched on their faces. For the third time, the calm yet insistent appeal of the Kariba air traffic controller crackled over the airwaves. "RH827 *Umniati*, this is Kariba Tower, do you read, over?" Dax looked through the open flap of the command tent. Separated by a quarter mile of blistering tarmac, he could see the modestly-sized tower perched atop the airport building. He willed the pilot of *Umniati* to respond. He checked his watch. It was 17:06.

Within minutes of receiving duPlessis' distress call, a sequence of emergency responses and actions was initiated across the country. Given her ongoing war status, the government relied heavily on the mobilization and deployment of several units of the Rhodesian armed forces to assist in the rescue.

Borne of bitter experience, the reaction to the situation was prompt and efficient. It was the second time in less than six months that an Air Rhodesia passenger plane had been shot down by a communist-backed terror group. The last time it happened thirty eight passengers were killed on impact. Shortly thereafter, ten survivors were gunned down in cold blood by the same group that had just shot them out of the sky.

Even with two of its sides rolled up to aid ventilation, the large tent suddenly felt claustrophobic. Dax felt sick to his core. The madness was spiraling. *Not again! How many this time?*

Manned by an assortment of army, police and air force personnel, the occupants of the tent all began talking at once. They were galvanized into action the moment they'd realized that flight RH827 was not responding. That single distress call had left them in no doubt as to the magnitude of the crisis.

Chillingly, everyone inside the tent had heard the same genial voice over the same radio less than ten minutes earlier. There was something reassuring about the way a proficient pilot conducts his radio patter. Being cheerful didn't equate to being unprofessional.

While Dax hadn't necessarily been paying attention to the dialogue between captain and tower, he'd nonetheless been reassured by the tone and timbre of their brief broadcasts. Still numbed by *Umniati's* silence, Dax wondered what had made him venture outside just a few minutes earlier. As a pilot, had he been drawn out by a subliminal urge to pay homage to a great aviator? Dax squeezed his eyes shut. He couldn't shake the vivid images of *Umniati's* last safe take-off. *May you have as many safe landings as take-offs.*

From the tower, less than four hundred yards from their command tent, the men listened silently as the air traffic controller tried in vain to raise the doomed Viscount. *Was it his fifth or sixth attempt?* All they heard in response was the hum of background static.

Barrel, as he was affectionately known to his colleagues, was a senior officer in the air force's helicopter squadron. 7 Squadron comprised a fleet of Alouette II and III choppers and its primary function was troop transport, medevac and fireforce augmentation. He had flown into Kariba earlier that day on a routine, whistle-stop tour of the country's Forward Air Fields. His visit was as much to keep an eye on his widely-dispersed charges as to maintain morale amongst the officers and men of 7 Squadron. Although he was an uncompromising task-master, he was regarded as an evenhanded leader. He'd quickly earned the unwavering respect of all the men and women he worked with at 7 Squadron.

While the officers and men huddled uneasily around the radio sets in the command tent, Dax noticed a stern-faced SAS major beckoning Barrel from the far side of the tent. The two of them stepped outside to discuss something in private. "Barrel, you know as much as I do that we are most likely dealing with another missile attack," the major wasted no time in getting to the point. "Loss of radio contact suggests to me that the plane's gone down, probably in the Vuti area. We need to get there ASAP to prevent the gooks from massacring any survivors … if there are any," he added ruefully.

"Apart from you Barrel, there's only Hunter here at the moment that can fly that Alouette," he indicated toward Dax's helicopter with his stubbled chin. "Can I take one of my chaps with me on Hunter's Alo and go recce the area?" The major didn't give Barrel any time to answer. "If I may suggest, you should probably stay-put here at the FAF. You'd be better equipped to take command of the search and rescue mission from here. Also, my sarge is a qualified field medic so he can triage if necessary."

Barrel took less than a second to make up his mind. "Dax!" he bellowed. "Prepare to get yourself and Beaver airborne." On top of the potential tragedy, another grim thought was troubling Barrel. Barely minutes before—as the Viscount was preparing to depart from Kariba—he had recognized the captain's voice during his exchange with the tower. Air Lieutenant DL duPlessis, the captain's son, had perished while flying a combat mission in 1977. Barrel felt ill: he knew both men.

Having been given the green light, the major hollered for his sergeant to come and join them. "Cargo, you're up." Cargo was an experienced soldier who'd already accumulated three years' service under his coveted SAS belt. A veteran of many campaigns, he was one of the regiment's most effective operators. While he acted like a regular clown around their base at Kabrit Barracks, the mercurial Cargo was capable of transforming into a ruthless, single-minded professional whenever he was deployed operationally. His cartoonish jaw had earned him the nickname 'Clutch Cargo' from his fellow soldiers. But 'Cargo' had stuck. The two young men hastened over to where their respective commanders were standing outside the tent. "Dax," said the major, "meet my sarge. You can call him Cargo. Cargo, this is Air Lieutenant Dax Hunter."

The two men shook hands and exchanged brief grins. The little interplay didn't go unnoticed by either Barrel or the major.

"Sir," said Cargo.

"Cargo," replied Dax. Protocol demanded that enlisted men refer to officers as 'sir.' In reality, the two young men were old friends—both hailed from the same farming district in Tengwe.

"Dax, you and Beaver are to load up the major and Cargo here, ASAP, you hear? I want you to find that damn plane. His Mayday came in six or so minutes after he was wheels up, so he can't be too far. We reckon he's about fifty clicks east-north-east of us, so that probably puts him in the Vuti area. As soon as you get a locstat on the plane, I need to know. Pronto." Barrel was in rapid-fire mode. "Make damn sure it's safe to land before you put down," he continued. "But I need to know your plan beforehand. Copy?" Dax listened intently to Barrel's orders. He nodded once. "No heroics. It's rough terrain out there. The gooks could be hiding and waiting for an opportunity to take you out. Keep the bastards away from that plane, whatever state it's in. We might have the makings of another cold-blooded massacre on our hands. That just can't happen." All four men had a clear recollection of the massacre that followed in the aftermath of the downing of Viscount *Hunyani*, five months before. "You don't have much daylight left, so get cracking. I'm also going to get a few Lynxes up there now to aid in the spotting," concluded Barrel.

The Reims Cessna 337—a spirited twin-engine utility aircraft—had been modified by the Rhodesians and carried an impressive array of armaments. It was a formidable weapons platform. Assigned to the air force's 4 Squadron, the fleet of Reims Cessnas had been renamed Lynxes. Barrel was about to put two of these aircraft aloft to help Dax in his search for the downed Viscount. Yelling to no one in particular, Barrel's booming voice filled the tent. "Somebody find me JK and King. Where are those Lynx pilots?"

"JK's airborne sir, he's on his way back from Centenary. Should be back here in about thirty minutes, sir," replied

Tyron. One of the lieutenant's responsibilities was coordinating deployments.

Despite having only earned his wings eighteen months prior, JK was already a seasoned combat pilot. Fergus Kincaid, the other Lynx pilot, had been on the same pilot training course as Dax. Initially nicknamed *Kin*—and later *King*—by his course mates, Dax and Kincaid were relative newcomers to the so-called *sharp-end*—slang for the Bush War's front-lines.

"Here he comes now, sir." Dax pointed over to where King was just exiting the hessian-sided latrines.

"Fucking hell, King!" Barrel's voice boomed across the open ground. "How long do you need to take a dump? Have you got any idea what's happened in the last five minutes?" Sometimes it was hard to tell when Barrel was joking. "Inside please gentlemen … I want to study the map before we send you out blindly." Instantly, he was back in command mode. "It looks like the plane's gone down in the Vuti APA."

During the early days of the colony, vast tracts of Rhodesia had been divided up into so-called APAs and TTLs: African Purchase Areas and Tribal Trust Lands. Venerated headmen and tribal chieftains were granted autonomy to preside over matters involving the traditions and mores within their particular societies. They, in turn, were managed by government-appointed District Commissioners.

Located in far-flung corners of the country, these APAs and TTLs were not only remote, but often inaccessible. Away from the prying eyes of the security forces, these isolated regions became fertile grounds for the recruiting of new terrorist insurgents.

Although they shared the common objective of liberating Rhodesia from its colonial leaders, the country's two main foes displayed little else in the way of unity. ZIPRA—the Zimbabwe People's Revolutionary Army—was the armed wing of the political party known as ZAPU. They followed the teachings and principles of Soviet Marxism and Leninism.

The Zimbabwe African National Liberation Army, or

ZANLA, served as the military wing of the ZANU political party. They followed Mao's doctrine. Each received support, training and matériel from their communist consorts—ZIPRA from the USSR and ZANLA from China.

Both armies excelled at the Procrustean tactics espoused by Marx and Mao. The authors of both these doctrines advocated the savage coercion of innocent civilians. The ideology of both armies required the complete propagandizing of the country's largely rural population. And they achieved their aim by means most foul.

Regardless of their victims' political persuasions, no one was immune to their fear-mongering tactics. Anyone who suffered—and survived—their brutish acts automatically became an unwilling poster-child for their vile cause. With bloodthirsty relish, they committed the majority of these acts against their own kith-and-kin. Given the insurgents' *modus operandi*, it was no surprise that the Rhodesian government chose to use the term 'terrorists' when referring to the guerrillas of either army. Despite their deadly acts of brutality, these terrorists—along with their liberal sympathizers around the world—preferred to use the term 'freedom fighters.'

With a growing number of terrorists entering the country, the Rhodesian forces were being stretched to the limits. As the conflict intensified, new strategies and tactics were regularly replacing old. One such strategy required that security forces be redeployed to defend the towns and cities, vital road and rail networks as well as the farms. This led to a vacuum in the APAs and TTLs. The void created by the redeployment of Rhodesian security forces gave free rein to the terrorists in these areas. Through their intimidatory tactics, ZANLA and ZIPRA commissars were able to preach the new communist gospel to their bewildered audiences.

Young men and women, often threatened with death, were force-marched across Rhodesia's borders where the governments of sympathetic neighbors offered safe haven to their communist-trained tenants. Once the reprogramming was complete, the new recruits were sent back to Rhodesia to continue the process of destabilization. Being so close to the Zambian border, Vuti was known to be one of the terrorists' favorite recruiting grounds.

Removing the rubber band from a rolled-up map, Barrel scavenged a stapler, a coffee mug and the major's spare 9mm magazine to weigh down the corners. King, Dax and the major stooped over the map. Using what little information they could glean from the captain's distress call, they discussed the Viscount's probable position and trajectory after it had been struck. With all factors considered, they quickly settled on the most likely search area. Using a blunt pencil, Barrel drew a palm-sized circle around an area about twenty five miles east of Kariba. The ring itself spanned a distance of about five miles from one side to the other. That was a large area to cover. With his search area now defined, Barrel threw down his pencil and looked over at Dax. Words weren't necessary.

Dax hurried out toward his helicopter. Beaver was already waiting for him. With nothing more than a grim set to his jaw, Barrel had projected an entire briefing to Dax without uttering a single word. *Set up a grid and follow a standard search pattern. Find that plane. Don't let the terrorists near the survivors … if there are any. Don't land unless it's completely safe to do so. Mark the location. Let us know its whereabouts. Stay with the Viscount until extra top-cover arrives.* Dax knew exactly what was required of him.

Hunter had already strapped himself into his seat and was priming the turbine for start-up. The heat clung to the air like a biblical threat. The haze continued to shimmer off the vast expanse of tarmac. Like sirens luring sailors onto the rocks, Dax became mesmerized by the mirages. He shook his head to clear the fog.

He had a pretty good idea of the terrain he was about to scour. Dax was somehow imbued with the uncanny ability to dead reckon his location from an assortment of cues. Even in flight school his instructors couldn't figure out how he could fly cross-country without so much as even a glance at his map. Dax recalled one particular instructor who was so infuriated by his technique—or lack thereof—that he'd threatened to fail Hunter on one of his cross-country navigation exercises. Once airborne, and with his SF260 instructor scrutinizing his every move, Dax merely made a show of raising his visor, peering at his map, tracing a line across his intended route then fastidiously studying his wristwatch. Although he might've fooled the instructor on that occasion, he still received a stinging rebuke during his debrief: *never lift your visor while you're airborne!*

Sifting through his memory, Dax was able to conjure up site pictures of the area he was about to search. He already knew the countryside well, but possessed more than just imprinted recollections of the topography. In his mind, even before he was aloft, Dax could visualize his aerial journey. Not only had he flown over the area dozens of times as an operational pilot, but also as a passenger in his dad's plane when he was flying PRAW duties. Each traverse that he made added to his mental library.

While the international trade embargo against Rhodesia was designed to bring the country to its knees, it actually had the opposite effect. Despite being landlocked, the country's collective 'can-do' attitude spawned hundreds of new inventions, ideas, modifications and tactics. In the face of punitive sanctions, the country's economy actually thrived through much of the 70s. Every new idea was worthy of consideration. One such innovation had been adopted by the air force.

Rather than waiting anxiously in their New Sarum hangars for the combat helicopters to come limping home for repairs and servicing, the squadron's technicians were instead deployed directly to the front-lines. Each helicopter was assigned a technician. Not only was each technician responsible for all field repairs and maintenance, but he was also trained to double-up as his helicopter's door gunner. Beaver was one of dozens of technicians deployed in this role. Like many of his contemporaries he was a resourceful artisan who lavished an inordinate amount of care on his helicopter. He viewed a badly-damaged machine as nothing more than a challenge. Not for the first time, Dax offered silent homage to the spirit of Daedalus for orchestrating his and Beaver's partnership.

Dax checked his watch. It was approaching 17:25. He would never forget this day—February 12, 1979.

Somewhat lackadaisically, the blades above Dax's head began to turn. The oily smell of burnt kerosene wafted into the cockpit and stung the back of his nostrils. Robotically attending to his start-up procedures, Dax was vaguely aware that he'd allowed his mind to wander. *Is it the heat? Is it the news of the downed Viscount? A combination of both?* He shelved the intrusive thoughts. *C'mon focus Hunter, focus.*

Strapped loosely under his chin, Dax's battered helmet barely concealed the shrill whine of the Artouste engine. As the rotors gathered momentum, he detected an almost imperceptible change to the pitch of the turbine. He was anxious to get airborne, but waited for the turbine to reach its working temperature. He tightened his harness, scanned his instruments, thumbed in his radio frequency and then exchanged a glance with Beaver. His technician was positioned behind the door-mounted machine guns.

Two members of the SAS were going to join them on this flight: the major and Cargo. They would make their way out from the tent as soon as they heard the distinctive whir of the fully-spinning disc. On cue, they emerged into the sunlight and took up the ready position on the edge of the scything arc. With his collective lever fully down, Dax gave a thumbs-up for the two soldiers to come to the aircraft. Ducking low under the wash of the blades, they quickly approached the chopper and climbed aboard. Both were stern-faced. Everyone was hardened by the uncompromising war.

At full rotational speed the chopper's three-bladed rotor system made a distinctive warbling sound. It filled their ears. Dax clicked his transmit button three times in rapid succession; a prearranged signal for Beaver to give the *all-clear* from his side. Barely audible above the clatter and radio static, Beaver grunted once. It was accompanied by a war-weary nod. *Left-hand side clear.* Hunter couldn't have been paired with a more dedicated airman; in lighter moments he joked that the man was capable of coaxing their helicopter aloft on nothing more than a keg of beer.

Dax's helicopter was relatively light; only four up, including himself. After Cargo and the major had boarded, he lifted his collective lever slightly and allowed the chopper's nose to swivel into the wind. Caressing the power lever in his left hand, he corrected the helicopter's natural yawing tendency with a nudge of his right pedal. With only the slightest amount of pressure, he eased the cyclic forward. As the chopper's spinning disc tilted downwards, it gave Dax a little forward momentum. He let the nose wheel kiss the tarmac as his aircraft gathered speed down the length of the taxiway. With his nose low through the transition and the helicopter starting to gain speed, Dax heard the satisfying metallic slap as Beaver cocked his door-mounted twin machine guns.

The taste of adrenaline burnt the back of their throats. With a stony set to their faces, the four warriors feared the worst.

11

STARLING TWO-ZERO

Straddling a narrow gorge in the Zambezi River, the massive Kariba dam wall held the distinction of retaining the waters of the world's largest man-made reservoir. With enormous turbines embedded deep within the wall, the dam's primary function was to generate hydro-electricity for the booming economies of Northern and Southern Rhodesia. Emerging from the structure's cavernous interior, high-voltage electricity cables snake their way across both countries. Suspended between giant lattice steel pylons, this network of cables was established to distribute much-needed energy to the hungry economies of Southern Africa's colonial federation. Flanking the pylons and cables, a wide swath of land had been cleared of all vegetation. From the air, the power lines were a useful aid to navigation.

Dax followed the lines eastwards for several minutes before making a small adjustment to his bearing. The Vuti African Purchase Area covered a large area and its northern part was located over to the north-east of his current position: if he'd continued following the lines he would have missed the track of the Viscount's intended flight path.

Even Morozov found it hard to contain his excitement. Within a second or two of the missile's deadly impact, he'd pounded Stix's shoulder. Equally as exuberant, the other comrades also gathered around. Using their mother tongue, they jabbered excitedly. Although Morozov didn't chide them, he was known for being intolerant of conversations that were conducted in anything but English. Given their elation, he decided to let it pass.

After downing the Viscount *Hunyani* in September the previous year, Stix had become a celebrity amongst his comrades. Morozov was well-aware of his legendary status. In an act that forever sealed his reputation, Stix went on to lead his men to the smoldering wreckage of the twisted Viscount. He'd beguilingly convinced the crash survivors to huddle together a short distance from the twisted aircraft. Shepherding them into a circle, Stix reassured the dazed survivors that he and his men would bring them water and blankets. Instead, he gave the order to gun them down in cold blood.

Cowering in the nearby bushes, a handful of lucky survivors heard those final, pitiful cries. They would forever be haunted by the sound of bullets ripping into human flesh.

Morozov ached to find out if there were any survivors on this aircraft. He also needed to ascertain if General Walls had indeed been eliminated. "Come comrades. We must get to that crash site quickly. It went down on the other side of those hills. We must go and finish what we started."

Heading south-east, Morozov set a grueling pace. Having judged its trajectory—as well as the point where it disappeared over the horizon—he reckoned they were no more than four to five miles from the crash site. He pushed the men hard.

Strapped into his Lynx, King had taken off from Kariba only a few minutes after Dax. He'd just spotted Dax's chopper a short distance ahead and below his own position. "Starling Two-Zero this is Dolphin One-Five, do you read over?" King called.

"This is Starling Two-Zero. I have you strength five," Dax replied.

"Eagle Seven has raised assistance from a chopper on fireforce mop-up operations in Karoi, as well as Dolphin

Eight, inbound from Centenary," said King.

Dax knew JK's call-sign was Dolphin Eight. Barrel was Eagle Seven. In the few short minutes since their departure from Kariba, Barrel had already put a plan into action. Dax was relieved to hear that Barrel was bringing a second Lynx into the search. *More firepower.*

A chopper from Karoi—less than fifty miles away—had also been lassoed into action. *That means four aircraft have now been dispatched to aid in the search.* Already, Dax felt better about their response plan.

"Not sure if Dolphin Eight will make it before sundown but it's all-hands. I'm starting a grid search from the southern end ... you commence yours from the northern end. Copy that?" asked King. Dax pressed his transmit button twice in quick succession; it was an acceptable form of acknowledgment. Dax adjusted his heading from 90 degrees to 75 magnetic, aiming toward the northern part of Vuti. King kept his heading and made for the southern portion of the search area.

While two aircraft of the Rhodesian Air Force had been dispatched within ten minutes of the Mayday call—and a further two, five minutes thereafter—there were at least another half dozen aircraft preparing to take off right at that moment. And that excluded the dozens of Police Reserve Air Wing pilots who'd been put on standby across the northern part of the country.

Rhodesian forces were being mobilized and put on full-alert. It was up to Dax or King to locate the downed Viscount as quickly as possible.

12

CARNAGE

To the others in the gang, Morozov seemed possessed. A blood-lust appeared to drive the Russian. He and his men had been slogging over rough ground for almost half an hour. Where the stony terrain was flat enough, peasant farmers had scratched small patches of earth so they might plant a few hardy crops. Morozov's gang had just reached the edge of a piece of badly-tilled land. Behind him, Morozov's men continued to share furtive glances; they would've been far happier with a less punishing pace. After all, it was late afternoon and the Rhodesians would be hard-pressed to arrange any sort of decent search-and-rescue so late in the day.

They were fifty yards from the crest of the rising ground when Morozov clicked his fingers and pointed ahead. A wisp of dark smoke wafted upwards from somewhere beyond the hill. Immediately vigilant, they crouched low as they approached the ridge. Morozov indicated for the others to lay low as he dropped to his stomach and inched forward. Using trees, rocks and shadows to break his outline, the Russian peered around the side of a large granite boulder.

The ground dropped away gently from his position. There was a dry meandering river bed less than a hundred feet below. About four hundred yards away, almost at his eye level, lay the twisted carcass of the downed Air Rhodesia Viscount. It was still smoldering.

Morozov could see that the fuselage had been rent open by

the force of impact. A jumble of bodies and debris littered the crash site.

Morozov felt his loins stir. A recollection—accompanied by a vivid image—surfaced in his mind's eye. It was the Cossack. Reflected in the mirror across the hotel room, he recalled his victim's face just as he twisted his neck like a farm bird.

Let there be survivors.

From his vantage point across the small valley, the Russian couldn't detect any hint of life. It was obvious that there had been a fierce fire. With the fuel having already burnt off, a few isolated fires still licked at the scattered luggage and seat cushions.

The initial fire must've burnt intensely. Even from this distance Morozov could see that it had melted parts of the aluminum fuselage. He also heard the occasional pop as heated rivets burst and snapped out of their housings.

The Russian beckoned for his radio man to come over. The terrorists seldom used radios on their missions into Rhodesia but Morozov had insisted on teaching them the benefits of listening into their enemy's transmissions. He'd taught his radio man how to scan the airwaves for transmissions. Most broadcasts yielded something of value; it was just a case of listening patiently. As they were never sure which channel the Rhodesians might be using, it was often down to chance whether they'd pick up any broadcasts. "Have you heard anything on the radio?" asked Morozov.

"Comrade, only the National Parks guys," answered Gadzire. "They are reporting a young bull elephant that has been caught in a snare. They need the vet in Kariba to come and fix it. Hauw! These Rhodesians," he scoffed.

Morozov checked his watch. It was just after six in the afternoon. *There's still enough daylight to go down and check the aircraft ... and little chance that the Rhodesians will be here within fifteen minutes. The radios have been quiet. That's all the time I need.* Morozov beckoned to his comrades to join him. Ever vigilant, he urged them to keep low and stay quiet.

The SAS major was sitting up front and to Dax's left. Like the pilot and the other two men seated behind, he was looking out for tell-tale signs of rising smoke. That could be difficult in these parts. For centuries, slash-and-burn has been Africa's preferred technique for clearing bush for farmland. Despite it being summer, the rains that year were late and the bush was still brittle; such fires would've been widespread. But they typically produce a blue-tinged smoke. What they were scanning for was a black smoke—the kind of smoke associated with burning fossil fuel.

The major saw it first. He tapped Dax's shoulder and pointed off to his left. Compared to the four or five other smoky palls that dotted the horizon, this one was different. Even from this distance—Dax estimated five miles—it looked thicker and a lot oilier than the others.

He banked his chopper and rolled-out onto his new heading.

13

A SPARTAN'S PACT

Down on the lee side of the gully, Morozov and his gang darted between trees and scrabbled over the rocky scree. Due to the sheltering affect of the terrain, they didn't hear Dax's chopper until it was almost upon them. As one, they all heard the slap of the blades as Dax loomed up from behind. No orders were necessary. Like cockroaches under the kitchen light, each of them dived for cover.

A hundred feet up and approaching fast, the four occupants' attention was focused on the horrific scene ahead. Had any of them looked down at that moment they might have spotted one luckless comrade scuttling for the last remaining bit of cover. As the chopper tore on overhead, the guerrilla realized he'd been lucky that day: the Rhodesians hadn't seen his clumsy dash.

Dax pulled the chopper into a high hover; he needed a bit of altitude to maximize his radio transmission. "Eagle Seven this is Starling Two-Zero, do you read, over?"

"This is Eagle Seven, go." Barrel responded immediately; back in the Kariba command tent, he had attached himself to the radio set.

"We have 827 visual. It's not pretty. I'm a hundred feet overhead. No sign of any surviving civvies, no sign of CTs." Charlie Tangos, or CTs, was the phonetic code for Communist Trained. "Stand by for a locstat." Dax drew his map from the pouch beside his seat.

Looking up to confirm his whereabouts, Dax recognized two distinctive hills: one was ten clicks north, the other five clicks east. Using them in conjunction with the river pattern below, he was quickly able to dead-reckon his position on the map. Running his finger to the left, he identified the two closest lines of latitude above and below his position. From this, he interpolated his southerly co-ordinate. "I am 16 25 00 south." Dax paused and repeated the calculation to determine his easterly co-ordinate. "And 29 26 00 east. Did you copy, Eagle Seven?"

Barrel read back the coordinates to ensure he'd gotten them right. As he clicked off, King made a transmission. "This is Dolphin One-Five, I am headed your way." King was no more than seven minutes' flying time from Dax's position.

"Eagle Seven to Starling Two-Zero," Barrel's voice crackled over the airwaves.

"Starling Two-Zero, go," replied Dax.

"Do a slow pass overhead and look for Sierra Oscar Limas." Barrel wanted Dax to check for any survivors—Signs of Life. "If that's a negative, then do a perimeter recce before putting down. Charlie Tangos might be waiting for a lucky shot."

"Roger that," said Dax.

Morozov and the others remained motionless. The Russian could only see four Rhodesians in the chopper, but he had three things to consider: their door gunner had a vicious twin machine gun; if there was one aircraft already here, there'd be many more coming before sunset; their cover was scant and he needed to somehow extract his gang before they were spotted.

With fingers curled across their triggers, the terrorists froze in position as the slow-moving chopper skimmed over their position. By that time the afternoon's shadows had lengthened and deepened across the southern slope of their hideaway. Such providence had spared them from being detected.

After completing his perimeter scan, Dax found a clearing a short distance from the twisted remains of the fuselage. He chose a spot where the grass had already been burnt by the fierce blaze. A runaway veld fire could engulf his chopper in minutes. Shortly before touching down, Dax called Kariba to notify them of his intention. In this location any transmission from the ground would likely be impeded by the rough terrain. Now only two minutes out, King advised both Dax and Barrel that he would hold a low circuit over the crash site and guide any subsequent arrivals to the spot.

The stanch-looking SAS major alighted first and strode purposefully toward the smoldering wreck. Cargo just shook his head. *How many times have I seen this guy wade into battle without first checking to see whether his boys have got his back?* Granted, this wasn't a battle, but 'the phantom,' as he was sometimes referred to, had no concept of personal safety. It was no wonder he was one of Rhodesia's most decorated warriors.

Cargo was the next off the chopper. Apart from the odd crackle emitted by the dying fires, an eerie silence hung in the air. He was immediately enveloped by a sepulchral sensation. He shuddered involuntarily. Off in the distance they heard the unmistakable drone of King's twin-engine Lynx. The welcome noise broke the reverential silence.

The four men split up and scoured the crash site for a sign that someone, anyone, had survived the terrific impact. The cloying smell was overbearing. But all they witnessed were burnt bodies. Primal thoughts of revenge bore down on Beaver like a Spartan's pact. He stood mutely in front of the charred body of a young girl. A cruel rictus disfigured her once joyous face.

Less than four hundred yards away, Morozov began weighing his options. *We cannot seek shelter here in Vuti ... the Rhodesians will be swarming over this place by first light and will flush us out. And we can't fight our way out of this.* Even if all eight of Morozov's guerrillas were marksmen, their AK-47s weren't accurate enough at this range. *If we open fire, that fucking Lynx overhead will have us all. We need to withdraw from here and make for the river tonight.* With a soft whistle, he signaled his men.

Interpreting his gestures, the men stealthily made their way to the summit. They were to congregate just over the rise.

At that moment, just a short distance from the terrorists' position, a troop of curious baboons had just made their way over the hill. Depending on Morozov's luck, that could be either a help or a hindrance. Although the sun sat low on the horizon, Morozov's men were still at risk of being spotted. He hoped that they would figure out that they needed to time their moves carefully, giving consideration to both the position of King's Lynx, as well as the four men on the ground.

Morozov bided his time. When the plane was at least half a mile south of their hideaway, and the four men below appeared to be looking down, he picked a short path to a nearby boulder. Crouching low, he hastened to his new position. Within a second or two, the others followed suit. They were able to complete three similar movements before the Lynx swung toward their position. Once it passed, they made their last short dash up-and-over the ridgeline. But just as the last terrorist was about to make the safety of the crest, one of the baboon sentries barked a warning call.

Dax was a farm boy. When he was old enough to handle the responsibility, his father had given him a .22 Hornet rifle. He was only allowed to shoot vermin, and baboons were top of the list. Over the years the boy had learnt to identify a variety of baboon vocalizations: *that* bark had sounded distinctly like a warning call. Dax looked up to the ridge and squinted. He recognized the familiar outlines as the primates bounded from rock to rock.

A little way off to their left, a shadowy figure scrambled over the lip of the hill.

Two hundred miles away in Salisbury, senior military staff at Combined Operations Headquarters had received urgent orders to return to work. At their hastily-convened special operations meeting, it was decided to task the SAS with coordinating the pursuit of the gang. The high-ranking HQ planners were enormously relieved to hear that the SAS major just happened to be deployed in Kariba at that time. Upon discovering that he was already at the crash site, his superiors in Salisbury ordered him back to the Kariba base. The major's orders were clear: coordinate the full-blown search and apprehension of the fleeing gang.

Dax knew there was a good moon out that night: flying back to Kariba after sunset wasn't going to be a problem. Back at his chopper, the pilot flicked on his battery and called King on the radio. He wanted to check whether Barrel had any new orders for him. Circling a few hundred feet above the crash site, King told Dax that the first chopper from Karoi was ten minutes out. It was carrying a stick of RLI troops: the men of the Rhodesia Light Infantry would secure the area until further reinforcements arrived.

Back at Kariba, Barrel could hear King's transmission but not Dax's. Sitting in a hollow, the chopper's signal was diluted. Barrel pressed his transmit button. "Dolphin One-Five, this is Eagle Seven."

"This is Dolphin One-Five, go," answered King.

"Tell Starling Two-Zero he is to head home immediately," ordered Barrel.

"Roger that." After breaking connection with Kariba, King relayed Barrel's instructions to Dax.

Now out of sight over the ridgeline, Morozov and his men started retracing their steps. They knew they'd have to put as much distance between themselves and the crash site. It would be an arduous trek, but they needed to make the river before sunrise the next morning. Any attempt to cross the river in daylight would be foolhardy.

Dax rounded up the other three and told them they'd been ordered back to Kariba. After completing his start-up procedures, he lifted the chopper and maintained upward pressure on his collective. The helicopter continued rising vertically. Once level with the ridgeline—the same ridge where he'd spotted the baboons—Dax nosed over and pointed his machine in a westerly direction.

But something was nagging at the back of his mind. *Why did the sentry bark a warning call? Why did a single baboon, far away from the sanctuary of his troop, disappear over the hill? And he was a big one too. If it was the alpha male, why was he leaving his troop unattended?* Baboons are cunning and opportunistic by nature. If an alpha male so much as turns his back for a moment, lustful lieutenants and crown pretenders will ravage his unattended harem in a heartbeat. *No, something's not right.*

Dax toggled his intercom button. Both Beaver and the major were wearing headsets. "Did you guys hear that baboon bark earlier?" enquired Dax.

"*Ja*," Beaver responded.

The major nodded.

"I don't like it," continued Dax. "I saw movement at the crest of the hill just as the baboon barked its warning call. The shape didn't look like a leopard." The leopard is the baboons' mortal enemy; its mere presence causes immediate distress within a troop. "It might be nothing, but the more I think about it, the more convinced I am that it wasn't a baboon. It might've just been an inquisitive villager." Dax acted on his own question before he'd even asked it. "You okay if I just fly on a northerly heading for a bit, just have a look-see?"

Before the others could even respond, Dax had swung the nose onto magnetic north

14

CONTACT!

Although faint, Morozov and the others heard the chopper the moment it came over the ridge. It was low against the horizon. As Dax adjusted his heading, so the slap of the rotors changed. The Russian also noticed that the helicopter's relative speed appeared to change; an illusion created by its altered direction. *Why is it coming this way when Kariba is over there?*

Initially confused, it took a few seconds for Morozov to compute. "Run!" he yelled. They were on open ground and needed to make it to a copse of miombo woodland about two hundred yards ahead. Morozov reckoned they had less than two minutes before the chopper was overhead.

Panting from the exertion, the men dropped to the ground as they reached the tree line. They had just made it as the chopper hove into full view. Or so they thought.

One of them—Morozov couldn't see who—had tripped on a small rock and rolled over his ankle. Grimacing from the pain, he'd hobbled toward the tree line, but not before being spotted by Dax and the major. He was caught in no-man's land. "Hold your fire," Morozov had yelled at the other seven, trying to make sure he'd be heard above the din. Their safety wasn't guaranteed, but there was no point in directing any unnecessary attention their way.

Caught in the open, the lone terrorist stood and faced the chopper. He'd have been spared if he'd thrown up his arms in surrender. Instead, the man foolishly raised his AK-47 to his shoulder.

Acting instinctively, Dax hauled the chopper's nose up and depressed the collective lever. Behaving like a massive air brake, the spinning rotor quickly slowed the machine to a walking pace. While gently easing the nose back down, Dax pulled on his collective and fed some power back to the disc. It immediately arrested the chopper's descent. He also needed to bring Beaver's door-mounted machine guns into play: Dax kicked his yaw pedal and presented the helicopter's left side to the lone gunman.

Beaver needed no instruction from his pilot. This aggressive aerial pirouette was only ever executed for a handful of reasons: Dax was either avoiding a high obstacle, or he needed to present a target to his gunner. Beaver prepared for the latter. He knew they were miles from the tall pylons that carried Kariba's electricity to the city.

The terrorist's first few rounds had pinged harmlessly off Dax's canopy. Due to the shooter's high angle of fire, combined with the curvature of the Perspex, the rounds had ricocheted up and away. Although relieved that they'd only left two telltale stars, Dax still had another concern. Deflected off the canopy, the tumbling rounds might yet cause some damage. A bullet strike to a spinning rotor was capable of causing a midflight de-lamination.

As the chopper spun sideways on, Beaver caught his first glimpse of the lone terrorist. He had no need to compensate for lead or lag; by then the chopper had settled and was at a virtual standstill. Looming ominously overhead, the gunman continued to fire. Beaver knew the familiar sensation; it was the strike of several Soviet 122 grain rounds peppering his side of the fuselage.

Let me have him.

Depressing the angle of his twin machine guns, Beaver raked the earth in front of the gook's feet. With a small adjustment, he slowly raised the barrels toward his target's torso. The technique served two purposes: it helped him sight the fall of his rounds; secondly, the shower of debris temporarily blinded the target. The terrorist jerked spasmodically as Beaver's next salvo tore into legs.

Without warning, the chopper lurched violently.

Beaver lost sight of his target as the helicopter began wobbling wildly off track. "You got him," yelled Dax, "but I think I took a round in my leg. Sorry for the bump."

As was customary amongst many operational pilots, Dax had long forsaken his flying suit in favor of camo shorts, a light flak jacket and a pair of ubiquitous *veldskoen* bush shoes.

The major looked down to check Dax's leg. The entry wound was neat and puckered, while the exit wound looked a little more ragged. But the major was more interested in the color of the blood coming out of the holes. Up by Dax's right ear, a splintered hole in the Perspex was framed by a fine red mist. "I'm okay," said Dax.

"Well it's not arterial," said the major. "You okay to go on?"

"Yeah, I'm fine." Looking back over his shoulder, the major indicated to Cargo to pass him a field dressing from their medic's bag.

Dax was about to speak when Beaver interjected. "Sir, we have fuel pissing out the side here … suggest we get outta the zone and put down so I can see what's potting." Dax checked his fuel gauges and saw that he'd need to nurse them back; more so now because of the leak. As he continued to scan his dials, a red warning light began to blink. To add to his woes, Dax's oil pressure was dropping.

The major made a quick evaluation. *This guy's ready to stay and fight but he's hit, we're losing fuel and a goddamn red light has just come on. I'm losing light and we haven't got any back-up.* He tapped Dax's shoulder, scribed three imaginary circles in the air with his forefinger, and then pointed toward Kariba. *Let's head back.*

As the last remnants of daylight sunk beneath the horizon, Dax realized the major was right. As they limped home, Dax raised Barrel on the radio. "Eagle Seven this is Starling Two-Zero."

"Go Two-Zero," responded Barrel. Two miles behind the

chopper, Morozov's radio man was twiddling his dials. He suddenly discovered a live channel.

"Comrade, come quickly," beckoned the radio operator. Morozov strode over and squatted beside Gadzire.

"Eagle Seven. We just made contact with one Charlie Tango approx two clicks north of the wreckage. May or may not be deceased. No sign of accomplices. We are hit but flyable. One wounded on board. You copy?" Dax toggled off and waited for Barrel's response.

"Starling Two-Zero, I copy. Who is hit?" enquired Barrel.

"Starling Two-Zero, sir," It was too late: Dax immediately realized how hammy that sounded. *Just like one of Barnes Wallis' pilots in The Dam Busters—stiff upper lip, old boy!* He cringed inwardly.

Eavesdropping on their transmission, Morozov made a mental note of the two call-signs. *Good! Not only have we discovered your operating frequency and two call-signs, but we have injured one of your valuable Rhodesian chopper pilots.*

As the helicopter receded from view, Morozov stood up and gathered his men around him. The men looked anxiously toward their fallen comrade: he was writhing in the grass a short distance away. The Russian was unmoved. "We are going to head north. It's now unlikely that we will make the river by sunrise. We must now aim to be there by noon tomorrow. We'll rest until sunset and return to Zambia under cover of darkness. That means we'll need to set a fast pace. We have a good moon tonight so we'll be able to see where we're going."

Under Morozov's watchful eye, the gang had endured months of arduous training: without it, they probably wouldn't have had the stamina to maintain the pace he now demanded.

"What will we do with Dennis Chifumbi?" asked Stix. He indicated toward the man squirming in the grass.

"I will give him something for the pain," answered Morozov, "but we'll have to leave him here. We can't carry him. Wait here."

Morozov walked over to Dennis. His torso was untouched but both his legs had been shattered by at least three of

Beaver's bullets. He moaned softly. The Russian stared at him for a few moments. *If the hyenas don't get him tonight, the Rhodesian doctors will be able to save his life, maybe even his left leg.* "You fucking idiot. You have compromised my mission," growled Morozov. "If they find you in the morning they will extract every last bit of intelligence out of you." Morozov un-holstered his Makarov pistol and cocked the weapon. "Because of you, the Rhodesians will be on our trail at first light." Morozov raised the pistol and aimed it at Dennis' forehead. "I told the others that I'd give you something for the pain."

Dennis Chifumbi looked beseechingly at Morozov. The last thing he saw was a small twitch in the corner of his comrade's eye.

15

EXFILTRATION

The army medic at FAF Kariba was satisfied that Dax had sustained nothing more than a flesh wound. Regardless, he still insisted that his patient be driven up to Kariba Heights to see the duty doctor.

Dax glanced over at the doctor's tray; some of the instruments looked like medieval torture devices. Wielding one of the tools like a clumsy carpenter, the doctor prodded and poked about in both holes. At least he'd had the courtesy to check that the anesthetic had taken effect.

After satisfying himself that his patient would survive, the doctor stood up and stretched his back. With a gloved and bloodied finger, he pushed his spectacles back up his nose. Dax wanted to laugh. *This is Pythonesque.*

"Mr. Hunter, you are indeed very lucky. Normally a tumbling bullet wreaks havoc inside the body. Due to its elastic nature, the flesh balloons and swells radially as the foreign body passes through. As you were shot from below, here, the bullet exited out of this hole, here, very quickly." Like a conductor wielding a baton, the doctor pointed at both holes in quick succession.

"Yes doc." Dax didn't know what else to say.

"Due to the short distance between entry and exit, you have only really suffered from what is known as the stretch mechanism. There appears to be little or no damage from the crush mechanism, which is usually associated with a longer passage through flesh or bones or organs," the doctor paused, "or all three." His afterthought didn't sound as ominous as he'd intended. "The passage of this bullet has left nothing more than a ragged hole through your leg. I'll patch you up and put a drain in, but our biggest fear with any gunshot wound of this nature is infection. I want you to get your medic to change the dressing regularly, and watch out for discolored seepage, understand?"

"Yes, sir," replied Dax.

"And take your full course of antibiotics, okay!" insisted the doctor. He clearly loved his job. "And I'm going to book you off flying duties for ten days. Understood?"

"Sir?" queried Dax beseechingly.

"And I also know my rugby players too, young man!" By now, the doctor was beaming. "So no rugby for you until the full season starts in April."

"Okay, sir, no rugby 'til April, I promise." Since joining the air force, Dax had already made an impression on the national rugby selectors. *This doctor must've seen me playing provincial rugby last season.* Dax still hoped he could somehow distract the doctor from penning a sick note.

Although the duty nurse had strapped Dax's leg from mid thigh to just below the knee, he was still able to flex it. With the anesthetic still lingering, he felt no discomfort as he walked out of the surgery. Before climbing into the Land Rover, Dax checked the two sheets of paper handed to him by the nurse. One was a prescription for extra painkillers. The other— addressed to the country's national rugby administrators— stated that Dax Hunter was not to play any sport until April 1st. Dax was elated not to be booked off flying duties.

Barrel looked skeptical. "Hunter, you sure you weren't booked off by the doctor?"

"No sir. He just told me no pre-season rugby training before 1st April, that's all. Oh yeah. Plus some technical stuff about it being no more than a superficial flesh wound."

"You know you don't have to fly, right?"

"Thanks sir, but I'll be fine." Barely fifteen minutes earlier, Barrel had observed closely as Hunter reported for duty. He certainly didn't look to be experiencing any discomfort. A crisp white bandage swathed his knee. There was no sign of blood.

"Okay. But I can't let you fly today though … the pain killers will still be making you woozy," said Barrel.

"Only had an anesthetic jab last night sir. No analgesics, I assure you."

Barrel furrowed his brow. *Well, this sure is one tenacious jockey. God knows I need every damn pilot today for the hot pursuit.*

"Okay, Dax," he conceded, "but take it easy," said Barrel. He immediately reverted to command mode. "You dropped off two PATU sticks in the valley yesterday, right? One stick found fresh tracks late yesterday heading south. Nine Charlie Tangos in total. If they're from the gooks who shot down the plane, they've likely been spooked by your contact last night. They'll definitely be wanting to get the hell out of Dodge."

"Let's hope they use the same path back down the valley," offered Dax.

"Ja," affirmed Barrel. "The first stick you dropped has reached the top of the escarpment and they've got an ambush set up in a tight ravine. I want you to fetch the second stick and take them close to the first, to bolster their firepower. Don't drop them too close though, I don't want to risk alerting the gooks to PATU's position in the ravine."

"Roger that," said Dax.

"By the way," said Barrel, changing tack. "While you were flirting with the nurse last night, Beaver was busy under the halogen lamp fixing your chariot. The man's a Trojan … he assures me your chopper is now fully serviceable. He even wiped your claret off the window. You owe him a beer or two."

The previous night, just an hour after setting off on their northerly heading, Morozov's gang had encountered a pride of lions. Although they couldn't see them in the darkness, the low, rumbling call of a dominant male had alerted them to the danger. Apart from not being able to see them, Morozov daren't fire his weapon to scare them off; the Rhodesians would be waiting for any telltale sign of their presence. Retracing their steps, the gang was forced to take a time-consuming detour. Even in the darkness, the men could sense Morozov's annoyance.

Approaching the main Kariba road in the moonlight, the fugitives could hear several trucks grinding their way through the tortuous Kariba-Makuti cuttings. Due to the widespread threat posed by terrorist activity, such nocturnal movements were rare. The only traffic that might risk driving that road at night would be military. Morozov guessed—quite correctly—that the vehicles were trucking troops into the area to assist in the follow-up operation. He and his gang were hunted men.

With their noisy engines and blazing headlights, any approaching vehicles would be impossible to miss. Despite the risk, Morozov decided to stay on the road and eat-up a few extra miles. It would also help mask their tracks.

They'd have ample time to dive for cover if they heard a truck approaching.

After about thirty minutes' hard march, Morozov decided to leave the road and strike north. Ahead, they faced over thirty miles of inhospitable terrain. Morozov gathered the men around him in the gloom. "Comrades. We are too easy to follow when we are so many. From here, we split up. Stix and Gadzire, you come with me. The rest of you, do what you do best … melt into the bush and disappear for a few days. At midnight on Saturday I will send the boat back to where it is now hidden. When you have crossed back over to Zambia, you are to report directly back to me at camp. Understood?"

The gang members offered a chorus of non-committal grunts.

16

THE ESCARPMENT

The Russian peered at his watch in the half-light. It was 04:42. An eerie dawn light was starting to nudge its way across the slumbering valley. Morozov checked his map. Even though they still had about eighteen miles to go, he was satisfied with their progress. He was still on track to cross the river that night. If the situation did turn nasty, he could always risk making a run for the Zambian side during broad daylight. It wasn't ideal, but the alternatives held little appeal.

The river was just under a mile wide at their crossing point. Of course, if they attempted a daytime crossing they risked being spotted by one of the army's observation posts hidden alongside the river. If they were marked by the Rhodesians, Morozov was certain they'd be sitting ducks in the water.

The Russian was a shrewd tactician. He'd already guessed that the Rhodesians would have an ambush ready-and-waiting for him. By his reckoning, it would likely be somewhere down the escarpment; somewhere with few escape options.

While making their way up the escarpment during the course of the previous day, Morozov had observed the two sticks being dropped behind his position. Having noted where they were dropped off, he guessed that the first stick had likely discovered his tracks soon after alighting. No doubt they would have initiated a pursuit, but bad light would have eventually stymied their progress. The Russian was certain that they would have been instructed to bivvy-up for the night and resume their chase at first light.

But it was likely they'd only chase so far.

The Russian began to assess his options. *The Rhodesians have flushed us, so they probably think we'll be coming back down this way to get out of the country as soon as possible. As sure as Rasputin was a Khlysty, they will find an ambush position somewhere through the escarpment, probably a tight passage where they can expect to splinter my group and overwhelm us with withering firepower.*

Ever observant, Morozov had noticed a perfect ambush spot the day before. It was in a narrow ravine near the crest of the escarpment. *If I was a Rhodesian commander, that's precisely where I'd put my ambush party.*

Since blowing a civilian aircraft out of the sky, Morozov knew the stakes had become immeasurably higher. He knew there would be a horde of Rhodesians chasing him down, and that they'd be leapfrogging small units ahead once they'd ascertained the direction and freshness of his tracks. Morozov's three-mile diversion along the Kariba-Makuti road would only fool the Rhodesian trackers for a short while. But by splitting his group, he hoped that he'd sow a little confusion amongst his pursuers. Morozov thought hard: he certainly didn't want to get caught in a classic pincer move.

"Gadzire, bring your radio here," he commanded. "Have you heard anything on the frequency you discovered last night?" he enquired.

"*Hapana nehurukuro*, comrade," said Gadzire in chiShona, "nothing," he added in English.

"Keep that radio on. At least we have the air force's channel. I need to know what they are up to," said the Russian.

"*Yebo*, comrade," said Gadzire sullenly. Dennis Chifumbi had been his best friend. Despite the callous act, none of the gang members could afford to be insolent toward Morozov. After witnessing the execution the night before, they all realized he was *kupenga* … insane.

Although he wasn't aware of it, Morozov's pitiless act had actually reinforced his status. The exertion of power through fear—more than charity and comradeship—is a compelling tool in African culture. Even with their superior numbers, none of Morozov's men would have dared usurp their new leader. The Russian was invulnerable.

Realizing that he was in a game of cat and mouse, Morozov decided to abandon the direct route down the escarpment. From his current position, he decided to follow an ox-bow detour. Initially following an easterly bearing, he planned to slowly swing northwards before eventually turning westwards. Scribing a large arc in this manner would circumvent the Rhodesian's most likely ambush site. It might also sow a little more confusion amongst their trackers. The ruse would be complete when the trackers discovered that the gang had splintered. By Morozov's reckoning, he and his two sidekicks would come back onto their game trail about half-way down the escarpment. From there, with some luck, they should be able to make the river in less than two hours.

After getting airborne out of Kariba, Dax turned onto a north-easterly bearing. They were on their way to collect the second PATU stick that they'd inserted late the previous day. After rendezvousing with this stick, they were to uplift and relocate them to a position close to Blue Stick One. Since early that morning, Blue Stick One had been lying in-wait in their well-chosen ambush position. It was the exact spot Morozov thought they might choose. According to the plan, Blue Stick Two was to join them and bolster their firepower.

Once over the escarpment, Dax transmitted to the PATU guys on the ground. "Blue Stick Two this is Starling Two-Zero, do you read, over?" Eight seconds passed with no answer. Dax was about to resend when the radio spat into life.

"This is Blue Stick Two, we read you strength five Starling Two-Zero."

Walking in single file, Morozov had taken-up position right behind Gadzire. The radio on his back was turned low. Upon hearing Dax's transmission, Morozov brought his small band to a halt. *Good morning Starling Two-Zero. So, you are up and about, despite being wounded by Chifumbi last night. Very brave of you. So what plans have you got today?*

"Relative to the position where I dropped you yesterday, where are you now Blue Stick Two?" asked Dax.

Morozov continued eavesdropping. *Very good radio procedure, Starling Two-Zero. I see you don't want to compromise the position of your team on the ground.*

In reality, Dax just found it easier to compute the second position relative to the first—the details of the latter were still clear in his mind from the previous day.

"Blue Stick Two is currently seven clicks south-south-east of yesterday's position," responded Stick Two's radio operator.

"Roger that. We'll be there in approximately nine minutes to lift you out. Can you find a patch for me to put down?" The guys knew the drill: it was their responsibility to identify a suitably-sized clearing for Dax to safely land his chopper.

Morozov nodded thoughtfully. *I wonder if he's picking them up and returning them to Kariba, or lifting them into a desirable ambush position?*

It was mid-morning. Morozov had almost completed his detour around the natural bottleneck—the one he considered to be the Rhodesians' best ambush option. As he approached from the east, he figured they'd intersect their original trail within the next thirty minutes. He also estimated that they'd cut the path about four miles below the likely ambush site.

Faintly, very faintly, the small gang made out the jangle of Dax's chopper. There was an almost imperceptible change to the tune of the rotors as Dax landed on Blue Stick Two's pre-arranged pick-up point. Morozov signaled for the other two to go to ground. They waited.

Thirty seconds later, as the chopper rose above the tree line, the sound of Dax's machine reached them on a favorable breeze. *Now, let's hear if you head south west back to Kariba, Starling Two-Zero.*

Five or six minutes passed. Although barely audible, the sound of the rotor was nonetheless distinct. Morozov couldn't tell which way it was heading. Running out of patience, he was about to resume their westward march when he heard the note of the rotor change.

Dax had found a suitable clearing about three clicks north of the ambush position. His PATU drop would have to tab up the trail to join forces with their companions from Blue Stick One. Morozov smiled. *Just as I thought.* It sounded as if the chopper had landed some way off to his eleven o'clock position, perhaps less than three miles away.

The men listened intently as the chopper rose from its landing zone; Morozov was anxious to determine the pilot's next move. To his immense relief, the sound of the chopper receded as it turned south and headed back in the direction of Kariba.

Morozov, Stix and Gadzire intersected their trail and immediately turned north onto the clearly defined animal track. These game paths had been used since time immemorial and were perfect infiltration routes for the guerrillas.

It was just before noon. Given their various delays, Morozov was confident they'd reach the river by 1:30 PM. Their trail would soon flatten out as it approached the Zambezi's broad alluvial plains.

There had been scant information shared over the airwaves by either Dax or his commander, Eagle Seven, during the course of the morning.

Since discovering Dax's radio frequency the previous day, Morozov had gained invaluable access to the Rhodesians' intentions. Despite the windfall, he derived little comfort from the fact that their most northerly-located pursuers appeared to be the two PATU sticks waiting in ambush. While he was confident they were well behind his position, he still worried about the Rhodesians' next move. *It'd be good if I knew what they were up to.*

17

COMMAND DECISION

Swinging in on a tight arc, his tail skid seemingly stroking the tarmac, Dax made a delicate adjustment as he settled the machine lightly on its tricycle landing gear. He was careful not to land too close to the command tent. Just last week, one of the junior pilots had hovered too close to the tent and practically ripped it out at the pegs. As was tradition in such situations, his bar tab that night bore the full brunt of his misdemeanor.

Dax had just completed his shut-down procedures when he noticed Barrel standing near the tent. He beckoned frantically.

Once his pilot was inside, Barrel got straight to business. "Our trackers got a bit confused this morning when they discovered the gang's tracks petered-out at the Kariba-Makuti road. It took them a while to find the tracks again. They stayed on the tarmac for about three miles before crossing over. We know they lost one guy last night, so the eight sets of tracks they found north of the tar road definitely ties to our gang. Not only that, the trackers were able to match several boot prints," said Barrel.

"Sir, I heard from one of the SAS guys this morning that last night's gook had been taken out, execution style," interjected Dax.

"*Ja.* 9mm between the eyes, never heard of them doing that before. But back to the gang. Our trackers have picked up that they've now split up. Three gooks are heading north—

probably trying to make a dash for the river. The other five have crossed back over the road and appear to be heading toward Vuti." Barrel indicated the various positions on the 1:20,000 ordinance map. "We know what that means," he continued. "If they melt into the community they're as good as gone. The SAS are all over this. The major doesn't want any of them slipping through, even the three that now appear to be heading north. He's tasked us with putting a stop group further north … almost too far, by my reckoning," Barrel demurred. "But the major argues that if we drop any men too close to the escarpment, we'll alert the gooks to our intentions." Barrel paused before adding, "He probably has a point."

"Are we dropping SAS guys, sir?" enquired Dax.

"The major can't spare any of his boys as they're concentrating on the five runaways. He wants us to take one of the PATU sticks and put them down somewhere south of the river. It'll be the gooks' last hurdle; let's see if we can make it count," said Barrel grimly.

"Sir, what about the PATU ambush at the top of the escarpment?"

"If the three fugitives had used the same path they used yesterday, they'd have triggered the ambush by now. If that was the case, we'd have heard from Blue Stick One and Two by now. I don't think our PATU guys are going to bag any charlies in *that* ambush. It's a damn pity," he added ruefully. "Now get yourself airborne, pronto. I want you to lift those PATU guys out and place them further north, about four clicks south of the river. Use that north-south trail as your reference; you know, the one that runs down from the gully in the escarpment."

"I'll get airborne as soon as I've fueled-up."

"No time," shot back Barrel. "You were full when you left this morning, right?" He didn't give Dax any time to answer. "My guess is you've already flown forty-five minutes today. You still have over two hours in the tank. You'll be okay to pick them up, leapfrog them to their forward position and then return here."

It was Dax's third attempt at raising the PATU guys in their ambush position. "Blue Stick One or Blue Stick Two, this is Starling Two-Zero, do you read, over?"

"Sir, I think they're still in ambush mode and are maintaining radio silence," ventured Beaver. Scudding low over the tree tops, Dax and Beaver were about fifteen clicks south of the ambush position. *Dammit, of course,* thought Dax.

Down on the ground, Morozov was relieved to hear Dax's call: his concern was that they might've switched frequencies. The Russian could sense Starling Two-Zero's frustration. *Ah, my Starling friend. Three unanswered radio calls tells me so much. Combining two call-signs in your transmission probably means that they're together or in close proximity. Is it the ambush party you bolstered earlier today? Your superiors have realized their trap is now futile. Do you want to lift them out and leapfrog forward?* Morozov's mind was working hard. *I know you can't pick up both sticks in your Alouette, so can I expect you to deliver four men, somewhere north of my position?*

Four on three. Morozov could handle those odds.

Dax had no choice but to hover directly over the PATU ambush position—or at least the position he *thought* they might be hiding in.

Earlier that day he'd dropped the second stick a short distance north of the ambush spot so that they could stealthily walk up into position. Dropping them directly on the spot would have been both dangerous and clumsy; dangerous because of the rocky terrain, clumsy because he would have compromised their location. Dax now had to guess where they had set their trap.

Dax knew the valley like his own back yard. His imprinted aerial image of the terrain didn't fail him. With a blend of luck, logic and location, he figured out the PATU guys' most likely ambush spot. He hovered overhead, waiting to flush them from their cover. No longer clandestine, Dax figured that the PATU guys would quickly conclude that their ambush wait was over.

Beaver caught sight of the first guy emerging from his leafy cover. He wasn't sure if the PATU guy below was waving at him or shaking a fist: *fuck you*, thought Beaver, just in case it was the latter.

After establishing eye contact, Beaver splayed the thumb and pinky of his right hand and lifted it to his face like an imaginary telephone. *Call me.* The man on the ground nodded an acknowledgement.

"Sir, I reckon you should move a little way off. They're going live on the radio but they probably won't hear us with this clatter overhead," suggested Beaver.

"Got you," responded Dax. With that he tracked off a short distance to reduce the ambient noise.

"Blue Stick One or Blue Stick Two, this is Starling Two-Zero, do you read, over?" Dax transmitted for the fourth time.

"This is Blue One, go," said the PATU radio man.

"Charlie Tangos ha..." six miles due north of Blue Stick One, Gadzire's batteries had just died.

Morozov cursed in Russian. "You fucking fool, quickly, put new batteries in."

"We have no more, comrade. They are all dead," pleaded Gadzire. Morozov glowered at his radio man.

Think Vladimir, think. "Okay. The Rhodesians must've figured out by now that we've split up. I suspect they'll concentrate their efforts on pursuing our five comrades, but make no mistake, they haven't forgotten about us. They probably know we're retracing our steps, so that last transmission was likely to be instructions to move one or both of the Blue Sticks further north along this path."

"What do you suggest, comrade?" asked Stix.

"Our next move then is to take another detour. We can't stay on this trail any longer." Detouring off the game path would make the going a lot tougher, but they had no alternative.

Hovering a short distance away from Blue Sticks One and Two, Dax conveyed their new orders. He needed to uplift them and ferry them northwards toward the river.

"Starling Two-Zero, there are no suitable landing zones around here for almost two clicks," said Blue Stick One's radioman. "I suggest Blue Stick Two leads us to the LZ where you dropped them this morning. It'll take us fifteen minutes to get there. Can you wait there for us, over?" enquired the radioman.

"Copy that," responded Dax. He didn't like it at all but he had little choice. Being shut down in a bush clearing with no perimeter defense was suicidal. Wasting fuel in an overhead hover not only reduced his airborne effectiveness, but also made him a perfect target. But it was the lesser of two evils.

Beaver concurred after Dax had shared his concerns. "Our closest fuel is back at FAF," said the door-gunner. "It's a forty-five minute round trip, and that excludes refueling time on the ground. It'll be the best part of an hour before we get back here. Giving the PATU guys more credit than they deserve, let's assume they *can* make it to our LZ in fifteen. With two-up, that's between eight and nine gallons burn."

Damn, Beaver's got a good head for this stuff! thought Dax.

"We then have to pick them up and fly six-up to the river, then make it back to Kariba." Beaver thought for a moment while he completed his mental calculation. "Plus, we've already completed one forty minute flight and some hover time on this tank already." He paused. "Sir, we'll be close to *bingo* but we should scrape through." Dax had already reached the same conclusion, but welcomed the confirmation. Beaver pressed his intercom button. "But I agree with you on us being sitting ducks ... whether we're overhead in the hover, or shut down on the ground."

Dax trusted his instinct: every fiber in his body was telling him not to land and shut down. They would just be too vulnerable on the ground. He decided to fly a lazy wide circuit around their rendezvous point. If he was to remain in the hover overhead the LZ, he first wanted to be sure that there was nobody around. Besides, completing the circuit around the LZ would not only kill time, but give him movement and momentum—a soldier's best ally.

Six miles north of Dax's position, Morozov, Gadzire and Stix heard the chopper. Its sound neither diminished nor increased. Morozov was certain it was in a holding hover. *This is good. It gives me time.* The Russian risked a quick glance at his map.

His decision to take a detour had probably added a further two miles to his journey. *A fucking waste of valuable time.* Morozov reckoned the river was now less than two miles due north of his position. But he still had to head upstream about a mile-and-a-half to reach the point where they'd concealed their boat almost forty hours earlier. Their landmark was easy to locate—their boat was secreted in the reeds diagonally opposite where the Kafue and Zambezi rivers converged.

Far behind their position, Morozov's gang could still hear the hovering chopper. *It sounds like he's preoccupied.* The Russian allowed himself a thin smile.

Dax was holding his hover thirty feet above the LZ when he noticed movement in the tree line about three hundred yards south of his position. Presenting the chopper's left side, he keyed Beaver and asked him to keep an eye on the approaching figures. They were probably the PATU guys, but he didn't want to assume anything. Just as he was about to call Blue Stick One to confirm, his own radio crackled to life.

"Starling Two-Zero this is Eagle Seven, do you read, over?"

"This is Starling Two-Zero, strength four, Eagle Seven," Dax responded. *Readable with practically no difficulty.*

"Two-Zero, an army lookout along the river has advised seeing three Charlie Tangos, do you copy, over?"

"This is Two-Zero. Three Charlie Tangos. I copy," replied Dax. He waited for Barrel to transmit their location.

"Their position as follows. One and a half clicks east of the confluence, and currently three quarters of a click south of the river. Seen heading west toward the confluence. Do you copy?"

"I copy that."

"One CT was reported to be carrying a tube-like device. That could be the missile canister. Apprehend at all costs. Copy?" Barrel's voice was tinged with desperation.

"I copy."

"Starling Two-Zero. Don't let the bastards get across that river."

Dax had to make a command decision. *Do I wait for the PATU guys to cover the three hundred yards, get onboard, then bear north with a few extra rifles pointing out my doors? Or do I head to the river with just Beaver's twin machine guns poking out the door?*

Dax pulled the chopper over aggressively and lowered his nose for the river.

18

PILOT HIT

If he'd navigated accurately, Morozov estimated they were no more than five hundred yards from where they'd concealed their boat. He and the other two could smell the wetness of the Zambezi. High elephant grass hugged the river's flanks. For several minutes they had been zigzagging down a maze of confusing paths that crisscrossed through the otherwise impregnable thicket. Although the tall grass obscured their view, the river's bouquet was unmistakable. Towering five feet above their heads, the swishing grass provided some cover, but also masked all other sounds.

Gadzire and Stix were anxious. They knew how hazardous it could be following such paths. Without a tree in sight, and nowhere else to go except backwards, confronting a large, wild animal down one of these paths was always a distinct possibility. The bush around them was rank with the odor of big game. Possibly the worst scenario would be a face-to-face encounter with a cantankerous old *dagga-boy*—a bull buffalo.

They never anticipated an aerial threat.

Skimming over the top of the tall grass, the chopper had come in low from behind their position. Its giveaway tune had been masked by the hypnotic susurrus of the millions of tall stems waving in the wind.

The chopper's untimely arrival was an insult to the Russian's vanity: for his part in the downing of the Rhodesian airliner, Morozov was already preparing his acceptance speech for the Order of Lenin.

Dax had seen the three figures in the tall grass. As he tore overhead, the three guerrillas bolted down the path. They reached an intersection; one branch bore northwards toward the water's edge. Veering right, they carried on sprinting toward the water's edge. Dax executed a high yaw turn maneuver barely a hundred feet overhead.

Although temporarily obscured from the pilot's view, Beaver had been able to keep the fugitives in sight. He shouted that he'd seen them breaking toward the river. In the turn, the chopper's initial forward momentum had carried it a hundred yards beyond where the three men had first been spotted. In the time that it had taken Dax to complete his maneuver—the quickest and most effective under the circumstances— Morozov and the others had burst out of the reeds onto a narrow sandy bank alongside the lapping waters.

Pointing ahead, Gadzire recognized the spot where they'd concealed their boat. It was only fifty yards from their position. "Comrade, you and Stix pull the boat out, I will distract them," he yelled above the noise of the buzzing chopper.

Dax was now tracking eastwards, parallel to the river, with his gunner facing the threat. But their enemy remained hidden from view.

Gadzire unleashed a short burst of machine gun fire. Beaver heard a couple of the rounds pinging into the metal around him. *Where the fuck are they?* He couldn't see the shooter. Lady Luck soon smiled on him. Amidst the next hail of bullets—a longer burst this time—a tell-tale, incandescent glow followed every fifth round. Gadzire had loaded tracer rounds into his magazine. Beaver sneered sardonically. *Tracers work both ways, fucker.*

Target unseen, Beaver squeezed off an angry burst. He aimed into the tall grass from where the tracers had originated. Moments later, a second burst rose up from the reeds, only this time it had been fired from about ten yards to the left of the original position. *Clever boy.* Beaver waited before unleashing another controlled burst, but instead of concentrating his salvo in one spot, he raked from right to left.

One of his rounds struck Gadzire in the left elbow. The lower limb was blown away, exposing a mangled mess of shattered bone and glistening tissue. Reeling from the pain, the terrorist staggered back out of cover. Beaver saw him looking down incredulously at his wet stump. Dazed, he looked over to his comrades for assistance. Time had distorted, sounds were echoing around him from the depths of a long tunnel. *Stix will help me. I need to get to Stix.*

Weaving drunkenly, Gadzire stumbled toward the boat. From a dense cluster of reeds, about thirty paces upstream, a raking arc of fire rose up toward the chopper.

During the distraction created by Gadzire's lone assault, the other two had finished pulling the boat from the bushes. Only the first few yards of the hull remained anchored in the sand. The rest of the boat lapped in the shallows. "Aim at the pilot, not the gunner," yelled Morozov above the chatter of Beaver's guns. Although counterintuitive, Stix realized that disabling the chopper was their only chance of making it.

Beaver swung the twin barrels onto the new threat and unleashed a torrent of lead. Seeking whatever shelter they could, Morozov and Stix dived behind some spindly trees. The trunks provided little ballistic cover, but the dense foliage managed to obscure them from view. Had Beaver known precisely where they were hiding, his rounds would have pulverized the trunks Using short, controlled bursts from behind their cover, Stix and Morozov continued firing up at the chopper. The incoming rounds hissed past Beaver's ears.

Aiming for the thicket, the door gunner let loose a speculative burst of fire.

Morozov stumbled back and cried out involuntarily. *I've been hit.* Looking around instinctively, Stix checked to see how badly his comrade had been wounded. Morozov's left hand was pressed up against his face. A copious flow of blood had already seeped between his fingers. "Keep firing at the pilot you fucking idiot," he snarled.

Stix knew what wrath those machine guns were capable of unleashing. He quickly realized that the Russian couldn't have taken a direct hit in the face—if he had, his head would have disintegrated like a melon. *It must've been a shrapnel ricochet.* While the foliage around him was being shredded, Stix took deliberate aim at the cockpit. As he depressed his trigger, he made sure to exert some downward pressure on the handguard. Without it, the weapon had a tendency to climb when fired on automatic.

Dax recoiled from the pain. His left hand had been violently knocked from the collective lever. *Fuck no! I'm hit.*

While the previous day's round through his thigh had stung, this one boiled all the way to his armpit. A bright explosion of lights sparkled across his peripheral vision. Lifting his left arm at the shoulder, Dax tried to test his reflexes: his shoulder joint functioned—in a fashion—but his forearm and left hand were devoid of sensation. His arm hung loose like a cut in a butcher's window.

Dax could see that he'd taken a round clean through the forearm. His left hand was useless. Unattended on the floor beside his left leg, his collective lever beckoned seductively. In the immediate aftermath of the bullet strike, Dax's arm had straightened reflexively. Driving the collective lever downwards, it caused the chopper to start descending. Not only was it dropping, but the initial jolt had also caused the helicopter to wobble precariously. He was furious. *I can't let those bastards get away. They just can't get away.*

"What in hell's name is going on up there?" Beaver yelled. He was still intent on putting rounds into the thicket, but the rocking chopper was making that impossible. In the absence of coordinated inputs, the helicopter lurched violently. Beaver lost sight of his target and spun his head around to see if Dax was okay.

"Beaver, I'm hit. My left arm's U-S. I can't operate the collective." In his right hand, Dax had thumbed the transmit button on the top of his cyclic stick, but he needed both hands to fly.

Curiously detached from his predicament, Dax's mind remained focused on his quarry. *I've gotta land this thing so Beaver and I can go after them on foot.*

If Beaver could get out of his harness he could scramble forward, take the collective and assist in putting them down somewhere. He knew how these darn contraptions stayed aloft: he'd definitely be able to handle one in just such an emergency.

But the wild bucking prevented him from being able to co-ordinate his own movements … he was a prisoner in his own harness.

Dax slid forward in his seat so he could grip the cyclic between his knees. *I gotta fly us safely to the ground.* Although his situation was desperate, he continued to ignore the searing pain: he could think of nothing else but annihilating the three terrorists. An angry red veil had started to descend. *We've gotta get them.*

With the cyclic stick clenched between his knees, Dax reached over awkwardly with his right hand. He managed to pull up on the collective. Due to the unnatural contortion of his body, Dax's twisting motion was transferred through his legs into the cyclic. The chopper started to roll left. Fighting to gain a modicum of stability, he pushed back slightly. His co-ordination was clumsy. Dax was too low to be able to perfect his improvised flying technique. *Fuck it. We're going down.*

All Dax could now hope for was that he could keep them level. He'd have to pull-up hard on the collective just above the beckoning tips of the elephant grass. With a combination of good providence and pilot skill, he was able to lift the chopper's nose above the horizon—but still the machine plummeted earthward. With the cyclic clamped between his knees, Dax managed to keep the chopper relatively level. With his body doubled like a contortionist, the pilot had to judge his height to perfection: at the moment critique, he pulled up hard on the collective with his right hand. His timing was perfect: Hunter's input arrested the chopper's headlong descent.

All he could hope for was that the tall elephant grass would cushion their forward momentum. Amidst the noise and fury, Dax had the presence of mind to reach forward and kill his battery and fuel switch. The chopper slewed through the thick reeds. Dragging on the spinning disk above their heads, thousands of tall stems helped retard the blades' rotation. As the tail rotor sliced through the grass and dug into the soft clay, Beaver heard his beloved gearbox grinding in protest. As the thick grass retarded the last of the machine's energy, the door gunner was jostled violently in his harness. His face was flailed by the sharp leaves.

Morozov squinted through the congealing blood. He was aware of a sharp pain in his face. The firing had stopped. He was vaguely aware that Stix was jabbering at him in his native tongue.

The Russian had looked up just as the chopper slewed overhead: it was wobbling precariously on all three axes. He knew it was doomed; it was just a question of whether it would crash on top of their heads or not. The chopper had been so close that Morozov had been able to read the serial number stenciled on the wheel strut.

The ungainly helicopter had disappeared from view over the top of the tall elephant grass. As it impacted with the earth, Morozov heard the stems of the thick grass tearing under the scything blades. He had been disappointed not to hear an explosion.

In the boxing ring, Morozov had taken a good few punches to the cheekbone, but nothing quite compared to the soreness he was experiencing at that moment. Despite the sting in his shattered face, he was slowly become aware of a second source of pain. It was a thick, dull ache that radiated up from around his groin.

Right at that moment, despite an urge to go for the jugular, Morozov was vaguely aware of a persistent voice of reason. *Get on that fucking boat and get back to Zambia.*

Gadzire was in a state of deep shock. Stumbling about in a stupor, he gabbled strangely in a low monotone. Despite his trance-like state, he'd somehow had the presence to locate the artery that had retracted into the mangled tissue. He pinched it shut with a slippery right thumb and forefinger. Stix ran over to him and steered him to the boat. "Gadzire," he yelled. The wounded man stared blankly at Stix. "*Kupinda*, get in."

Morozov and Stix pushed the boat the rest of the way into the water. After scrambling aboard, Stix took up position at the helm. With the wheel in one hand and the throttle in the other, he primed the carburetor. He then twisted the key. *Chug chug chug*. Resisting the temptation to pump the throttle a second time, he tried again. *Chug chug chug*. He daren't look at Morozov. The boat was starting to drift. Up ahead, Stix noticed a change in the pattern of the wavelets: they were at risk of running aground on a submerged sandbank. On the third attempt the motor coughed, then fired into life.

Having notified FAF Kariba of the gang's presence just a little over thirty minutes before, the same sentry was presently distracted. At that precise moment he was concentrating on sending a rescue appeal for the downed chopper. Had he been looking toward the river, he might have noticed a battered old boat slipping into the current of the Zambezi and pointing its nose toward the sanctuary of the far bank.

19

THE OATH

Crouching low in the boat, Stix manned the tiller and directed them toward deeper water. He was convinced that he was in the cross-hairs of a Rhodesian marksman. Up front, Gadzire was still keening softly. Morozov appeared to be fiddling with something in his lap. Although Stix could see blood on the front of Morozov's combat pants, he'd assumed that it was where the Russian had just wiped his bloodied hands. With his face still covered with congealed blood, Morozov continued to fumble with the front fastener of his webbing belt. As the adrenaline started to wear off, the dull ache in his groin had intensified.

Wet from his own blood, Morozov's fingers fumbled with his belt buckle. Unleashing an angry snarl, he eventually managed to loosen the front of his pants. Lying on his back, the Russian squirmed out of his combat pants. He inched them down toward his knees. Unrestrained by the tight-fitting garment, Morozov ran his right hand over his genitalia. *My cock is okay, but what the …*

Morozov blanched. He sat up and looked down at his groin. One of the door gunner's rounds had passed high-up between Morozov's legs and nicked his right testicle. A soupçon of body fluids oozed between the folds and tatters of the exploded organ. Swollen and discolored, the opposite sac looked like an overripe avocado. The Russian began to rage. With his trousers still crumpled about his knees, he stretched

forward to retrieve a field dressing from one of his pockets.
Using his teeth to tear open the cellophane wrapper, he removed the sterile wad and placed it in position over his scrotum.

Working gingerly over his wound, Morozov eased his combat pants back up to his waist. Once fastened, he stood unsteadily in the middle of the boat. Wild eyed and foaming, he faced the receding bank and began to unleash a vile storm of Russian curses. "Starling Two-Zero, you son of a fucking whore. I will come back to find you. I will kill you. I will slice you like my great grandfather butchered the Romanovs. You hear me? You fucking hear me?" As the spittle flew from the deranged Russian's lips, his left eye began to twitch uncontrollably.

20

THE REVEAL

The Russian opened his eye. It took him a few moments to realize he was in a private hospital ward. He tried to raise his head off the pillow but it collapsed back weakly; he was light-headed and not a little confused. The last vestiges of anesthetic still chilled his blood.

Outside the window, as throngs of Lusakans hailed buses, dodged hooting cars, hawked their wares or begged from passersby, the nation's capital was just awakening. Already, the stench of a thousand coal fires mingled with the nonmelodious hubbub.

In small, disjointed increments, Morozov started piecing together the events of the previous day. Having made it across the river, Stix had moored their launch a short distance up the Kafue. After tying-off the boat against a crumbling jetty, he'd scouted around the small fishing village. He discovered an off-duty taxi driver snoozing in his parked minibus. Indignant at being woken, the bewildered driver had initially been reluctant to make the long journey to Lusaka. He quickly recanted after Stix had menacingly waved his AK-47. After loading his two wounded comrades into the taxi, Stix urged the driver to make Lusaka by nightfall.

Still smarting from being rudely commandeered, the driver's confidence had soon recovered. Raising his voice to emphasize his point, he'd threatened to double his fee in order to cover the cost of washing all the blood off his tacky vinyl seats.

With an hour still to go before they reached Lusaka, their taxi approached the small town of Kafue. Although there was a reasonable clinic in the town, Stix had intuited that Morozov would require better hospital care than was available in the sleepy little town. But by that stage of their journey Gadzire had become catatonic from blood loss. Stix ordered the taxi to make a small detour to the clinic. Without urgent medical attention, his friend would probably not make it to Lusaka. Making a small diversion, they dropped Gadzire outside the Kafue clinic. Using the persuasive power of his AK-47, Stix urged the disgruntled driver to continue onwards to Lusaka.

Since tying the boat, the drive to Kafue had taken them a little under three hours. It had been just over four hours since Morozov and Gadzire had both taken hits.

For the remaining hour of their journey, the driver gagged theatrically as the stench of gore and cloying blood permeated the cab.

Ditch the scrubs, put on a pair of sandals and wrap yourself in robes. You're Gandhi's Doppelgänger. Morozov thought he was being hilarious. Unsurprisingly, the effects of the anesthetic hadn't quite worn off.

Short of stature and sporting owlish wire-rimmed spectacles, the balding East German doctor could've easily been mistaken for the famous Indian ascetic. Rising up on his toes, he peered at his patient lying propped-up in his hospital bed.

The East German doctor had studied medicine in Leningrad and his Russian was accented but good. "Ah, comrade Morozov, I see you are joining us," joked the doctor. "And how are you this morning?"

"Let's cut the idle chatter, doctor," he groused. "Tell me how the operation went." Morozov's speech was slightly slurred. A massive wad of gauze had been taped over his damaged cheek and also extended up over his eye. Despite his intoxication, Morozov sensed a rising dread. "What's wrong with my eye?"

"Your eye is fine, comrade. This is just a precaution to entirely disengage all the muscles in the area around your wound. I will check in a few days to see if it is safe to remove the cover," reassured the doctor.

"And my cheekbone?" enquired Morozov.

"Your cheekbone was badly shattered. I had to remove a large fragment of shrapnel from your sinus cavity. Any higher, and you would have been blinded."

Ah, Doctor Gandhi has just pulled the speculative-scenario card. Is that meant to make me feel better? Still trippy from the anesthetic, Morozov quietly applauded his wry wit. "How will it heal?" he pressed.

"There will be a noticeable indentation once the skin has repaired, but it will be possible for a maxillofacial surgeon to restructure the cheekbone in a few months. That kind of work is beyond my pay-grade, comrade." The doctor paused. "Besides, specialists like that only visit Lusaka every few months."

Using his good eye, Morozov squinted at the doctor's name badge. "Doctor Spielmann, tell me about my right testicle."

"Your right testicle was a mess. There was nothing to save. The miracle is that your left testicle is undamaged. You are lucky …" The doctor paused for effect.

Morozov rolled his one eye. *Here it comes.*

"If that bullet was half an inch higher." With a wistful look, the doctor shook his head in fraternal solidarity. He deeply grasped his own implication.

Clearly you're not a fatalist, Dr. Gandhi. "What will it look like when it's healed?" asked Morozov.

"I have used very fine suture material to gather and repair most of the thin scrotal skin. Much of the skin on the right side of the raphe had to be ablated and what was left has been carefully closed and stitched over the empty sac," said the East German.

It sounds like he knows what he's talking about.

"But if I may suggest, comrade. When you have healed, a surgeon can take a skin graft to remodel your scrotum and insert a prosthetic testicle. I am confident that your left testicle will function as normal, and you will be able to father many sons." Doctor Spielmann allowed himself a small chuckle, "You will just be a little … let's say, unbalanced. That's all."

Like every army throughout history, the Rhodesian forces had their share of subverters and traitors. With a growing number of Rhodesia's clandestine operations turning into lemons— failed missions—it was becoming obvious to the hierarchy that they had a mole, or several, embedded within their senior ranks.

After their ordeal on the banks of the Zambezi, and the subsequent taxi ride to the capital, Stix had deposited his Russian casualty at the Lusaka General Hospital. Before departing, Morozov had given Stix a hastily-scrawled note. He was instructed to pass it on to one of Morozov's colleagues in Lusaka. "Make sure he gets this tonight," ordered the Russian.

Despite being inherently bureaucratic, the Soviet's global intelligence-gathering network was stupendous. Morozov knew this and needed to tap into it. They, in-turn, would merely reach out to their network of Rhodesian moles.

Morozov was getting agitated. But despite his confinement, he hadn't been able to fight off the waves of fatigue that engulfed him. Since the operation, he had slept on-and-off for almost three days.

Morozov was still groggy when his Russian colleague eventually came to visit. His mood pepped up when he noticed a thin manila folder tucked under his associate's arm. The nondescript visitor wore a ubiquitous powder-blue Crimplene safari suit; standard casual attire for the majority of middle-aged white men across colonial Africa. He dropped a sturdy canvas zipper bag at the end of Morozov's bed. "Comrade, the things you asked for." His head tilted slightly toward the canvas bag. "There is a padlock in there too."

Since neither man was socially adept, they sacrificed any pretense of inquiring about each other's wellbeing. The visitor got straight to the point.

"Here's the information you were seeking, comrade. It was an unusual request and certainly outside normal protocols. I will ask no questions. If anyone ever asks, you are to assure me you will never link me back to this information," intoned the quintessential gray man.

"I won't. Thank you, comrade," said Morozov. Both men knew the meeting was over.

Morozov waited as his comrade's footsteps receded down the long corridor. He was flushed with a heady brew of eagerness and loathing. His testicle started to ache. Unable to contain his anticipation, he flipped open the folder.

An oversized paperclip held two loose pages of typed notes together. A black-and-white photograph was wedged under the clip in the top left corner. Morozov's eye was drawn immediately to the picture of an open-faced, personable young man.

The picture was grainy. It was a head-and-torso shot and the young man in the photograph was wearing a rugby jersey. The trimmed shoulders of two people appearing either side of the man suggested that the picture had been enlarged from a team photograph. The man's arms were folded across his broad chest. Despite the loss of detail, Morozov could see the sparkle of self-assurance in the young man's eyes.

The blood in Morozov's veins began to pump harder. His pupil shrunk to a pinprick and his eyelid narrowed. His mouth curled menacingly. As the rage gathered, his chest began to tighten. Barely audible, a feral sound rose from the back of the Russian's throat.

He flipped the photograph out from beneath the paperclip to reveal the name of his nemesis. *Dax Hunter. Dax Fucking Hunter. I know your name. I look forward to the day when I can watch you beg for my mercy.*

When the CIA sent Field Agent Elroy Matthews to Zambia, they probably thought their guy from Jackson, Mississippi would blend in perfectly amongst the local African population.

But their logic was defective for one simple reason: at six feet seven inches, Matthews was almost a foot taller than the average Zambian male.

Soon after his arrival in the city, Elroy had come to the conclusion that it would be almost impossible for someone of his stature to fly below the radar. Despite the clandestine nature of his work, he needed to craft a credible back story. To anyone asking, he described himself as the American-educated son of a Zambian woman. In reality, he was not only the proud descendant of one of America's oldest surviving Buffalo Soldiers, but also a Morehouse alumnus.

With his CIA-sponsored import-export agency offering him a requisite amount of legitimacy, Elroy soon became a recognizable figure around Lusaka. His masquerade appeared to be foolproof. Although highly lucrative, Elroy had to keep reminding himself that the business was nothing more than a front. Quick to sequester the proceeds from the dummy operation, the CIA bean-counters redirected the profits to an unofficial account simply known as 'Contingency Reserve.' Boosting the liquidity of the CIA's African slush-fund was dependent on such ad-hoc injections.

Sitting casually on a bench outside the Lusaka hospital, Elroy pretended to read a copy of the *Times of Zambia*. At the very moment that a nondescript white man walked past him, the big American made a show of turning the page and vigorously shaking his newspaper. The unremarkable pedestrian was dressed in a blue Crimplene safari suit.

Elroy checked his watch. It was almost an hour since he'd flicked his newspaper. Waiting under the flame-colored canopy of a blooming Spathodea, Elroy had parked his car just off Burma Road. It was a short distance from the city center. He checked his rearview mirror. A fresh wave of cars had just been released by a favorable traffic light. *There he is.* Elroy's Russian contact was approaching from behind. It was precisely one hour since he'd signaled the man in the gardens outside the hospital.

Without slowing, the Russian drove right past Elroy's car. Fifty yards further up, he made a left turn into Fir Road. Elroy waited a full three minutes. During that time, nobody else had turned into the small street. Firing the engine, Elroy joined the traffic on Burma Road and immediately indicated his intention to turn left onto Fir. As he turned he could see the Russian's car parked up on the left. It was about two hundred yards further up the road. He drove past without slowing. The Russian waited three minutes. Once satisfied that Elroy wasn't being followed, he made a u-turn then a quick right into Cedar Road. The American's car was already approaching from the opposite direction. Parking on the verge outside an empty lot, they both climbed out their cars.

Elroy had a large roll tucked under his arm. Sliding off the rubber band, he unfurled an architectural drawing across the hood of his car. Like high-rolling property developers, the two men began to pore over the drawings. For the benefit of anyone watching, Elroy pointed randomly toward the empty plot every few minutes. "My friend, are you well?" Elroy asked quietly.

Maxim's relationship with the CIA had been cultivated over more than a decade. He'd first become a double agent while serving in England in the late 60s. Keeping up appearances in his Swiss Cottage community on the outskirts of London, he'd met an English girl and soon fathered a son. Emotional detachment is the hallmark of a skilled KGB operative. Maxim had always been cold-hearted: until, that is, he became a father. Upon discovering the real reason behind their agent's reluctance to return to Moscow, Maxim's superiors had threatened to liquidate his family. Fearful for their safety, he arranged to meet with someone from the CIA's London office. The liaison was fraught with danger. Although Maxim eventually acquiesced and returned to Russia, his deal with the Americans had secured a bright future for his wife and beloved son. With all the benefits of the witness protection program,

Maxim's small family was soon introduced to their new home in rural Minnesota.

"I am as well as can be," said Maxim.

"So tell me *Sotto Voce*, what news do you have for me?" The big American had given Maxim the cipher soon after arriving in Zambia. It meant *Quite Voice* in Italian. For the sake of appearances, Elroy turned and pointed at the far corner of the empty property.

Maxim shook his head vigorously and pointed toward the opposite corner. To anyone observing, the two developers looked like they were in total disagreement. "Well, you remember a few months ago I told you about the arrival here in Lusaka of a KGB colleague?"

"Yes. Vladimir Morozov. Named after Lenin. Alfa branch. Special Purpose Center to the Africa desk," said Elroy. Maxim raised an approving eyebrow. "What's he been up to?" asked Elroy.

"I was just visiting him in hospital. I heard from his sidekick Stix Mbudzi a few days ago. He gave me an encoded note from Morozov. It said that he needed some information from me." Elroy had heard of Stix.

"Go on," said the American.

"Stix was cagey at first … I couldn't get him to open up. But eventually he alluded to the fact that he and his gang had something to do with the shooting down of the Air Rhodesia Viscount a few days ago." Elroy whistled softly.

"I'm not surprised. He's been sent behind the Iron Curtain a few times. So why is your man Morozov in hospital?" asked Elroy.

"Stix says they were shot-up by a Rhodesian Air Force helicopter as they were trying to escape back to Zambia. Morozov got hit twice. So if Morozov and Stix were together when they skirmished with the Rhodesians on the banks of the Zambezi, it's a fair bet that Morozov was there at the downing of the Viscount as well."

Elroy bit his lower lip pensively. "Carry on."

"Just before they managed to shoot down the helicopter,

Morozov was hit in the face by shrapnel … and also his nuts," added Maxim.

"Sorry, no sympathy there."

"No, of course not. But here's the interesting thing," continued Maxim. "Morozov's message to me said he'd managed to read the serial number on the chopper as it went down. He wanted me to identify the pilot who was flying it that day. It's a very unusual request. The only logical explanation is that he wants to take out his revenge on this pilot."

"What did you find out?" pressed Elroy.

"I was able to discover the name of the Rhodesian pilot," said the double agent. "In fact I had just handed Morozov a short dossier on the pilot when you signaled me outside the hospital. His name is Dax Hunter."

After carefully recording all the details of his clandestine meeting with Maxim earlier that day, Elroy Matthews sent an encoded dispatch to the Head of the CIA Central & Southern Africa Desk. As per procedure, he also filed a copy with CIA HQ in Langley, Virginia.

Deep within the CIA's retrieval system, the *Persons of Interest* archive was predominantly made-up of Russian and East European agents. Through Elroy's latest entry, the name *Vladimir Morozov* had just found its way into the CIA's database. And highlighted within that file was the name of a certain Rhodesian helicopter pilot.

It had been a week since news of Morozov's hospitalization had reached Dar es Salaam. His KGB handler in Tanzania would have come to Lusaka sooner but he'd been busy.

If the Dar es Salaam agent had chosen to sit down in the chair next to his subordinate's hospital bed, he'd have been positioned lower than Morozov's eye level. That was simply unacceptable. Instead, he stood a few feet from Morozov's bed.

The handler had taken careful note of Morozov's barely-disguised agitation. His junior agent clearly didn't like the news he'd just heard.

Hell-bent on pursuing his vendetta, Morozov seethed when he heard that he was to be sent back to Moscow for further surgery and physical recuperation. Despite this, he knew it would be prudent to disguise his rage. "But comrade, you'll be attended to by the finest doctors back in Moscow," countered the handler. "You will be well taken care of."

"Yes comrade, this might be so, but I know many of these doctors are sent to the African frontlines for extra trauma training. Surely it can be arranged that I can see one of these specialists here in Lusaka or Dar es Salaam?" There was an unmistakable edge to his plea.

"Comrade, I note your persistence." The rebuke was subtle but unmistakable. "But your condition is still regarded as serious and my superiors," he paused to let Morozov grasp the implication, "they are insisting on providing the best possible care to hasten your recovery." It was Morozov's cue to accede to his handler's wishes.

"Comrade, thank you," said Morozov grudgingly. Without pause, Mr. Hyde had segued into Dr Jekyll. "I will go back to Moscow to recover. But may I ask that you look favorably on my request to return to Africa when I have recovered sufficiently? I am very eager to continue my assignment here," said Morozov charmingly.

"I will see to it that your request is appended to your file, comrade." With that the handler bade him farewell.

Morozov's physician was a stickler for procedure; he knew how the system worked. In his professional opinion, his patient should have been kept under his qualified care for at least a further seven days. The persuasive KGB operative from Dar es Salaam thought otherwise. "Dr Spielmann, very few of our Eastern Bloc doctors relish the thought of serving their mandatory three month's duty in the Frontline States." The man's every word was carefully measured. "It was unusual, therefore, when we received your request for permission to extend your stay by a further three months." Spielmann started to feel uncomfortable; the KGB man's tone had a menacing edge. "So we checked. And what we found, Dr Spielmann, was very interesting. Does your loving family back in East Berlin know you have a ... how can I put this? A cozy relationship with a rather buxom Zambian lady?"

The short Gandhi-lookalike squirmed. "So, Dr Spielmann, you will simply sign the papers and discharge Comrade Morozov with immediate effect."

Thirty minutes after Morozov's discharge papers had been signed, Elroy received a call from the hospital. Having cultivated a useful network of informants, the friendly matron at Lusaka General didn't disappoint him. "Your friend will be departing within the hour," she told Elroy cryptically.

He had to move quickly. For the sake of completeness, Elroy wanted to add a photograph to the recently-created dossier on Vladimir Morozov.

21

APPLE

Trey was putting his women's soccer team through their final paces. They were due to face their long-time rivals—the Auburn Tigers—at Saturday's big game. As head coach, he truly believed that his University of Alabama side had a good chance of lifting the 1977 All State Cup that coming weekend. "Pass to Apple. She's open," he hollered. "Look up, Lizzy. Apple's open." Lizzy heard his instruction and executed a perfectly-timed pass to the team's talismanic player.

"Good, Lizzy. Good," he encouraged. "Bring it up now Apple, drive it forward."

Playing out wide, Apple shimmied around her opposite number. Her dazzling footwork left her opponent floundering.

"Shoot, Apple, shoot," he beseeched.

Apple nudged the ball into position so she could drive it with her left foot—her natural side. Glancing up one last time, she dipped her head, shifted her weight onto her right foot, leaned into the strike and swung her left leg down onto the face of the ball. Watching from the sideline, the coach just shook his head in disbelief. *How does she arc that dang ball?*

Zipping past the goalie's flailing arms, the spinning ball creased the back of the net. Accompanied by a chorus of compliments from her team mates, Trey blew a short, trill blast on his whistle. "Alright team, good practice. Everyone gather around. Take a knee."

After a short pep talk with all twenty two, Trey dismissed

them for the afternoon. "Apple," he called, as the group started dispersing, "one moment please."

"What's up coach?" she asked, still perspiring from the exertion.

"Good work out there today. Hey, listen, there's a guy up there in the grandstand." Trey indicated with a tilt of his head. "Kinda self-important dude. Says he needs to chat." The coach couldn't disguise his suspicion. "Privately," he added sneeringly. He was protective of his team. "You talk to me first before you sign any deals, you hear?"

"Thanks coach," said Apple breezily. Trey was about to walk away.

"Hey, Apple," he half turned. "I'll be hanging about the field for a bit. Just shout if the guy makes you feel … uncomfortable."

"Thanks coach," replied Apple, turning toward the stands. "Really," she added, after taking a few steps. On a whim, she decided to wait in the center of the field.

As Trey stalked off, Apple noticed the guy in the stands get up from his seat and descend slowly to the field. She held her ground as he sauntered toward her. He didn't appear to be in any hurry to make her acquaintance.

"Simone Lacroix?" The man enquired, as he approached Apple.

She reckoned he was in his mid-forties. Already thinning, he'd combed his wispy gray hair up and over his pink pate. Like a spindly aerial, one thin strand stood up proudly from somewhere near the crown of his head. His heavy-rimmed spectacles were dated—he looked like one of J Edgar Hoover's G-Men. All that was missing was the fedora. The man's dress-sense was less than impeccable: the checked, short-sleeve shirt bore evidence of an earlier encounter with a hotdog. Hanging well-short of his belt buckle, a plain black tie clashed with his gray shoes. *Is this dude for real?* she thought sardonically. *He needs a make-over, man.* "Yes it is, and who, may I inquire, are you, sir?" A Southern gal never forgot her manners.

"I heard your coach call you Apple. May I call you that, Simone?"

"Sir, indeed you may. But only if I can address you by your name." Apple could be feisty, but she always managed to do it in the most disarming manner.

"I am Akron Wilberforce Sneddon." Up to this point the stranger hadn't offered his hand. "Forgive me," he eventually offered his hand. "You can call me Sneddon."

A nerdish name for a geeky guy. Apple pushed the thought to one side. "Mr. Sneddon. Pleased to make your acquaintance sir. How can I help you?"

"Miss Apple, I'll get straight to the point. My organization is always on the lookout for exceptionally talented individuals like you."

Oh boy, another offer for a sports scholarship to one of the ivy leagues. Apple stopped herself from rolling her eyes.

"We've checked your GPA and spoken with a few of your professors already," he continued. Truth-be-told it wasn't only her Grade Point Average that he'd checked; he'd also conducted a thorough background search. "It is apparent to us that your profile and intellect would make you an ideal recruit for our organization," he said.

"A recruit?" Apple was genuinely confused. "Sir, I am sorry. What is this about? Your organization? What organization? This is not about a sports scholarship, is it?" Her mild annoyance was accentuated by a small crease in her brow.

"Apple, can I count on your discretion?" Before she could fire another salvo of questions, he continued. "Regardless of the outcome of this meeting, I need to ask that you don't discuss this with anyone else … it's a matter of national security." *That* caught Apple's attention. "Come, let's walk a bit." He didn't wait for an answer. Despite his disheveled appearance, Akron Wilberforce Sneddon was someone who was clearly used to being obeyed.

Over at the far side of the field, Apple stopped abruptly. She turned and looked at Sneddon. "I should learn to trust my instincts more, Mr. Sneddon," she said wryly. "I actually thought *FBI* when I first saw you. I thought you looked like a G-Man," she chuckled. "But you're quite serious aren't you sir? You really want to recruit *me* for the CIA?" She could barely disguise her doubt.

"As soon as you've earned your degree, yes, you will be enrolled on the next Professional Trainee Program. That's only four months away. If you make the grade—and I have no doubt you will—you will then be assigned to my Clandestine Service Trainee Program for further development. But again, I must emphasize the point: you must only consider this offer if you are wholly committed to the idea of putting your country first, and then the CIA before your own self."

"Mr. Sneddon. This is a lot to digest. May I please have a few days to consider your offer?" asked Apple.

Sneddon dug in his breast pocket. "Call me when you've thought about it," said Sneddon, offering her his card. Apple was disappointed. Although she didn't know what to expect, the business card bore nothing more than the man's number, name and initials.

Apple's father was a proud *Créoles de Louisiane*. His ancestors had settled in Louisiana's Bayou Têche Region after their part in the successful Haitian Revolution. Like his father and grandfather before him, he ran the family's prosperous fisheries business.

Apple's mother was a true bibliophile: from the day she graduated from college, she worked at the Municipal Library in downtown Lafayette. Her greatest honor was when she was appointed head librarian.

Through her mother's influence, Apple also developed a love for books. She read extensively—if not indiscriminately. In the process she acquired an encyclopedic knowledge on all manner of subjects and learnt how to embroider her arguments with a slew of impressive facts.

Her father—a natural and hot-headed debater himself—would often capitulate in the face of his little girl's well-reasoned arguments. "Simone, you know honey, you are the apple of your daddy's eye." He'd used the refrain ever since she was a toddler.

With an emphasis placed on 'apple,' she would mimic her father every time he uttered the words. "I am the *apple* of my daddy's eye."

To the Lacroix's friends and family it came as no surprise that the epithet eventually stuck.

22

BOARD OF ENQUIRY

After being airlifted to Salisbury, Dax underwent a series of operations on his damaged forearm. Two weeks later—and still facing a lengthy recovery process—he found himself amongst a dozen other wounded soldiers at Tsanga Lodge.

Running north-south along Rhodesia's eastern border, the Inyanga mountain range is regarded by locals as a deeply spiritual place. Resident shamans and wise tribal elders counsel against taking leisurely hikes up the slopes of Inyangani—the country's highest peak—without first seeking the ancestors' blessings.

It wasn't just voodoo folklore either: over the years, too many people had mysteriously vanished off the mountain for the elders' advice not to be taken seriously. Despite its eerie mysticism, the area and its surrounds are breathtaking. Peppered with dolerite and sandstone outcroppings, the strange peaks sit like a pantheon of gods presiding over the misty dells and dark forests that hug their slopes.

Tsanga Lodge was nestled in the foothills of the Inyanga range. It was chosen by the army for its isolation, serene surroundings and brisk but healthy climate. Wounded Rhodesian soldiers requiring longer-term rehabilitation were sent to Tsanga to recuperate.

Hunter had been an inveterate joke teller from a young age. While the jokes were always good, his forte lay in the ability to turn a simple joke into a humorous story. With years of practice, he had raised his talent to an art form.

Although Tsanga Lodge provided the perfect setting for wounded soldiers to rehabilitate, the circumstances under which they got there were invariably quite harrowing. The collective mood at Tsanga was always fluid. On any given day the ebb-and-flow of each soldier's emotions would have a bearing on the overall atmosphere. As one war story followed another, Dax noticed that each story teller's sole objective was to be more graphic, more gruesome, than the last. It was obvious how the despair could take root.

One day, as the mood in the room plummeted, Dax had an epiphany. He quickly realized that it was the agonizing stories that were darkening the ambiance. In that moment of clarity, Dax decided that he'd only ever share cheerful stories. If morose stories could depress the mood, it made sense that stories with a positive theme would have the opposite effect.

Digging into his memory banks, Dax proceeded to regale the group with his best jokes. Unaware of his experiment, the soldiers responded positively to his stories, just as he'd predicted.

In the days that followed, Dax made up his mind to start a series called 'Joke of the Week.' By pollinating each situation with a humorous anecdote, he hoped to break the discouraging cycle of pessimistic stories.

Dax leaned over the artist's shoulder. "Hey china, that's one helluva painting," he said.

"*Ja*, china, thanks." Dax was expecting more but the artist's reticence lingered.

Maybe he's just engrossed in the artistic process. "You been painting long?" enquired Dax.

"About thirty minutes before you came along, china," replied the artist sarcastically. Despite his gruffness, Dax liked him already.

"Ah, multitalented I see … an artist *plus* a regular Jack Benny," riposted Dax. During this exchange of light banter, Hunter had been leaning over with his hands resting on his knees. He stood up and took a quick peek at the artist's body. He bore no wounds that Dax could see. *Maybe they're underneath his shirt?* "What you in for?" asked Dax, making light of their circumstances. Without uttering a word, the wounded soldier stretched his leg out from beneath his stool. Dax looked down. The artist's lower right leg was encased in a steampunk contraption. Stainless steel rods burrowed through the skin and anchored in the bones deep inside his damaged leg. "Looks painful. How long you been here?"

"About a month," said the artist. "Hey, you remember *Hogan's Heroes* on TV?" He switched subjects effortlessly.

"*Ja*, of course," replied Dax.

"Remember how the POWs were always digging new tunnels under *Stalag 13* to escape from Colonel Klink?" pressed the artist.

"Sure do," said Dax, wondering where this was going.

"Well, can *you* dig?" asked the artist, a mischievous twinkle appearing in the corner of his eye.

"What? Like tunnels underneath this lodge? Are we prisoners here?" Dax decided to play along.

"No, dude!" The artist remained deadpan. "A couple of my Rhodesia Light Infantry buddies here are growing some weed out back … we need volunteers to help us dig the beds." It was corny but Dax still chuckled.

"I'm Dax Hunter, by the way," he thrust his hand out to the artist.

"I know who you are, china," said the artist. "You've flown me a couple of times on fireforce deployments … once or twice at Kariba, and a few other times out of Karoi. Might've been more, but I've lost track. Anyway, I'm Bone, Craig Bone," said the artist, extending his hand.

"Well Craig Bone, I can see what *you're* going to do with your life when this war's over," predicted Dax.

The sergeant major in charge of Tsanga Lodge truly cared for his patients. With so many activities available at the recuperation center, he insisted that all his charges immerse themselves in at least one pastime. It was part of the rehabilitative process. Craig Bone had chosen canvas, brushes and an easel. Some did workshop, others even wrote poetry.

Heedful of his surgeon's advice, Dax knew that he had to continuously strengthen his arm. It was as important exercising the damaged tissue as it was stimulating the nerves. Dax decided to try his hand at archery. Although the lodge provided only the most rudimentary equipment, it soon became apparent that Dax was a bit of a natural.

Hunter's father had insisted that his sons learn to shoot properly from a young age. Instilling in them all the necessary techniques of good marksmanship, he paid equal attention to the safe handling of their weapons. During the school holidays, if he wasn't hunting vermin, Dax was out practicing on his metallic silhouette targets. On the front lawn of his mother's garden, he'd also honed his clay-pigeon shooting skills. With the incessant *boom! boom!* of her husband's double-barrel Purdy, Dax's mother was forever lamented the lack of birdlife in her otherwise inviting garden. It was in this environment that Dax sharpened his formidable eye for aiming and shooting.

Dax only stayed two weeks at Tsanga. He'd called Barrel and convinced the squadron boss to let him rejoin the team. Desperate to get back into the fray, he'd offered to help with *anything* around the hangar.

But Dax's homecoming wasn't as welcoming as he'd hoped. In his absence, the so-called *corridor commodores* at Air Force HQ had convened a Board of Enquiry to investigate his crash. Although it was standard procedure, what annoyed Dax was that he discovered they were already nearing their conclusion—and they hadn't even interviewed him yet. Dax was eventually invited to a formal hearing where he was given the opportunity to present his account of events that day.

While the board's final verdict didn't heap the blame

entirely on his shoulders, he didn't escape unscathed. Dax was officially admonished for not first picking up the four members of the PATU stick—Blue Stick One—to offer more firepower at the scene of the contact. "Your impetuousness not only caused a crash, but you probably forfeited a good opportunity to apprehend or eliminate three of the CTs responsible for the downing of the *Umniati*," said one of the Group Captains on the panel.

Hunter received formal notification that his next promotion review would be suspended for three months.

Back at the hangar later that afternoon, Dax was checking the flight logs for one of the choppers. Beaver spotted him and sauntered over. "Didn't see that coming sir," said Beaver. "Sorry man."

"Ugh, it's the way it is with head office brass. Damned if you do, damned if you don't," said Dax. He wasn't too upset about the outcome.

"For what it's worth, I told them that if we'd waited for the PATU guys we probably would've missed the gooks at the river altogether. I told them I agreed with your decision for us to go alone. So did Boss Barrel, by the way." Dax had a feeling Barrel would back him. "They also tore a strip off Barrel for letting you go up again the day after you took a round in the leg," added Beaver. "Said you should have been medically-relieved from active duty for at least ten days. Jesus man, what's with those fuckwits?" Beaver shook his head scornfully. He was well-aware that Dax could report him for such insubordination.

There was a pregnant pause. Dax knew Beaver well enough to know that there was still something playing on his mind. "Spit it out, buddy. What's eating you?"

"Sir, it might be nothing, but after I blew the first guy's arm off, I directed my fire into some thick bush a little way off to the left. I was getting some heat from that direction."

"Go on," said Dax, intrigued by Beaver's tone.

"Well I definitely hit one guy, or at least wounded him. Just before we started spinning out of control, the guy stepped back out of cover. He was holding his hand up to his face … looked like there was a lot of blood. I only saw him for a second or two, but I still got a good look."

"And?" said Dax.

"Well, I swear he was a European," said Beaver.

"C'mon Beeves, you know we've come across a few albino CTs over the past few months. Hell, you've been on the squadron longer than me; you must've seen a few, even before I came along?" said Dax.

"*Ja*, but I've seen enough albinos to know the difference sir. I'm telling you, this one was fair-skinned. He definitely had pigment."

"You put this in your report?" enquired Dax.

"No sir, not until I had a chance to speak to you about it," answered Beaver.

"Thanks Beeves. Let me talk to Barrel and ask him what he thinks."

Although he wasn't back in the cockpit yet, just being back amongst his friends was a close second for Dax. He soon discovered that the husband of one of the squadron's admin clerks was deeply involved in the local archery scene. Dax asked her to arrange an introduction. The following weekend he headed out on the Golden Stairs Road to one of the club's local events.

Travis's wife had told her husband that there was an injured pilot on their squadron who'd developed an enthusiasm for the sport. Motivated by a vague sense of pity for a wounded soldier, he extended an unenthusiastic invite for Dax to come out to the range.

After letting fly a mere six arrows, Travis whistled softly. *This guy's a frigging natural. Even with that half-healed, angry scar crisscrossing his forearm.*

With his interest piqued, Travis took Dax to one side. He started to explain the mechanics of the compound bow and how the pulley and cam system imparted its huge mechanical advantage. Being technically-inclined himself, Dax understood precisely what Travis was saying. Thinking his explanation might have been too detailed, Travis offered to go over it a second time. "Only one way to learn, Travis ... put me on the horse," joked Dax. From a distance of fifty yards, Dax unleashed a quiver-full of fiberglass arrows. The target bristled like an agitated porcupine. For the rest of the afternoon Dax demonstrated that it hadn't been beginner's luck.

It was early March 1979 and the country's political situation was in a state of flux. Eager to try and broker the next-best deal to save Rhodesia, an assemblage of self-important foreign politicians, clerics and noblemen evanesced across the world's stage. As international pressure mounted, so Prime Minister Ian Smith began to realize that the pieces on his chess board were tumbling. In a move aimed at hastening a fair dispensation for the country's majority, the cornered Smith conceded to demands for the staging of the country's first democratic elections.

While the two main exiled parties of Joshua Nkomo and Robert Mugabe chose to continue fighting, the largely peaceful elections in 1979 yielded a new leader and a new country. Bishop Abel Muzorewa became the prime minister of the newly-formed nation of Zimbabwe-Rhodesia in June of 1979.

Margaret Thatcher had initially promised her country's unconditional recognition of whichever party won the election. Her cabinet later reneged and insisted that the elections be retaken, this time with the inclusion of the two communist stooges, Mugabe and Nkomo.

Stung by the betrayal, Zimbabwe-Rhodesia's newly-elected government was still-born. Everyone remained in political limbo. The Bush War not only continued—it intensified.

With Britain's pandering interference, Mugabe's ZANU party and Nkomo's ZAPU party were both given a free pass to the high table: a galling turn-about since both had rejected earlier invitations to participate in the first democratic elections.

Using their respective armies, Nkomo and Mugabe embarked on a systematic campaign of coercion to win the hearts and minds of the masses. Thousands more lost their lives in the ten months following the country's first all-inclusive elections.

The workload on the army and air force soon became unsustainable. For the first time, both within the armed forces as well as the general public, morale was starting to falter. In order to prevent the precipitous flight of cash and assets, the government had placed economic restrictions on the removal of all manner of valuable items. With badly-disguised intentions, the volume of holiday traffic to South Africa mushroomed as Rhodesians made multiple trips to their southerly neighbor. On each visit, another stash of silver tea-sets or dodgy emeralds was spirited across the border.

After a full three months of convalescence, Dax was allowed to resume his flying duties. The surgeons' successful repairs had seen a reinstatement of 95% of his fine-motor skills, as well as full opposable use of his thumb.

Hunter's reputation as a raconteur had grown. Amidst the usual banter, he was repeatedly called upon to tell one of his Jokes of the Week.. "You idiots don't get it do you? How can I possibly tell more than one Joke of the Week?" These lighter moments were essential for morale: finding a release valve was essential for everyone's sanity. They were all still embroiled in a vicious war and many believed they were still fighting for their country; and with it, everything they held dear. Good men continued to die valiantly.

Dax's new-found escape was archery. Just prior to resuming his flying duties, he had taken a much-needed holiday to the coastal town of Durban in South Africa. After a few enquiries he managed to locate a specialized sports equipment outlet that sold a range of the latest, new-fangled compound bows.

Travis proved to be the perfect coach. Dax's archery improved to the point where he was soon selected to represent

Mashonaland, his provincial home. Around the clubhouse, members still jokingly referred to Dax as the 'newcomer.' But he soon silenced his new-found friends when he cleaned up at the inter-provincial championships.

At the post-event party—an essential component of Rhodesian sporting life—the chairman of the national archery association approached Dax. Fashioning himself on an English aristocrat, Archie Binswald looked the part in his navy blue blazer and silk cravat. "Young man, have you ever noticed how many really talented sportsmen and women have had to sacrifice one sporting code in order to pursue the other?" Despite his pomposity he was a likeable old gent; definitely old-school colonial. "They are usually equally good at both, but the demands of either discipline will eventually impinge on the other. Tell me if I'm wrong, old cock, but don't you think that describes you?" He didn't give Dax a chance to answer.

"I know talent when I see it and you're a natural archer. Don't get me wrong, I think you'll be a shoo-in for the national rugby side, but come on fellow," he beseeched, "just look at how many ruddy injuries you rugby chaps pick up each season." The avuncular chairman patted Dax on the shoulder. "Those ruddy damaged knees never quite come right afterwards, do they now?" he pontificated. "Give it some thought, won't you?" With that, the genial old gent veered off toward the nearest group of ice-tinkling gin swillers.

The country was on edge: it was February 1980 and the nation was about to go to the polls for the second time in less than ten months. Across the globe, interest had piqued in the ongoing Zimbabwe-Rhodesia drama.

Accompanying a huge foreign press contingent, the poorly-named Commonwealth Monitoring Force also jetted into the country. Their dual objective was to supervise the ceasefire arrangements and also oversee the electoral process. In the case of the latter, their primary aim was to ensure that the elections were conducted in a free-and-fair fashion. In this regard, they failed dismally.

Through a contemptible process of fear-mongering, Mugabe and Nkomo's hatchet-men worked their evil charm on the electorate. With the sole aim of influencing the ballot, they reinforced their sinister message by publicly executing dozens of innocents. With a collective shrug of their shoulders, the Monitoring Force blithely described the loathsome acts as being unfortunate, isolated incidents. To add insult to injury, elements of the foreign press glibly wrote-off the accusations of wrong-doing as nothing more than sour grapes from the Rhodesians.

The country's new history was being writ bold in blood.

Although the Rhodesian public knew that there had been widespread intimidation throughout the lead-up to the elections, the final results still beggared belief. Against all predictions—even some assurances—the avowed Maoist, Robert Gabriel Mugabe, achieved a landslide victory. Whatever its new name, the beloved land would never be the same again.

Along with many other servicemen and women, Dax had decided to stay on and serve in the newly-constituted Air Force of Zimbabwe. He was prepared to give the new leaders a fair crack at running the country. For each one that stayed, two or three opted to resign their commissions in the aftermath of the elections. Most had headed south to join the South African Air Force.

The South Africans were more than willing to help hundreds of ex-Rhodesian servicemen and women reintegrate into their new careers in the South African Defense Force.

Eager to give his erstwhile enemy the benefit of the doubt, Dax decided to wait a year before making a longer-term commitment. The new Zimbabwe was already attracting huge direct foreign investment and the aviation sector was booming: the world just couldn't seem to get enough of Zimbabwe's famed exports. If the air force didn't work out for him, he could always go and fly commercially.

Recently graduated from N°33 Pilot Training Course, the junior officer jumped up to answer the phone in the 7 Squadron crew room. Seniority had its privileges. "Dax, it's for you," shouted Scholvinck.

Dax was hunched over a backgammon table when the phone rang. He was just about to bear-off one of his checkers when Scholvinck called him. He stood up and took the phone. "G'day, this is Hunter speaking."

"Dax, how are you old cock? This is Archie Binswald from the Rhodesian National Archery Association," there was an embarrassed pause. "Dammit, sorry, *Zimbabwean* National Archery Association," he corrected himself.

Dax smiled. "Hello sir, how are you?"

"Spiffing, absolutely spiffing old cock. But more importantly, how are *you*?"

"Thank you for asking. I am fine. How can I help you, sir?"

"Well Dax, I'm not sure if you've been listening to the news today, but it's just been announced that the USSR has cleared the way for Zimbabwe to send a team of athletes to the Moscow Summer Olympics in July. That's just over one ruddy month away." He paused to let the fact sink in.

"That's fantastic news, sir … thank you for letting me know." Dax still hadn't figured out the purpose of Binswald's call.

"Wake up, old cock. I don't think you're getting my drift. If you can shoot like William Tell at this weekend's competition, you'll be going to the ruddy Olympics." Dax was speechless. "We don't have much time though, old cock. They only allow recurve bows at the Olympics. I've only ever seen you use that god-awful compound contraption."

23

CIA RECRUIT

Five candidates had already been scrubbed and only thirty two remained. The head of the academy assured the class that at least five more would wash-out before the program had ended. The stakes couldn't be higher.

It was Easter of 1980. Apple was excelling on her Professional Trainee Program. It was the first of two intensive CIA recruits' courses on her route to becoming an active agent.

Apple was lost in thought. Outside the classroom window, an early spring flush had already started to transform the trees that surrounded the Langley headquarters. She was thinking about the fifty two hostages being held in the US Embassy in Tehran. Since the violation of US sovereign property in November the previous year, the Iranian incident continued to consume the nation. Five months on and it still featured in the headlines of the world's most influential papers.

The students were already formulating the characteristics of good CIA agents. At every opportunity these agile young minds debated the merits of a negotiated solution versus military intervention. Fueled by scuttlebutt in their wider environment, the students soon started hearing rumors that a rescue mission was imminent.

Amidst the classroom gossip, Apple heard the name Jim Rhyne mentioned for the first time. Hailed as one of the CIA's top pilots, he was touted to fly the first covert recce team into Iran as a precursor to a full-scale military assault: if indeed the

President decided on that course of action.

Some of the older agents around the office—McCarthy-era stalwarts who'd cut their teeth during the Second Red Scare—advocated the full-on use of force. Some even speculated that an interdiction might include members of the army's newly-formed Delta Force.

Apple's distraction was short-lived. In order to emphasize a point, the lecturer had just slammed his palm down on the table. Apple jumped reflexively. "Secretary of State Vance has stated categorically that there's to be no military intervention in the Iran hostage drama. As if it's his damn call," he scoffed. It was almost five months to the day since the Iranians had stormed the US Embassy in Tehran. It was obvious that their lecturer didn't care much for politicians. "Insiders on the Hill reckon Vance will resign if the Commander-in-Chief actually goes ahead and authorizes the cavalry into Tehran. Personally, I think the USA needs to toughen-up and resume its rightful role as global cop." The lecturer also had clearly-defined ideas on America's wider geopolitical role. And those ideas, by extension, involved the CIA. "Who knows, we might even have a new Secretary of State within a few weeks," he mused, "and maybe *he'll* have the balls to play a wider role on the international stage ... and not sit on his goddamn hands like Cyrus Vance," he added.

As things transpired, the lecturer's words proved to be prophetic. On President Jimmy Carter's orders, the US military launched *Operation Eagle Claw* two weeks later. Their objective was to secure the release of the US hostages still being held in the US Embassy building in Tehran.

Sadly, while still in the staging area, an unfortunate string of technical problems beset the operation. Before a shot had been fired in anger, the brass decided to abort the mission. Worse was to follow. As the soldiers were preparing to leave, an unfortunate collision involving a helicopter and parked Hercules transport plane claimed the lives of eight US servicemen.

The lecturer had also predicted that Secretary of State Cyrus Vance would resign if a military operation was indeed launched into Tehran. Again, their lecturer was vindicated: Vance resigned four days after the failed bid.

Apple found it uncanny. She desperately wanted to know how these guys could foretell such events; not only predict them, but how they managed to do so in such detail.

24

ZIMBABWE GOLD

With only twenty seconds to go to the start of the ceremony, the athletes started counting down in anticipation of the commencement of the Olympic Games. Gathered in the car park outside the main arena, Dax was standing amongst more than five thousand athletes. He absorbed the atmosphere with child-like wonderment: the healthy faces, the gleaming smiles, the honed physiques. There was an atmosphere of perfection: an aura of youthful vitality with a touch of mythological invincibility.

Dax craned his neck. Barely visible through the stadium's tunnel, he could just make out a portion of the expectant crowd. They too were watching the large screen. It carried a live feed of the Kremlin Clock from downtown Moscow. With their attention drawn to the screen, the crowd too was counting down to the big moment. Due to a combination of acoustics and distance, the chant from the stadium echoed a split second after the athletes' own countdown.

The 1980 Moscow Summer Olympics were due to begin at precisely 4 PM. Waiting eagerly for the big moment, tens of thousands of spectators had filled the Central Lenin Stadium.

A moment after the Kremlin Clock chimed the hour, a band of trumpeters heralded the grand opening with a rousing rendition of *Moscow Fanfare*. Outside the stadium, the athletes waited impatiently: any moment now they could expect to be summoned onto the stage of the world's greatest sporting event. It felt as if they'd already been standing for hours. But the festivities would only start once the compère had dispensed with the formality of introducing and welcoming Leonid Brezhnev, the president of the USSR. After the brief but sycophantic welcome, everyone rose respectfully to listen to the Soviet national anthem.

While the trumpets flourished, a stirring procession of artistes entered the stadium. Grouped together in the main stand, several hundred performers dazzled the world with their choreographed drill involving the sequenced display of different colored cards. With well-rehearsed precision, the colored cards were changed in quick succession to depict a series of different images.

One slick act followed after the other. Dozens of toga-clad Grecians—each one bearing a bountiful platter—strode into the arena in an arrow formation. The impressive phalanx included bearers of the giant symbol of the Olympics; the five interlinked rings. Behind them, proud teams of strutting charioteers joined the procession. To rapturous applause, the athletes were eventually ushered in for the Parade of Nations.

As a tribute to Greece—the creators of the Olympics—that nation's athletes were the first to enter the stadium. Each subsequent nation entered in accordance with their order in the Cyrillic alphabet. This put the Zimbabwean athletes in slot twenty-five, followed directly by India's athletes.

Proudly bearing the colorful flag of his newly-independent country, Abel Nkhoma—Zimbabwe's marathoner—led his teammates into the stadium. Many of the Zimbabwean athletes were disappointed to see that thousands of athletes had ignored the official request banning personal cameras at the opening ceremony. Waving joyously to the appreciative crowd, the team continued their stroll around the track. The stadium fizzed with atmosphere: Dax had never before been quite so overwhelmed.

The vast Soviet team entered last; with four hundred and eighty nine athletes, theirs was the largest contingent of the eighty participating nations.

As the final echelons took up their positions in the center of the field, President Brezhnev approached the microphone and solemnly announced that the 22nd Games of the Olympiad had begun. The vast stadium erupted in thunderous applause. Before the triumphant arrival of the torch bearer, a series of traditions and rituals were performed by various attending dignitaries. With the cauldron aflame, the Olympic Oath was taken by one of the Soviet gymnasts.

As the early euphoria wore off, and the pageant began to wind-down, the order was given for the athletes to start filing out of the stadium. Behind them, scores of performers continued to entertain the spectators.

The USSR women's field hockey side considered themselves a shoo-in for the gold medal. It was to be the first time in the history of the games that women's field hockey was to be included in the sporting line-up.

With a record seven straight victories coming into the games, everyone was aware of the much-vaunted reputation of the men's hockey side from India. What they didn't know was whether the men's success would have a talismanic affect on their female counterparts. Just to be safe, the Soviet field hockey coach penciled in the Indian women's side as a credible threat to their march to glory. While Poland would probably put up a spirited fight, they weren't likely to be able to absorb the Soviet's aggressive style and tactics. Along with India, the USSR identified Czechoslovakia and Austria as their most dangerous rivals.

And then there was Zimbabwe. The Soviet coach had sneeringly dismissed the Zimbabwe women's side as a bunch of tourists. "They've been handed a sympathetic invitation because their poxy little country has just been freed from its imperialistic chains," he said, patronizingly. "They only heard they were coming to Moscow a month ago," he sneered. "One fucking month! Not only that—these girls haven't played one game together as a team ... not one." It was entirely true. The Zimbabwean women's side had been chosen a week before the opening ceremony of the Olympic Games.

With its idyllic year-round weather, there was no need for artificial turf on any of the thousands of sports fields scattered across Zimbabwe. Accordingly, none of the women had ever played on a synthetic pitch before. Still in the process of getting to know each other, this side was about to represent their nation without having conducted even a single team practice, let alone ever played on a synthetic surface.

With a few games scheduled against one or two enthusiastic local Moscow club sides, the Zimbabweans had six days to prepare for their Olympic debut.

Each of the other five contesting teams relished the thought of picking up maximum points against the Zimbabwean women's hockey side. With USSR and Czechoslovakia certain to battle for gold, it was up to the other three to fight over bronze, and Zimbabwe to bring out the oranges at half-time.

While Dax was no slouch in front of the target, he faced a challenging four days. Each archer would shoot two hundred and eighty eight arrows at four standard distances: ninety, seventy, fifty and thirty meters. Contestants would be scored using the double FITA format, and each archer would be required to use a modern recurve bow.

After receiving Archie Binswald's phone call, Dax had less than two months to master the recurve bow. With the exception of some Paralympics events, it was the only type of bow permissible at the Games. After a hasty conversion, Dax had barely sufficient time to adapt to his new bow. He nevertheless acquitted himself well in tough company. After the first day he realized he had a long way to go—and a lot to learn—before he could compete with the likes of the Fin, Tomi Poikolainen, the eventual gold medalist.

The women's field hockey event was scheduled to take place over seven days, with two rest days allocated in between. On day one, USSR and India won their respective games. To everyone's complete surprise, Zimbabwe managed to beat Poland. Outside of their tight-knit unit, nobody had expected the Zimbabweans to start their campaign with two points on the log.

After drawing 2-2 with Czechoslovakia on the second day of competition, Zimbabwe had earned an impressive 3 points, while the table-topping Indians had netted 4 points. The USSR and Austria shared third spot on 2 points apiece.

Wary of putting the kibosh on their chances, the Zimbabweans' self-belief nonetheless started to ignite. The women began dreaming a little: maybe, just maybe, a bronze? By the end of play on Monday—the third day—Zimbabwe was no longer a dark-horse. They were now credible medal contenders. After having stunned the Soviets 2-0, they topped the table with 5 points.

Zimbabwe's fourth match was against the Indians. The team from the sub-continent had been rallying and Wednesday's match looked like it was going to be a doozie. With grit and determination, both sides fought a closely-contested battle. Neither side was able to gain the ascendancy and the final whistle blew with the score drawn at 1-1. With just Austria and Czechoslovakia still to play that day, each team waited anxiously for the final result to see how it would affect the overall table.

After receiving the penultimate day's results, the scorekeepers quickly recalculated the table: Zimbabwe topped the log with 6 points, India and Czechoslovakia shared second spot with 5 points, and the USSR, along with Austria, had 4 points apiece. With a medal almost guaranteed, the Zimbabweans' last hurdle was against Austria the following day. Their coach, eager to work out all the permutations, became an accomplished statistician overnight.

No one really believed Poland could upset the Czechoslovakians: if the pundits were right, Czechoslovakia should secure top spot by the end of the final day's first game. But if—and it was a big ask—Zimbabwe could beat Austria, they'd take an unassailable lead and, of course, the gold medal.

With the USSR due to play India last in the following day's program, even a Soviet win could only secure them the bronze medal. If however the Indians won, they'd most likely share second spot with Czechoslovakia.

That night—30th July 1980—the Zimbabwean women's hockey team dreamed big, audacious dreams.

Their day had arrived. Few of the Zimbabwean girls had slept the night before, but their resolve was undiminished as they took to the field for the day's second game. The outcome against Austria would determine who took gold.

It had been a tight affair but, as predicted, Czechoslovakia had beaten Poland 1-0 in the earlier game. Now, of course, the Czechoslovakians' gold medal hopes rested on the outcome of the next game. They began to pray for an Austrian win. One more game—surely Austria could prevail.

With an invisible hand seeming to propel the Zimbabweans up-field throughout the game, the girls from Africa prevailed in emphatic fashion. The final score was a resounding 4-1.

They had dared to dream. And they'd won. It was a fairy-tale victory.

Whichever way the game went between USSR and India, the gold belonged to Zimbabwe.

Tearful, jubilant, relieved, even overwhelmed; the Zimbabwean women were swamped by team mates, coaching staff, traveling friends and fans. Even a small horde of Zimbabwean athletes—not competing that day—joined the mêlée. They bounced and hugged at the side of the field until officials eventually had to usher them out to the buses waiting to transport them back to the Olympic Village.

Still involved in their own events around the city, it didn't take long before other Zimbabwean athletes started learning of their team mates' stunning victory. It was Tomi, the Finnish archer, who first broke the news to Dax. Although it was only the second day of the archery competition, Dax and Tomi had already struck up a friendship. The Zimbabwean was mentally exhausted. Even he was surprised by the high levels of concentration required for competition archery. It took a while for Dax's tired mind to absorb what his Finnish companion was saying. "So I see your country has taken its first gold," Tomi had said in his thickly-accented English.

"What you talking about?" enquired Dax.

"Your women's field hockey side … they just took gold," said the eighteen year old.

Dax was elated to hear about his teammates' stunning victory. As the athletes' bus wound its way home through the Moscow streets, he could only imagine the scene that was unfolding back at the girls' compound in the Olympic village.

Eager to assimilate their new identity, the Zimbabwean team had already started referring to themselves as 'Zimbos.' Dax was proud to be part of this select group of talented individuals. He knew the Zimbos would party hard that night—or at least those who didn't have events the next day.

As the bus approached its stop outside the athletes' village, Dax noticed that a small throng had gathered on the steps outside the women's residential block. As he got off the bus, Dax could hear the girls' jubilant voices drifting over toward him.

"Dax! Over here," beckoned Patricia. Dax and Patricia knew each other well. They both represented Old Hararians, their sports club in Zimbabwe's newly-named capital of Harare.

As Dax sauntered over to where the team was gathered, an over-bearing Russian press photographer started hustling the delighted group of girls. He insisted that they gather around for a photograph. "Quick, quick you make happy face all people. Make happy face," he instructed.

Like seasoned Klondike prospectors testing the malleability of their nuggets, some of the girls posed with their medals clenched between their teeth. After the Russian had snapped half-a-dozen photographs, Patricia insisted that he take a couple more, but this time with their fellow Zimbabwean Olympians included in the shot. Along with four other

Zimbabwean athletes, Dax happily posed alongside the victorious women's field hockey team.

The photograph appeared the following day on the front page of one of the city's large-circulation tabloids, the *Moskovskij Komsomolets.*

ZIMBABWE TAKES GOLD! declared the headline.

25

ACHILLES

Although he'd grown up as the child of an Athenian shipping tycoon, Achilles' greatest endowments were the lessons bestowed on him by his father. He'd also received the best education possible, but spoilt he was not.

At the tender age of twelve Achilles' father had started his working life in the harbor of his picturesque fishing village on the island of Salamis. By age seventeen he'd purchased his first fishing boat. Fixing up the leaky old tug by himself, he soon managed to get it seaworthy. Three months after taking ownership, his reconditioned boat was plying its trade on the azure waters of the Mediterranean.

Having missed out on an education himself, Yiannos Fotakis had spared no expense ensuring his son's academic development. Along with an education, Yiannos had also taught Achilles the value of hard work. The boy was not going to get lazy off the back of his pappá's fortune.

Achilles was billeted in the room across the hallway from Dax. A sign—affixed to every door—displayed the athlete's name and country of origin. When Dax had knocked on Achilles' door on the first day of the Games, he hadn't expected his Greek neighbor to be so adept at English—let alone so eloquent.

Achilles looked like a natural athlete. He was tall and broad and Dax suspected he might be a water polo player or butterfly swimmer. In fact he was his country's national javelin champion. Dax and Achilles clicked immediately. The Greek had a sharp mind and his humor infectious. Within a short period of time, up-and-down their corridor, athletes began to look forward to the exchange of banter with their new friends from Harare and Athens.

It was Thursday evening. Achilles and Dax were drinking coffee in Dax's room. They'd exhausted the current topic— Zimbabwe's spectacular hockey upset—and their talk began drifting aimlessly from one topic to the next. "Tell me about those scars on your arm there, my friend," said Achilles. He paused to take a sip of coffee. "And those ones there on your leg."

Not one to indulge in war stories, Dax hesitated. He wondered if he could make up some cock-and-bull story about a farming accident. But he didn't like lying either. "Ah, nothing really," he answered casually. If Dax's intention had been to play it down, he'd already failed with his stoical John Wayne opening. He cringed inwardly. "I'm actually a pilot in the Zimbabwean Air Force. I got shot-up a few times, that's all," he said, trying to recover.

"Like in a real war pilot?" Achilles was impressed. "Do you fly war planes?"

"No, I'm a helicopter pilot," smiled Dax.

"That's even better," said Achilles impressively.

At the Greek's playful insistence, Dax eventually relented and gave him an abridged version of what had transpired over that two-day period, seventeen months before.

"Hey Dax, I was going to ask you earlier, but you interrupted me with your jibber-jabber about your heroic hockey girls." The influence of Achilles' private English tutor was evident in many of his colloquialisms.

"*Ja?* What's that?" asked Dax.

"It's my step-mom's birthday this Sunday and my dad has insisted I get home for the party at our house," said Achilles. "I told him about you and I asked him if I could invite you to come and stay for a few days. He says it'd be a pleasure to host you."

"But that's the day of the closing ceremony," Dax countered. "Aren't we all meant to be in the parade?"

"It's usually only the medal winners who parade. In any case, there are plenty of athletes who've finished their events and have already left. Those still here in Moscow who aren't in the parade get to watch from the grandstand," said Achilles.

Dax performed a quick calculation. Prior to departing for the Olympics, he had checked his leave status with the payroll department at Air Force headquarters. With several weeks owing to him, he'd decided to apply for an extra seven days after the Games. *This might work, but then again* ... "I don't know, Achilles, I'll have to check with the team manager. Besides, I'll have to purchase one-way tickets. First to Athens, then Harare ... that's kind of expensive doing it that way," he added. As the words left his lips, Dax realized how it had sounded: sometime prior, Achilles had made mention of the fact that his father was a shipping tycoon.

Before he could retrieve his words, the Greek interrupted. "No Dax. I am also meant to be flying home with my team on Monday morning, but my father insists I must not miss my step mother's birthday party. That's why he's sending one of his private jets to fetch me ... us," he corrected.

With several of his large boats on lease to various Russian operations around the Black Sea, Yiannos had enough sway with the Moscow bureaucrats to get clearance to fly a private jet into Sheremetyevo airport at short notice.

"And also, my father has many connections with Olympic Airlines. He can arrange a special deal for you to fly back to Johannesburg with them." Achilles was building his case.

"Okay," said Dax, folding. "But on one condition. Only if our team manager says he's okay with it."

Achilles reached over to shake his friend's hand.

26

THE PARROT

On his return to Moscow at the end of February 1979, Morozov underwent a series of intensive debriefings. His superiors at Directorate 'A' FSB Alfa wanted to hear in detail all the events surrounding the shooting down of the Viscount, as well as Morozov's fortuitous escape back to Lusaka.

The agent's superiors had been impressed with his ability to recall even the tiniest detail. What Morozov had omitted to tell them was that he'd managed to identify the name and particulars of his archenemy, the Rhodesian helicopter pilot.

As the debriefing had progressed, Morozov became more agitated. Just three weeks prior—while lying prostrate in his Lusaka hospital bed—Morozov's KGB handler had said that he'd petition Moscow to consider sending Morozov back to Africa. It now appeared as if the debriefing committee had no intention of doing so. "Comrade, there are two considerations," intoned one of the committee members. "Firstly, you are yet to undergo a series of medical procedures to rectify the mess on your face," he'd coughed embarrassingly before adding, "and your balls."

In fact Morozov had already made a decision. He wanted his disfiguring scar to be a constant reminder of the revulsion he felt toward Hunter. Having his face repaired was tantamount to forgiving him, and Morozov certainly had no intention of doing *that*. "Secondly, we expect that once you have recovered and are fully functional again, the Rhodesia issue will have resolved itself," the interviewer had continued. "In the face of such political, economic and military pressure, it is almost impossible for them to hold out much longer. By the grace of Lenin's ghost we will soon have another communist ally in Africa. We will send you back, eventually, I promise. Our final step in the Africa strategy is to secure South Africa. In the meantime, you are being transferred to the Third Chief Directorate for a two-year deployment."

One of the Soviets' major considerations throughout the Cold War was ensuring the political fealty of the officers and men in control of the military machine. This function was organized through an intricate network of KGB-controlled departments known as the *Osobye Otdely*. Officially regarded as a military counterintelligence organization, the network was supervised by the KGB's Third Chief Directorate.

This was to be Morozov's new home for the following two years.

The Third Chief Directorate's mandate actually extended far beyond counterintelligence: it encompassed the comprehensive surveillance of the military, as well as military security duties. It was imperative to the Soviet cause that the hierarchy be able to depend on the assured loyalty of the men and women running its military apparatus. Any hint of subversion would derail Moscow's ultimate plan to usurp the Americans as the world's dominant power.

With the exception of a nuclear threat, political paranoia fueled the Soviet's mistrust of the West. They were acutely aware of the CIA's technique of using ideological sabotage to promote doubt and instability within the Soviet ranks. The USSR knew about the West's bourgeois propaganda and their sinister methods of subverting the convictions of key Soviet individuals.

Infatuated with their unofficial uniform—black leather jackets, black turtle-neck sweaters and black pants—Morozov and his team went about the duty of surveilling their fellow countrymen.

Boris Sokolov was a low-life criminal. Although he'd been on-and-off the militsiya's radar for a couple of years, he'd never gone so far as to invite the curiosity of the KGB's Third Chief Directorate. But Boris was getting sloppy … and greedy.

With a string of strip joints and underground brothels across Moscow—and a reputation for disciplining his girls with burning cigarettes—the egregious Sokolov was starting to expand his empire. With the demand for underage Russian girls booming across Europe, Sokolov's prurient realm was poised to expand beyond the Berlin Wall.

But he needed help.

One of his regulars at *The Gentlemen's Club* was a colonel with a penchant for sadism and bondage. He had long hinted to Sokolov that he'd be interested in acquiring shares in the lucrative operation. After a series of clandestine meetings in smoky basement offices, Sokolov and the colonel hammered out the details of their new joint venture. Business had boomed over the following eighteen months.

Secreted away between huge cases of otherwise legitimate military hardware, badly-ventilated crates of drugged children were shipped over the border to the USSR's Eastern Bloc allies. From there, a sinister underworld network of Bulgarian and Romanian mafiosi spirited the frightened children across their borders. Like expendable commodities, the kids were distributed to seedy fleshpots located across Europe.

Morozov and his team had unearthed the existence of this wicked business. Through their own insidious spy network, the KGB had discovered that the vulgar pimp, Sokolov, had been operating with the assistance of a high-ranking business partner. Rumored to be a senior army officer, the KGB was eager to unearth the identity of the mysterious man. Having established that Sokolov's partner was in the military, the shady operation triggered the interest of the Third Chief Directorate.

It was time to pay Sokolov a visit.

Sokolov had long felt the need to protect himself. His brutish bodyguards—two Mongolian thugs each with a string of convictions—stood like implacable statues on either side of the door to his basement office. Upstairs, as the throbbing music filled the smoky room, vacant-looking dancers slid up-and-down unhygienic poles. Whereas his partner had been intrigued, Morozov was disgusted.

The two KGB agents—menacing in their dark garb—descended the stairs. Both guards' hands had been clasped in front of their crotches. As the two black-clad men approached, the Mongolians freed their hands and let their arms hang loosely at their sides. It wasn't only their matching black outfits that raised the guards' suspicions: both newcomers wore tight-fitting black leather gloves.

"KGB. We're here to see Sokolov." Morozov's partner flashed his card.

"Do you have an appointment?" asked one of the meatheads, moving in front of the door to block Morozov's progress.

"The KGB doesn't make appointments," snarled Morozov. "Out of my way." As he stepped forward to reach for the door handle, the bodyguard raised his open palm to Morozov's chest.

With blinding speed, Morozov raised both his hands. Seizing the man's thick wrist in one hand, he splayed the fingers of his free hand. In the same fluid movement he angled the raised arm down and away, then crashed his forehead onto the Mongolian's ample nose. He felt the cartilage explode. Before the bodyguard could recover from the searing pain, Morozov slid his free hand up behind the Mongolian's elbow and forced his arm into a locked position. Morozov maintained his firm grip on his opponent's right wrist. Glancing down, he was able to make out the telltale angular outline under the bodyguard's jacket. *A right-hander. Always good to disable that side first.*

Using the Mongolian's straightened arm as a lever, Morozov propelled his foe backwards toward the door.

Simultaneously lifting with his left hand, Morozov pushed the bodyguard off balance, but also forced him up onto his toes— a very unsettling position in close quarter battle.

Although graceful in its execution, there was nothing benign about Morozov's intentions. With cat-like agility he brought the man's hand up, twisted it sideways, then used his right hand up to execute a lock on the big man's wrist. Over the hypnotic sound of the music, all four men heard the man's wrist snap under the pressure.

But Morozov wasn't finished. Splaying the fingers of his right hand like the claws of a panther, he drove his extended digits into the man's eyes. For the first time, Morozov heard the brute grunt in pain.

In the five seconds that had elapsed since the doorman had raised his pudgy hand, his accomplice had barely had time to react. Stunned by the brutality of Morozov's attack, the second guard had only managed to stare in disbelief. Eventually gathering his senses, he fumbled for his concealed pistol. Instead of concentrating on his threat, the man's eyes had been drawn to the crumpled form of his defeated accomplice. In that moment of indecision, the man was doomed.

Morozov turned on him. The second Mogolian was wearing a polo shirt beneath his loose jacket. His neck was heavily muscled. Although barely discernable between the man's collarbones, Morozov was able to make out the indentation of the Mongolian's jugular notch. It was his landmark. Extending his index finger, Morozov drove it hard into the man's trachea. With his breathing interrupted by the ensuing spasm, the Mongolian gasped like a landed fish.

Both bodyguards had been armed; the second man had shown his intent to use his firearm. In Morozov's mind, that was sufficient justification to negate the threat with a commensurate amount of force. Drawing his Matsuda combat knife, he plunged the blade behind the Mongolian's collarbone. It punctured his subclavian artery.

As if performing a sumo ritual, the Mongolian bowed his head momentarily; he then looked up slowly. He wore a look of bewilderment. He'd just sensed his own demise. As the man slumped to the floor, Morozov leaned over and casually extracted the blade. He wiped it across the man's pants. The KGB agent looked impassively at his partner. The man just shrugged.

Sokolov had heard the muffled voices outside his door. He also heard the short scuffle and brief silence in the aftermath of the seven or eight-second commotion. Sokolov was unperturbed: he had fully expected one of his guards to knock politely on his door. *The small problem outside has been taken care of, sir.* Instead, two strangers burst into his office. Sokolov recoiled. He was cornered. There was only one way in-and-out of his basement office. His gut instinct told him they were KGB. *Fuckers!*

Morozov strode into the room and grabbed a fistful of Sokolov's lank hair. Pulling him from around his desk, he forced the pimp down onto a wooden chair in the middle of the room. From outside the office, Morozov's partner dragged first one, then the other bodyguard into the room. Like a butler retiring discreetly from a stately dinner, the KGB man quietly closed the door behind him.

Up against the wall, perched atop his open bird cage, a talkative African grey parrot bobbed and commented annoyingly. "Comrade Sokolov, it looks like you will be requiring some new bodyguards, no?" Morozov tilted his head disdainfully in the direction of the two men. The one had already bled out.

Sokolov's mind was churning. There was no doubting his visitors were KGB; they had that telltale, menacing aura about them. This was serious. *These guys are loose cannons—just look at how ruthless they were with my men.* He had no idea that it was Morozov alone who had neutralized the two guards.

For the sake of his miserable life, Sokolov knew not to annoy his captor. "What do you want from me comrade?" asked Sokolov. "This business is very lucrative. I can cut you in, comrade," he fawned.

Still slumped on the floor, the surviving Mongolian started

to stir. "I want answers Sokolov, details of your operation. I want to know everything," said Morozov softly.

"I don't know what you mean, comrade. I run a chain of strip joints. It's that simple. What you see here, this is my top club. I have seven others in the city. I have no quarrel with the KGB comrade, no quarrel." His reedy voice had registered an octave higher.

"Don't fucking lie to me," Morozov shot back. "And who says we are KGB?" With that he struck Sokolov with the back of his gloved hand. "Give me the name of your partner … the one you call the colonel," insisted Morozov.

"I don't know who you mean, comrade. I don't know this colonel." Morozov knew when a man was lying. He struck him a second time.

Bobbing on the top of its cage, the parrot joined the conversation. *"Grigor wants to fuck a whore. Grigor wants to fuck a whore."* The parrot reached up with a prehensile claw and scratched the top of its head.

"Stop fucking with me, you idiot. I know about your sick operation with the colonel," spat Morozov.

"Comrade. Really. Let's talk. How about we bring you into our little operation? There is enough to share." Morozov thought him contemptible. Not because he traded in young Russians, but because he had managed to compromise an officer's ethical obligation to uphold the integrity of the Motherland. Morozov's Motherland. He couldn't imagine anything more treasonous.

Still groggy from his beating, the Mongolian shook his head. His eyes still watered from the vicious finger strike. Morozov reached into his pocket and withdrew his knife. Wide-eyed, Sokolov noticed it still bore a thin smear of blood. Heaving upstairs, the floorboards above their heads trembled to the deep bass of the dancers' music. Without warning, Morozov plunged the knife into the bodyguard's upper thigh. The man yelled. The music played on. The Russian released his grip on the handle and left the knife embedded deep in the man's groin. The Mongolian was still screaming. Morozov squatted down next to him and slapped him a few times across the face: he wanted the man's undivided attention. "Are you listening carefully?" Morozov asked conversationally. Biting his lip, the guard nodded frantically. "I have cut into your artery. Take that knife out, and you will certainly bleed to death. Leave it in … well it might just plug the hole. The choice is yours," he offered reasonably.

The KGB man knew it was a lie—no steel blade would plug an arterial wound in that manner. After the chest cavity and pelvis, Morozov also knew that the leg was the next largest part of the body capable of concealing internal bleeding.

The Mongolian was slowly dying.

"Do I have your attention yet, Sokolov?" asked Morozov, standing up from beside the Mongolian.

Morozov listened intently as Sokolov spilled the details of his sleazy operation. At one stage the KGB man had to tell him to slow his garbled confession for fear of missing out on important points. He memorized the name and particulars of the colonel.

"Comrade, please, I have shared everything," pleaded Sokolov. "What are you going to do now? The colonel, he is the one you should go after. Please. Comrade, please," beseeched the criminal.

Again, the parrot scratched vigorously at its balding head. *"Grigor wants to fuck a whore …"*

Morozov snatched the scrawny bird off the top of its cage. With its wings pinned by its side, the African grey squawked indignantly as it struggled in his grip. "Please comrade. Not my Grigor," pleaded Sokolov.

Without warning, Morozov's left hand shot out. He gripped Sokolov violently around his neck. Using his thumb and forefinger to press down on the man's carotids, Morozov shut-down the blood pressure inside Sokolov's brain. His eyes lolled and his head began to swim. Within a few seconds his head flopped to the side and his mouth drooped open. Sokolov had slipped out of consciousness.

Morozov thrust the screeching bird deep into Sokolov's throat. While the man twitched and convulsed, the bird's claws slowly clenched and unclenched.

Both were dead within minutes.

Pale and afraid, the Mongolian looked on as Morozov rifled through Sokolov's desk drawers. The KGB agent found nothing of interest. On a whim, he forced his fingers into Sokolov's mouth and levered the bird out. A few loose feathers clung to the victim's blue-tinged lips. Taking one step toward the bird cage, he was about to drop the avian corpse inside when something caught his eye.

It can't be. That's impossible. Morozov froze. Staring up at him from the bottom of the cage was an unmistakable image: an image that was forever etched in his mind. The face of a man that embodied everything Morozov loathed. The smile even appeared to taunt him: *It's Dax fucking Hunter!*

If it hadn't been for the bird's poor aim, Hunter's face might otherwise have been hidden beneath a yellowish smear of bird shit. Taut with rage, Morozov lifted the folded paper out of the bottom of the cage and spread it open on Sokolov's desk.

It was a copy of the *Moskovskij Komsomolets*: *ZIMBABWE TAKES GOLD!* Morozov checked the date at the top of the page: 1st August. *What is today? 3rd August. The final ceremony of the Olympics is later today. Cyka, blyat! Let him still be here in Moscow. Please.*

Morozov had no need to read the article—it was immaterial who'd won gold. He knew Dax was a sportsman and he knew the face. Beyond any doubt, he knew it was Dax Hunter. Even if the headline hadn't confirmed the association with Zimbabwe, Morozov still would've known it was him.

Creasing the news-sheet carefully around Dax's head, he reached for a letter opener and sliced out the picture. Morozov's neurotransmitters fizzed like sherbet powder on a child's tongue: he could feel the familiar rage starting to brew.

The Mongolian's head had started to droop—he was losing

consciousness. As he stepped over him, Morozov reached down and pulled his knife out of the man's leg.

After letting himself out of the room, the Russian nodded to his KGB colleague. "Let's go." Morozov flipped the mechanism on the handle and checked to see that the door was locked behind them.

Crashing through the gears, Morozov wove recklessly through the midmorning traffic. Inside the drab green Lada 1200, both men could smell the over-cooked engine. Morozov's partner had already asked what had made him so mad in Sokolov's office: the driver simply glowered.

Another irate driver hit the horn and waved his fist out his open window. *Let one more bastard honk his horn and I'll pull his fucking eyeballs out.*

Morozov pulled into a car park outside a dilapidated carpet factory. It was located on the southern outskirts of the Moscow Oblast. Patches of weed and grass grew out of the network of cracks that radiated across the surface. "Take the rest of the day off, I have an urgent matter to attend to," he told his colleague.

The carpet factory was nothing more than a front: behind its crumbling façade, thirty men and women of the Third Chief Directorate—Moscow Branch—were busy at work. To complete the charade, the front office actually did stock a few rolls of cheap polyester carpets. Detachedly filing her nails, a glum-looking saleslady glanced up as Morozov walked in. Without saying a word, she buzzed him through the heavy metal door at the back. Morozov forgave her sullenness: every week, each female in the department had to fake an interest in carpets.

The steel door clanged shut behind him. With barely enough room to move, Morozov squeezed into a tight cubicle. There was another door right in front of him. Besides the two doors, the other two walls were bare.

Above his head, a speaker crackled into life. "Look into the camera and state your name, rank, number and today's password." Embedded in the second door, the lens of a standard peephole was in fact a hidden camera.

Located somewhere deep in the back of the building, an unseen operator must've been satisfied with Morozov's responses. To the right of his shoulder, a carefully concealed door clicked open. Even on close inspection it would have been difficult to detect, especially given the confined space.

A dozen or so junior agents—each one wearing a set of headphones—sat in front of a bank of oversized reel-to-reel tapes. It was part of the KGB's endless mission to eavesdrop on all the private or salacious conversations taking place across the city. Morozov walked past them and approached the Assignments Desk. "Comrade, I need some assistance." Brevity was always encouraged, if not appreciated.

Morozov's reputation as an effective 'closer' afforded him a few privileges. With a little luck the clerk would overlook his interruption, make a quick call, and then simply hand him the information he needed. He didn't want to attract unnecessary attention to his request, and he certainly didn't want to open a case file. He checked his watch. 10:47. "What is it you need, comrade?" asked the pinch-faced clerk.

"One of my sources has heard that there may be a Russian athlete planning a defection after tonight's ceremony. He thinks the defector might have already shared some of his plans or intentions with an athlete from the Zimbabwean team. This athlete's name is Dax Hunter. I would like to meet the Zimbabwean and ask him if he knows anything about this possible defection. All I need is the Olympic Village address and room number for this athlete."

On the surface, the request appeared to be innocuous enough. Had the clerk stopped for a moment and considered it more carefully, perhaps she might've wondered why someone from the Third Chief Directorate was getting involved in investigating a possible defection; or how an informant could so accurately identify a foreign accomplice but not have the vaguest idea of the perpetrator's identity. Luckily for Morozov she was willing to oblige; and too careless to delve a little further into his odd request.

It was 11:04. Despite being immune to emotion, Morozov was getting impatient. *Play it cool Vladimir, don't annoy the bitch.*

Six minutes later, armed with his information, Morozov left the building the same way he'd entered.

27

THE GENTLEMEN'S CLUB

The city's bureaucrats had gone to extraordinary lengths to emphasize the need for Muscovites to put their best foot forward. After all, they *were* hosting the Olympic Games. Sixty-five nations had chosen to boycott the Games because of the USSR's recent invasion of Afghanistan. The last thing the officials wanted was any further embarrassment to their showpiece. Dutifully fulfilling the party's orders, even the taxi drivers desisted from taking foreigners via the scenic route.

Dax knocked on Achilles' door. "I'm ready," he shouted. "We better hurry, or we'll miss the next bus to the airport."

"I'm coming, but don't worry about the bus. We'll take a taxi," responded Achilles from beyond the closed door. "Besides, I honestly don't think my dad's pilot will be leaving without us."

There were still a few athletes hanging around on their floor. Ortiz from Mexico was impressively strong. Embracing Dax with a sweaty farewell hug, the weightlifter hoisted the Zimbabwean clear off the floor. "You wait here, Dax. Wait!" insisted Ortiz. Disappearing into his room, he emerged moments later with a large sombrero. "For you, *mi amigo*, to remember me by," said the big Mexican. Dax was sure he saw Ortiz's eyes brimming.

Squashing the colorful hat down onto Dax's head, the weightlifter playfully punched him on the shoulder. *Goddamn, that hurt.* After bidding them all farewell, Dax and Achilles descended to the ground floor and headed out across the park toward the security gate.

Getting out of the athlete's compound was easy; getting in was always a tedious process. After the 1972 massacre of Israeli athletes at the Munich Games, every subsequent organizing committee had been obliged to introduce strict security measures around the athletes' villages. Already paranoid, the Soviets took their security obligations to a new level. Other than athletes, coaches, judges and team officials, it was practically impossible to get inside. Taxis had been forced to stage-up a short distance away from the compound.

Shortly after exiting through the checkpoint, Dax and Achilles noticed a black-clad man sprinting their way. Although he was trying to weave between the throngs, he still managed to jostle a number of pedestrians. He didn't even have the courtesy to slow down or shout an apology. *That guy's on a mission,* thought Dax.

Ahead of them, pedestrians parted like the Red Sea. "Come on, out my way," the man growled. His English was accented. Sauntering toward him, Morozov was aware that *this* pair of athletes was making little effort to move aside. *Move, you fucking Mexican.*

Sprinting past them, both Dax and Achilles couldn't help notice a livid scar across the man's left cheek. "Would give anything to know what that was all about," said Dax.

The two friends made their way toward the orderly line of taxis parked-up less than half a quarter mile from the Olympic village checkpoint. Dressed more like a concierge from a top hotel, an engaging man ushered them toward the first taxi in the front of the queue. "Tell me, you two fine athletes, are you going to the airport?" he enquired. Contrary to the taxi drivers' usual habit, there was no hooting or hustling on this occasion.

"Sheremetyevo airport please," instructed Achilles.

A chorus of angry objections rose from the line of athletes and officials as Morozov shouldered his way to the front of the queue. Blowing on his whistle and raising his hand, one of the security guards made a move to block his path. Morozov thrust his badge under the guard's nose. "I am sorry comrade, I didn't realize," he groveled.

"Quick, where is Men's Apartment Block C," demanded Morozov.

As he'd expected, there was a guard posted at the main door to Block C. Morozov ran right up to him. For the second time in as many minutes, he took out his KGB badge and waved it at the door guard. The badge was very persuasive. "Comrade, I need your help. You are to say nothing to anybody about this." Morozov stared into the sentry's eyes. Mesmerized by the snake charmer's aura, the guard nodded dumbly.

"Of course, comrade," he said, pleased to be taken into the agent's confidence.

Morozov reached into the inside pocket of his leather jacket and removed the folded newspaper cutting. "This athlete, I believe he stays in this apartment block, no?" asked Morozov.

For a moment the guard's eyes lit-up. He then became cagey. "Indeed comrade, but this man, he's done something wrong?"

Morozov read the small cues. *Fucking Hunter, you probably already know this guard's kids' names.* The agent decided to reel the guard in with his cover story. *If it can fool a KGB clerk at the Assignments Desk, it'll work on this imbecile.*

After explaining that the Zimbabwean might have information about a possible defector, the guard nodded enthusiastically. "Yes comrade, that sounds like the Zimbabwean. Everyone here knows him, and they all like him too. He's a good person, Hunter. The kind of guy everyone wants to share their story with."

"Good comrade, thank you." Just hearing about Dax's string of agreeable traits made the KGB man angry. Careful not to alienate the guard, Morozov moderated his tone. "And do you know if this Zimbabwean ... you said his name is Hunter, right? Is he here in the apartments right now?"

"Ah, you have just missed him comrade. He and his Greek friend left for the airport no more than ten minutes ago. You might have even passed them on your way here. Hunter was wearing a big sombrero."

On this occasion, Morozov didn't even bother alerting people to move out of his way. *Too bad if they don't fucking hear me coming*, he thought, as he bulldozed his way through. Morozov was raging.

Morozov knew that his fury was dimming his powers of reasoning. With great effort, he managed to contain his anger; he needed to start filtering his options. *If they'd gone by bus, they would have taken the other footpath to the terminal and I wouldn't have seen that fucking Hunter with his stupid sombrero. Therefore they must've taken a taxi.* Morozov swerved off the path and headed toward the taxi rank. *I must find out which airport they are going to.*

With two international airports servicing the city's Olympic influx, Hunter's flight could be departing from either Sheremetyevo or Vnukovo.

At the front of the rank, a flamboyantly-dressed man was controlling taxi dispatches. Morozov knew that he'd be his most likely source of information. Again, the KGB badge elicited respect. "Yes comrade. They must have left here maybe fifteen minutes ago. This one here," the taxi usher pointed at the photograph in Morozov's hand, "I remember him. He was the one wearing the big Mexican hat."

"Quickly comrade, where did their taxi take them?"

"Sheremetyevo," said the usher without hesitation. Morozov checked his watch. It was 12:13.

As he saw the third overhead sign to the airport, a thought flashed into Achilles' mind. *Shit! We aren't departing on a commercial flight.* "Driver, please, we are flying out on a private charter. We are not going to the main terminal," explained Achilles.

"You fly private jet?" said the driver, his English passable.

"Yes, yes. Private jet," confirmed Achilles.

"Too late. We go around," said the driver, shaking his head and muttering to himself in Russian. They'd just missed the turn-off to the private charter terminal.

Factoring in the usher's estimate that he'd dispatched the cab about fifteen minutes earlier—plus the travel time to the airport—Morozov calculated their likely arrival time. Since they were flying international, they would be expected to check in at least an hour prior to departure. *I still have time to apprehend Hunter before he boards his aircraft.*

Morozov sprinted toward his car.

For the inconvenience of having been given a route change mid-fare, Dax was convinced that their driver had taken a decidedly circuitous route back to the charter terminal. He watched as the meter clicked-over and a few more rubles were added to their charge.

They eventually pulled into the car park outside the private charter terminal. Achilles checked his watch. "My father said his Learjet is scheduled to leave Sheremetyevo at 1:15. See, we made it with half an hour to spare."

"How long's the flight to Athens?" asked Dax.

"A little over three hours. Perhaps the helicopter will be waiting for us. If it is, we'll be at my father's house before five. My step-mother's party starts at seven," said Achilles.

Dax did a quick mental calculation. "So there's no time difference between Moscow and Athens?"

"No," said Achilles.

With his hand hovering over the horn, Morozov drove aggressively through the Moscow traffic. All the roads leading to Sheremetyevo were busy. Although the Games' final ceremony was only scheduled for later that evening, the majority of the European-based visitors wanted to be home in time for the start of a new work week. Despite the congestion, Morozov made it to the airport by 12:55. Swinging aggressively into a tight opening in the drop-off zone, he leaped out and slammed the door behind him. A nearby policeman was about to remonstrate. Morozov flashed his badge. "Official business," he said, running inside the building.

Morozov had already served in three different branches of the KGB. He knew exactly where in the airport he'd find their offices. Turning down a narrow corridor off the main concourse, Morozov noticed a slovenly looking traveler slouched against the wall. His face hadn't seen a razor in at least five days. A cheap cigarette dangled from his lips. To complete the charade, a grubby rucksack lay at his feet. As he approached, Morozov discreetly flashed his badge. The man nodded and tipped his head in the direction of an unmarked door.

The air inside the office had been fouled by a fug of stale smoke and rancid body odor. Morozov went straight over to a heavy-set man. He was working the keyboard in front of his glowing terminal. The display screen was alive with an ever-changing pattern of luminous green characters.

After a brief exchange, Morozov got to the point. "Comrade, I need you to check the flight details of a witness in a case I am working on. His name is Hunter. Dax Hunter. Nationality … Zimbabwean."

The man's fingers flashed across his keyboard. The minutes ticked by. Morozov was getting frustrated. "Comrade, there is no Dax Hunter on any manifest out of Sheremetyevo today. Not even Vnukovo. Nothing. But he is due to fly out tomorrow on Air Zimbabwe. Are you certain he's flying today?"

"Fuck!" Morozov was furious. He banged his palm down on the tabletop. *Think, Vladimir, think*. He checked his watch. *1:12*.

"Wait!" he shouted. "Do private flights list all their passenger names?"

"Yes," responded the computer operator. "But that list is only available to the Customs and Immigration guys located in the private terminal on the other side of the airfield."

Morozov reached over and snatched a heavy black phone

off its cradle. He thrust it at the computer man. "Call them," he demanded.

After Morozov explained his request, he heard the official place the phone down on the counter top. Although he could hear him conferring with a colleague, he only caught indistinct snippets of their conversation.

"Hello. You still there?" asked the customs official.

"Yes."

"Comrade, Learjet 23, registration SX-B11, bound for Athens, got airborne at 1:08."

Consumed by the unfolding drama, the agents in the office had been watching discreetly. As Morozov slammed the phone back onto its cradle, he looked up challengingly. "What?" he shouted. Embarrassed, they hurriedly looked away.

Morozov strode across the airport concourse toward where he'd left his car. His frustration devoured him. Hunter had been so close. The KGB man was already scheming. He needed to concoct a reason to fly to Athens. Then it came to him. *The colonel.* But there were some loose ends that he needed to take care of first.

It had just occurred to Morozov that he'd been careless in Sokolov's basement office earlier that day. *I left the fucking newspaper on the desk with the picture of Hunter cut out.* Morozov needed to go back to tidy up his crime scene. Unclipping the two-way pager from his belt, he sent a short message to Anatoly, his KGB colleague.

Unfinished business. Meet me outside the strip joint in 40 minutes.

Morozov was waiting on the corner opposite *The Gentlemen's Club.* He had a small back pack slung over his shoulder. He checked his watch again. He was getting agitated; Anatoly was already two minutes late. His partner arrived a few moments later. Shepherding him across the street, Morozov explained why it was necessary for them to return to the office. Doctoring crime scenes was part of their stock-in-trade.

Anatoly gave a customary shrug of his shoulders.

The seedy club appeared to be functioning as normal. There were no police in sight. As Morozov had expected, Sokolov probably forbade any of the staff from ever venturing downstairs to his basement office. Upstairs, so many men came-and-went during the course of business that it was unlikely that anyone would specifically recognize the two men who'd visited earlier that day. Both KGB men slipped their gloves on as they descended the creaky stairs.

Hours before, Morozov had locked the door as he and Anatoly had left Sokolov's office. Testing the handle, he made sure the door was still locked. He reached into his jacket and dug out a small leather pouch. He selected a small brass tension wrench along with a finely-wrought pick. After inserting the wrench in the keyhole, he applied a small amount of torque on the handle. He then slid the pick over the tension wrench and gently scrubbed back-and-forth on the concealed pins. The door eased open. The overbearing smell of cigarette smoke still filled the room, but it couldn't quite mask the new scent of cloying blood. Morozov closed the door behind them.

"Comrade, I just want to check these bodyguards' pockets … can you check Sokolov's cupboards for any documents that might identify the colonel," directed Morozov.

Anatoly was unaware that Morozov had already extracted the colonel's identity from Sokolov during their earlier visit.

While his colleague rifled through Sokolov's desk drawers, Morozov squatted next to one of the bodies. With his back to Anatoly, he discreetly withdrew a pistol from his jacket pocket. Before arriving at the strip joint he'd screwed the silencer onto the end of the barrel. "Anatoly, come and look at this," said Morozov excitedly. He stood and turned to face his colleague.

Anatoly looked up as he stepped toward his comrade. *What the fuck?* Morozov's weapon was pointed directly at his chest. The pistol coughed twice. Anatoly toppled forward onto the floor, a half-formed oath still on his lips. *Fucking bastard. I should have known … he never calls me by my first name.*

Morozov's weapon wasn't standard KGB issue—it was one

of several he kept for just such situations. It had been wiped free of prints. Manipulating one of the dead Mongolian's fingers, he pressed a number of prints over the pistol's handle, slide and barrel. Unscrewing the silencer, he then left the gun in the loose grip of the dead bodyguard.

Taking the folding combat knife out of his pocket, Morozov carefully wiped off all his own prints. He then removed both Anatoly's gloves and closed the dead man's fingers around the handle. Clasping the knife between his gloved thumb and forefinger, Morozov wriggled the blade back into the Mongolian's original thigh wound. He allowed some congealed blood to smear across the blade before tugging gently on the handle and sliding it back out. Stepping over to the other Mongolian, he inserted the knife blade into the neat hole above the big man's collarbone. This time he left the knife buried to the hilt.

Morozov loved his Matsuda knife, but he could always buy himself another one.

Now functioning at its best, Morozov's mind was working furiously. He created a pile of items that needed to be removed from the crime scene: the one Mongolian's weapon—Morozov had given him the planted weapon; Anatoly's pager—it contained Morozov's earlier message; the newspaper—it had Hunter's photograph cut out; the loose feathers still clinging to Sokolov's lips; the silencer; and, finally, Anatoly's gloves—why would a KGB agent have conducted a routine investigation with gloves on? Morozov thought through every scenario.

He then started filling his back pack with the various items. As he reached for Anatoly's pager, he paused and thought for a moment. Using that pager, he quickly sent a message to his own. From beyond the grave, Anatoly had just sent Morozov a message revealing the name of the colonel. *The KGB will be proud of you Anatoly. Before succumbing to your wounds, you were able to send your partner crucial details of the case we were working. It's just such a pity you opted to go into the lion's den without backup.*

The next part of Morozov's scheme was going to be tricky: he needed to mask the sound of a gunshot. The silencer he'd just used was incompatible with the weapon he needed to fire. He looked around the room. A soiled couch was wedged into the corner of the room. Morozov could only imagine what the bastard pimp did on it. Three un-matching cushions lay on top.

Morozov removed Anatoly's weapon from beneath his jacket then shifted the dead weight into a sitting position. Kneeling behind him to prevent him from toppling over, he placed the weapon in his colleague's limp grip. He then used his free hand to smother the weapon with the cushion.

With his mouth still stretched open, Sokolov sat slumped in his chair. Aiming up at his chest, Morozov carefully inserted a gloved finger into the tight-fitting space behind the trigger guard. Anticipating the next musical crescendo from the DJ upstairs, he waited for a moment. Timing it perfectly, he pressed back on Anatoly's index finger and fired once into Sokolov's lifeless body. He quickly stuffed the cushion into his back pack.

The last thing to take care of was the fire. Choosing a half-finished cigarette from Sokolov's overflowing ashtray, Morozov blanked out his revulsion as he lit it and inhaled. Once burning, he tossed it casually onto the carpet. Careful not to make it too obvious, he left a small pyre of combustible material just close enough to fuel the flames.

Stuffed with the various items he needed removed from the scene, Morozov shouldered his back pack. Another thought occurred to him. *If the investigators happen to link my crucial pager message to Anatoly's last dying deed, they'll want to know where his pager disappeared to.* He dug in his bag, retrieved the pager and tossed it close to where the fire had started to take hold. *The flames will melt the circuitry.* He checked the room one more time. Spotting the parrot on Sokolov's desk, he picked it up and threw it back into the bird cage.

As the flames started licking upwards, Morozov closed the door behind him. He didn't lock it this time.

Morozov drove straight back to the carpet shop on the southern side of the city. He needed to build an alibi. Once inside, he risked calling his boss at home. "Comrade, I am sorry to disturb you on a Sunday afternoon," said Morozov, "but a short while ago I received a message from Anatoly."

"Continue," said his boss.

"He has somehow discovered the identity of the mysterious colonel. The problem is that I have tried to page him several times after I received his message, but he has not answered. Has he reported anything to you on this matter?" Morozov feigned mild concern.

"Why was he operating independently this morning?" asked Morozov's superior.

"It is unusual comrade, but I don't know why."

"You were pursuing this lead through the scumbag Sokolov, correct?" asked the KGB boss.

"That is right, comrade," answered Morozov.

"Keep trying Anatoly's pager. In the meantime, find Sokolov. Keep me informed." With that, the boss put down his phone.

Morozov walked over to the clerk at the Assignments Desk. She looked up as he approached. "Second time in one day, comrade?"

"Yes comrade." Morozov hoped to capitalize on the rapport he'd developed earlier that day. He slipped her a piece of paper with the colonel's name on it.

Within minutes she produced the man's address and phone number. More importantly, she'd also given him the location of his private dacha in the exurbs. *That might be useful.*

Morozov paged his boss about forty-five minutes later. It was an urgent appeal to come as quickly as possible to an address just outside the Garden Ring.

After sending the pager message, Morozov walked toward a bank of pay phones. They were across the street from the charred remains of Sokolov's seedy club. Morozov watched as the firemen started rolling up their reels; they were about to make way for the police investigators. In the wake of the fire crew, the police were itching to swarm over the gutted remains of Sokolov's notorious club.

Morozov fed several coins into the pay phone and dialed a number. It rang four times. "This is Colonel Alexeev."

"Comrade Colonel," said Morozov, making no effort to disguise his voice. "Listen carefully. I am a friend of Sokolov's. He has unfortunately revealed your name to some unsavory members of the Moscow mafia." Instead of using the common underworld description, Morozov had carelessly used an esoteric term to describe the Moscow mafia. The phrase was rarely used outside of military and police circles. As he said it, Morozov hoped that the colonel hadn't noticed. The last thing he wanted was for Alexeev to suspect that the state authorities were onto him. "They want to take control of yours and Sokolov's business," continued Morozov. "I have heard they will kill you both if necessary. I suggest you disappear for a while." Morozov hung up before the colonel could ask him any questions.

Morozov's boss arrived just under an hour after receiving his agent's pager message. With the loss of one of their own, the KGB alone would be responsible for solving the crime.

Flashing his ID badge at the senior police investigator, Morozov's boss ordered him to stand down. Up at street level, the coroners were waiting for the order to come down and remove the bodies.

Stepping over the sooty mush that had pooled in the basement, Morozov and his boss went about investigating the crime scene. Before bending down to examine one of the crisply-burnt bodies, Morozov's boss smeared some Tiger Balm ointment under his nostrils. He'd never gotten used to the smell.

Using an instinctual rather than an evidentiary approach to assessing the crime scene, the senior KGB man quickly pieced together the sequence of events. Barring the mild irritation of having to file an official Murder Document, he told Morozov that he believed it was essentially an open-and-shut case. "There's not much investigative work needed here," he confided. "The evidence at the crime scene points compellingly to a routine call having gone horribly wrong. Sokolov's bodyguards precipitated the carnage by overreacting to the presence of a KGB man. Firstly a knife had been drawn in self-defense, and then shots were fired. A burning cigarette fell on the shag carpet and the ensuing inferno engulfed the rest of the building."

To appease the invisible grey bureaucrats deep in the KGB apparatus, Morozov's boss ordered an autopsy on Anatoly. "What about these three pigs, comrade?" Morozov enquired. He knew that if an autopsy was performed on Sokolov it would reveal a very different end to the one suggested by the bullet hole in his chest. Furthermore, the coroner would have no difficulty proving that the two Mongolians had curiously died several hours before Anatoly had succumbed to his gunshot wounds. Morozov waited for his commander's answer.

"These fucking pigs don't even deserve a pauper's grave, let alone an autopsy," said the KGB boss. "No! No autopsy required on these criminals. But I do want you to intensify your search for this colonel."

Early the next morning, Morozov advised his superior that the elusive colonel must have fled after receiving an anonymous tip-off. Under pressure to solve the case, Morozov's boss ordered his junior to redouble his efforts in the search for the fugitive officer.

Using the KGB's sinuous spy network, Morozov's first task was to trace the owner of the Greek-registered Learjet. After a bit more digging he was able to determine that Dax's Greek friend—the Olympic athlete—was the son of the tycoon who owned the aircraft.

Finding their address in Corinth, outside Athens, had been easy. Almost as easy was Morozov's ability to fabricate a story about the colonel's whereabouts. Concocting a plausible yarn, he convinced his KGB boss that the colonel had fled to Athens after discovering that he'd been compromised.

According to Morozov's ongoing investigations, Athens was apparently the hub of their iniquitous European trafficking ring.

Morozov's superior was well duped. He ordered his agent to leave for the Greek capital on the first available flight. It was less than twenty hours since the fire department had been called to Sokolov's *Gentlemen's Club*.

28

ISABELLA

With the captain attending to the shutdown procedures, the co-pilot unlatched the cabin door and lowered the Learjet's stairs to the apron. The Fotakis' jet had just arrived at Hellinikon airport on the outskirts of Athens. Stepping out into the late afternoon sunshine, Achilles saw his father's Long Ranger helicopter parked close by. Zephyr, one of the company's pilots, was standing alongside his gleaming machine. As he saw Achilles emerge, he walked over to greet the two athletes. He offered to load their bags while the two men went inside the private terminal to have their passports checked.

With the formalities complete, Dax and Achilles walked back toward the helicopter. As they approached Zephyr, Achilles called out. "Hey Zeph, Dax also flies. He's in the army." Dax cringed. "You should check out all his battle scars." Zephyr smiled politely. "Let him fly us home."

Before Zephyr could respond, Dax rescued himself from potential embarrassment. "I don't think that's a good idea, Achilles. Zephyr will tell you that there's a big difference between the French-built helicopter I fly and this American-designed helicopter."

"That's not a problem," said Zephyr, realizing Dax was a helicopter pilot and not a fixed wing pilot. "I'll hold my hands and feet softly on the dual controls; you'll pick it up very quickly, I promise."

Achilles' brow furrowed. "So what's the big difference then—a helicopter's a helicopter, right?"

"The rotor blades in American-designed choppers rotate in one direction, but in European-built helicopters they spin the other way. Basically you have to use your pedals the other way around," explained Zephyr. His English was almost as good as Achilles'.

Dax picked up the technique very quickly; he instinctively responded to the helicopter's movements with just the right inputs and pressure on the yaw pedals. With Dax flying the desired bearing and altitude, Zephyr took care of the radio. After about fifteen minutes aloft, the Greek pilot pointed out the helipad where he wanted Dax to put down. The Zimbabwean whistled impressively. The helipad lay on the last of six large, sculpted terraces that descended from the main house. Carved into the rock face and leading down from the last terrace, a precipitous set of steps accessed a private cove. The horseshoe inlet protected the cobalt waters of the Mediterranean.

After gently touching down, Dax handed control back to Zephyr: he would manage the shut-down procedures. Squinting through the Perspex canopy, Dax noticed a small party of enthusiastic servants waiting to greet their returning Olympian.

Try as he might, Dax was unable to wrestle his bag and bow-case from the servants. They happily allowed him to carry his sombrero though. Zigzagging their way up the stone-flagged steps, Dax could better appreciate the splendor of each of the manicured terraces. Breaking the ascent for the less energetic, the landscaper had placed a number of small alcoves along the path leading to the house. In each alcove, vivid flamboyant trees cast great shadows across the pathways and carved stone benches. Those requiring a little more time to recover could idle away their day admiring the sculptures adorning the edges of the fronded fishponds.

Looking up toward the mansion, Dax noticed that it

appeared to be designed in the style of an old monastery. While the main structure was painted entirely in white—so bright, it dazzled—the gates, low fences and domed cupolas were painted an electric indigo. Still gazing upward, Dax caught a brief glimpse of a striking women looking down on them from her window. She hurriedly withdrew into the shadows. *I wonder if that's Achilles' sister?*

Achilles' father was a consummate host. After enfolding his son in a warm hug, Yiannos turned his attention to his guest. He ignored Dax's hand, instead embracing him in a similar manner. Thrust among so many people of different cultures during the preceding two weeks, Dax had quickly overcome his discomfort of this uniquely continental habit. He was starting to respond a little less awkwardly with each successive hug.

The gregarious tycoon slapped Dax on his back and told him to make himself at home. Politely excusing himself, Yiannos moved-off to start greeting the early arrivals.

Dax was not entirely comfortable being a novelty; his embarrassment rose as Achilles paraded him around the party. At each introduction, he deflected his Greek friend's lavish praise. Having chosen to abstain during the lead-up to his participation in the Olympics, Achilles' tolerance for alcohol had weakened. Succumbing quickly to the ouzo, he clumsily interrupted two of Dax's conversations. Close to becoming bothersome, Achilles accosted Dax for a third time and led him off to meet some-or-other daughter of a government minister. The Zimbabwean was about to have a private word with him when Yiannos' booming voice echoed out across the room. The hubbub of a hundred conversations quickly died away.

Yiannos had ascended halfway up the spiral staircase to address his guests. "Ladies and gentlemen, honored guests, welcome, welcome. Thank you for coming to celebrate the occasion of my beautiful wife's birthday. Before I announce her arrival, may I briefly say a special welcome home for my son Achilles and his good friend Dax, both of whom returned today from Moscow where they represented their countries at the Olympic Games." The crowd cheered warmly. "And now ladies and gentlemen, may I introduce the birthday girl, my darling wife Isabella."

Waiting out of sight at the top of the stairwell, the elegant Isabella emerged from the shadows. Dax recognized her immediately; she was the woman he'd seen fleetingly in the window. As the guests applauded, she walked gracefully to where Yiannos stood. Stooping slightly, she delicately brushed each of his cheeks with her own. Standing by his side with their arms interlaced, she faced the room and accepted the guests' flattering ovation.

Disguised behind their jealous stares and false smiles, it wasn't difficult interpreting the women's non-verbal signals; some were so threatened they subconsciously pulled their partners in a little closer. Dax's observation of the men's body language was equally perceptive; their ruminative gestures telegraphed their basest thoughts. "Now we celebrate," proclaimed Yiannos.

Dax wasn't much of a drinker, but the few beers he'd had were starting to make him light-headed. He grabbed a coke from the bar and ventured out onto the vast balcony. Leaning back on the railing, he scanned the partygoers. "There you are," said Achilles, weaving toward where Dax stood. "How are you enjoying the party, my friend?" Achilles was starting to slur.

"It's good, Achilles. All good," replied Dax. "Hey, you didn't tell me your step-mom looks like Sophia Loren."

"My friend," he whispered hoarsely, "that woman is actually King Juan Carlos' second cousin, and has apparently earned some fame as a Spanish actress," he scoffed. Despite the impressive résumé, there was a distinct lack of enthusiasm in Achilles' tone. "So what does a washed-up forty-year old actress do when her star starts to fade?" he asked sarcastically. "She looks for an older millionaire Dax, that's what she does." Just at that moment, Isabella sashayed over to where the two were standing. "Ah, speak of the devil." Even Achilles realized the inappropriateness of his greeting. "Isabella, I was just telling Dax that you are the King of Spain's cousin ... forgive me, have I introduced you?"

"Dax Hunter. Pleased to meet you." He offered his hand.

"As am I Dax." Her accent was enchanting. She held his hand a moment or two longer than was fitting. Of all her allures, Dax found her fragrance most captivating.

Isabella was statuesque. She held Dax's gaze intently. Her long auburn hair cascaded softly onto her exposed shoulder, accentuating her décolletage. Her tight lamé dress had no doubt been chosen to draw attention to her curvaceous figure. Dax detected a small but sensuous parting of her mouth. Her lips were like exotic fruit, her appeal intoxicating.

While not entirely immune to her affect, Dax still managed to resist the temptation to look down. She smiled enigmatically. Dax wondered if he'd just passed a test. "So Dax, you are an Olympian and I see you're a helicopter pilot too?" she purred. Before Dax could answer, she glanced over at Achilles. "Be a darling Achilles, go and fetch us two glasses of champagne." Dax immediately sensed the power play.

He used the interruption to change the subject. "Achilles tells me you're also an actress. Is that stage or cinema, or both?" he asked.

"You are such a delightful young man, Dax, trying to deflect my question." Isabella raised her chin slightly and laughed delicately. Subliminal or not, Dax was convinced it was an immodest invitation to ravage her throat. It immediately reminded him of Meatloaf's song, '*You took the words right out of my mouth.*' In the song's opening dialogue between Meatloaf and a sultry temptress, the singer asks, '*Would you offer your throat to the wolf with the red roses?*' Dax loved that song. He smiled at the imagery.

Yiannos was working the crowd when he spotted his wife and Dax outside on the verandah. Even as he approached from across the balcony, he was talking. "My darling wife ... I see you have eventually been introduced to Dax."

"Yes I have," she said breezily. "But he's just too modest

for my liking. I can't get him to talk about himself at all." Yiannos appeared to like both those facts. He put an arm around Dax's shoulder and squeezed him affectionately.

"Ah, there's Dimitri Galanakis, please, excuse me," said Yiannos. He clutched his wife's waist a little too tightly and kissed her wetly on the cheek. Dax noticed a fleeting look of distaste.

The dog marks its territory.

It was 07:30. The three men were sitting at the breakfast table and one of them was decidedly under-the-weather. Achilles had been picking half-heartedly at his plate of fresh oven bread, feta and boiled quails' eggs when Yiannos chided him good-humoredly. "Ah, my son. You want to drink so much after being off the liquor for so long? Why are you up so early, anyway?"

Achilles groaned. "Pappá, I need to fly into Athens with you after breakfast. I can't face driving there later this morning. All the athletes from Moscow land at 11:45 this morning and the whole team has been invited to the Prime Minister's residence for lunch. I would invite you Dax, but it's a team affair only."

"I'll be fine, honest. I'll take a walk around the town … maybe go to the beach," said Dax.

"Excellent," said Yiannos, wiping his mouth on a napkin, "let's all go out to my favorite taverna for dinner tonight. Come my son, we must get going."

While Dax hadn't exactly overindulged the previous night, he was still feeling the after effects of the liquor. After donning his swimming trunks, Dax grabbed a towel and headed down the path to the private cove he'd spotted the previous day. A swim would be a good antidote. It was just a little after 9 o'clock and already the mercury was climbing.

From the top of the stone stairs leading down to the sand, Dax admired the picturesque setting. It would've easily served as the cover of a Greek tourist brochure. Cocooned by the rugged cliffs, the cove curved out and away to form a large horseshoe, the spits eventually angling in to embrace the sheltered bay.

Once down on the sand, Dax stepped out of his flip flops. He loved the ocean. Unlike Durban, where you could body-surf the big swells, the sea here was benign. Considering a triangular swim, Dax estimated the distance to be a little under a mile. After wading out to a suitable depth, he dived into the tepid waters and struck out for the tip of the left spit.

Shaded by her broad straw hat and Jackie-O sunglasses, Isabella watched from the cliffs above the cove. Delicious thoughts started to fill her head.

The salt water was starting to sting Dax's eyes. Keeping his eyes closed underwater, he looked up to check his direction after every sixteenth stroke. He had been in the water just over twenty-five minutes when his arm suddenly connected with something in the water. From its movement, he knew it wasn't flotsam. He experienced a quick flush of anxiety. Still underwater, he opened his eyes to identify the threat.

Treading water beside him, a bikini-clad body had swum out a short distance to intercept him. Dax lifted his head out the water and wiped his eyes. "Hey Isabella," he managed to mask his relief, "you gave me a fright. What are you doing out here?"

"Maybe I need rescuing," she said coquettishly. With that, she raised her arms and allowed herself to sink below the surface. As she bobbed-up next to him a moment later, she pouted theatrically. "Where's a chivalrous knight when you need one?" she complained, splashing water in his face. "Come, race me," she challenged.

Just as they reached shallower water, Dax grabbed her ankle. Instead of kicking hard to break his grip, she allowed him to pull her back. They both stood. The water lapped at their waists. Without taking her eyes off his face, Isabella raised her hands, pulled her ponytail up into a twist and squeezed out the water. Her head was tilted to one side as she wrung out her hair. Her lips parted slightly. On this occasion, Dax allowed his eyes to drop down. He knew her gesture was an invitation. Like a provocative Siren on the rocks, Isabella had patiently lured her sailor into her irresistible embrace.

Pressed against the fabric of her bikini, Isabella's nipples were hard with desire. She lowered her arms slowly and reached forward, encircling his neck. Although Dax was no saint, he knew the rule about forbidden fruit. But a primeval instinct was driving Dax's ardor; it taunted his last remnants of restraint.

Isabella drew Dax's head close to her lips. Her mouth was inches from his ear. "My husband is no longer capable of satisfying me ... can you Dax? Can you satisfy the ache?"

Everyone erupted in peals of laughter as Dax finished telling one of his stories about farm life in Zimbabwe. It was one of his favorite Jokes of the Week. The mood around the breakfast table was light and cheerful. As if by arrangement, both Dax and Isabella were managing to feign their disinterest in each other. Despite this, their steamy tryst on the beach the day before still played itself out in succulent detail.

"So, Achilles and I have to fly to Nicosia today on business. We have a dinner meeting which means we are unfortunately only able to return tomorrow," said Yiannos. "Dax, I promise you, after tomorrow I will give Achilles a few days off so he can show you around our beautiful islands." Dax nodded and smiled. "Isabella, perhaps if you are not busy today, you two could take a trip to the Acropolis?"

Dax walked down to the helipad with Yiannos and Achilles. When they got there, Zephyr was just completing his pre-flight walk-around. After they'd climbed aboard and strapped themselves in, the pilot went through a series of memorized start-up checks. As the engine started to whine, Dax could visualize all the procedures Zephyr was following: feeding fuel, checking temperatures and monitoring engine percentages. Once the blades were whirring at full speed, Zephyr glanced at the windsock one more time. As the pilot lifted the collective lever, Dax saw the plane of the blades alter to form a shallow cone. He gave them a wave as the Long Ranger lifted effortlessly off the helipad and set course for Athens. With the exception of Sunday's short joyride, it had been nearly three weeks since Dax had flown. He was starting to itch for the exhilaration of unfettered flight.

Dax strode back up to the house. He was about to make his way back to the kitchen when Isabella intercepted him at the bottom of the staircase. "I haven't finished my breakfast yet," she said, winding her forefinger into the collar of his tee-shirt.

Upstairs, the two of them stood silently and searched each other's eyes; both of them were transfixed. As if under a hypnotist's spell, Isabella took an involuntary step toward him. The gesture broke Dax's stupor. He stepped closer into her space and wrapped her in a tight embrace.

Dax pushed his body hard against hers. He tilted his head down to find her warm lips. They kissed deeply, their tongues probing and exploring. Isabella was aware of the throb of Dax's tumescence. Her own hips gyrated softly at first, then grew more urgent. She thrust herself against his manhood. As their lust intensified, they feverishly unfastened and unbuttoned each others' clothing.

Dax reached behind her and found the clasp of her bra. Released from their lacy confinement, he stepped back and admired the wholesome swell of her breasts. Like decadent chocolate buttons, Isabella's tight nipples were perfectly framed by her dark areola. Gently cupping a breast in one hand, Dax lowered his head and softly closed his mouth over the firm curve of her flesh. She clutched his head tightly against her bosom. During their brief foreplay, the exquisite anticipation had produced a slight sheen of perspiration on their chests. Succumbing to the familiar tingle, Isabella could feel the warm seep of erotic passion. Dax's tongue flicked over the briny luster between her breasts. "Taste me everywhere," she breathed hotly in his ear.

He kneeled in front of her. While Dax's hands caressed her

firm derrière, his tongue slowly flicked down toward the tuck of her navel. Isabella arched her back. Her head began to swim as she succumbed to the cascade of sensations. He slowly brought his hands around and tugged gently on the elastic of her lacy underwear. He slowly inched them down toward her ankles.

Intoxicated by her feminine allure, Dax's lips were drawn to Isabella's womanhood. He inhaled her heady fragrance. She arched her back and pressed herself closer to him. She needed him; she ached for him. Slowly, ever so slowly, he moved down. He found the crease of her womanly folds.

Isabella jerked involuntarily as a crescendo of exquisite sensations cascaded over her body.

As Yiannos' helicopter approached the far side of Hellinikon International, its occupants saw an Aeroflot Ilyushin-Il-86 passenger plane touching down on the threshold of runway 33 Left.

Looking out from the window seat of his commercial jet, Morozov made out the tiny shape of a helicopter coming in to land on the opposite side of the field. Although he was traveling light, he'd taken the precaution of packing his weapon in his suitcase and not in his hand luggage: the 70s had been a good decade for hijackers and airports were starting to tighten their security protocols. After clearing customs and immigration, he went over to the Avis counter and hired a car. They threw-in a complimentary road map of Athens and its surrounds.

Morozov took a leisurely drive on the E94 toward Corinth. He wanted to check his surrounds before settling on a plan of action. Parking up in an alley leading off the town's main road, the Russian headed for the bustling central market. He eventually found a local storekeeper who could speak English. Morozov handed him a piece of paper with Yiannos' address scrawled on it. "I am Achilles' friend from Moscow. We met at the Olympics," said Morozov.

"Ah, yes. This is Yiannos' house. You play in the Olympics like Achilles?" asked the friendly Greek. "You look like boxer or wrestler."

"No, I am a shottist," Morozov lied smoothly.

"You win medal?" the Greek persisted.

"Fourth place," said Morozov, barely suppressing his agitation. "You can tell me which way to Achilles' house, please?"

"Yes, yes. The house, it is only a few miles up the road." The shopkeeper pointed down the main street in the general direction of Yiannos' house. "Look for the olive grove on the left-hand side. Turn right at the end of the trees. Go one mile then right again at the old well. Theirs is the big blue gate on the left-hand side. You can't miss it."

After turning at the olive grove, Morozov wound his way down the narrow road. A bright red Alfa Spider convertible swept past him heading in the opposite direction. If he hadn't been so intent on keeping an eye out for the old well, he might've recognized the passenger.

Morozov found the house. He drove a short distance further up the hill, turned the car around, found some shade, then settled back to observe. It was forty minutes before he saw any movement. Appearing at a side door, a maid began vigorously beating a small rug with a hand-held brush. *That's one.* Twenty-five minutes passed before he saw any more activity. A man appeared in the doorway of the kitchen. From his apron, Morozov guessed it was the chef. He was joined a moment later by the same maid he'd seen earlier. From their gesticulations, Morozov could tell they were conducting an animated conversation. While holding forth on some point or other, the chef smoked his cigarette. *That's two.*

Morozov was in no rush. He needed to assimilate as much of his new surrounds as possible. His patience was eventually rewarded. An hour and twenty minutes after parking, a short, rotund maid bustled out the house. She was carrying an overstuffed laundry basket. Her two colleagues were still jabbering outside, the chef already on his second cigarette. Based on the short woman's body language, Morozov could tell she was frustrated with the malingerers. She tapped her wrist several times to emphasize her point. After remonstrating with the other two, she started hanging a large number of bed sheets on the clothesline.

Morozov nodded to himself. *So there are three. The fat one has chided the other two because there is much work to do in the house—a sign of a busy household. And she hung six bed sheets out to dry in the breeze.*

Even though Morozov had no intention of going down to the house at that stage, he remained in the car to check if any of the occupants might appear. After a full fifteen minutes with no further activity, he started the car. *It is foolish to stay here any longer. I look forward to seeing you later, Dax Hunter.*

Morozov slipped down the hill and headed back to Corinth. He needed to find a motel where he could get some rest.

The afternoon shadows had grown long by the time Isabella and Dax returned to the house. Isabella had insisted on taking several Polaroid photographs of them visiting the Acropolis. "You never know," she had told Dax, "it might please Yiannos to see that we actually came up here."

Inside the house, the servants were finishing up their daily chores. Isabella also dismissed the chef for the night, telling him that she and their guest would probably take a trip to one of the town's local restaurants.

Outside on the road, Morozov had just cruised past the house. He parked a little higher up the road on this occasion, seeing that there were a couple of other cars parked there already. Further down, his lone car might've looked suspicious. Morozov waited and watched. From his vantage point he was able to see the three servants leave for the day. He wanted to wait for the sun to disappear before going to investigate.

Laughing and touching the entire day, Isabella and Dax hadn't once mentioned Yiannos' fortuitous overnight business trip.

But the anticipation was never far from their minds. When they got home, Dax told Isabella he wanted to go and swim his one mile course. "I'm going to luxuriate in a bubble bath then, my Zimbabwean stud," she purred.

As the last of the Mediterranean light slipped beneath the horizon, Morozov left his car and headed down toward Yiannos' property. He checked up-and-down the road one more time. Vaulting over the barrier, the bright blue fence around the mansion surrendered easily to the athletic Russian. Keeping to the shadows, he prowled around the perimeter of the vast property. He heard gentle music coming from one of the upstairs rooms. Up on the verandah, Morozov tested the front door. It was unlocked. He cracked it open slightly and listened. No voices. But still the music. Tiptoeing upstairs, he got to the door leading to Isabella's bedroom. It was open. Inside, he could hear a woman humming gently to the music. Peering slowly around the corner, he could see clear across the vast bedroom and into the adjoining bathroom. Above a profusion of iridescent suds, Morozov could see the back of a woman's head and her naked shoulders. A fluted glass stood next to her elbow. The contents effervesced delicately on the surface of the beige liquid.

Dax's guest room was adjacent to the main house. Although adjoining, it had its own separate entrance. After completing his swim, he'd walked up the winding path from the cove and quietly entered his own room. On an impulse, he decided to call Isabella on the house phone.

Fixed to the bathroom wall, the phone next to Isabella's elbow started ringing. Having detected nobody else in the house, and with Isabella's back to him, Morozov risked moving closer to the bathroom door. He wasn't to know that this particular ringtone signified a call from within the house. Shielded from view, he listened to Isabella's conversation.

On the off-chance that one of the servants had returned to the house and needed to call upstairs for something, Isabella chose a neutral response. "Hello," she said languorously. She wasn't expecting it to be anyone other than Dax, but discretion was preferable.

"You still in the bath?" asked Dax, letting his tone betray his intentions.

"Dax, my handsome stallion," she said huskily. The blip on Morozov's radar glowed brightly. His shoulder muscles tensed involuntarily.

"I'm going to have a quick shave and freshen up. Then I'm going to come up there and ravage you, my condesa," said Dax.

"We have the house to ourselves my semental. I'm here all night, but don't be long. I'm waiting," she said throatily.

Morozov's nerves starting singing like tension wires in a hurricane. *I will wait outside in the shadows until Hunter's car gets here. I'll let them get naked first then I'll subdue him and make him watch as I carve my name on his whore's tits. And then, Hunter, you will suffer. I will fucking make you suffer.*

Morozov could see a vehicle approaching. He slid down behind his steering wheel. As the car turned into the driveway, its headlights swept over him like a lighthouse beam. He could hear the gate motor rumbling as the car idled out on the road. He stayed low. Only once the car had disappeared into the garage did Morozov risk raising his head.

Dax was just closing the door to his guest room when he heard men's voices coming from upstairs. He stood rooted to the spot. Alarm bells jangled in his head. Then he heard Achilles' familiar laugh. *Fuck! They're back. They must've canceled the Nicosia trip.* Dax quietly let himself back into his room ... *I should call Isabella to warn her?* His heart was thumping. *That was too fucking close. You're playing with fire Hunter.*

Through his open window, Dax heard Achilles walking down the steps toward his cottage. "Hey Dax. Are you in there?" Achilles called out.

"Yeah, come in brother," Dax forced his best casual tone.

"So our client canceled on us at the last minute. Pappá had already told Zephyr he could take the day off, so we drove home. Tell me all about your day," insisted Achilles.

Upstairs in her boudoir, Isabella had been sitting in front of the mirror brushing her hair. Even over the music, she was sure she'd detected the sound of the automated garage door opening and closing. Guessing correctly, she figured that her husband's trip had been canceled and he was home early. Her second thought was relief—relief at not being caught red-handed—and her third was disappointment. Her final thought was that she hoped Dax had also heard them returning and didn't come bounding upstairs with nothing on but a hard-on.

"My darling, are you up there?" Yiannos was already halfway up the stairs when he called out.

"Yes my dear. Everything okay? You cancel your meeting?" Isabella's voice bore no sign of guilt or panic. Unfazed, she carried on brushing her hair.

On the pretext of rounding everyone up for dinner, Yiannos had sent Achilles to go and fetch Dax from his cottage. He suppressed the urge to check under his bed. He kissed his wife on the cheek. "Did you get a chance to go into Athens today?" It was a poorly-disguised question and Isabella sensed the inference. Looking into the bathroom, he noticed the single champagne glass next to the bath. On the dressing table, he noted the level of the liquid in the green bottle. *Barely a glassful missing, this is good.* Yiannos had been cuckolded once before; his ego couldn't face a repeat performance.

Still under the illusion that it was only Dax and Yiannos' wife at home, Morozov stealthily re-entered the house. On the landing outside the upstairs bedroom, he steeled himself. He heard the muted voices coming from the boudoir. *It would've been so much easier if they were both in the bath.* Drawing his weapon, Morozov made his move.

It was an inopportune time for Yiannos to turn and leave the boudoir. He was barely one pace past the door when he saw a menacing intruder surge into the room. Instinctively, he yelled out.

Moments before, Dax had feigned the need to go to the bathroom. He promised Achilles he would follow him upstairs shortly. Truth-be-told, he was still anxious of Yiannos' unannounced arrival and likely reaction to discovering his wife lounging seductively across her divan.

Achilles was already inside the house when he heard his father's scream echoing from upstairs.

Upon hearing her husband's scream, Isabella shot up from her stool and rushed across the boudoir to see what had caused the commotion. No more than a few seconds had elapsed since Yiannos had yelled out. As she burst into the room, Isabella also screamed in terror.

Downstairs, Dax heard both screams in quick succession. Hunter was schooled in warfare. He knew how to harness and direct his adrenaline. His reaction was instant. He'd already hit the door by the time Isabella's muffled scream had been cut short.

For the first time in Morozov's twenty-two years, he experienced something akin to panic. Like a spinning-top on the verge of wobbling out of control, his paradigm had betrayed him. In that utterly perplexing moment, Morozov had been confronted by a short, portly Greek, and not Dax Hunter. His focus evaporated as his spinning-top tumbled off its axis. Forfeiting control of his actions, his silenced pistol took on a life of its own. It belched twice. Two copper-coated slugs tore into Yiannos' belly.

Morozov sprinted from the bedroom, confusion wracking his brain. As he skidded out onto the landing, he noticed a dark-haired man bounding up the spiral stairs toward him. Placing one hand on the balustrade, Morozov vaulted over the edge and dropped four yards to the floor below. He landed with the agility of a gymnast.

"Hey!" Achilles shouted from the top of the stairs. Morozov didn't have time to aim properly; he fired once toward Achilles. Ducking for cover behind a decorative Corinthian piece, the round splintered the cornice above Achilles' head. He heard the intruder's footsteps receding down the hallway.

Dax burst into the house right at that moment. "Achilles," he yelled out, "what's going on?"

"Dax. Go after him. But be careful, he's got a gun," warned Achilles.

Don't worry. I heard it! By the time Dax made it to the fence, there was no evidence of anyone outside. Without a flashlight, searching further was futile. He had just returned to the house when he heard the screech of car tires a short distance up the road. It was pointless trying to read the number plate; the driver hadn't turned his lights on.

Achilles was on the phone when Dax got upstairs. He was speaking frantically in Greek. Dax looked around and took in the scene. Sitting on the floor, Isabella was cradling Yiannos' head in her lap. She was smoothing his hair and talking softly to him in Spanish. Two dark spots of blood tinged the front of her husband's white shirt.

The ambulance only had room for one patient and a single family member. Gently but firmly, the paramedic insisted that Achilles follow the ambulance in his own car. Achilles had to bite his tongue. *She's a money-grabber, not a family member.*

As they loaded Yiannos into the ambulance, Achilles came over to where his friend was standing. He clutched Dax's upper arm firmly. "Listen carefully to what I am about to tell you Dax." Achilles' face was stern. "Are you listening?" he repeated himself.

"I am." Dax gave him his full attention.

"Do you remember on Sunday before we flew out of Moscow, a crazy guy dressed in black sprinted past us heading toward the athletes' village?" Of course Dax remembered. *Everything* about the episode was remarkable.

"*Ja.* He shouted at us to get out of his way as he sprinted toward us. I remember the guy. Why do you ask?" said Dax.

"Can you remember anything more specific about him?" Achilles urged.

"Yeah. He had a scar like a spider's web across his cheek."

"On my grandmother's grave Dax, I swear the guy tonight is the same man." Achilles' face was grim.

Dax put his arm on Achilles' shoulder. "You're absolutely

certain?"

"It was him Dax. That bastard must have some kind of fanatical vendetta against my pappá, or maybe both of us." Achilles shook his head in disbelief.

Dax squeezed his shoulder reassuringly. *Man, what kind of crazy shit is this family involved in?*

In the convoluted folds of Morozov's brain, he'd always known that he was beyond reproach. Throughout his life, he'd found it easy to deflect responsibility onto someone or something; he was never to blame. Granting himself absolution was never a conscious decision—it was hard-wired into the illogical matrix of his personality.

But as he fled from Yiannos' house, Morozov experienced a worrying, alien sensation. His familiar and perpetual sense of anger was now accompanied by the unsettling notion that he'd erred. *I have fucked up. How could I have fucked that up so badly?* He slammed the steering wheel violently. He couldn't care less that he'd shot the wrong man in his moment of confusion. What worried him was that he'd shot him in the first place: unlike every other time, it hadn't been premeditated.

Morozov simply regarded himself as too good to screw-up. He was trying to work out how he got so easily misled by the information he'd gleaned from Isabella's half of the phone conversation. *What the fuck did I miss?* Morozov shifted that thought to one side for a later analysis. *I shot the fat fuck in the stomach ... he'll survive. That means three people can identify me.* Morozov cursed aloud and banged his steering wheel violently. This time it caused the car to veer dangerously toward the shoulder. *Hunter, you get to breathe another day.*

Morozov's thoughts turned to how best to get out of Greece.

In conjunction with his recollection of events at Yiannos' mansion, Dax was able to give the Greek police a description of what had transpired outside the Olympic village a few days earlier. Between them, Dax and Achilles were able to describe

Morozov well enough for a police artist to create a very good likeness. When shown the identikit, ground staff at Hellinikon International were also able to positively identify the man they'd served early the previous day.

Given the nature of the gunman's unmistakable scar, plus the credibility of the two key witnesses, the police reached the same conclusion as Achilles. The investigators were in no doubt that the black-clad man with the disfiguring scar was after one, perhaps both of the Fotakis men. Privately, the police suspected it was connected to a soured business deal.

Under the watchful eye of a round-the-clock protection team, Yiannos was ordered to stay in hospital for a full six days. He'd undergone an emergency operation after doctors discovered that one of the slugs had nicked his liver. As a further precaution, Achilles also ordered that the house be put under 24-hour surveillance.

Dax's leave was about to run out; it was time to bid the family farewell. The magic between him and Isabella had evaporated.

Due to his father's enforced lay off, Achilles was required to take the helm of the vast maritime empire. "Dax, my friend, I know you'll understand. In my father's absence, I have to run the business. You don't mind if I ask Isabella to take you to the airport?"

The two Olympians bade each other farewell in the driveway of the tycoon's mansion.

29

COLONEL ALEXEEV

Morozov avoided the embassy. The help he needed would have to come from a far more covert source. Reaching out to an Athens-based colleague in the KGB underworld, he explained that he was unable to leave the country via conventional means.

Pointed toward an Aegean dawn, Morozov's malodorous ride chugged out of Porto Rafti harbor. He was aboard a Russian trawler bound for Istanbul and the Black Sea.

Alighting in Istanbul harbor, Morozov caught a taxi to the airport and just made the last flight to Moscow. He landed a little after midnight.

Morozov found his vehicle in the airport car park. He ignored the two tickets stuffed under his wiper blades. Before reversing out of his bay, he extracted a piece of paper from his top pocket. Peering at it under the feeble glow of the car's interior light, he checked the address scrawled on the paper. He fired the engine and set course for Colonel Alexeev's private dacha in the exurbs.

There was another loose end to take care of.

Killing the lights and engine, Morozov allowed the Lada 1200 to cruise silently to a halt. The area was sparsely populated and only a few lights were burning. He sat for a moment and allowed his eyes to adjust. Reaching back behind him, he grabbed an old cassette recorder and stuffed it into his small backpack. He then flipped open the glove compartment and scratched around for his torch filter; a simple device that fitted over the head of his torch. Instead of a clear glass lens, it had a red-colored film of regenerated cellulose. Morozov got out of the car and closed the door quietly. Crouching down, he snapped the filter over the torch and aimed it at the underside of the car. He flicked the switch on. A diffuse red glow lit the gravel beneath the chassis.

Shouldering his bag, he headed for the nearest dacha. Morozov stepped off the gravel road; it was quieter walking on the grassed verge. Twenty paces ahead, a bare bulb glowed weakly over a narrow porch. Off in the distance, a domesticated red fox yipped at the half moon. Working the shadows, Morozov eased up to the side of the dilapidated house. He peered around the corner to look for the house number on the front door. The first of the three brass numerals had long since fallen off the door, but whatever the missing digits, it wasn't the colonel's address. Morozov deduced that Colonel Alexeev's dacha was the next one down.

The plots in the exurbs weren't much over an eighth of an acre in size. Morozov noted that even senior military officers weren't exempt from the Soviet's strict building regulations: only single storey dachas with mansard roofs were permitted. Morozov squatted down behind the lone vehicle parked in the front. Shielding the torch, he flicked on the light and checked the car's registration number. The plate bore six characters, one less than a civilian-registered vehicle. This was a military car. Morozov nodded approvingly. He withdrew his standard-issue Makarov PM pistol and crept toward the house.

One of the porch timbers creaked as Morozov tested his weight. He slowly eased off the pressure. Slipping down the side of the dacha, he went to try the back door instead.

He turned the handle gently. As the mechanism twisted in his hand, Morozov also applied a little pressure to the door. It was unlocked. He left it ajar and stepped away to the side. With his pistol at the ready, he held his position for several minutes.

Barely audible at first, he soon detected the familiar sound of a semi-anesthetized vodka snore. It triggered a distant memory: he'd last heard his father snore like that. Morozov felt no regret at the loss of his father; he did however believe they would've understood each other well. Only one image ever materialized when he thought of him: the one with a meat cleaver protruding from his chest. He shook his head to clear the image. Not because it disturbed him, but because it distracted him.

Morozov tested the hinges to see if they would squeak. They appeared to be oiled. He pushed the door wide and stepped inside. Abruptly, the colonel's snoring snagged on a lost breath. All went silent. Five, six, seven seconds passed. In the recesses of his autonomic folds, Alexeev's survival functions suddenly reawakened. A guttural splutter, followed by three short gasps, restored his breathing rhythm. Morozov remained immobile throughout the colonel's obstructive apnea attack.

Alexeev mumbled in his sleep and shifted his position. In the darkness, Morozov was aware there was a chance that he might bump into an unseen object. Since he couldn't afford to compromise his presence, he risked turning on his torch. Lying on the floor, barely inches in front of his left foot, an empty vodka bottle reflected in the eerie glow. The colonel's snoring rose by a few decibels. Morozov slowly raised his wrist. The arc of light cast a surreal glow over the surrounds. Although it was a two room dacha, the colonel had collapsed in a drunken stupor on the sofa in the small living area. After checking that the other two rooms were empty, the intruder gave up any further pretense of being stealthy. Morozov flipped the light switch on and clomped over to where the colonel was lying.

"Hey you! Fat fuck. Get up." Morozov slapped Alexeev's cheek.

"Wha … what the fuck is this?" he said groggily. The overweight colonel struggled to sit up.

"Wake up you fat dolt," urged Morozov. By the time the colonel's eyes had focused, it was too late to reach for his pistol: the barrel of the intruder's weapon was pointed directly at his forehead.

"Who are you? What is this about? Do you know who I am?" demanded the colonel.

He attempted to stand up but Morozov shoved him back down. "I will be asking all the questions tonight, do you understand?"

"Do you know I am a colonel in the Soviet Army?" Undignified in his pair of grubby shorts, Alexeev's professed authority was risible. Morozov's smirk further riled the officer. "You lay another finger on me and I will personally see you dangle on the gallows," he threatened.

Morozov answered him with a stinging backhand. "Shut up, you traitor," he spat. The menace in his voice silenced any further protest.

Just a few days earlier the colonel had received an anonymous phone call. Based on the caller's tip-off, he'd fled to his dacha on the outskirts of Moscow. The colonel had known that his situation was dire. He'd absconded without notifying his family or superiors. The criminals that his nameless caller had warned him about had clearly managed to track him down. *Fucking mafia.* Alexeev concluded that this midnight caller was here about his seedy business dealings with Sokolov.

Morozov's old Parus-301 cassette recorder had seen better days. He pulled the battered appliance from his bag. The colonel assumed that Morozov wanted to play him a recording of a private conversation. *Perhaps something compromising? Use it to bribe me?* He decided to adopt a more placatory approach. "Comrade, whatever it is you want me to listen to, I am sure between me and your organization we can come to some equitable arrangement," the colonel fawned.

"*Cyka blyat!* I am not Moscow mafia," growled Morozov. For the second time he used the lesser-known jargon to describe the Moscow mafia: terminology used mainly in law enforcement circles.

The colonel's head shot up. "Wait! It's you! You used that

term before. You were the one who called me last Sunday. Yes! I recognize your voice. You were the one who suggested I hide for a while … who are you? Fuck man, who *are* you?" A confused look creased the pudgy man's face.

Morozov produced his badge. "This is an official KGB investigation. It will be in your best interests to cooperate fully." With his pistol still pointed at the colonel, Morozov pulled a chair out from beneath the kitchen table. He placed it in front of the colonel and sat down. "Now slowly, very slowly, reach under your cushion and pass me your weapon. No funny business." Morozov had guessed correctly. The colonel's weapon was indeed stashed under his cushion. The KGB man took the weapon and placed it on the table. "I am going to ask you questions. Don't lie to me because I will shoot you in the balls." He leant closer and thrust the barrel between the colonel's legs. Morozov turned the recorder on. "Give me your full name and rank, which army and regiment you serve in," instructed Morozov.

Over the following thirty minutes, with the muzzle of a Makarov thrust against his testicles, the colonel described the illicit operation in great detail. Along with the names of Russian accomplices and middle-men, Morozov also extracted the identities of their foreign collaborators.

Well-schooled in such matters, Morozov had been careful to conduct the interview in a professional style. He addressed the colonel in a manner deserving of his rank. Apart from the influence exerted by the hovering Makarov, at no stage did he swear, humiliate or verbally threaten the colonel. Morozov spoke politely, but with authority. To anyone listening it would've sounded like a well-conducted, routine interrogation.

Morozov bided his time. He was waiting for the precise moment when it became apparent that the flow of information was about to peter-out; that moment when he sensed that Alexeev had revealed all he knew. When it came, he caught the colonel completely unawares. "Colonel, why haven't you mentioned your Athens partner, Yiannos Fotakis?" For the first time in the interview, the colonel looked genuinely confused.

Before Alexeev could react in any way to Morozov's odd question, the KGB man stood up abruptly. His chair scraped across the floor. "Colonel, no!" he shouted. "Sit down! Colonel … put down your weapon." Alexeev looked utterly bewildered. Before the colonel could utter a word, Morozov kicked over a lamp. Pandemonium had broken loose; except the colonel was a puzzled spectator, not a participant. With his head turning like a ventriloquist's doll, he sat dumfounded while the demented KGB agent raged around him. Morozov let out a rasping snarl, followed by a credible imitation of the colonel's voice. "Fucking KGB pig … I kill you."

Morozov raised his pistol and double-tapped the colonel; two rounds ripped into his heart. He purposefully bumped the table on which the recorder was standing. Reaching for the colonel's weapon, Morozov retreated silently to the main bedroom. From across the living room he shouted at the dead man. "Colonel, put down your weapon or I'll fucking shoot." Armed with Alexeev's weapon, Morozov turned and fired one shot into the wall behind him. He waited two seconds. "Put down your weapon," he ordered again. Stepping back out of the bedroom, Morozov turned and faced the door he'd just exited. He double-tapped two rounds into the woodwork around the door. *Perfect.* Morozov waited almost ten seconds. For the benefit of his future audience, his grand finale had to be convincing. The tape continued rolling. "Colonel … I'm coming out. I have you in my sights. Do not try to resist any more." The microphone picked up faint footsteps. Then, as the gravity of the situation hit the KGB agent, he could be heard whispering a single, drawn-out expletive. "Fuck!" It was just loud enough to be detected on the recording.

Morozov silently applauded his performance. He waited a full thirty seconds before switching off the cassette recorder. Several neighborhood dogs had started to yap. Morozov heard muffled voices from across the street. He had to work quickly.

Pulling an oily rag from his backpack, Morozov wiped his own prints off the colonel's weapon. He was careful not to bump the trigger; the weapon was still live. He then reached for the dead man's right hand and pressed his fingertips all over the same weapon. The colonel's body was slumped back on the sofa, his weapon hanging loosely in his hand. Two black holes, no more than an inch apart, had punctured his sternum. Casting one last glance around the room, Morozov went outside to speak to the neighbor. "I am from KGB," he showed his badge. "Everything here is under control. Do you have a phone in your dacha?"

Morozov held the immaculate belief that he only ever spoke the truth. Howsoever caused, the wiring within his brain could only be described as chaotic. He felt an unconscionable indifference to notions such as empathy, morality and scruples. In his world, grandiose fantasies were nothing more than achievable objectives. Identifying such pathologies is the domain of trained clinicians; not KGB supervisors.

Morozov's report was meticulous. After digesting all its contents, as well as listening to the cassette recording, the head of the Moscow branch of the Third Chief Directorate sat back in his chair. He was mightily impressed with the caliber of his young agent's work. He nodded to himself. *Despite losing a close colleague, this young man went on and single-handedly solved this filthy racket involving Russian kids.*

Over the past few days, Morozov's boss had been placed under mounting pressure. Besides his superiors in Moscow, senior KGB officers in Athens were also insisting on answers. It hadn't taken much scratching to determine the motive for his clandestine visit to Greece. Convinced Morozov had gone rogue, they were demanding answers: why hadn't they been informed that he'd been granted authority to come onto their turf? Why had he shot a highly influential member of the Greek business community?

Trusting his agent implicitly, the KGB boss deflected their persistent appeals. He had asked them for an extra day to find out, first-hand, what had transpired.

Morozov's report, supported by the cassette recording, was

compelling. It brought all the pieces together. More than just relief, the boss felt vindicated. Morozov was squeaky clean.

Of course, the boy from Sverdlovsk felt no remorse for implicating a completely innocent Greek man in a contemptible act of which he knew nothing. Such were the benefits of Morozov's condition.

Morozov's reputation on the Red Square had been secured: the Bucharest affair; the downing of the Viscount; and now the cracking open of an international child-trafficking ring. A few Kremlin die-hards believed he bore his ugly scar as a symbol of his valorous feats. Some staffers even suggested he was deserving of the Hero's Gold Star.

With his reputation sealed, Morozov had earned the right to choose his career path. While he pretended to listen patiently to their petitions, he chose to ignore the advice of his superiors. Morozov was determined to return to Africa.

Morozov sat opposite the head of KGB Third Chief Directorate, Moscow Division. After lighting a bootleg cigarette, his boss waved the match to extinguish the flame. He inhaled deeply, his eyes squinting through the blue haze. He looked at Morozov ruefully. "Comrade, it saddens me that you want to leave my division and return to Africa. You have acquitted yourself in an exemplary fashion and your record bears testament to your fine skills. I cannot convince you to reconsider?" The supervisor was genuinely hopeful that his appeal might sway his subordinate.

"Thank you comrade, but my decision is final. I must thank you for facilitating my wish to transfer back to Alfa Directorate A."

The head of Third Chief Directorate had encountered no resistance when he petitioned on behalf of Morozov. The senior staff officer at the Alfa unit was indeed honored when he discovered that Morozov wanted to rejoin his former division. "Good luck back in Africa, Comrade Morozov. I believe there are many exciting opportunities there at the moment," concluded the agent's superior.

Morozov was attired in his full KGB dress uniform. The royal blue piping distinguished him from other units of the Soviet military. Placing his cap on his head, he stood to attention and saluted. His boss stood and returned the salute. *In the name of Trotsky, why didn't he ever get his fucking scar fixed?*

30

TAGMA GROUP

Sneddon held the edges of the polished table like a pinball machine. He leaned back in his swivel chair and exhaled loudly. Three other people sat around him. On the far side of the conference room, the fifth person present stood uncomfortably in front of the wall-mounted screen. The room was deep in the bowels of CIA's headquarters in Langley.

"Chuck, I want to thank you for a most informative presentation. Would you give us the room please?" Chuck was the junior in the room and had felt mildly overwhelmed by the august company in which he found himself. Relieved to be dismissed, he excused himself and closed the door quietly behind him.

Amongst his CIA peers, Sneddon was regarded as probably one of the best-informed agents when it came to the Latin American region. The three remaining people had all been hand-picked by Sneddon. Not only did they possess in-depth knowledge of Central American affairs, but were all skillful in the arcane craft of geopolitical manipulations.

They called themselves the Tagma Group, named for the ancient Byzantine Empire's elite soldiers.

Their ghostly existence was known only to a select group of people in the CIA. Among its hand-picked members there was an earnest belief that their decisions allowed Americans to sleep safely at night.

"Here are a few more facts I'd like to add to Chuck's

summation of the situation as it currently stands in the region." Sneddon cleared his throat and continued. "You may well have heard of the Japanese businessman Shigeo Nagano. His name's been cropping up quite a bit recently. He may well be an octogenarian, but this guy is inspiring the hell out of Omar Torrijos right now. He's proposing a new canal across the Panamanian isthmus. And it's not only Torrijos who's excited by this proposal. By all accounts, even his top engineers are sold on Nagano's concept of a second canal across the country."

"For Chrissake, why on earth would Panama want to build a second canal? They've got a perfectly good one already," said Sergio Teves, a senior geopolitical analyst.

"First up, Sergio, the Americans have been evaluating alternative canal options across Panama for decades. Did you know that our own Atomic Energy Commission was tasked with investigating the use of PNEs—peaceful nuclear explosions—to blast a canal across the isthmus? It was known as *Operation Plowshare*."

"Heck, I wasn't aware of that," said Sergio sheepishly.

"But back to your original question," said Sneddon. "There are a couple of reasons. Let's look at history first. Torrijos and President Carter signed the canal treaties in 1977. Torrijos was hailed in some quarters as a champion for securing the ultimate sovereignty of the canal, plus the adjacent unincorporated territory known as the Panama Canal Zone. But his detractors—and he has many—accuse him of being a sellout. They still blame him for conceding to America's demand that gives us the right to defend the canal in perpetuity.

"Let me give you an example of just how much latitude the USA has got here. If a container so much as falls overboard and threatens to block sea traffic, we forever hold the right to swoop in and fix it. Even, and especially, *after* this treaty relinquishes full control of the canal to the Panamanians at the end of this century." Sneddon paused to top up his glass. "Torrijos' political foes argue that that kind of meddling is tantamount to interference in their right to govern their asset as they see fit. Expressed in another way, it is seen as a violation of their right to self determination."

"So what's that got to do with Shigeo Nagano?" asked Lynn. She was a senior psychologist who had previously worked with Sneddon during Noriega's recruitment into the CIA.

"Torrijos himself is embarrassed by this clause. It hangs like an albatross around his neck. Nagano's ambitious design has the potential to free Torrijos from his all-consuming guilt. The Japanese industrialist proposes a so-called sea-level canal. That means there are no bothersome and time-consuming locks to negotiate."

"Just like the Suez Canal?" asked Lynn.

"Exactly. Which means it'll be cheaper to build and operate. Not only would the project create thousands of jobs, but it would forever erase the embarrassment of Torrijos' negotiating blunder. In one fell swoop he wins back the hearts of his people *and* assuages his own guilt."

"And what's so bad about that?" Like Sneddon, Denton Styles liked to be referred to only by his surname. He'd been quiet up to that point of the discussion.

"The new canal has the potential to render the old Panama Canal almost obsolete," said Sneddon. "It'll be able to route supertankers between the Pacific and the Atlantic in record time. The cost of passage would be enormously reduced and it would dilute our influence—or, more importantly—our right to exert our influence in the region. Right now, we pretty much control and sway affairs as we see fit. But here's the worst part. Not only does a new canal have the potential to emasculate us, but the project will be designed and built entirely by a consortium of overseas companies. Because of his perceived failure at the negotiating table, Torrijos is vehemently anti-American right now. You can bet your last dollar he'll make sure that no engineering work comes our way. That's a multi-billion dollar project we're talking about."

"But surely the economic benefit of having a more efficient canal would translate to cheaper landed goods in our own market?" persisted Styles.

"Yes it would," agreed Sneddon, "but in this case, let me make myself absolutely clear. Given the current situation, the United States' regional strategic interest trumps economic benefits, hand-over-fist." He paused to let the statement sink in. "But there's still more I want to share. This man Torrijos is clearly a bit of an egotist. He got a lot of attention—I'm talking worldwide attention—during his Panama Canal negotiations. Lynn will tell you that it's hard for any man to just walk away from the limelight—it becomes intoxicating. And the lust for recognition becomes even more alluring when they harbor such an inflated opinion of themselves. Just last week he was back in the spotlight, this time brokering a deal with the Vatican, Argentina and Spain. Under the terms of the agreement he's just brokered, the Argentines have agreed to release former President Isabel Martinez de Perón from house-arrest so she can take up exile in Spain. And let's not forget the fucking US embassy fiasco in Tehran two years ago."

Lynn pulled a face. *That's the first time I've ever heard him curse.*

"God rest his soul but the Shah of Iran caused us a great deal of pain and embarrassment. Against President's Carter's better judgment, we gave sanctuary to the Shah here in the US of A so he could seek medical attention. The revolutionaries in Iran were so incensed by our support of their reviled 'King of Kings,' 'Light of the Aryans,' and 'Head of the Warriors' that they eventually stormed our embassy and took our citizens hostage."

"Hell, the man had as many vainglorious titles as Idi Amin," quipped Sergio.

Sneddon ignored the interruption and continued his monologue. "And it was just last year that our generous friend Torrijos allowed the same exiled Shah to live on the island of Contadora. Indignant over Torrijos' high-handed decision to allow the Shah into their country, demonstrators then rioted in the streets of Panama City. As you may recall, Torrijos ordered his National Guard to quell the uprising. After using rubber hoses and clubs on his own citizens, anti-Torrijos sentiment swelled amongst the rank and file."

"Yeah, I remember that," said Sergio. "The guy's like an unguided missile."

Sneddon was starting to get irritated with Sergio's inane interruptions. "In my opinion, he's trying too hard to be the world's new Mister-Go-To-Guy. And the trouble is he's a novice trying to play chess with the masters. I don't know if it's altruism that motivates him, but our Mr. Torrijos definitely doesn't possess an intellectual frame of mind," said Sneddon. "Although these examples might appear as low-grade affairs, his meddlesome tactics have the ability to backfire badly. We all know how delicately poised international politics can be. A warm handshake over here has the potential to spark an incident over there." In quick succession, Sneddon pointed imprecisely at opposite ends of a world map hanging on the side wall.

"I myself am still not convinced about which ideology General Torrijos represents. He seems to vacillate between the two ends of the political spectrum. America should be particularly alarmed by his fresh visits to Cuba. Not only is he flirting with Fidel Castro, but he has also made recent overtures to Libya's leader, Colonel Muammar el-Qaddafi. After Leonid Brezhnev and Kim Il-sung, I am hard-pressed to think of any world leaders more reviled than those two." Sneddon paused for a full seven seconds and stared intently into the eyes of each of his three colleagues. "I am therefore going to take the unprecedented step of recommending that Omar Torrijos be liquidated forthwith."

"And how do you propose we orchestrate the succession?" asked Sergio.

"That's a reasonable question," said Sneddon, relieved that Sergio was at last making a meaningful contribution to the discussion. "Noriega is happy for us to facilitate the termination, but suggests that a façade of democracy—perhaps as long as two years—might help allay any suspicions that Torrijos' death was manufactured. Noriega certainly doesn't want to ride in on his chariot with that specter hanging over his head. Right now he practically runs the country's armed forces. He's perfectly positioned to keep an eye on the loyalty and discipline of his men. We therefore have no worries about a renegade or upstart trying to usurp his current power base. In terms of his own political aspirations, Noriega is prepared to bide his time and use the event as an expedient ladder to his own ascension." The others nodded their understanding.

"Are there any dissenting voices then?" enquired Sneddon. The room remained silent. Then I will see to it that the wishes of the Tagma Group are duly granted. With that, Sneddon and the others rose from the table.

Four days later, on August 2, 1981, a headline on the obituaries page of The New York Times caught Sneddon's eye:

PANAMA LEADER KILLED IN
CRASH IN BAD WEATHER

31

SEYCHELLES

The pressure during both her courses had been unrelenting, but by mid-August of 1981 Apple had not only completed them, but she'd graduated in the top five of her intake. She was poised on the first rung of the department known as Clandestine Services. After all the preparation and training, she was now ready to embark on a career with the CIA.

Tidying her desk, Apple was humming a Francis Cabrel tune when Sneddon materialized at her side. He startled her. "I have an assignment for you," he said without greeting or preamble. "I need you to get up to speed on the political situation in the Seychelles, how the factions are stacked up, and how it affects our overseas interests." Apple could barely contain her excitement. "Something's brewing down there and it looks like we might have to exercise some leverage to protect our interests in the Indian Ocean region." Sneddon dropped a thin folder on her desk. "Here's the brief but you'll need to pull some more background information out of that confounded computer downstairs. I've highlighted the areas you are to pay particular attention to."

Sneddon started to walk off but paused briefly. "Seychelles will be a good assignment for you to cut your teeth on." With that, he turned and strode away.

Apple couldn't figure out why so many organizations assigned their computer departments to the basement. *C'mon people, this is the future. They don't belong in the basement.*

Downstairs, in the bowels of the building, Apple approached the geeky new guy who'd just joined from MIT. "Hey Art, how you doin?" she inquired genuinely.

"Hey Miss, I mean hey Miss Apple, I mean Apple," he stammered awkwardly. *Oh my God. It's Apple. She has to be the coolest lady in the galaxy.* Apple knew the pimply kid had a crush, and winced every time she talked to him: not because she felt awkward with his harmless infatuation, but because she sincerely wanted him to develop a bit more confidence.

"Art, I need to pull some information out of Big Blue ... you able to help me?" If anyone could massage the IBM's inner mind, it was Art. After all, he was recruited into the CIA after they learnt of his prodigious talent for hacking corporate computers.

While she knew her request would fall into the *Medium Priority* queue—and hence only be processed in a day or two—she was counting on Art's hormonal fascination to impress her with a quicker turn-around.

He personally delivered a sheaf of papers an hour-and-a-half later.

With a glass of iced water at her elbow, Apple sat down to study the printout in minute detail.

STATUS: Top Secret

DESK OF EMANATION: Africa, Indian Ocean & Rim

ORIGINATION DATE: August 5, 1981

CONDITION REPORT: Vulnerability of US assets in Indian Ocean vis-à-vis USSR interests & actions

PREAMBLE

DIEGO GARCIA

The largest of 60 small islands in the Chagos Archipelago, Diego Garcia is an atoll located just south of the equator in the central Indian Ocean. It lies at the southernmost tip of a vast submarine mountain range known as the Chagos-Laccadive Ridge. The atoll is located at 7°18' 48" South & 72°24'40" East.

After the Napoleonic Wars, the former French settlement was transferred to British rule. Prior to 1965 it was administered as one of the 'Dependencies' of the British Colony of Mauritius. Between 1968 and 1973 the United Kingdom intimidated the locals and forcibly removed them from the islands. Those who left were denied the chance of returning. Many were deported to the Seychelles and Mauritius.

Following the forced removals, the United States built a large naval and military base on Diego Garcia. It has been in continuous operation ever since. The population is composed of military personnel and supporting contractors.

On 1 October 1977 US Navy command established Naval Support Facility—Diego Garcia. Although the Naval Communications Station (NAVCOMMSTA) was the primary tenant, others were commissioned as new facilities were completed, namely the expanded anchorage and mooring area, and later the extended airfield.

The Navy established a Near-Term Prepositioned Force of 16 ships in August 1980 and further force extensions will occur as more deep-water anchorages are developed. The naval air facility will be commissioned in the latter part of 1981. Further development and construction will occur during 1982, the majority of which will be undertaken by a consortium of civilian contractors, two of which have already been pre-vetted: Raymond International, and Brown & Root & Molem.

No women have lived on the island since 1971.

Apple paused to let that fact sink in. *Stuffy old naval commanders; watch us make our mark this decade!* She carried on reading.

SEYCHELLES

> *The Republic of Seychelles is an independent country located on an archipelago comprising 115 islands. They are located in the Indian Ocean 932 miles east of mainland East Africa. They lie 4°37' South & 55°27' East. The capital is Victoria. With only 65,200 inhabitants, it has the smallest population of any sovereign African country.*

> *The US Naval Base on Diego Garcia is approx. 1130 miles east-southeast of the Seychelles.*

Reaching for her water, Apple continued scrutinizing the facts and figures contained in the brief. Jumping off the page of the document, a familiar word immediately caught her eye.

> *Population Breakdown:*

> *92.7% Creoles*

Apple put her glass down. She reached up and back, interlaced her fingers and then stretched her lissome body. *Wow! My people make up 92.7% of all the islands' ethnic groups.*

She continued speed-reading through the section on the islands' socio-economic affairs, then moved quickly on to the island's political history.

> *Portuguese Admiral Vasco da Gama passed through the archipelago in 1502 and named them the Amirantes after himself (Islands of the Admiral). His was the earliest recorded sighting by Europeans.*

Working at some autonomic level, Apple's mind was carefully filing all the facts into easily-retrievable compartments. She continued to read about the islands' early history: how it eventually came to be administered by the French, only to be sequestered by the British thirty eight years later in 1794.

In the years following WWII, Seychelles' nationalist agitators pressed the United Kingdom to consider granting independence. In a move aimed at placating the campaigners, the country was granted the right to hold elections for its first legislative council in 1948.

In 1964, the islands were allowed to form their first political parties. France-Albert René led the Socialist Seychelles People's United Party (SSPUP) while James Mancham led the Seychelles Democratic Party. In 1966, and again in 1970, Mancham's party won both elections.

On 1st October 1975, Britain granted the Seychelles the right to self-govern and on 29th June 1976, Britain granted full independence to the Seychelles.

After celebrating their Independence Day on 31st July 1976, the country was governed by a coalition comprising James Mancham as President, and France-Albert René as Prime Minister.

On 5th June 1977, while visiting London on official business, Mancham was ousted by a coup d'état. The sixty men who conducted the coup had purportedly received communist-style training in Tanzania beforehand. While France-Albert René vehemently denied any knowledge of the coup, he was quick to allow himself to be sworn in as president of a newly-formed government.

René quickly established a Socialist one-party state, censored the rival newspaper, and abolished religious, fee-paying schools. Popular resentment rose as his controversial policies included the creation of a large security apparatus, as well as the creation of an army.

Thousands of Seychellois went into exile, while many more attempted to form a credible opposition capable of ousting the dictator. In April 1978, some of Mancham's followers attempted to overthrow the government while René was on a state visit to North Korea and the PRC. René's army quickly quelled the uprising.

In 1979, René enacted a new constitution and turned the Seychelles into a one party state.

Following René's acceptance of the role as new president in 1977, many affluent Seychellois fled to South Africa (SA) as exiles. Corroborated intel reveals that since 1980 to the present time, James Mancham's South African-based supporters have been petitioning a number of high-level SA government officials—purportedly with Mancham's blessings.

This group (known as Mouvement pour la Résistance) has proposed their own counter-coup to oust René. Latest intelligence available reveals that they are currently seeking South Africa's cooperation and assistance in organizing the coup. In their talks with the SA government, the group has stated categorically that their sole objective is the reinstatement of democracy on the islands. Furthermore, the group has emphasized that they are both willing and capable of financing the operation themselves.

The CIA's own Core Collectors have reported from SA that some individuals within the Resistance movement have also reached out to Colonel 'Mad' Mike Hoare (†) to test his willingness to lead a mercenary-style coup to the Seychelles.

Apple stopped reading and rocked back in her chair. *'Mad'*
Mike Hoare. What a nickname. She flipped to the annexure
section at the back of the document to read up on the
swashbuckling colonel.

> *(f) Thomas Michael Hoare was born in British India on 17*
> *March 1919, but received his education in England. At the*
> *outbreak of WWII he joined the London Irish Rifles and*
> *served in India and Burma as an officer. He eventually reached*
> *the rank of major. After the war he completed his training as*
> *a chartered accountant and qualified in 1948. He later*
> *immigrated to Durban, South Africa where he ran safaris, but*
> *his reputation as a soldier-for-hire led to several opportunities in*
> *various African countries.*

The report went on to detail Mike Hoare's exploits as a
mercenary during the Congo Crisis in the Republic of the
Congo between 1960 and 1965. With opposing factions in the
crisis being supported by the Soviet Union and USA
respectively, the report explained how the escalating struggle
became another proxy conflict in the Cold War.

> *It was during the Congo Crisis in the 1960s that Hoare*
> *earned the epithet 'Mad' Mike. Whenever referring to Colonel*
> *Hoare in their radio broadcasts, the East German propaganda*
> *station would precede their commentary with 'The mad*
> *bloodhound, Mike Hoare.'*

The report detailed his various escapades in Katanga in 1961,
as well as his role in the Simba Rebellion in 1964.

Reading further, Apple learnt that in 1977 'Mad' Mike was
brought in as technical advisor for the English-directed film
titled *The Wild Geese*; a fictional story about a group of
mercenaries who are hired to rescue a deposed African
president.

The principal character, Colonel Alan Faulkner, was
patterned on Hoare himself and the role was played by

multiple Academy Awards nominee Richard Burton. Starring alongside him in the film was legendary English actor Roger Moore, as well as the talented Irish actor, Richard Harris. Most of the other actors who were cast in the movie's mercenary roles had served time in various elite military regiments. Several had actually served under Hoare in the Congo.

Apple smiled to herself. *You can't make this stuff up.* She flipped back to the body of the report.

CURRENT STATUS

'Whoever attains maritime supremacy in the Indian Ocean would be a prominent player on the international scene.' Rear Admiral Alfred Thayer Mahan (1840-1914). US Navy Geo-strategist

The islands comprising the Diego Garcia archipelago are of enormous strategic importance to the United States of America. With continental USA possessing both western and eastern seaboards, the country's ability to project and extend its influence into both the Pacific and Atlantic Oceans is assured. The Pacific region is further bolstered by major bases in Hawaii, Okinawa, Japan and Subic Bay, Philippines.

The USA's strategic ability to maintain and/or project its presence in the Indian Ocean region is limited by the fact that we only have one (fixed) base in the region. While the Indian Ocean naval base on Diego Garcia comprises both fixed and mobile assets, its current force-projection capabilities would have to be augmented by one or more of the Navy's nomadic battle fleets in the event of a major conflict. Despite their tactical endurance, such fleets require replenishment. The USA is reliant on its regional allies to provide the necessary anchorage to facilitate the replenishment of the carriers, frigates, submarines and support vessels that make up a battle fleet.

The short to medium-term cooperation of our existing coastal allies (located around the rim of the Indian Ocean) is politically assured. But it would be prudent to remember that such assurances extend only to free and unhindered access to their deep-water ports, not their direct military involvement.

Elsewhere around the rim, many countries have forged unfavorable ideological alliances with the USSR. This, combined with general political instability along Africa's eastern seaboard, adds to the tilting imbalance.

If a situation requiring force projection were to arise, the USA could petition the cooperation of Australia & South Africa. While Singapore claims a policy of strategic non-alignment, their recent economic emergence and national prosperity can be traced to the charitableness of a succession of US administrations. They can be prevailed upon to open their port.

India's strategic non-alignment is clearer: there is little or no likelihood of any support coming from that quarter.

In the context of the Indian Ocean theatre, the USA's capacity to project its global responsibility is largely dependent on two key factors:

- *It is absolutely imperative that we maintain the operational functionality of our military base on Diego Garcia. That ability must not be nullified or compromised in any way, whether by political or military means*
- *Our ability to counterpoise the threat currently posed by the USSR's military base on the Socotra Archipelago (strategically situated in the Gulf of Aden) must not be undermined.*

Apple found the enormity of the situation a little unsettling. Put in the context of the ongoing Cold War, the implications were far-reaching. America simply could not afford to allow any regional upheavals to unsettle the delicately-poised balance in the Indian Ocean region. Apple was engrossed; she carried on reading.

> *With the implementation of a one-party system in the Seychelles, along with the stated socialistic principles promulgated by its president, the islands' political ideologies make them a perfect target for further exploitation by the USSR.*

> *Since its establishment, Diego Garcia has been revictualed from the Seychelles. Any further hardening of René's socialistic views may herald the restriction or closure of Diego Garcia's vital supply links. The USA should also factor in the possibility of the Seychelles acceding to a USSR request for the establishment of a substantial military base on the islands.*

Apple exhaled softly. *That'd be a double whammy: the disruption to Diego Garcia's vital supply-lines, as well as the insertion of another USSR base in the Indian Ocean. And so close to Diego Garcia too.*

RECOMMENDATION

> *Engineering a favorable military coup d'état in the Seychelles appears to be the most effective means of securing American interests in the Indian Ocean. An arm's-length deal with South Africa may yield the most beneficial outcome.*

> *With his 'off-reservation' reputation, Colonel 'Mad' Mike Hoare instantly selects himself for the role as leader and coup coordinator. Any political splash-back that might occur could easily be ascribed to his colorful and quixotic reputation. The South African-based Seychellois exiles (Mouvement pour la Résistance), have already pledged their willingness to finance the operation. They have petitioned the South African government and have secured their tacit agreement.*

> *The selection of Southern African mercenaries is crucial to the*

exercise—there must be no ties, either personnel or matériel—to the Agency or to this country.

In the context of strategic interests and global balance, this report has described why the USA has compelling reasons to secure its interests in the mid Indian Ocean region. An overt intervention by the USA, at this point, is not a favorable option. The most prudent approach would be to cooperate fully with the South African government and assist them in ousting the René regime. Deposing that regime will be mutually beneficial. Based on verifiable information acquired by our Core Collectors, South Africa has already conducted a feasibility study into a possible military-styled intervention in the Seychelles. Assisting them would ensure that we secure the right to promote our own regional agenda.

South Africa's motivation for supporting a military intervention in the Seychelles is summarized as follows:

- *Strongly opposed to South Africa's apartheid policies, René has already withdrawn Seychelles' landing rights for South African Airways' long haul flights to the Far East. A more favorably-disposed government would quickly reinstate such rights.*
- *René has also reduced his country's economic ties and trade volume with South Africa.*
- *At worst, René's socialist ideologies render him vulnerable to sinister exploitation by the USSR. At best, he becomes their puppet and agrees to allow his island nation to become a spring-board for trained operatives to further destabilize South Africa's government.*
- *Tanzania is one of the OAU's (Organization of African Unity) most outspoken critics of the South African regime. Of all the member nations, they currently provide the most meaningful support to South Africa's agents of destabilization—the ANC*

guerrillas. *If South Africa plays a favorable role in the reinstatement of Mancham's party, they will have closer physical access to Tanzania and therefore the ability to strike at and neutralize those bases currently training the ANC guerrillas.*

- *The Cape sea route remains one of South Africa's most valued strategic assets. With the backing of a well-disposed ally in Seychelles, South Africa could extend their control of that critical sea route by basing some of their naval assets in the Seychelles.*

CONCLUSION

In light of recent developments, this desk requests that Agency considers vetting and sanctioning a plausibly deniable intervention to mitigate any further deterioration of the situation in the Seychelles.

Apple's mind was whirring. This was heady stuff. *This is what I signed up for Mr. Sneddon ... just point me in the right direction.*

32

ONDJIVA

1960 was known as 'Africa Year.' Across the continent, seventeen countries had recently achieved independence. It appeared as if the zeitgeist of that period had eventually caught up with the politicians. Perhaps in an effort to assuage their collective guilt, a host of European nations started surrendering their former African colonies. As the wave of liberation swept down the continent, hopes were high that the few remaining colonies would also be granted their independence.

But as international pressure mounted, willful politicians in Pretoria, Salisbury and Lisbon held an opposing view of Southern Africa's future. They argued that if the economies of South West Africa, South Africa, Rhodesia, Angola and Mozambique were to be nationalized—or worse still, plundered for personal gain—it would invite untold suffering on tens of millions across the entire region.

How right they were eventually proven to be.

As nationalistic fervor grew—and these countries' leaders became more intractable—so the liberation organizations were forced to rethink their strategies. In quick succession, each of Southern Africa's liberation movements reached the same conclusion: in order to hasten their independence they had no choice but to instigate an armed struggle against their oppressors.

Armed members of Angola's liberation movement attempted to spring their fellow dissidents from the Luanda prison in February of 1961. The skirmish heralded the beginning of the armed struggle for independence across Southern Africa.

Under the pretext of offering support for a just cause, the USSR identified Africa's wider liberation struggles as an ideal way to promote their own agenda on the continent. While the Soviets claimed the moral high ground for supporting a noble and just cause, their real motive was to further their anti-imperialist struggle against their nemesis, the United States of America. By the early 1960s, the People's Movement for Liberation of Angola started receiving much more than just moral support from the Russians. It was soon apparent that the communists had a clearly-defined strategy regarding their future role in Africa.

Over the following two decades, the Soviets succeeded in wheedling their way into the fabric of Angola's existence. Members of the Soviet armed forces were as likely to get a transfer to Luanda as they were to Labinsk.

It was against this backdrop that Morozov found himself on a plane bound for the capital, Luanda, in late 1980.

Although Morozov's glowing reputation in Moscow had opened doors—after all, he'd managed to engineer a transfer back to Africa—he hadn't been able to convince his superiors to send him to Zimbabwe. This was a source of great frustration for Morozov. Zimbabwe had gained independence earlier that year and a slew of Eastern Bloc countries were falling over themselves in their rush to romance Mugabe's new socialist government. Even putting his personal vendetta to one side, Morozov was convinced that someone with his skills could be put to good use in Africa's newest independent nation. But his superiors had been adamant that he was needed in Angola. Morozov reconciled himself with the fact that he was at least being posted to a Southern African destination. At the closest point, the Angolan border was only a hundred and twenty miles from Zimbabwe.

Within days of arriving in Angola, Morozov was sent to Ondjiva, a small town near the country's southern border with South West Africa. His record bore testament to his success as an instructor while based in Zambia a few years before. On reputation alone, he was handed the task of training members of PLAN—the People's Liberation Army of Namibia.

PLAN represented the armed wing of SWAPO: the South West African People's Organization. As a political party, their sole objective was to hasten their country's independence from South Africa.

Angola—itself a former colony—sympathized with SWAPO's political objectives and readily offered them safe haven within her own borders. Throughout the course of 1981, SWAPO had intensified their war effort against South Africa.

In late August 1981, under the overall command of Brigadier Rudolf Badenhorst, combined units of the South African defense force launched a series of attacks on key positions in southern Angola. The South African raid—aimed at SWAPO's military wing—was code-named *Operation Protea*.

On August 26, the day before the planned attack on Ondjiva, a 'Skyshout' aircraft of the South African Air Force dropped thousands of pamphlets on the town. The message, aimed at civilians as well as Angolan soldiers, warned that an attack was imminent and that they should evacuate the town. The pamphlet also stated that South Africa's premeditated attack was directed solely at PLAN soldiers. The South African combat pilots who'd been tasked with carrying out the following day's raid were unimpressed by the planners' insistence on broadcasting their intentions.

Soon after the pamphlets had fluttered to earth, one of Morozov's recruits brought him a tattered copy of the leaflet. After reading the message, the Russian hawked-up a wad of phlegm and dropped it in the dust by his feet. "Fucking South African pigs," he said, toeing his sputum into the dirt.

Although the inhabitants of Ondjiva had been forewarned—and the military base placed under a heightened state of alert—the brutality of the South African attack still appeared to catch most of the soldiers by surprise. But not Vladimir Morozov. Having anticipated a dawn raid, he rose early and headed across the airfield to the anti-aircraft emplacements located north of the Ondjiva runway.

On cue, two SAAF Mirage IIIs streaked in from the east at precisely 7 AM. As they unleashed a salvo of 68mm rockets from beneath their delta wings, Morozov raised a Strela missile launcher to his shoulder. *Fuck Stix and his two Viscounts, I'm going to claim a fighter jet today.*

In the corner of Morozov's peripheral vision, a small light alongside the iron sights began to blink. A moment later a buzzer began to protest. *Time to fire the weapon.* With the warhead's internal gyros stabilized, he squeezed the trigger. Morozov watched transfixed. From his perspective it looked as if the missile was losing momentum. But as the booster motor ignited, the rocket accelerated viciously toward the receding target.

The missile warning device shrieked in the pilot's headset. Straining against the 'G' forces of his exit maneuver, he twisted his neck left and right. Streaking up from the ground, a growing red dot loomed large on his tail. Although he wasn't yet clear of the danger zone, the Mirage pilot had no choice but to cut his afterburner to reduce his heat signature. He banked hard but the tenacious missile wasn't about to relinquish its quarry. Two seconds later, Captain Rynier Keet's Mirage was struck in the tailpipe and lower rudder.

Keet felt the airframe shudder. He looked down. Almost every light in his alarm panel was blinking in protest. As the aircraft's hydraulic control dampers popped, he felt his stick stiffen up in his right hand. His first thought was to fly the aircraft as far away from Ondjiva as possible: hordes of angry men would have relished the opportunity to torture a downed pilot. Easing up alongside the crippled plane, Keet's wingman escorted the damaged Mirage safely back to base.

On the ground, rockets were still exploding around Morozov's ears. Satisfied that he'd struck the fighter jet, he ran toward the bunker. He was mildly annoyed by the fact that the aircraft hadn't disintegrated in a fiery midair explosion.

Over the next seventy five minutes, waves of South African jets unleashed their ordnance over a number of targets in-and-around the town. For several hours after the air assault, Ondjiva was subjected to a sustained barrage of artillery and infantry attacks.

By the time the sun had started dipping toward the horizon, the initial onslaught was starting to ebb. Tacticians on both sides knew that the South Africans were poised to take the town. Weary soldiers began to dig in for the night.

Ondjiva's senior-ranking Russian was fearful for the safety of his soldiers and their wives. Sometime after midnight he ordered his men to gather in the control room. "Comrades, our situation is dire. At sunrise, we can stand and face the South Africans." He looked briefly into his soldiers' eyes. "But I assure you it will be our last stand." The colonel furrowed his brow as if contemplating something of great importance. "Alternatively, we could surrender to our enemy tomorrow … but as long as I am in command, that option is unacceptable. It is apparent that PLAN offered little or no resistance to the South Africans today, so we can no longer rely on their help. I have therefore arranged for a convoy of trucks to take us northwards to Anchanca at 4 AM. That means we depart in just over an hour's time. Apart from just the most important documents, you and your wives will have to leave all your personal belongings behind. Go to your quarters now and fetch what you must, but hurry. Are there any questions?"

While protocol dictated that he should defer to the colonel's seniority, Morozov owed his loyalty to no man—besides, he was KGB and this man was mere army. His arrogance got the better of him. "Comrade Colonel. To leave tonight, even under the cover of darkness, is suicidal. Right now the South Africans are chewing their biltong and cleaning their rifles, but they'll have sentries posted on all the roads out of town. Even if you are lucky and slip past their ambushes, you run the risk of being spotted by their scouts. You'll still be on the road at sunrise and they can call in their aircraft to strafe your convoy. You'll be like pigs on a skewer."

The colonel flashed a look of contempt. "Comrade Morozov, due to the gravity of our situation, I will ignore your impudence. If you have a better suggestion, I am willing to hear it."

"Comrade Colonel. I will stay in Ondjiva and take my chances with the South Africans tomorrow. I would rather be able to look in my enemy's eye when he shoots me." There was an awkward silence as Morozov left the room.

Laying back on his cot, Morozov stared up at his ceiling. There was a knock on his door. "Enter," he said. Two acquaintances let themselves in.

"Comrade Morozov, you are either a fool or a hero," said Nikolai Pestretsov. "We wish you well tomorrow. Tell us truly, will you surrender yourself to the South Africans?"

Fucking Nikolai ... he doesn't know me well enough to know that I don't take kindly to such insinuations. "No Nikolai, I assure you. I will not surrender."

"Comrade Morozov, the colonel made me send a radio message to headquarters in Luanda a short while ago," said Andre. He was the senior Russian signals officer on the base. "The message said that all Russian military staff, with the exception of one man, will attempt to exfiltrate within the hour. Comrade Morozov of the KGB Alfa Directorate A has chosen to stay and fight the South Africans."

Still lying on his bed, Morozov heard the departing convoy rumble past the station's main gates. He got up and walked toward the maintenance depot. Apart from the receding sound of the colonel's convoy, the base was quiet. It had been abandoned by both PLAN and the Russians. Morozov checked his wristwatch. The sun would be up in just over an hour and a half.

Fumbling in the dark, Morozov found the light switch near the side entrance. As the overhead tubes flickered into life, he could see that the workshop's main roller door had been left wide open. The two mechanics must've scampered for their lives as the first bombs started falling early the previous day. The senior mechanic, a jovial old Madeiran, had abandoned his much beloved GAZ-67. Leaning over to check the panel, Morozov was relieved to see that the key was still in the ignition. He climbed behind the wheel, pumped the pedal twice and turned the motor. As expected, it fired enthusiastically.

Just after daybreak, South African scouts of the famed '32' Battalion spotted a convoy of tanks, trucks and armored personnel carriers fleeing northwards. They immediately called in an air force strike. After SAAF Mirage and Impala jets had strafed the convoy, a fleet of Alouette gunships swept in to clean up.

In the direct aftermath of the attack, mop-up teams discovered the bodies of two Soviet officers, four Russian men and two civilian women. '32' Battalion scouts also pulled a grieving man off his wife's torn and broken body. He offered only his name and rank to his captors.

"Sergeant Major Nikolai F. Pestretsov," said the heartbroken man.

"*Ja swaar, jy's 'n regte fokken commie, nê?*" intoned one of the '32' Battalion lieutenants. *Yes dude, you're a real fucking communist huh?* Pestretsov wasn't technically a POW as South Africa wasn't at war with the Soviets. He was however afforded all the rights of a POW in accordance with the Geneva Conventions.

Around midday, just as the final head-count was being completed, South African soldiers had added a further seven Soviet military advisors to the list of fatalities.

Crudely tied to a bracket high up in the minaret, the old Sony speaker screeched into life. Summoning the believers, the mullah's voice wailed across the rooftops of Ondjiva. In the hours preceding the South African attack, many of the townsfolk had heeded the pamphlets' warning and had fled northwards. But many had decided to stay, including some of the mullah's faithful adherents.

Using only the pale dawn light to guide him, Morozov had driven the short distance into the town center. Killing the engine, he cruised to a halt in a quiet alley. Using the deep shadows to mask his presence, Morozov worked his way through the town's small commercial district. A hundred yards from where he'd hidden the GAZ, he waited in the gloom. From a discreet distance he watched as Ali the merchant emerged from his general dealer's store. The sandaled man turned and locked the front door of his shop. As he stepped into the street, a scrofulous mongrel groveled toward the Pakistani. Without breaking stride, Ali kicked it maliciously in the ribs. He had to hurry or he'd be late for the first prayers.

Ali returned from mosque about half an hour later. As he rounded the corner he saw Morozov sitting on the curb outside his trading store. "*As-Salaam-Alaikum* Mister Russian, and how are you this fine morning?" Ali's head wobbled from side-to-side. Try as he might, he just hadn't been able to master the pronunciation of Morozov's name. They'd come to an agreement many months before that he'd just address him as 'Mister Russian.'

"*Wa-Alaikum-Salaam* Ali, I am well this morning," responded the Russian.

"What brings you into town? The bombing … is it finished now?"

"No Ali, I am certain the bombing will start again soon. These South Africans will come into town to make sure there are no more soldiers hiding here. Tell me, why didn't you escape when you had the chance?"

"Ah, Mister Russian. I am a simple businessman." Ali's head continued to teeter. "I pray to Allah that the South Africans will leave me in peace. They have no need to fear a harmless trader like me." Ali pulled a face. "Besides, my shop is my livelihood. If I leave it unattended too long, these Angolan types, you know, they can rob me blind in a jiffy."

"This is true Ali." Morozov nodded knowingly.

"So how can I be helping you this fine morning, Mister Russian? You want your favorite sveeties, yes?" Ali had trouble pronouncing 'sweeties.' He was referring to candy.

"Yes Ali. Maybe a few other items as well." Morozov stood up from the curb.

Ali unlocked the door and led Morozov inside. A medley of aromas permeated the small shop: a waft of exotic spices; a hint of overripe fruit; the tang of cheap tobacco; and the sickly-sweet bouquet of patchouli oil. In a small room leading off the main part of Ali's store, the shelves were crammed with zinc buckets, pick handles, cheap radios, garments, bicycle parts and a hodgepodge of other items beside. While Ali went about rearranging the smaller pieces of merchandise on his over-crowded countertop, Morozov stepped into the room crammed with the assortment of commodities.

"Ali, please. I need your help," called Morozov.

"Right away, Mister Russian."

Every time he thought about it, Morozov still felt a pang of regret over having to leave his coveted Matsuda knife embedded behind the Mongolian's collarbone. Soon after the Sokolov incident he'd gone in search of his black-market fence. After tracking him down in one of the seedier parts of Moscow, Morozov placed an order for a new Matsuda.

Of his own volition, the fence had gone above-and-beyond the call of duty: he had arranged to have Morozov's initials engraved onto the handle of his new knife. Never in his entire life had Morozov experienced such an act of generosity. With something akin to fondness, he recalled the moment the fence had handed him the new Matsuda. He kept on turning it over in the palm of his hand, each time stopping to admire his initials etched into the handle: *V I U M*. Morozov had promised himself that he wasn't going to leave *this* knife protruding from *anyone's* body.

As Ali stepped into the side room, Morozov lunged toward him. "Mister Russian, no …"

Aiming for the point just below the center of Ali's ribcage, Morozov plunged the blade deep into his abdominal cavity. Perforating both the front and back wall of his victim's stomach, he drove the six inch blade toward Ali's abdominal aorta. The blade sliced through the artery. The Pakistani slumped but Morozov held him up as if in a brotherly embrace. Ali tried to gasp—his mouth moved but no sound escaped. He looked questioningly into his killer's dark eyes. The Russian waited as his victim's life force flickered and spluttered like a dying candle.

Morozov withdrew the knife and carefully wiped the blade in the loose folds of Ali's robe. He folded it and put it back in his pocket. Bending down, he lifted Ali under the armpits and dragged him into the tiny back office. Before wedging the body under the table, he removed the Pakistani's fez. Rearranging a dozen bolts of calico around the table, Morozov hid the body from casual detection. Somewhere in the distance he heard a low rumble as a convoy of trucks surged into town. *Exactly as I expected … South African infantrymen. They will be starting their door-to-door search in the next few minutes.*

Stepping back into the shop's side room, Morozov went straight to the shelf displaying a selection of men's garments. Rummaging through the range of cotton robes, he checked each of the tags for their sizes. He pulled the largest one off the shelf. It was a traditional Muslim's thobe. He could already hear voices approaching from down the street. Before stripping down, he removed the knife from his pocket. *I might need that later.* The Russian bundled his fatigues into a zinc bucket and repositioned it high on the shelf. After pulling the thobe over his head he grabbed his knife.

The voices drew nearer. Morozov was about to go to the front of the shop when he remembered the fez. *Fuck!* Rushing back to the office, he placed the knife on the table and grabbed the fez off Ali's desk. He jammed it on his head. He was about to make his way to the front of the store when two South

African soldiers entered cautiously, weapons at the ready.

"Whoa!" said Morozov in mock surprise. He immediately threw his arms up in surrender. The soldiers leveled their R4 rifles at his belly.

"Hey! Put your hands up," shouted Piet, the shorter of the two soldiers. His English was heavily accented.

My hands are already up you fucking idiot. Morozov had to be careful not to respond too readily to anything they said to him. He didn't want them to know that he understood English, nor did he want them to hear his accent.

"*Hy's net 'n fokken smous,*" said Harries, the taller of the two soldiers. *He's just a fucking hawker.*

"*Ja. Hy's nog 'n fokken Patel,*" said Piet. *Yes. He's just another fucking Patel.* Because of his dusky features and traditional outfit, Piet had wrongly assumed that Morozov was an Indian. Amongst the Indians, Patel is a common surname. In Piet's worldview, if every second Indian was named Patel, and every second Indian was a hawker, then every hawker was a Patel. Using the name Patel in this manner, Piet's undertone was intentionally condescending.

Morozov had no clue as to what they were saying, but a combination of his swarthy features and his traditional Muslim garb seemed to have them fooled. He was also thankful that the unflattering robe hid his physique: soldiers the world over seem to believe that a well-built man represents a challenge to their masculinity.

"Do you speak English?" asked Harries slowly.

Morozov mimicked Ali's head bob. "No English, sir." He even affected Ali's accent.

"We're wasting our time here," said Piet. "Keep an eye on him. I'll check the back."

Harries waited as Piet disappeared; first into the side room, then the office. With his arms still raised, Morozov waited, calculating his options. "Everything okay back there?" Harries called out.

From the back room he heard his friend's response. "*Ja,* let's go," said Piet, as he pocketed the knife on Ali's table.

Just as they were about to depart, Morozov called out after them. "Sveeties, sveeties?" He pointed toward the jar of candy sticks sitting on top of the counter.

Having finished their sweep through the town, the soldiers of Battle Group 20 boarded their trucks and headed for the outskirts of Ondjiva. Morozov suspected they'd have been given orders to garrison the town for a few days. After his two visitors had left, he locked the doors to the shop and helped himself to a few items off the shelves. It was pointless going back to the airbase at this stage. He knew that members of South Africa's Intelligence Division would be swarming over Ondjiva for at least a day, perhaps even longer. Morozov made himself comfortable and tried to get some rest.

Still in jubilant spirits, it was apparent to the South African soldiers that the Battle of Ondjiva had been a resounding success. Around their temporary camp—set-up on the outskirts of town—members of the elite '32' Battalion intermingled with their fellow infantrymen, artillerymen and engineers. The air of elation had grown as word spread of the thirteen Russians killed earlier that day, as well as the captured sergeant major.

With the general threat level now greatly reduced, the soldiers needed to find a way to expend some of their nervous energy. Harries and Piet found themselves in a poker game with two men from '32' Battalion. Bored of gambling with matchsticks, the '32' Battalion corporal felt it was time to ratchet up the ante. "Come *ouens*, let's make this game a little more interesting," said Fonseca. "One game. Winner takes all." Fonseca rummaged in his backpack and produced a whole slab of Cadbury's chocolate. The other three salivated.

His colleague dug into his own bag. "I see your slab of chocolate and raise you an unopened carton of Lucky Strikes," he said, tossing it into the middle. The others eyed the cigarettes covetously. Initially reluctant, Harries eventually parted with a precious tin of condensed milk. They all turned and looked expectantly at the last man. Piet reached into his pocket and withdrew a Matsuda combat knife. He unfolded the blade and held it up for inspection. In the sulfur glow of the hissing lamp, everyone leant in to admire the weapon.

After winning the bounty fair-and-square, Fonseca generously divided the chocolate and cigarettes between the four of them. Harries managed to use his share of the cigarettes to trade back his condensed milk, but Fonseca refused to horse-trade his newly-acquired combat knife.

Satisfied that their route south was clear of landmines, the convoy of triumphant soldiers left the battered town of Ondjiva two days after their initial air strike. Counting their spoils of war, they left Angola with an estimated four thousand tons of captured equipment.

Holed up in Ali's shop, Morozov raged over the theft of his prized knife. To add to his anger, even the store's perfumed mélange couldn't mask the rank odor of Ali's putrefying body.

Peering out of the store's small barred windows, Morozov checked for any signs of life. Up the street he saw a small band of looters crowbar the lock off the door to a shoe repair shop. *If the looters are out, the South Africans must have left.*

The Russian bundled his fatigues into a small bag that he'd taken down from one of Ali's shelves. Making use of the extra space, he filled it with an assortment of basic provisions. Still dressed in his thobe and fez, Morozov locked the store and walked to where he'd left the GAZ. To his relief, both the looters and the South Africans had overlooked it.

Hoping his disguise would hold up if he was stopped in a South African roadblock, Morozov drove out to the main road and turned north toward Luanda.

After an arduous twelve hour drive, Morozov headed straight to the KGB's secret location on the outskirts of Luanda. He had to wait almost thirty minutes before an aide came and ushered him into the supervisor's office.

Morozov stood to attention in front of his KGB controller.

He'd changed back into his military issue fatigues. "So comrade Morozov, you disobeyed a commanding officer's direct order to return to Luanda by convoy?" He jabbed his finger at a Teletype message lying on his desk. "KGB received a copy of this army message four hours after it was transmitted." He was clearly disgusted by the delay. "Less than two hours after we received it, we got confirmation that the colonel's entire convoy had been decimated. Were you aware of this?"

"No comrade, I was not."

"Comrade Morozov, let me tell you. That army commander made a fucking poor decision. I praise your bravery for disregarding his order. I say 'disregarding' and not 'disobeying' because KGB does not answer to anyone except our illustrious leader, the General Secretary. I hope you killed at least one South African in your escape from Ondjiva?" queried the supervisor.

"I did kill one man, comrade." Morozov said flatly.

"This is good." The supervisor nodded approvingly. "Comrade, your record of bravery just grows and grows." He pulled Morozov's open file toward him and read off the top sheet. "First the Bucharest Affair, then the Rhodesian Viscount, then the international child trafficking ring, and now this act of individual bravery ... and you are still in your twenties."

Sensing his supervisor's upbeat mood, Morozov risked a bold interruption. "Forgive me for cutting in comrade, but I'd be grateful if you could check our intelligence to see if my direct missile strike caused the South African Mirage to crash."

The supervisor shook his head in mock disbelief. "Indeed comrade. Another addition to your growing list of achievements, huh? But let me continue. I had to keep you waiting outside because I needed to wake up our division commander in Moscow to discuss your future in Alfa FSB. He tells me you have an overarching desire to work in Africa. In light of this, he has decided to reward you with the best possible posting in the whole of Africa."

Morozov's pulse quickened. *They have finally decided to grant my wish and send me to Zimbabwe.*

"In two days you will be transferred to the islands of the Seychelles. Their president is a fellow socialist and has shown a willingness to explore closer ties with Moscow."

Morozov clenched his jaw. *I don't fucking believe it.* He hardly heard the rest of what his supervisor had to say.

"Our politburo believes he could be a very useful ally in the Indian Ocean region. Before you depart, I will draw up a detailed description of your duties for the new position. Congratulations comrade." Rising partially from his seat, the supervisor offered his hand to his subordinate.

Morozov could barely contain his frustration.

33

FATHER'S MOUSTACHE

As a self-exiled tenant during the latter part of the Bush War, Zimbabwe's new president was somewhat indebted to his Mozambican host, Samora Machel.

Toward the closing stages of the Bush War, much of Rhodesia's wrath had been directed at Mugabe's terrorist camps located in Mozambique. But that all changed after Zimbabwe's independence in 1980. Despite the promise of peace in the region, President Machel's woes were far from over. Internally, militias from the organization known as RENAMO were hell-bent on destabilizing his communist regime. In recognition of Mozambique's loyal support during his own campaign, Mugabe offered to send Zimbabwean troops into Mozambique to suppress the RENAMO rebels.

After returning from the Moscow Olympics, Dax continued to serve on in the Air Force of Zimbabwe. Although no longer at war, select units of Zimbabwe's defense force had found themselves deployed in various military roles in neighboring Mozambique. Dax's new foe was a determined band of rebels attempting to overthrow the Mozambican government. It wasn't his war, but it was his job.

Although a few of Dax's skirmishes in Mozambique had been intense, none were as exhilarating as the battles he'd fought during the latter part of the Rhodesian Bush War. Hunter hankered for action. Boredom soon set in and he started contemplating a move to South Africa. Dozens of his flying colleagues had already headed south and were quickly integrated into the various South African Air Force squadrons.

With both Russia and Cuba intensifying their support of the Angolans, South Africa's Border War was starting to ratchet up. It had been left to South Africa to stand firm against the Soviets' inexorable march down the continent.

Dax Hunter had developed an itch and only the buzz of pitched battle could assuage it. In September of 1981 he resigned his commission and left the Air Force of Zimbabwe. Aside from a few casual enquiries, he hadn't formally applied for a flying post in the South African Air Force. His friends however had all assured him that the SAAF would welcome him with open arms.

With a healthy chunk of change in his bank account, Dax was in no rush to sign up; besides, summer had just started and the waves off Durban beckoned. He figured that he'd take a few weeks off before making any overtures to the brass at SAAF headquarters. Naturally gregarious, it wasn't long before Hunter reconnected with a number of friends who'd also headed to Durban after the end of the Bush War.

Socializing with his band of old buddies, comrades and ex-team mates, Dax soon started picking up on a persistent rumor: plans were afoot to launch a covert, military-styled mission into an unnamed country somewhere in southern Africa. It was penciled to happen within the next two months. Although the details were sketchy, talk was that the cloak-and-dagger operation had the backing of the South African government.

Amongst the more talkative members of his circle, conjecture was rampant. Some speculated that the operation might involve a coup to oust Mugabe. Dax knew the military capabilities of the newly-formed Zimbabwean apparatus; he quickly disabused his friends of such a folly. The rumor had generated an enormous amount of interest amongst his circle of friends. Judging by the gossip, it appeared as if all his buddies were eager to become soldiers of fortune. Excited by the prospect of their involvement, reports of handsome payouts also abounded. Whatever their fee, operators were guaranteed a sizeable reward. Dax was more than just interested—he wanted in.

Although Dax pressed his friends for more detail, each one of them was incapable of offering more than just a dumb shrug. But they were unanimous about one thing; if he wanted to find out more, he should speak to Dev.

With the exception of moustaches, the old Rhodesian military regulations required each soldier to be clean-shaven. But there was *one* unit which was exempt from this ruling. Members of the vaunted Selous Scouts regiment were actually *encouraged* to grow beards.

In their eight year history, the secretive regiment had built a staunch reputation. Like all special force units, they never divulged their exploits. In the vacuum where details were thin, it was inevitable that urban legends began to flourish. The less the Scouts strutted, the more intriguing they became. Heroic deeds were soon embellished to the point where their derring-do was mythologized in popular culture. It added to the fashionable notion of a band of semi-invincible warriors at the vanguard of Rhodesia's defense.

One of the regiment's idiosyncrasies was their preferred form of communication; conversations were typically conducted in either of the country's two indigenous languages. Dev liked to tell anyone who listened that his nickname 'Dev' derived from the word *ndebvu*, meaning 'beard' in Shona.

Eighteen months after the disbandment of his legendary unit, the bewhiskered soldier still couldn't bring himself to shave off his unruly beard.

Dev had also recently moved to Durban. Tracking him down was easy; he not only socialized in the same circles as Dax, but also happened to be an old rugby mate from Salisbury. Dax got his number from a mutual friend and called him up the next morning. After a brief exchange, Dev suggested the two of them get together for a beer. They agreed to meet at Magoo's bar later that afternoon.

Seated down at the end of the bar, the two men spoke in hushed tones. The barman had just finished pouring their beers when the first few regulars started shuffling in. As he moved off to go and serve them, Dax and Dev raised their glasses in a toast. "To fallen Rhodesians," intoned Dev.

"Fallen Rhodesians," repeated Dax.

"So Dax, you been playing any rugby lately?" enquired Dev.

"*Ja.* I turned out for Old Hararians this last season … also played a few games for the Air Force side. What about you?"

"*Ja*, china. A whole bunch of us ex-Rhodies are playing for Berea Rovers," said Dev. What he lacked in skill on the sports field, Dev definitely made up for in aggression. Like many of the Rhodesian Diaspora, his war was still waging: nightmares; passive-aggressive behavior; inexplicable anxiety attacks; flashbacks; and aberrant indulgences. It wasn't just a yearning for the fight that troubled men like Dev. Over-and-above their post-traumatic stress, a great number of combatants felt a pervasive sense of loss. Although Rhodesia had valiantly pushed-back against the advancing Soviet tide, duplicitous world leaders had sold the country to a tyrant for thirty pieces of silver. At the end of the fourteen year war, thousands had lost their lives; many survivors felt they'd lost theirs too. Material possessions could be replaced; what they'd lost were their very identities.

At the end of the Rhodesian Bush War, men of Dev's caliber had been actively recruited by the South Africa military. Dax listened intently as Dev told him what he'd been up to since leaving the Selous Scouts. It was clear to Dax that his old mate had landed feet first. He had quickly worked his way into the structure of the South African Defense Intelligence Division and, in Dev's own words, had done pretty well for himself. In terms of military gossip, he was a veritable mine of information. But there were some things he didn't share.

Dax wasn't to know that his old Selous Scout buddy had been tasked with vetting all prospective candidates for the forthcoming mission. Supping their ales, Hunter was naively oblivious to the fact that Dev was actually interviewing him.

One of the priorities on Dev's shopping list was a military-trained pilot. Although the operation was to be executed without aerial support, the planners believed their mercenaries might succeed in commandeering an aircraft or helicopter. If that were the case, it would significantly bolster their force projection capabilities. Of course, they'd need a pilot.

After half-an-hour of talking, Dev had made up his mind: he wanted Dax on the team. Before sharing any more details, he secured the pilot's commitment to the mission. "So there's a bit of internal politics going on right now between two South African agencies. I'm with DID, Defense Intelligence Division, and we have been tasked with organizing the manpower for the coup." Dev hadn't yet revealed the name of the country they were going to invade, but he'd given Dax his assurance that it wasn't Zimbabwe. He told Dax that details surrounding their final objective would be revealed closer to the time.

"Tell me then, who is this other crowd muscling in on your turf?" asked Dax.

"So up to now the NIS, that's the National Intelligence Service, has been doing all the detailed planning. While they've been doing that, me and my guys at DID have been tasked with selecting, training and equipping the men. The NIS guys are sour because they feel the whole operation should come under their jurisdiction. To be honest, it is a bit of a fuck up when you have two competing agencies working on the same task, especially when both teams refuse to cooperate. But I promise, it won't really affect the mission either way. It's going to go ahead regardless."

"How can you be so sure?"

"Because this whole fucking mission has the complete backing of the South African government," said Dev, just a little too loudly. Dax narrowed his eyes; he disapproved of Dev's careless outburst. It must've registered: Dev lowered his voice conspiratorially. "But not only South Africa. It also has the blessing of the CIA. They support it to the hilt but they don't want the USA to be involved militarily. It's Cold War chess, that's all. It's another proxy conflict between the forces of good and evil, east versus west, capitalism versus communism." Dev's philosophical eloquence had been well-oiled by his third beer.

"Who's commanding the raid? A Dutchman?" asked Dax. A fair portion of South Africa's white population could trace their ancestral roots back to the country's early Dutch settlers. These Afrikaners, as they were known, had a proud military heritage and naturally gravitated to the South African defense force. Their English-speaking brethren often used the mildly pejorative term 'Dutchmen' when referring to the Afrikaners.

"Not even close. You've heard of Mad Mike Hoare, right?" asked Dev.

"*Ja*, of course."

"Well who better to lead the party than Mister Mercenary himself?" Dev quaffed the last of his beer and called the barman for two refills. Hoare's exploits were legendary and practically everyone in Southern Africa had either heard or read of his escapades in the Congo.

Marty Docheck slammed down the phone. He wasn't a happy man. Elroy looked across Marty's wide oak desk to see if he'd broken the cradle. "What's up man?" asked the big American.

"Fucking bureaucrats and politicians," cursed Docheck.

"Don't I know it," consoled the CIA agent. Elroy Matthews had been in South Africa for almost three months. The Agency needed to replace a retiring field agent and Elroy had leapt at the chance to interview for the post. It didn't matter a whit to him that he might end up working in apartheid South Africa. Being an employee of the world's preeminent spy agency wouldn't guarantee him immunity from prejudice, but in his mind he couldn't imagine it being any worse than what he'd experienced growing up in the deep south of good old USA.

In the main, South Africa's spy apparatus was populated by dedicated and hard-working professionals. Matthews knew there were a few hard-core operators working in one or two of the country's shadier outfits, but thankfully their paths seldom crossed. Relations between the CIA and South Africa's State Security network appeared to be cordial in nature. In the three months since his arrival, Matthews hadn't once been treated any differently from his European colleagues. The irony wasn't lost on him.

"That was the fucking Prime Minister's personal aide," bemoaned Docheck. "*Die groot krokodil* has just growled."

"Dee what?" asked Elroy.

"*Die groot krokodil* means 'the big crocodile' in Afrikaans. It's our nickname for the Prime Minister," explained Docheck. Elroy could tell it wasn't intended to be complimentary.

"So what's he said that's made you so pissed?" asked Elroy.

"With immediate effect, the Defense Intelligence Division is to assume *full* control of *Operation Angela.*" Angela was the code-name for the planned Seychelles coup. "After all the fucking hard work and planning NIS has invested in this coup d'état. *Poes!* I can't believe it." Docheck's jowls shook with rage. "And it's on the Prime Minister's express orders, *nogal!*"

With a vested interest in the outcome of the coup, the CIA had been working in close cooperation with South Africa's National Intelligence Service—and Docheck in particular. With some concern, Elroy wondered how things might change now that a new internal agency had been tasked with overall command of the operation. He had first-hand experience of how competing jurisdictions could derail a perfectly good case.

"Hey Marty. Cool down just one second. My team might be able to swing some dick here. Let me make a few calls. Let's meet here same time tomorrow. Okay?" Elroy leant forward and shook Docheck's hand. He could see the man was still simmering. Just before reaching for the door handle, Elroy turned back toward Docheck. "Hey Marty … one last thing. I have a colleague flying in tonight from the States. She's going to be shadowing me on this operation. I'll bring her around tomorrow to meet you." As he left, Elroy stooped slightly to get under the door's head jamb.

Docheck's office was on the tenth floor of an austere, block-like structure in the city center. Indulging his love of fine architecture, he'd positioned his antique oak desk so that he could savor the view of Sir Herbert Baker's masterfully designed Union Buildings, located less than a mile away. Visitors experiencing the panorama for the first time were invariably taken by the buildings' grandeur. Apple was no different. Standing in front of the large window in Docheck's office, she admired the splendid view. The jacarandas had just come into bloom and the city's celebrated purple canopy stretched for miles in every direction.

Elroy and Apple had arrived just minutes before. After the introductions, Apple was naturally drawn to the window. "This view is beautiful Mr. Docheck. What a magnificent building," said Apple.

"It is indeed. It's a masterpiece. A timeless masterpiece ... forgive me, I am easily mesmerized by the buildings' grandness. It compensates for the excuse of a building that we're housed in here. Coffee, Miss Apple?" Docheck had lifted his receiver and was poised to call his secretary. Elroy was relieved to see that Docheck was in good spirits. He'd briefed Apple on the turn of events that had so enraged the South African the previous day. He'd warned her that they may well encounter more of the same at their follow-up meeting.

As promised, Elroy had made a phone call late the previous day. He hadn't been at all happy with the South African's last-minute change to the coup's command and control arrangements. Through Elroy's hard work, the CIA had quickly formed a strong accord with Docheck and the NIS. Both parties sought the same outcome but for completely different reasons. With delicate maneuvering, Docheck and Matthews had found that elusive common ground that satisfied both parties' objectives. Not only had Docheck invested a great deal of time and energy in the planning of the coup, but he'd opted to work candidly with his CIA counterpart. In the world of espionage, that was considered highly unusual. But it had made Elroy's job so much easier.

Even if it *was* an arms-length operation, it was still a CIA-sanctioned event. While on the phone to his supervisor the day before, Elroy had argued that to sideline Docheck now would not only be foolhardy, but potentially disruptive to the whole operation. Especially so close to D-day. After carefully explaining this to his field supervisor, Elroy concluded his appeal by suggesting that some form of high-level CIA intervention might be prudent.

After putting down the tray, Docheck's secretary left the office and closed the door behind her. Marty took a sip from his mug then placed it down carefully on the coaster. "Elroy, I don't know who you called, what you did, or what you said, but whatever it was, thank-you man."

"I'm glad my phone call made a difference Marty, but I have absolutely no idea why it's made you so happy," said Elroy.

"You're kidding, right?" said Docheck. Elroy pulled a face and shrugged his shoulders. "Your people must have some impressive leverage over my people. That's all I can say," said Docheck.

"C'mon dude. Spill the beans. What the hell's happened since we last spoke?" asked Elroy.

"Well, *Die Groot Krokodil's* original order still stands firm: *Operation Angela* is to be handled entirely by Defense Intelligence Division. But they've been told by someone very high up the totem pole that I am to be granted full access to the continued planning and execution of the operation. Although my own NIS might be completely out the loop, *I* still get an invite to the ball. I'm going to the Seychelles!" Docheck's face cracked into a wide grin.

"Hallelujah, my man! Well done." Elroy was immensely relieved. His project was back on track. But his grin was short-lived. He looked sternly at Docheck. "Listen up Marty. Your man Colonel Hoare is holding his first informal meeting with the mercs at a bar in Durban tomorrow, is that right?"

"That's correct, yes," confirmed Docheck.

"And you're okay with these boys getting together in such a large group, in such a conspicuous place, to do a meet-and-greet?" Elroy was dead serious.

"They're all professional soldiers, Elroy. Hand-picked. Most come from special force units and know the drill. Besides, they've got a good cover; they're pretending to be a team of rugby players. We're good, I assure you." Docheck tried to sound convincing but Elroy harbored reservations. After discussing a few further details, the meeting drew to a close. They agreed to meet again in a weeks' time.

Elroy and Apple headed back across town toward their offices in Menlyn Park. Elroy hadn't spoken since they'd left. Apple had been happy to just take in the sights of Pretoria. Besides, she knew he was deep in thought and didn't want to interrupt him. It was only after they'd passed the university that Elroy spoke. "I want to send you to that bar tomorrow. I'll find a few lady colleagues to go in there with you for moral support. No guys … they'll scare the men off." Elroy chuckled then got serious. "I'll tell you this much, Apple. I'm not happy that the colonel is being so cavalier over this whole thing. Yeah, I know Marty said they're gonna disguise themselves as a bunch of rugby players and all, but this is taking the charade a bit too far in my book." Apple nodded but let Elroy continue. "So I want you and the other girls to position yourselves close enough to this group to make sure that they don't start blabbing off about the mission to their buddies. If they so much as mention the word Seychelles, I'm gonna call off the whole damn mission. Liquor has a funny way of loosening tongues. I want you to keep your ears open for any careless talk, got it?"

"I got you," said Apple. Although she was still feeling the effects of jetlag, Apple was exhilarated by the thought of jumping straight into the action.

Elroy and Apple flew into Durban early the next day. They were met at the airport by Cathy, one of Elroy's local field agents. The CIA was sponsoring her post-graduate study in political science at the University of Natal in Durban. Upon being introduced, Apple was immediately reminded of Sammy Jo Carrington, one of the characters in the popular TV soap *Dynasty*. The two hit it off immediately. While driving out of the airport, Cathy told Apple that she'd been recruited by the CIA while in her senior year at college in Kentucky. Apple guessed they were of similar age. "Wouldn't by any chance have been by a guy named Sneddon?" Apple enquired.

"Oh my goodness, yes it was!" said Cathy, laughing. "Don't tell me he recruited you as well?"

"Sure did."

"Come ladies. Let's concentrate on today's mission," Elroy chided lightly. "Cathy, you manage to arrange two friends to join you tonight at the nightclub?"

"Yes sir, I have indeed."

"Good. For the sake of appearances I want you all to get into a carousing mood. But Apple, you need to remain sober—and vigilant. But don't be a killjoy, alright?" He didn't give her a chance to answer. "If anyone asks, or if anyone offers, you're drinking vodka, lime and soda, okay?"

"Without the soda?" interjected Apple.

"No dammit, the ..." It took Elroy a moment to realize that Apple was messing with him. "Vodka," he trailed off. Apple had been a performer since she was a child. If anyone could convince an audience of her insobriety, it was her.

After dropping Elroy at his hotel, the two girls drove to Cathy's campus residence just beyond the city center.

From the car park it was a short walk up to where Cathy stayed. Ambling up the road toward Mabel Palmer, the two girls chatted like old friends. In honor of the suffragist and acclaimed academic, one of the women's residential blocks on campus had been named after Ms. Palmer. "If they only see two girls out on the town, South African guys will typically deduce that the pair are simply out to enjoy each others' company, and aren't interested in partying. If there are four girls however ... well then, sister, we have us a party. So I've invited two of my friends to join us at the nightclub," announced Cathy.

Having been selected as her residence sub-warden, Cathy qualified for one of the more well-appointed rooms in the block. Apple whistled as she was ushered in. "These South Africans certainly know how to look after their students," said Apple. From beyond the closed door, the two women heard voices, followed shortly by a knock. Cathy went over to answer the door.

Cathy greeted the newcomers and led them into the room. She introduced Apple as her American cousin, visiting Africa for the first time. The two friends hailed from Zimbabwe— both students had opted to further their education at a South African university. Although both had formed a close friendship with Cathy, neither was aware that she led a double life as an international spy.

Apple immediately warmed to the two Zimbabweans. *This is going to be a fun evening.* After freshening up, the four young ladies departed for the Golden Mile—Durban's beachfront promenade and home to its glitziest nightspots.

Dominating the skyline of the Durban waterfront, the Malibu Hotel is an unmissable beacon toward the end of the Golden Mile. Every night, as if fulfilling some innate ritual, streams of revelers were drawn to *The Father's Moustache*—the hotel's raucous, basement nightclub. Arriving sober was optional; departing drunk was inevitable. Down in the hotel's receiving area, a constant flow of delivery trucks ensured *Fathers'* beer taps never dried up—despite the merrymakers' best efforts.

Flinders and Vogt, the two resident bouncers, were struggling to keep the crowd orderly. As ever, the queue outside *The Father's Moustache* snaked its way up to the Marine Parade. Inside, the club was already heaving; it had the makings of another profitable evening. Like a covey of Medici bankers, the Malibu's management team greedily rubbed their hands together.

Colonel 'Mad' Mike Hoare was anxious about his boys keeping up appearances. They all knew the drill; they were just a rollicking bunch of rugby players out for their end-of-season celebrations. It was a big team—over forty men. While queuing to get inside, Hoare had insisted that his lads don the polystyrene boaters that came with the price of the entrance fee. There was a good reason why the colonel had chosen *The Father's Moustache* as the venue for their first meeting.

Bert Temple was an ex-English soldier and silk-merchant. In 1924 he survived a life-threatening operation performed by the noted surgeon Sir Alfred Fripp. Eager to honor his surgeon, Temple established a humorous charitable drinking club known as *The Ancient Order of Froth-Blowers*. They abbreviated their name to AOFB. Their aim was 'to foster the noble art and gentle and healthy pastime of froth blowing amongst gentlemen of leisure and ex-soldiers.' All funds raised by the *Blowers* were donated to children's charities nominated by Sir Alfred Fripp. Their motto was '*Lubrication in Moderation.*' The AOFB disbanded when Temple died in 1931.

Colonel Hoare rose from his chair at the head of the long table in *Father's Moustache*. With mock pomposity, he raised his beer mug and repeated the AOFBs traditional toast. "Gentlemen of ye Ancient Order of Froth Blowers: ale fellow, well met!"

"Ale fellow, well met," chorused the group. Under the guise of a defunct charity, the spoof Order had just been revived—but goodwill was not their métier. Instead, the clinking of two-score beer mugs heralded the creation of Africa's latest league of warriors.

In just over a month's time, these dogs of war would stage an audacious coup to wrestle the Seychelles from its socialist leader and hand the nation back to the deposed moderate, James Mancham.

Their Trojan horse was beguilingly simple. The mercenaries planned on arriving in the Seychelles disguised as members of a rugby team. Each player also happened to belong to a benevolent society known as the AOFB. As was customary amongst the original *Blowers,* Hoare's compassionate band of hirelings was there to distribute toys amongst Seychelles' needy. Hoare's plan was to use false-bottom bags. Each soldier would stuff his bag with a number of bulky toys. He'd already settled on the idea of using rugby balls for this purpose. But concealed in the bags' secret compartments would be an arsenal of deadly hardware.

Dax was in good spirits. He wasn't alone. After raising his mug to his newfound AOFB companions, he chugged back his beer. Fonseca, the South African sitting next to him, immediately refilled his glass from the pitcher beside his elbow. Corporal Fonseca was a member of South Africa's elite '32' Battalion. While many of the mercenaries were former members of crack regiments, Docheck had insisted that a significant portion of the raiding party be drawn from serving members of '32' Battalion—South Africa's renowned special forces unit.

Having just completed a medley of fifteen songs, the Blarney Brothers announced they'd be taking a ten minute break. Accompanied by a chorus of good-humored heckling and booing, the band members vacated the stage. Getting up from their long table, the lads from the AOFB started introducing themselves to their new brothers-in-arms.

Lubricated by a cascade of amber liquid, the mood in the nightclub was jovial. Amped up by the liquor—and their testosterone crying for attention—some of the soldiers had already scoped the crowd for unattached females. Dax wasn't surprised to see that six of his colleagues had gravitated toward a small group of women seated near the *Blowers'* long table. Unsure as to whether they should be flattered or insulted by the passel of suitors, the four women stoically bore the barrage of corny pick-up lines. The fleeting image of gorillas beating their chests brought a wry smile to Dax's face.

Including himself, Dax counted nine ex-Rhodesian soldiers in the group of legionnaires. Dev had only needed to introduce

Dax to two of them, the rest he knew. The bulk of the raiding party—twenty-seven individuals—were drawn from South African special force units. Fonseca was one of the twenty seven.

Detaching themselves from the general revelry, seven older men sat cheerlessly at the end of the table. They were talking quietly amongst themselves when Dax went over to introduce himself.

"*Howzit* gents! My name's Dax." He offered his hand to the closest man. Making little effort, each of the grizzly men offered a hand, a name and a brief nod. Despite the awkward reception, Dax decided to persevere. He was about to pull up a chair and insert himself into their clique when Colonel Hoare appeared at his elbow. Immediately—and without exception— the seven men straightened their backs: only in military circles would men react like that to the arrival of a superior officer.

"Ah, Dax. So I see you've met my boys," said the colonel.

"Yes, sir. I have," *Boys indeed!* Dax thought.

The colonel leant in close to Dax and lowered his voice. "You mustn't address me as *sir* when we're in public. Remember, we're keeping up appearances here." He slapped Dax's back.

"Got you."

"So these brutes all served with me in the Congo back in the 60s. Fine soldiers, every last one of them." The colonel's voice was still low. "You saw the movie *The Wild Geese?*" asked Hoare.

"I sure did," answered Dax.

"Well Grayboy and Rhett over there," the colonel pointed the two men out, "they actually played themselves in that movie. Can you believe it? These two ugly oafs … movie stars?" All of them laughed at the colonel's jibe. Rhett's face cracked to reveal two missing teeth. "Look at that face Dax; only a mother could love that. Hey Rhett, what happened to those lovely ivories the director made you wear during filming?"

"Aw boss, I still got 'em … but the ladies find this very

stimulating," answered Rhett lewdly. Laughing a little louder, the group was starting to loosen up a little.

"Dax, perhaps one day you can get Rhett to tell you the story of how he lost his pearlies," said Hoare.

Playing along with the other three, Apple flirted with the six men clustered around their table. The girls were sitting in one of the booths located along the far wall of the nightclub. "So what brings so many hunky men together in one place?" Apple batted her eyelids.

"We're a team of rugby players. It's our end-of-season celebrations," said the talkative one. "Hey, I like your accent. Which part of the States you from?"

"I'm from Louisiana and Cathy here is from Toledo, Ohio," answered Apple. "You've probably gathered from their accents that my other two friends are Zimbabweans. Where are you guys from?"

"We're all Rhodies. Rhodesia? You've heard of it?" said their self-appointed spokesman. He looked at the Zimbabwean girls reprovingly.

"Yeah, we know where Zimbabwe is," said Cathy pointedly. She knew enough ex-Rhodesian students on campus to know that some of them were still quite touchy about their national identity.

"So is this whole rugby team from Zimbabwe?" asked Apple.

"Nah. A whole bunch of us Rhodies emigrated here quite recently. Most of our players are from South Africa, and a few of the boys come from overseas."

The latest Brit invasion to hit US shores was a pop duo called *Wham! UK*—at least that's how they were marketed in America. Members George Michael and Andrew Ridgeley had spawned a worldwide craze for bouffant hairstyles. Surrounded by so many short-haired men, Apple wondered why the trend hadn't yet hit South Africa's shores. "Why have so many of your team mates got such short hair?" asked Apple, pointing at the cluster of South Africans sitting at the table.

The six rugby players laughed. "Those guys are still in the South African Defense Force. It's a requirement that every able-bodied male in South Africa does compulsory national service. These blokes are still off playing soldiers for their country." The chatty one paused. "Heck I'm sorry. I'm Dave." He offered his hand. After everyone had been introduced, Dave caught a waiter's attention and ordered drinks all around.

"Who's the salt-and-pepper haired guy in your group?" asked Cathy.

"You like the older men, huh?" Dave wore a lecherous grin.

Cathy smiled but was unfazed. "No, I just thought he was a bit too old to be playing rugby, that's all."

"He's Mad Mike. He's our coach," said Andrew, trying to muscle Dave off his podium. The other four men appeared to be happy just sipping their beers and staring at the four beautiful women.

"What on earth was he toasting earlier? Froth Blowers something-or-other?" Apple asked.

Dave started to answer before Andrew had even drawn a breath. *I can piss further than you.* "Ye Ancient Order of Froth Blowers. It's an old English charity that used to raise money for kids way back in the 20s. I guess the founder just wanted an excuse to quaff beers with his mates every Friday night. But it was a noble cause and they genuinely did good work for charities. Anyway, the joke amongst us rugby players is that Mad Mike was a former member, back in the day. He's a benevolent old sod who now just wants to revive the old tradition. So we play rugby, we drink hard, and we raise money for various charities."

"Very noble indeed," said Apple, making a mental note to research this ancient order. Their drinks arrived just as the band started coming back on stage.

"We'll chat some more during the next break," suggested Dave.

Although it had started out as an awkward introduction, it hadn't taken Dax long to win-over the colonel's seven crusty stalwarts. With the band returning to the stage, he excused himself from the group. "Hey Dax, you come back here and chat later huh!" Grayboy called out. In ten short minutes they'd struck up a good rapport.

The six Lotharios had just left the girls' booth and were also meandering back to their seats. Making his way to his own seat, Dax passed within a few feet of where the girls were sitting. Glancing casually in their general direction, he couldn't help notice the four attractive ladies chatting and laughing amongst themselves. But his attention was immediately drawn to Apple: her high cheek bones; her ready smile; the luster of her olive skin. She was truly striking. Their eyes met.

Dax was not only the product of a society that valued good manners, he was also an officer and a gentleman. Having been well-schooled in the niceties of etiquette and chivalry, he knew that staring was considered rude. But Dax stared. And Apple held his gaze. He forgot to look where he was going and stumbled clumsily as he bumped into an unseen chair. Somewhat self-consciously, he forced a smile. *Fuck! Nice way to make an impression, Hunter.*

In return, Apple offered him her own enchanting smile: *I love that you blushed; I like that I mesmerized you for a fleeting moment in time; I think you and I have just connected.*

Dax's reverie was rudely interrupted: Paul McIlroy—the band's lead singer—had just witnessed his awkward stumble. "Oi, you there with the two left feet. Yes you!" He was pointing directly at Dax. "Get yourself up on stage here. Looks like you're in much need of another pint." Dax's team mates all started chanting in unison.

"Dax, Dax, Dax ..."

"Somebody from that long table of crochet blanket salesmen ... pass him a pint, will ya," instructed Paul.

The rugby players hooted at the slight on their masculinity. Up on the stage, with a beer in hand, Dax waited for his cue to down his pint. Any self-respecting reveler at *The Father's Moustache* knew the drill. The band struck-up their stock-in-trade drinking song. "*We'll drink-a-drink-a-drink to Lily the pink-a-*

pink-a-pink ..."

As the band finished playing the ditty, the audience picked up the tempo. To the chorus of "one, two, three ..." Dax started gulping down his beer. Upon downing its contents, he completed the tradition by placing the empty glass upside down on top of his head.

Some of his team mates felt he'd committed an unforgivable sin. "Spillage ... spillage," they heckled good-humoredly.

Inhibitions were being cast aside as the liquor started flowing in earnest. Keeping the crowd on the crest of the wave was what the Blarney Brothers did best. The audience had started to sing along with gusto. As the band tore into *Wild Rover*—a popular Irish drinking song—a hundred merrymakers heartily banged their mugs on the tables.

Dax leant back and craned his neck. He could see her in profile from across the room. Still captivated by her striking smile, he discreetly admired her from a distance. As if knowing she was being watched, Apple turned her head and met his gaze.

Dax didn't want to risk waiting until the next break; he knew his six goatish buddies would definitely go back to try and charm the fine ladies. The band was between songs and Paul had just pulled someone else on stage; the guy was celebrating his birthday and was about to participate in another beer-guzzling ritual.

As a military man, Dax understood the advantages of a preemptive strike: steeling himself, he stood up and walked over to the girls' booth. "Good evening ladies. Would you mind if I joined you?" Dax had already braced himself for a rejection, but it was a gamble he was willing to take.

Inside their booth, and with a table between them, each of the padded bench seats could comfortably fit three people either side. "Scooch on down a bit, honey," said Apple in response to Dax's question. One of the Zimbabwean girls bounced down the long seat to make some space, quickly followed by Apple. Through the seat of his pants, Dax could feel the warmth from where Apple had just been sitting.

"Well, you're probably all wondering why I've called this meeting." Dax didn't know what else to say. He was still recovering from the shock of actually being invited to sit with them. But his quip worked. The girls laughed.

"Okay, Mr. Chairman," said Cathy, playing along, "don't you think you'd better introduce yourself first before you launch straight into business?"

"Ah! A fair question and one that in recent weeks 'as been much on my mind." Dax did his best Eric Idle impersonation. Although the Pythonesque humor was lost on all four of them, it still managed to raise a giggle. "I'm Dax. Dax Hunter." The four ladies introduced themselves.

"Apple, Nova, Fiona, Cathy." Dax shook each of their hands. "It's a pleasure to meet you all. Apple? It's unusual ... I like it. Is that a nickname?" asked Dax. Apple smiled and briefly explained how the name had stuck from when she was a child.

Dax's forearms were resting on the table in front of him. "So, Mr. Dax Hunter, honorable member of ye Ancient Order of Froth Blowers, how does a beer-drinking rugby player get to earn such an impressive scar as that?" Apple pointed at Dax's left forearm. The other three immediately leant in to scrutinize the scar.

Dax never liked situations like this. *Honesty's always best, son.* His father's words were forever etched across his soul. He decided to cross his fingers and go with black humor instead. *Why spoil a perfectly good mood with war stories?* "My evil stepmother tried to sever my hand with a shovel after she caught me stealing marshmallows from the jar, but the shovel was blunt." The girls grimaced in mock horror. Although well disguised, Apple sensed his disquiet and moved to change the subject. She respected the deflection and what it said about his character.

"So your friends who were over here earlier, they're from Zimbabwe. Are you also a Zimbabwean?" asked Apple.

"I certainly am. And you two are both American—that's obvious—and you two are Zimbos, right?" There were subtle differences in regional phonologies; once you knew what to listen for, it wasn't that difficult identifying the origins of a person's accent. A waiter materialized at Dax's shoulder. "Anyone for drinks?" asked Dax.

Each person gave the waiter their own order. "I'll have a vodka, lime and soda again." Apple smiled enigmatically at the waiter. Dax was looking casually in the waiter's direction as he wrote down their order. As Apple finished placing hers, he could've sworn he saw the waiter wink. *A bit familiar*, he thought, but didn't dwell on it.

Apple let her leg brush gently against Dax's thigh. When their eyes had met earlier, there was little doubt in Apple's mind that she was attracted to him. But now she was certain: he was even better up close. Intoxicated by the attraction, she hadn't stopped to consider the danger of mixing business with pleasure. She reconciled her action by convincing herself that nobody—with the exception of Dax—was aware of her flirtatious move below the table. But a vague yet persistent thought kept nagging at the back of her mind: she was still on official business.

Apple had allowed her state of rapture to interfere with her powers of reasoning. In the short time that Dax had been in their company, she had already convinced herself that he was a steady and dependable character. With a supreme effort, she forced herself back into work-mode. She decided now would be a good time to test her assumption. Apple truly hoped he'd match her expectation. "So Dax, earlier on this evening one of your friends said that you guys were going on a charity tour sometime soon." Cathy stiffened. She was certain that neither Dave nor Andrew had mentioned anything of the sort. And the four mute sentries certainly hadn't said anything either— they had just stared dumbly at the girls' cleavages. Although she was alarmed by Apple's fib, she didn't allow her face to betray her concern.

"Oh, *ja?*" answered Dax. His eyes narrowed momentarily.

Inside, Dax seethed. He was furious that the other guys had been so reckless. *Dammit, think Hunter, think.* "*Ja*, we go on these charity tours at the end of every year," he said blandly. Apple had seen the flicker in the corner of his eye. She knew she'd hit a nerve but was both impressed and relieved that he hadn't divulged anything.

Nice move Mr. Hunter. You've just answered me by rephrasing my own question. "So where you guys going then?" she asked. Cathy's alarm bells jangled.

"Didn't the guys tell you already?" Hunter prayed for the right answer.

"No," said Apple airily, "just that you were going on tour someplace." The knot in Dax's stomach eased fractionally.

"I don't remember those guys mentioning anything about a tour," said Nova innocently.

Fiona was just about to say the same thing, but remained silent. *What's with this American girl?*

"Oh, I think it might've been when the waiter interrupted us to take our order," said Apple. *Heck. That was a dumb-ass thing to do.* Apple chided herself for being so clumsy. *Stop letting your ovaries interfere, girl.*

"So how long have you been in South Africa?" Even though Dax knew he needed to change the subject, a section of his brain was trying to process what had just happened. *One girl fishes about our destination while another denies the lads even mentioned it in the first place. Tread warily, Hunter, this girl's up to something.*

"Please excuse me for a moment. I'll answer that when I get back. Which way's the bathroom?" asked Apple. She felt an overwhelming urge to splash cold water on her face.

"I need to go too, I'll come with you," said Cathy.

The two CIA agents entered the bathroom. Cathy quickly pushed each of the four stall doors inwards. Satisfied they were alone, she spun around on her colleague. "Apple, I barely know you. You strike me as being a very capable operator and Elroy speaks highly of you. But in Jesus' name, what just happened out there? That was downright amateurish. You are here to do a job tonight, not flirt with the fucking Rhodesians. Goddamn it, you're meant to be the sober one here."

Apple was contrite. She was about to take ownership of her blunder when the door pushed open and two older ladies stumbled in. It looked like their faces needed repainting. "So I told her, 'Janet honey, you can have him … he's got herpes anyway.'" Cathy changed gears effortlessly; in a split second she segued from international spy to a loose-tongued gossip monger.

"Amen to that," slurred the larger of the two lushes.

Cathy gave Apple a sisterly hug and whispered in her ear. "Just be cool, that's all." They returned to the table.

Returning from the bathroom, the two Americans slid back into their seats. Although Dax had been chatting amiably with the two Zimbabwean girls, the conversation became wooden after the two Americans rejoined the party.

Apple's spontaneous smile had evaporated. The whole episode had toppled Dax's gyro. Certain that she was following some hidden agenda, the pilot started doubting her sincerity. But there was another part of him that still wanted to reach out and get to know her better—he couldn't deny the attraction he felt toward her.

But somewhere in the recesses of his memory, Dax recalled the story of the bewitching Mata Hari—a bohemian seductress who purportedly played both sides during World War One.

34

ELANGENI

Apple had been in South Africa a little over a fortnight. She and Elroy had relocated to Durban in order to be closer to Colonel 'Mad' Mike Hoare—the coup's principal logistician and leader. Although still part of the planning team, it was apparent that Marty Docheck hadn't quite reconciled the fact that his agency, the NIS, had been supplanted by the Defense Intelligence Division. Professional jealousies obviously ran deep. On more than one occasion Elroy had to exercise his powers of diplomacy in order to keep the peace. Without them, the project ran the risk of veering off the tracks.

The Seychelles coup was scheduled to launch in two weeks. Although everything still appeared to be in order, something was nagging at the back of Elroy's mind. "Apple, I want you to do a background search for me on one of our soldiers. His name is Dax Hunter."

Apple's breath snagged at the back of her throat. "Sure Elroy." She disguised her alarm. "There a particular reason why him?"

"His name keeps on scratching at my memory banks but I just can't seem to place it." He rubbed his chin contemplatively. "Listen, the South Africans have already given us a dossier on each of the members in Hoare's party. I think it'd be wise if we spread our search a little wider. Don't only focus on Hunter. I want you to perform a CIA check on every mercenary. If anyone on this team is even vaguely left-leaning they could leak word to the Soviets. Not only does it put individual soldier's lives at risk, but it could jeopardize the whole mission. A failed coup attempt will do irreparable damage to South Africa's reputation on the international stage. It'll do us no harm to double-check the Defense Intelligence Division's background checks."

Apple exhaled slowly. In the days after the *Father's Moustache* incident, she had waited anxiously for a rebuke from Elroy. But none had been forthcoming. Cathy had chosen not to inform Elroy of her colleague's professional indiscretion. Apple owed her one.

Complying with an array of protocol checks, Apple eventually established a secure connection with the CIA mainframe in Langley, Virginia. After each prompt, she punched in a sequence of codes. Any incorrect entry would automatically block her access for three hours. Thirty seconds passed. *REQUEST APPROVED*. Apple pushed *SEND*. She knew from experience that the to-and-fro exchange could take several minutes. She drummed her fingers anxiously while waiting for Langley to respond.

At precisely the same time, over two thousand miles away, the printer in the KGB's office in Victoria started chattering. From his new office in the Seychelles' capital, Morozov had made contact with a KGB colleague in Harare just hours before. He had requested information on the whereabouts of one Dax Hunter, last known occupation, Air Force of Zimbabwe pilot.

Line by laborious line, the carriage inked, then re-inked each string of text. Morozov drummed his fingers impatiently.

Routing via Criggion, the top-secret Cold War communications base in Wales, Apple's encoded message surged along the network of undersea cables. Originating in the CIA's Headquarters, the information zigzagged across the Atlantic Ocean, eventually routing to a terminal in Durban, South

Africa. Several minutes later her newfangled HP laser printer blinked into life. Apple collected her three page document from the tray and turned toward her desk. *Three pages?* She wondered.

Morozov tore off his document at the second perforation and walked over to the coffee urn. He scanned the document while refilling his cup. The first two pages revealed nothing he already didn't know. Then the bombshell:

> *Air Lieutenant Dax Hunter (Force #44820) Air Force of Zimbabwe, 7 Squadron pilot, resigned 15 August 1981.*

Morozov checked the date. *Less than two fucking months ago.* He could taste the hatred sticking in his craw. He forced himself to read the last few lines.

> *Subject is believed to have emigrated to South Africa with the intention of joining the South African Air Force.*

The document ended with a short footnote.

> *CIO advises that subject should be held for interrogation by this department if he tries to re-enter Zimbabwe.*

After independence, Zimbabwe's Central Intelligence Organization had become paranoid about the intentions of ex-Rhodesian security force members trying to return to their country.

Apple hurried back to her desk. She was eager to discover how or why the CIA had already accumulated three pages' worth of background intelligence on Dax Hunter. She started reading the document. Her brow furrowed. *This is not about Dax Hunter.* Despite her carefully encrypted request for information on LAST: *Hunter*, FIRST: *Dax*, NATIONALITY: *Zimbabwe*, the CIA system had spat out a three page profile on a known KGB operative: LAST: *Morozov*, FIRST: *Vladimir*, NATIONALITY: *USSR.*

Frustrated by the mix-up, she flipped to the second page, then the last. A photograph of Morozov's disfigured face stared back at her from the page; she shuddered involuntarily. As Apple scanned the rest of the document, her eyes widened in disbelief. Dax Hunter's name sprang off the page.

> *SOURCE OF INFORMATION: KGB 'Sotto Voce'*
> *POINT OF CONTACT: 'Ampersand#12'*
> *DATE OF ORIGINATION: 02/19/79*
> *TIME OF ORIGINATION: 2140 Zulu*
> *OFFICE OF ORIGINATION: CIA, Lusaka.*
> *REPORT: Morozov, Vladimir (KGB Directorate 'A' of FSB Special Purpose Center to Africa) was admitted to Lusaka General Hospital on 02/13/79 for serious facial and abdominal injuries. Wounds likely sustained in an encounter with a Rhodesian Air Force Alouette III gunship following the downing of Air Rhodesia civilian passenger aircraft on 02/12/79. Source is confident that Morozov led the team that fired the Strela-2 missile (Russian code), SA-7 Grail (NATO code) that struck the aircraft, killing all 59 souls. Source reports that pilot of Alouette III helicopter has been positively identified as Hunter, Dax. Source speculates that Morozov is obsessed with avenging the injuries inflicted upon him by Hunter, Dax.*

After reading the entire report, Apple hurried over to Elroy's office. "Boss, this is important." She knocked but didn't wait for his response.

"What's up?"

"You know you said earlier that Hunter's name was so familiar, but you couldn't place it?" Apple had to control her breathing.

"Yeah."

"And your designated cipher in Zambia was *Ampersand Twelve*, right?"

"That was me," he said, looking at her quizzically.

"And *Sotto Voce* was your Russian double agent in Lusaka?"

"Yeah, Quiet *Voice,* but c'mon girl, get to the point," demanded Elroy.

"Well, sir, here's a report you might remember. You filed this from Lusaka on February 19, 1979. In it you describe how your mole informed you about a KGB agent in Lusaka who's fixated on taking his revenge on Dax Hunter." Apple looked smug as she offered him the last page of the report.

Elroy took a minute to scan the sheet. "Jesus! How could I have forgotten that damn name? Of course I remember the Russian guy's name … darn, I should've remembered the Rhodesian though." His voice trailed off as he handed the sheet back to her. "I remember taking that goddamn photograph. Does the last paragraph tell us anything about Morozov's latest whereabouts?"

"Yes boss. He went back to Moscow after his hospital discharge and transferred over to the Third Chief Directorate for a while. He then transferred back to the Alfa team and took a posting in Angola in September 1980. He certainly gets around."

Elroy held a clenched fist up to his face. Apple knew it was his thinking pose. "I get the feeling something's not right here Apple. He's been in two KGB divisions that we know of, and he's come back to Africa a second time with Alfa team … two postings to Southern Africa in quick succession? Even for the unpredictable KGB, that doesn't add up."

Elroy sat back in his chair and gave her a look she knew well. *Here comes a challenging assignment.* She relished those the most.

"I want you to call up all our resources and find out where the hell this guy Morozov is right now, and what he's up to. Even reach out to my man *Sotto Voce,* if that'll help. Morozov's taken his injuries personally and I reckon he's hellbent on revenge. He's probably working off-reservation and my guess is that he's using his KGB status to provide just the right amount of camouflage to fulfill his quest. Angola's not that far away. If he's been using it as a base to track Hunter's whereabouts, odds are he could've discovered something about *Operation Angela.* Apple, we simply have to ensure that this mission to Seychelles isn't compromised in any way." As Apple turned to leave, Elroy called out to her. "One last thing, I want you to arrange a meeting with Dax Hunter. Soon … and make it somewhere discreet. South African spies get jumpy when they see a white guy in public with a black dude."

Down in the lobby of the Elangeni hotel, Dax waited for the next elevator to whisk him up to the ninth floor. The Elangeni was next door to the Malibu—the same hotel where he'd met the enigmatic American woman at the *Father's Moustache* just a few weeks prior. Part of him regretted not asking her for her number, but her odd behavior that night had quelled his interest. Despite the strange encounter, Dax still struggled to get her out of his mind.

Entering the elevator, Dax's mind switched to the conversation he'd had with Dev the day before. Weary of phone taps, Dev had called Dax and told him to meet for a beer at their local watering hole. Over a cold Lion Lager, Dev informed him that he was required to meet some of the senior coup planners in the Elangeni hotel the following day. It was three days before the mercenaries were due to launch their Seychelles mission. Like some of the other soldiers, Dev noticed that his friend was getting uneasy. He gave Dax every assurance that it was a routine meeting and that he had nothing to be concerned about.

Dax pressed the bell for room 921. A few moments later, the door was pulled open by a tall black man. "Forgive me," said Dax, "I must have the wrong room."

He was already turning away when Elroy responded. "Dax. Dax Hunter. You have the right room, please come in."

Although caught off-balance, Dax's only reassurance was the man's American accent: he knew the Yanks were secretly sanctioning the coup plot. He entered warily. Elroy checked the corridor then hung the *DO NOT DISTURB* sign on the handle. Dax was still watching the big American and hadn't yet noticed the presence of a third person. Still cautious, he turned to enter the room. The Rhodesian was caught entirely off guard as Apple rose from her chair. "Oh, it's you," was all he could manage. *What the hell is this about?*

"Hello Dax, good to see you again." Apple offered her hand.

"Glad to see you two have already met. My name's Elroy. It's a pleasure to meet you Dax." They shook hands. "Won't you take a seat?" Elroy poured each of them a Coke. After dispensing with the pleasantries, he moved straight to the point. "Colonel Hoare has no doubt told you and your team that this operation has been sanctioned by the South African Prime Minister. While this is entirely a South African initiative, the Americans have a vested interest in the outcome. We are not physically involving ourselves in any way with this plot, but we nonetheless appreciate the fact that the South Africans have allowed us to monitor its progress from the sidelines. Unofficially, Apple and I represent the USA's interests in this venture." Although Elroy didn't say as much, Dax assumed they were CIA. The American continued speaking in general terms and spent a few minutes talking about the forthcoming putsch.

Elroy was competing for Dax's attention: with Apple's unexpected presence, the pilot had to force himself to concentrate. *Stay focused Hunter. Apple is CIA? I should've guessed. It all makes sense now.*

With Apple a mere observer, Elroy pressed Dax for some of his thoughts regarding the plot. The Rhodesian sensed it was merely a preamble. "Dax, enough of the chit-chat ... before I explain exactly why you're here, I need to clarify something of great importance. I need you to tell me everything that happened on the day after the downing of the Viscount in February 1979. You'll understand why in a few minutes."

For the second time since entering the room, Dax was

caught off-guard. He didn't even bother asking how the Americans knew that he was involved in that *particular* follow-up operation. *Fuckers probably know my bowel movements.*

Calculating his options, Dax elected to be candid. He explained the sequence of events that had led up to the encounter on the banks of the Zambezi River, and his and Beaver's subsequent crash into the tall elephant grass.

"Can you give us a description of the three guys that you encountered on the river bank?" asked Apple.

"I can't describe any of their physical characteristics. We were being shot at from behind thick cover and ..." Dax paused. In a moment of clarity, he recalled a conversation he'd had with Beaver. It had been in the hangar shortly after his convalescence in Inyanga. "Wait a minute," he said. "My door gunner told me something about a month later that I never bothered to follow up on."

Both Elroy's and Apple's attention piqued. "Go on," Elroy encouraged.

"Beaver—he was my door gunner—said he was absolutely certain that one of the guys shooting at us was a Caucasian. I argued that it must've been an albino but he was adamant it was a Caucasian."

"Did Beaver say whether he injured the guy or not?" pressed Elroy.

"Yeah, actually he did. He said the guy had a lot of blood on his face." Dax paused and looked at each of them. "Okay, now it's your turn to tell me what this has to do with Seychelles?"

Elroy looked at Apple and nodded. After taking a sip of her Coke, she opened a folder that lay in front of her. "Dax, have you ever seen this man before?"

Dax felt light-headed as a flood of tiny icicles surged through his veins. The back of his throat tasted like rusty iron. "Holy shit! I know that man. I've seen him before. Is this the guy from the river?" Dax knew he was gabbling. "Hold on! I saw him in Athens. What the fuck is going on here?" Ordinarily, Dax would never curse in front of a woman, but his anger had gotten the best of him.

"Okay, cool down Dax. I'll tell you everything we know. Everything," assured Apple. "But firstly, you said you know him. How?"

Dax had to gather his thoughts; he was still reeling from the shock of seeing the man's face. After gulping down the rest of his drink, he began to explain how he and Achilles had seen the man sprinting past them as they were leaving the Olympic village. "Wait a minute, you're an Olympic athlete?" interrupted Apple. Elroy shot her a look.

"*Ja*, archery." Dax went on to describe the incident on the evening Achilles' father was shot. He told them how they'd been convinced that the intruder was after Yiannos, Achilles, or perhaps both of them. "Of course it never occurred to me that this guy was after me."

"We've discovered that he holds *you* responsible for his disfiguring scar," said Elroy. "Apparently he was also badly injured in the groin. Dax, it appears he wants to exact his revenge on you for his injuries. Based on what you've just told us, I think it's obvious that his infatuation with your demise indicates a deep-seated psychological problem. My guess is that he has sociopathic, perhaps even psychopathic tendencies," ventured Elroy.

"Who is he?" asked Dax.

"He's a Russian KGB operative by the name of Morozov," said Apple. "We know he came back to Africa soon after the incident in Greece, and his last known location is Angola. We suspect he managed to engineer a transfer back here to hunt you down. We're desperately trying to establish exactly where he is now. The thing is, whatever his assignment is in Angola, you are at the epicenter of his troubled world."

"Wait-a-fucking-minute," yelled Dax angrily. "This bastard shoots down a plane load of *my* people ... innocent civilians, and he's coming after *me*? Fuck him! I'm going to go after this goddamn psycho myself." A volatile brew of rage and revenge was clouding Dax's judgment. He fought to contain his emotions.

There was a long pause before Elroy spoke. "Dax, we're really sorry to have to do this to you, but I just can't let you go to the Seychelles."

"What do you mean?" Dax was incredulous.

"Odds are that Morozov's vendetta against you could easily compromise the Seychelles job. It's not only him that's preoccupied with you, but you're now also distracted by him."

"Well Elroy, distractions like this would cause most men to become dazzled by the headlights, wouldn't they?" Dax was grim. "But these circumstances are as extreme as you can get." Dax didn't realize he'd bunched both his fists. "I assure you, I'm not distracted in the slightest. In fact, my mind couldn't be more focused than it is right now."

"I understand that Dax. But until we get hard evidence, we can't be certain that Morozov is still in Angola. Besides, with the resources at his disposal, he's probably been tracking your movements. God forbid, but there's even the chance that he might've found out about your forthcoming involvement in Seychelles." Elroy let that fact sink in before continuing.

"Since we've discovered the link between you and him, we've ascertained that he's served in three specialized KGB units. That's three times the training of the best elite soldier out there. Dax, this guy is a loose cannon. What makes him more dangerous is that he appears to be operating outside of his assigned ambit. Dax, eliminating you is definitely not the kind of task that the KGB would consider sanctioning. Sorry to tell you this, but you're just not *that* much of a threat to the Soviet Union right now." Neither Apple nor Dax appeared to appreciate Elroy's wry humor. "But seriously Dax, you are in grave danger, regardless of whether you go to Seychelles or not."

"Well it's pointless waiting for *him* to come and find *me*. He'll always have the advantage, won't he?" It was a rhetorical question. "I have to be proactive. The way I see it, I'm on my own here … I'll just have to go after him myself."

"Well then Dax, what I have to say next might just be music to your ears," said Elroy cryptically. Dax looked at the

American inquiringly. "Let's talk about the real reason we called you here today." Elroy looked intently at Dax. "We want to offer you a job with the CIA."

"You want to do what?" Hunter was astonished.

"Are you familiar with the current situation in Nicaragua?" Elroy asked.

"Not particularly, no."

"Former President Somoza was no angel but the USA found him, how can I put this?, easy to work with. Ever since the Cuban Revolution, a sympathetic wave of avant-garde fervor has swept across Central America. Care to guess what ideology these revolutionaries share?"

"Communism," said Dax.

"Correct. In July 1979 Somoza was ousted by just such a group: they call themselves the Sandinistas. After they seized power, the majority of Nicaragua's middle class fled the country, fearful of this group's communistic intentions." Elroy paused to take a sip of his drink.

"*Ja*, I've heard of the Sandinistas," said Dax.

"Carter, our last president, was initially eager to work with the new Nicaraguan regime. He sent them heaps of aid money. Only problem there was that we soon discovered that the Sandinistas, in turn, were supporting communist rebels in neighboring El Salvador. In effect, we were funding the communists. And America wasn't going to tolerate that!

"Meantime, dissatisfaction with the Sandinista regime was starting to foment amongst a significant part of the local populace. They felt as if the new government was betraying the popular ideals upon which they'd ridden into power. And so arose the so-called Contras—militant right-wingers opposed to the left-wing Sandinista government. Right now there are several Contra groups, but all share the same goal ... to oust the Sandinistas. And we, the Americans, are going to help them achieve that goal. One of our objectives is to try and blend these ragtag Contra entities into one big happy unified force."

"And you want me to do what, precisely?" asked Dax.

"This is a delicate situation for the Americans. We're

engaged in another proxy Cold War conflict. Of course we can apply sanctions to destabilize their economy, but we can't go in directly with guns blazing. With Reagan's blessings, the CIA has established a number of front companies to train, clothe, supervise and support the Contras in any way possible. The CIA has already established training facilities in neighboring Costa Rica and Honduras. If you join us you will be employed by one of these front companies. Along with flying duties in-and-out of Nicaragua, you'll also get involved in devising, coordinating, implementing and training the Contras in their new protocols and strategies."

Dax looked unconvinced. "You're forgetting there's a madman out there trying to kill me. I need to figure out how to deal with that, don't I? Then maybe I'll consider your offer."

"Dax, this drama has already played-out on a wide stage," said Apple pragmatically. "Clearly Morozov doesn't intend resting until you're eliminated. The hallmark of a psychopath is the quest for immediate gratification. He won't simply forget about you as time goes by. He's coming after you, probably even as we speak, and he won't stop until he's found you."

"He's a KGB professional capable of drawing on a formidable network to help him hunt you down," interjected Elroy. "The only hope you have of meeting the threat head-on is if you too can draw on the resources of an equally formidable network. If you join us, I'll assign Apple as your handler. The CIA will do everything in its power to help you track Morozov," said Elroy earnestly.

"You've got me over a barrel, haven't you?"

"No Dax. This is two-way. While you work for us, you get to tap into the world's preeminent spy agency. I guarantee you'll need *that* kind of backing if you want to find Morozov."

"When would you want me to start?"

"You don't even want to know the package we're offering you?" smiled Elroy.

Given the revelation of the Greece incident, Dax realized he was now a hunted man. His life had taken a wholly unexpected turn. Under the circumstances, Elroy's offer was his best chance. "Your assistance in helping me locate Morozov is sufficient compensation," said Dax, semi-seriously.

"You could start right away," said Elroy. "This whole CIA operation in Central America is headed-up by a colleague of ours ... a guy called Sneddon. He recruited Apple into the CIA a few years back. All-round good guy. We've already spoken to him about bringing you on board and he has sanctioned the whole idea. You and Apple could leave for the States later this week ... get yourself processed into the fold, as it were. Then make your way down to Costa Rica as soon as possible."

A few days prior, with Sneddon on speaker phone, Apple and Elroy had discussed Dax's recruitment in detail. Privately, Apple had harbored doubts that the ex-Rhodesian would accept their proposal. However, with the way the conversation in the hotel room was unfolding, she was almost certain he would come aboard. In the moments after Dax had indicated his interest in their offer, Apple's face had flushed with expectation. She hoped neither of the two men had noticed her reaction.

In the build-up to the coup, Colonel Hoare had encouraged his disparate bunch of Seychelles mercenaries to forge soldierly bonds. But there was a caveat: he didn't want them socializing in large groups. The risk of detection was just too great. Their earlier gathering at *Father's Moustache* had been the one exception. After their night of revelry a month before, Dax and Corporal Fonseca had formed a strong friendship. Both were avid surfers and had spent many enjoyable hours testing their skills off Durban's Battery Beach. While Dax wasn't at liberty to discuss the details of his conversation with Elroy and Apple, he nevertheless wanted to meet with his new buddy face-to-face. Besides offering some kind of explanation, Dax also wanted to tell Fonseca to watch his back in the Seychelles.

"Yes Fons, I'm pulling out," said Dax.

"Man, I can't believe it," Fonseca shook his head. "Why so late?"

"The South African Air Force has made me a firm offer.

It's a career decision. Their own Intelligence Division is aware of the island mission and they've said they'll withdraw the offer if I involve myself with the plan." Dax felt terrible. Regardless of whether Fonseca was a friend or not, he just hated lying. But Dax simply couldn't tell his friend the truth.

Although Fonseca tried to force a smile, Dax could see his buddy was upset. But the corporal's eyes quickly lit-up as he shifted on his barstool and dug in his pocket. "Here. This is a present for you. I want you to have it. That old air force survival knife of yours is so Daniel Boone." Fonseca reached over and pressed the Matsuda knife into Dax's palm. "I won it in a game of poker in Angola. It's a Matsuda ... I hope you appreciate it's crafted by a Japanese master," he said with a twinkle in his eye.

Dax opened the blade and heft the knife in his palm. From the look and feel alone, he could sense that it was a beautifully crafted tool. "I can't Fons, really. This is ..."

"No. This is yours. It's a gift. You can't refuse a gift," insisted Fonseca.

Dax folded the blade away and turned the knife over in his hand. "What's *V I U M?*" he asked, reading the inscription etched into the handle.

"Fuck knows. As I said, I won it in a poker game. It looks like Latin shit or something."

Dev got lucky. With barely two days to go to launch, he desperately needed to find a military pilot to replace Dax. Fortuitously, his network of ex-soldiers provided the lead he sought: Baz—also an ex-Rhodesian Air Force pilot—was hastily recruited onto the team and apprised of the coup's final plans.

With members of the advance party already inserted in the Seychelles, Colonel Hoare and the rest of his band of AOFBs boarded a Royal Swazi National Airways charter flight on November 25th, 1981. They were scheduled to land in the Seychelles later that afternoon.

In the three days since their meeting in the Elangeni, Elroy and Apple had doubled their efforts to track Morozov's whereabouts. Reaching into their worldwide network of informants, associates and deep-level agents, the best they got was that he was still in Angola.

Cathy had just finished her final university exam. Unburdened of her academic responsibilities, Elroy had called her to come and assist them in the office over the duration of the coup. The next few days were likely to be both busy and stressful. They all knew they were in for a few sleepless nights. Apple had brought some bedding to the office so they could rotate shifts on the radio and get some rest in between.

Against Elroy's better judgment, Hoare had elected to fly into Seychelles with their arsenal of weapons. The CIA man had pleaded with Hoare to ship them over in a container beforehand. Their first hurdle would be to successfully smuggle seventy-five AK-47 rifles, twenty-four thousand rounds of ammunition, forty hand grenades and a hundred rockets aboard their Royal Swazi charter flight. Exerting some of his considerable influence, Docheck had arranged for both the Head of Airport Security, as well as the Senior Air Traffic Controller, to keep Elroy apprised of Colonel Hoare's progress through the airport.

Elroy and his two colleagues had been immensely relieved to hear that the Royal Swazi flight had eventually departed without incident.

It was a five hour flight to the islands. The aircraft had been airborne for just under two hours when Elroy's bulky satellite phone began buzzing. In order to guarantee a good line-of-sight connection, the phone stood near an open window. Elroy strode over to retrieve it off the desk. He checked the code on the small screen. "It's Langley," he murmured. He pushed the RECEIVE button. "This is *Exclamation Twelve*," he answered. All the agents' ciphers were changed regularly. A long period of silence followed as Elroy listened intently to his caller. His mouth started to fall open. He looked across at his two colleagues. They could sense the news was bad. "Alright, thank you Langley," he said glumly, killing the connection.

"What is it? What's happened?" insisted Cathy.

Elroy shook his head as if to clear the unpalatable news. "You're not going to believe this. Morozov was recently transferred to the Seychelles. It's just too much of a damn coincidence. He must've found out about Dax 's participation in the coup and wants to be there in person to take him out." Elroy turned and looked out the window. It took him all of eight seconds to reach a decision. "This mission has been compromised. Get hold of my counterpart at South African Defense Intelligence Division. I need to tell him to call that plane back."

Perched on a table next to Morozov's desk, the Teletype machine beeped four times. *Fuck it! It's 5:30. I want to go and find a whore.* The machine came to life a few seconds later. Morozov waited impatiently for the printer to spew-out its message. The missive originated from the KGB office in Nairobi.

> *Beechcraft Super King Air 200C Reg N821CA owned by Bill Parkinson (Kenyan national and known British agent), scheduled to fly Mombasa to Seychelles Nov 26 1981. Pax listed as American tourists:*
> *Mr. & Mrs. Morgan*
> *Mr. & Mrs. Bowman*
> *Mr. Nescott*
> *All are fake names. Mr. & Mrs. Morgan are aliases and have been identified as Mr. James Mancham and his wife. HE IS THE DEPOSED PRESIDENT OF SEYCHELLES.*
> *Parkinson's aircraft is leased to Sunbird Aviation. Sunbird is owned by Lord Andrew Cole, 7th Earl of Enniskillen. Cole has close ties with Kenyan Constitutional Affairs Minister, Charles Njonjo, and both have been linked to international arms dealer Adnan Khashoggi. Gerard Hoareau—a cabinet*

minister in Mancham's deposed government—was seen meeting with Njonjo in Nairobi on Nov 5 1981. Paul Chow, also a known associate of Mancham, arrived in Nairobi on Nov 13 1981 for further meetings with Hoareau and Njonjo.
Be aware that signs indicate a potential and imminent coup d'état in Seychelles. Analysts believe Mancham's arrival will coincide with the declaration of a possible new government.

Morozov checked his watch. *Fuck it. 17:38. It'll take me more than half an hour to get to the airport.* He picked up the phone and dialed airport security. One of Morozov's responsibilities had included an evaluation of Seychellois security at key installations—one of them being the airport. All the staff knew about the hard-man from Russia. The phone rang six times before being picked up. "This is Morozov, do you know who I am?" he growled into the phone.

"Yes sir, I know who sir is. Can I help you, sir?"

"This is not a drill. This is not an exercise. I want you and your security team to examine every passenger, and I mean *every* passenger, that comes through Customs and Immigration. Do you understand? This is urgent. I will be there in thirty minutes." Morozov was about to hang up. "Wait! So far, what passenger aircraft have come in this afternoon?"

"We've had Air India from Bombay, Air Seychelles from Düsseldorf and a Royal Swazi Airways charter flight from South Africa, sir," said the security official. Morozov calculated the odds.

"When did the flight from South Africa arrive?"

"They are coming through customs right now, sir."

"Fuck it! Check every one of those passengers. Now!" Morozov slammed down the phone and sprinted out the office.

The shirt buttons over the customs official's belly strained to contain his enormous girth. With little enthusiasm for the task at hand, he dabbed incessantly at his shiny brow. There was no indication that he intended rising from his chair anytime soon.

Using his free hand, he signaled for the next tourist to come through. Sidling forward in the queue, Fonseca had been watching him distractedly. *This is going to be like clubbing seals.* Scanning the other queues in the arrivals hall, Fonseca noticed that the majority of the AOFBs had already passed through the other customs checkpoints. Including himself, there were just three more mercenaries to clear the final obstacle.

Looking beyond where the large man sat, Fonseca noticed a faded sign nailed to an office door. *AIRPORT PERSONNEL ONLY.* The door suddenly burst open. A gangly, dark-skinned official poked his head out. He shouted something in Creole. Working his limbs like an upended tortoise, the fat man struggled out of his seat. "Next," he beckoned for Fonseca to step forward.

Fonseca kept his composure. *Okay, be cool Fons.*

"Anything to declare?" asked the sweaty tortoise man.

"No, just a whole bunch of toys for distribution to the local children's charities around Mahé," said Fons.

"Please open your bag," demanded the official. Fons endeavored to lift the bag as effortlessly as possible. It was weighed down by a concealed AK-47 assault rifle, along with half a dozen grenades. He unzipped the top compartment. The official rummaged around inside and found nothing but toys. Satisfied that all was in order, he slid the bag down the steel table to make space for the last tourist's bag. Notwithstanding his general apathy, even the fat guy could tell that the weight of the bag exceeded the expected weight of the toys. Using both hands, he lifted the bag an inch off the table and let it drop. *Clunk!*

Despite his training as a special-forces soldier, Fonseca froze.

Working the seams of the canvas bag with his sausage fingers, the official found the concealed compartment. Drops of sweat pooled on the steel surface as he gingerly opened the hidden zipper. The fat man bent forward to peer into the dark recess. A muzzle stared menacingly back at him. With an agility belying his size, he turned and sprinted for the sanctuary of the security control room. He screamed like a ghoul denied redemption.

Trevor, the last mercenary in the queue, had been watching closely. He withdrew his AK-47, cocked the weapon and fired at the retreating official. Pandemonium broke loose. The rest of the team, by now safely through customs, heard the gunshots ringing out. They grabbed their bags and sprinted back into the hall.

Colonel 'Mad' Mike Hoare's ambitious coup plot had just been thwarted. And it had also claimed its first casualty. One of Trevor's rounds had accidentally struck Fonseca. Dax's friend lay dying in a pool of blood on the floor of Seychelles International Airport.

35

FORENSICS

The Soviet Army's Head of Forensics wasn't exactly renowned for his tempo; it was no surprise therefore that he faced an enormous backlog. But what he lacked in speed he more than made up for in thoroughness. Although it frustrated his superiors enormously, his success rate appeared to justify his pedestrian approach.

All of the physical evidence collected at Colonel Alexeev's dacha had been locked in the department's vault for over a year. Dr Kuznetsov scanned the register in search of his next case. Armed with a reference number, he unlocked the vault, found the corresponding crate, removed the file and repaired to his office. His first task was to familiarize himself with the details of the case.

The first page was written by the Head of the Moscow Branch of the Third Chief Directorate. From the tone of his report, it was apparent that the *Osobye Otdely* was entirely satisfied with the circumstances under which their agent, Vladimr Morozov, had apprehended and extracted a confession from Colonel Alexeev. The report concluded that the ensuing gunfight had left Morozov no choice but to shoot back in self-defense.

The forensic expert remembered the incident and was inclined to agree that it was an open-and-shut case. Even the unflappable Dr Kuznetsov had been repulsed by the colonel's reputed links to child trafficking. But, as in the past, his training forced him to keep an open mind.

He took almost an hour to digest and memorize the details and photographs contained in the report. He was troubled by the fact that the KGB-Third Chief Directorate had elected to withhold certain physical evidence: the old Parus-301 cassette recorder, as well as the cassette on which the colonel's confession had been recorded. A footnote simply stated that the transcript alone, appended to the file, would suffice. *I wonder what other evidence the KGB has buried?* He soon discovered from the Physical Evidence List that they'd also withheld Morozov's Makarov PM pistol.

As far as interrogations went, Kuznetsov was inclined to think that the dialogue between Morozov and Alexeev was straightforward and routine: but what he really wanted to hear was the mood and nuance between the two men on that fateful night. He made a mental note to get his superior to request the cassette from the KGB; perhaps even Morozov's weapon. He knew he was being ambitious. There was no love lost between the two entities.

After clipping the enlarged images of Alexeev's fingerprints into the wall-mounted light-box, Kuznetsov proceeded to lift the prints off the cartridges recovered from the scene. He did the same with the colonel's vodka bottle. As expected, two of the cartridges bore the fingerprints of an unknown individual. *Presumably Morozov's,* deduced the doctor. *Another omission from the case file—a set of Morozov's fingerprints.* He then turned his attention to Alexeev's personal weapon. A sarcastic smile creased the doctor's mouth. *Luckily for me this is military property … the KGB couldn't withhold this piece of evidence.*

After two hours of painstaking analysis, the forensic expert placed a call to his superior.

Smirnov was young for a lieutenant-colonel. Tracking his stellar progress, it was obvious that his superiors had rewarded his aptitude and dedication. He was renowned, if not feared, for his penchant for challenging the system. He bustled into Kuznetsov's laboratory. "This better be important comrade."

"*Podpolkovnik*, I think you will be interested in this." As an added mark of respect, Kuznetsov addressed his superior by his rank. "I was able to lift a perfect set of prints off the colonel's weapon. There was no contamination. I found the prints of four of his fingers on his weapon, which in itself is strange, but not entirely unexpected. If the thumb is used to pull back the hammer, it will of course leave a thumbprint. But that action is not a prerequisite for firing a semi-automatic pistol. Regardless of that, the odds of a shooter's thumbprint *not* appearing on his weapon are very slim."

"What is the relevance? Come to the point please doctor."

"Please bear with me *podpolkovnik*. According to my ballistics analysis, I can prove that the bullets extracted from the walls in the dacha were indeed fired from Alexeev's weapon. So far there's nothing untoward there. But that very fact suggests that Alexeev's weapon must have been cocked beforehand in order to be able to fire."

"That is obvious doctor ... you are speaking to a soldier, remember?" Smirnov was getting impatient.

"Yes *podpolkovnik*, but the prints all over the outside of the weapon are from Alexeev's right hand only. I know there are single-handed techniques used for cocking a weapon, but that is a technique used in extreme circumstances when one hand has become disabled for whatever reason. The prints on Alexeev's vodka bottle are from both hands ... that suggests that both his hands were fully functional in the time leading up to his death. From the crime scene photographs of Alexeev's body, I can see no evidence of injury to either hand."

"This better be leading somewhere conclusive doctor, I am a busy man. Sometimes soldiers practice the technique of disassembling and reassembling their weapons with one hand. It improves dexterity; it hones martial awareness; it increases weapon familiarity and prepares the soldier for unforeseen battleground situations. I am not convinced that you have discovered anything unusual here at all, doctor. Unless you have something conclusive, I will bid you good day."

"Please *podpolkovnik*, just one more minute. I beseech you."

Smirnov turned around reluctantly. "Yes, I understand everything you've said about single-handed weapons drills. But here's the interesting bit. Firstly, I would argue that practicing dexterous weapons drills would not be the colonel's priority when he has a bottle of vodka to entertain him. Secondly, the reason the prints were so clear is because the weapon had not been cleaned in a long time. There was barely any gun oil evident on the weapon. Why practice such advanced reassembling techniques if you aren't going to spend some time ensuring the serviceability of your weapon?"

"I believe you might be right, doctor. With due respect to the deceased, he was way past his glory days as a hero of Stalingrad," said Smirnov. "Please. Go on."

"I then disassembled the weapon and dusted all the internal parts for prints. I find it very strange that the prints from a single hand appear all over the *outside* of the weapon, yet the prints of *both* his hands appear all over the *inside;* on the components that remain hidden, unless the weapon is disassembled."

"I concede that does sound strange," said the lieutenant-colonel.

"But this is the best part *podpolkovnik*. The prints on the outside of Alexeev's weapon are from his right hand. His personnel file says the colonel was left handed. To support this, there are several photographs on record that show him signing documents left-handed."

"So what is your conclusion, doctor?"

"I am of the belief that Alexeev's weapon was wiped clean before being pressed into his right hand. As it turns out, it was the wrong hand," concluded the doctor.

Smirnov narrowed his eyes and thought for a moment. "What do you suggest doctor?"

"The circumstances are beyond suspicious. I believe we should insist that the KGB hand over the missing cassette as well as Morozov's weapon. More importantly, they must bring him in for routine questioning … by our own investigators. The report shows that the KGB made no effort to interview him after the incident. For the sake of thoroughness I would also need permission to exhume the colonel's body."

Holding the mouthpiece eight inches from his face, the Moscow chief of Alfa Directorate 'A' raged down the phone. "Let me give you a little history lesson, Comrade Smirnov. The man you are asking me to hand over is a hero of the Motherland. In fact I am recommending him for the Order of Lenin. He has done more in his four year career than most men achieve in a lifetime of service. He prevented the rape of a Soviet official's wife in Bucharest, he infiltrated deep into Rhodesian territory and shot down an enemy plane, he solved an international child trafficking ring involving our own children, he single-handedly faced the might of the South African army, he shot down one of their Mirage jets over Angola, and just last month he prevented the fucking South Africans from pulling off a coup in the Seychelles. Are you fucking mad?"

Smirnov waited until the chief had finished his tirade. "Comrade, I will elevate my request to the highest level if necessary." He lowered his voice menacingly. "Unless General Secretary Brezhnev himself tells me to back off, I will not relent. Good day, comrade."

36

SOVIET ARMY ORDERS

Colonel Hoare knew that it was just a matter of time before army reinforcements would be summoned to the Seychelles International Airport. He and the other mercenaries had rushed back inside the airport terminal building the moment they heard Trevor's first shots ring out. Barricading himself in the control room, the obese customs official had managed to raise the alarm. As reinforcements poured into the area, a sustained exchange of gunfire ensued between the putschists and members of the militia. Hoare knew he was running out of options. Realizing he needed a bargaining chip, he ordered the taking of seventy hostages.

Colonel Berlouis, Chief of the Seychelles defense force, ordered the disabling of the mercenaries' Royal Swazi aircraft. By that stage, several mercenaries had seized the control tower. The battle continued to rage around them.

Hoare sensed their luck might be changing when an Air India Boeing 707 requested clearance to land. Fearing that the plane was carrying reinforcements, the army endeavored to block the pilot's efforts to land. Low on fuel, the captain had no choice but to ignore the warning flares fired in his direction. Despite insufficient runway lighting, he managed to maneuver the aircraft onto the apron, but not before sustaining some superficial damage to his starboard wing.

Through their impromptu negotiations, the mercenaries managed to persuade the pilot to fly them back to South

Africa. Hoare had no choice but to abandon seven members of his advance party to their own fate. They'd already been on the island a week and were probably still blissfully unaware of the fiasco taking place at the airport.

One of them was Marty Docheck.

All seven were eventually rounded-up and taken into custody. In the aftermath of the debacle, the South African authorities vehemently denied any knowledge or involvement in the coup. Given their denial, Docheck began to believe that he'd been abandoned by his government. Sensing that he was being sacrificed on the altar of political expediency, he eventually opted to cooperate with his captors.

A new interrogator entered the dimly-lit room. Without saying a word, he withdrew a pack of cheap cigarettes and offered one to the disheveled South African. Lifting his manacled hands as far as the chain would allow, Docheck gratefully withdrew a cigarette from the crumpled pack. He lent forward to insert it between his lips. The interrogator lit the tip.

"So Marty, it is good that you have decided at last to cooperate with us." Marty was repulsed by the ugly scar on the man's face. He recognized the accent as being Russian.

Using his connections within the Seychelles establishment, Morozov had managed to get permission to interview each of the seven prisoners. "You are correct ... the South Africans have abandoned you and your friends. We have decided to honor your request for a meeting with the ANC representative here in Seychelles." Since his incarceration, Marty had become a desperate man. If engineering his freedom meant selling his soul to the devil, then so be it. The African National Congress was Pretoria's archenemy. They now represented his only hope.

"Please sir. Can you undo my handcuffs? I can't smoke this cigarette properly."

"You will manage just fine Marty. You know, you and I, we are so similar. We come from the same background. You know how it works: you give me something, I give you something."

Sitting down opposite his prisoner, Morozov withdrew a piece of paper from his top pocket. In the aftermath of the attempted coup, he'd discovered that nine of Hoare's raiding party comprised ex-Rhodesian soldiers. Morozov needed to determine whether any of them had meaningful links to Hunter. "So Marty, you recognize this piece of paper, huh? It was found in your possession when you were arrested a fortnight ago." During the course of their investigations, the Seychelles police interrogators had already ascertained that Docheck was one of the coup's top planners. Morozov had decided to start his interview process with the senior prisoner. "Let's go through this list, okay?"

"I've already explained the contents of that list to the other interrogators," pleaded Docheck. Morozov's hand crashed down onto the surface of the steel table. Docheck jumped.

"It wasn't a fucking request Marty."

"Okay, okay … I'm sorry," Docheck groveled.

One-by-one, Docheck gave a description of each-and-every member of the mercenaries appearing on the list. Morozov was biding his time. He could barely disguise his arousal as they came to the eighteenth name on the list.

"Baz is an ex-Rhodesian air force pilot. Most of his flying was on operational duty in the Bush War, but he also served briefly as a pilot instructor at their station in Gwelo. He was recruited only two or three days before the attempted coup. I didn't know anything about it because I was already here in the Seychelles. I got a message from Colonel Hoare that he was replacing a guy called Dax Hunter." Morozov's stomach muscles tightened. "It was a last minute decision. There, you can see his name crossed-out on the list and replaced by Baz's name. That's my handwriting," said Docheck.

"So tell me everything about this man Hunter. Why do you think he pulled out at the last minute?"

"As I said, I came to Seychelles a week before the planned coup. This last minute change took place after I arrived here. All I know about Hunter is that he's also an ex-Rhodesian Air Force pilot. He flew choppers. He came to South Africa around August, maybe September this year. I think he was planning on joining the South African Air Force right after the Seychelles job. I have absolutely no idea why he pulled out at the last minute." Docheck thought his interrogator looked distracted.

Morozov stood up abruptly. "I must go. I will be back later." He raised his voice, "Guard, let me out."

For two days Morozov had carried a copy of Docheck's manpower list. He was enraged that fate had once again dangled his quarry so tantalizingly close. In the privacy of the warder's staff room, he smashed his balled fist into a guard's steel locker. The indentation was as large as a coconut.

It took Morozov almost thirty minutes to quell his anger. Once in check, he summoned one of the guards. "You can take the next prisoner through to the interrogation room for me." Two of the seven captives were ex-Rhodesian soldiers. Morozov was about to speak to the first one.

The battle-hardened soldier was intractable. Morozov was unable to extract any further information from the uncooperative prisoner. But he soon made headway with the second. In exchange for a host of prisoner privileges, he eventually hit pay dirt. The man just happened to live in a block of apartments across the road from where Hunter lived on the Durban Berea.

The Russian had to anchor a piece of paper while the manacled man clumsily wrote down Hunter's Durban address. If he'd been capable of expressing his emotion, Morozov might've said he was elated.

Morozov left the prison and returned to the KGB's office in Victoria. Like the old office back in Dar es Salaam, this one also operated as a front company: West Indian Ocean Import & Export Inc. The secretary handed him two envelopes as he walked in.

Tearing the first one open, he withdrew a telex message

from his regional supervisor in Tanzania. He read the printout: *Leave request approved: 10 Dec '81 to 19 Dec '81 inclusive.* Even before he'd managed to secure permission to interrogate the prisoners, Morozov had decided he was going to take some leave and visit South Africa. With the fortuitous discovery of Hunter's address, his quest had suddenly become a lot easier.

Turning the second envelope over in his hand, he recognized the wax seal on the back. It had originated in Moscow but had been routed via the Soviet Consular Office in Victoria. *What the fuck is this about, my Order of Lenin medal?* He ripped open the letter.

> *Pursuant to the resolution of the incident involving Comrade Colonel B. Alexeev & Comrade Agent V.I.U. Morozov in the Moscow exurbs on the evening of 11 Aug 1980, the Chief Military Procurator's Office requires that Comrade Agent V.I.U. Morozov attend a formal enquiry regarding events leading up to the death of Comrade Colonel B. Alexeev on the night stated above. As this is an enquiry only, it will not be necessary for Comrade Agent V.I.U. Morozov to appoint a counsel.*

The hearing was five days hence. Morozov was unastonished by the message. Although he hadn't expected it, it still didn't come as a surprise. *Idiots took over a year to open that case. I think it's time for me to disappear permanently from the radar.*

Morozov left the office and went to his rented room above the Korean takeaway. After throwing a few items of clothing into his duffel bag, he positioned a chair in the center of the room and stepped onto it. Stretching up, he shifted an asbestos ceiling panel to one side and reached into the void. He took down a small bundle of US dollars, an air ticket to Johannesburg and his three passports. Each one bore a different name, and was issued by a different country.

37

RIDGE ROAD

Repercussions from the failed Seychelles coup had started to reverberate around the world. In the immediate aftermath of the bungled attempt, the disgraced Colonel Hoare had already started accusing the South African government of being complicit in the affair. They, in turn, vehemently denied any involvement.

As each tension-filled day passed, Elroy kept his fingers tightly crossed: the last thing he needed was for Hoare to implicate the CIA. Amidst all the claims, counterclaims and accusations, the CIA had somehow managed to stay out of the crossfire. Elroy nevertheless found himself in the stressful role of damage controller. Despite the distraction, he, Apple and Cathy were still able to plan and compile the finer details of Dax's job offer with the CIA.

A fortnight after the Seychelles fiasco, Dax and Apple boarded a plane bound for JFK International in New York.

The Durban taxi driver recognized the name of the apartment block on Ridge Road. He drove the Russian straight there. After settling his fare, Morozov walked across the street and approached the entrance to the large block. With his right hand thrust in his pocket, he stroked the cheap Chinese folding knife. He'd bought it at the market in Victoria a few weeks before.

Inside the main atrium, Morozov found what he was

looking for. Affixed to the wall, a large bank of electronic buzzers appeared alongside each apartment number. With no concept of privacy, each occupant's name also appeared beside the corresponding apartment number. Morozov scanned the list. He angrily checked it a second time after his first search proved futile. *There's no fucking Hunter here.*

Morozov heard voices echoing from the stairwell. *Two females.*

A metal security gate separated the atrium from the main apartment block. The two ladies buzzed themselves out. Morozov returned his attention to the board. "Hello, can we help you?" said one of the women.

Morozov turned and forced a smile. "Thank you. I am an old friend of Dax Hunter. We competed in the Olympics together last year. I thought I'd surprise him but I see that his name isn't on the list. This is the address he gave me in our last correspondence." The girls both giggled. *Yes, of course … they both fucking know Dax Hunter.*

"Sure … we know Dax," said one of the girls dreamily. "But I'm afraid you've just missed him. He moved out two days ago. Let me buzz the landlady for you. I'm sure she's got his forwarding address."

Content with the knowledge that everyone knew and loved the Zimbabwean, the gullible landlady happily handed Dax's forwarding address over to the Russian. It was actually Apple's aunt's place: an old double-storey overlooking the Potomac, close to where Apple worked. "You know, that lovely boy even left me with a pile of money to cover the cost of forwarding his mail to his new address in America. Here we go young man … I hope you two meet up again sometime soon," chuckled the old woman.

38

BRUTUS

Eager to stretch his legs, Morozov left his seat in the dimly-lit cabin and headed toward the galley. Soaring thirty-one thousand feet above the Atlantic, his passenger jet was making its way toward South America. Given the short notice and proximity to Christmas, he'd had no choice but to fly via Buenos Aires.

Stooping slightly to peer out of the small window in the emergency exit door, a wiry man with swarthy complexion sensed someone was coming toward the galley. He straightened up to make way as Morozov approached. They nodded at each other. "Can't sleep either?" asked the shorter man in Spanish. He looked to be of similar age.

"Sorry, only English," offered Morozov, hoping to deflect any further need for conversation.

"English, yes. But I detect an accent. Can I ask where you are from?"

Since leaving the Seychelles, Morozov had traveled on his fake Kenyan passport. "Originally Bulgaria," he said brusquely. Also fake, it appeared in the passport alongside the false name of Vladimir Chenkov.

"My name is Santiago ... but people call me Brutus—you know, like the cartoon character?"

Morozov didn't know of Brutus; in fact he didn't know any cartoon characters. "My name is Vlad. People call me Vlad," he said humorlessly.

"What takes you to Argentina? Vlad."

There was something about the way the man emphasized the name. Morozov continued studying the shorter man. His eyes appeared to betray a dark malevolence. Both his physique and body language suggested he knew how to handle himself. Although still wary, Morozov intuited something familiar in Brutus' demeanor. *No harm in being civil. Besides, I have nothing else to do.* "I am passing through on my way to America. Brutus." Through the passive-aggressive interplay, each knew they were being sized-up.

Six hours later, Morozov stepped off the jet bridge and started following the deplaning passengers down a long corridor. He veered off and entered the men's bathroom on his left. The corridor was almost empty when he exited five minutes later. Morozov bristled when he noticed Brutus standing against the opposite wall.

"Relax Vlad. You know, your reaction there has just confirmed my earlier suspicion," said Brutus.

"And what is that meant to mean?"

"C'mon Vlad. Your demeanor tells me you are military, probably special forces. Am I right?"

Morozov started walking in the directions of Customs and Immigration. Brutus fell in step alongside him. "Okay, so you don't have to tell me if you're military or not. But if I'm right—and I know I am—then you might be interested in what I have to say."

"I am not interested in what you have to say," said Morozov, knowing full-well that he was already a mildly-interested participant in Brutus' game.

"Ah, so you are not denying that you are military, huh? I knew it. I can spot a trained professional a mile off."

"So, *if* I am military, as you seem to think, why are you talking to me?"

"Vlad. I don't know what work you do, but someone from the Eastern Bloc is immediately going to be treated with suspicion by the Americans. Russian, Bulgarian ... you're all the same to them. Remember, they think there's a communist hiding under every bush. You got a convincing back story?" Morozov stopped walking and fixed Brutus with a stare. The shorter man appeared unfazed. "My guess is that you're going for a short visit ... I saw the size of the bag you checked in at Johannesburg airport. If you are as ... versatile as I think you are, I would like to explore whether it is worth my while offering you a permanent job with my organization. That is, after you have finished whatever it is that you are going to do in America, of course."

"Brutus, you are starting to annoy me. We are finished talking," said Morozov brusquely. He was about to walk off.

"Vlad. Please. My organization sells goods all over the world. We have connections that run deep into the corridors of practically every government in the world. I sit at the right hand of our illustrious chairman. I am responsible for recruitment. If my hunch is right, you look like someone who would fit perfectly into our family."

"And what exactly is this perfect fit you speak of?"

"Vlad, you look like someone who doesn't take shit from anyone. I see it in your eyes. I see it in the way you walk. Even the way you talk. I will level with you. If I am wrong—which I doubt—we will part ways and forget we ever had this conversation."

As a fresh wave of arrivals bore down upon them, Brutus steered Vlad by the elbow to the edge of the corridor. He lowered his voice. "But the only reason you haven't walked away so far is because you are intrigued that I have figured you out. I can sense that you are highly trained. You are disciplined. You are precise and you are capable of executing orders. I am serious about offering you a role."

"Who is your organization?" asked Morozov.

"Let's collect our bags and meet on the other side. How long is it before your connection to the USA?"

"Three hours," answered Morozov.

"There are cameras here and airport security will be watching. I will shake your hand and then go to the men's room. We were just old friends talking. Meet me at the coffee shop on the left as you clear through passport control."

Brutus took a sip from his cup. "Before I go on Vlad, humor me, please. Tell me whether you are military special forces or not?"

"I am," Morozov nodded.

"Ah, thank fuck! My instincts ... they haven't betrayed me yet." Brutus' smile lacked any trace of humor.

"Why is that so important?"

"By its very nature Vlad, our organization has to be run with military precision. I will tell you more, but I need to know if I can trust you to honor the professionals' code? If nothing materializes from this conversation, we walk away from this meeting and never talk about it again, right?"

"I give you my word," said Morozov, wondering if that was what he was meant to say.

"That is good Vlad ... very good." Brutus took another sip of his coffee. "My organization is headed by a man named Escobar. Pablo Escobar. Have you heard of him?"

"Yes, I have heard of him."

"Our organization controls eighty percent of the global cocaine market."

"You are called the Medellín Cartel, I believe?" Statistics never impressed Morozov.

"*Si*, that is correct. And the only reason we control so much of the market is because we are ruthless in the way we deal with the opposition. I am Escobar's top *sicario* ... you know, his chief enforcer. Our organization runs a small army. But we need a bigger army ... a stronger army. We need to train our soldiers to the highest levels. They must be capable of engaging the forces of law and order and neutralizing them. Do you think this is something you want to be a part of?"

Although Morozov was on official leave, he hadn't bothered to respond to the Chief Military Procurator's Office regarding his hearing. In defying the order, he knew it would unleash the very worst of the KGB's wrath. Morozov was just days away from being classified as a rogue operator—to be ruthlessly hunted by every foreign KGB agent around the globe. *What better way to disappear than bury myself deep in this underworld organization?* "Yes, Brutus, this is something I would like to be a part of," answered Morozov.

"Excellent. Let me make a suggestion. Let's go and see if we can change your ticket to Bogotá. I want to help you improve your cover for your American visit. I can't afford to have you detained by the authorities when you land there. Once you have finished whatever business you have in the States, you can come back to your new home in Colombia." Brutus smiled triumphantly.

"Tell me Brutus. Why did your travels take you to South Africa?" enquired Morozov.

"Some product from the Far East was starting to interfere in our South African market. We found out that the head of the Vietnamese cartel was paying a visit to South Africa. It was messy, but I managed to persuade his cartel to consider moving into textiles."

39

MEDELLÍN

It took Brutus only three days to arrange a new passport for Morozov. For the purpose of his forthcoming American trip, his new identity came with a whole new persona. As the trade representative of a Chilean copper company, he was traveling to Morenci mine in Arizona to explore international business synergies.

Soon after their arrival in Medellín, Brutus took his new hire into the jungles to visit over a dozen coca farms and as many processing factories. The Russian was impressed by the sophistication of each operation: the final processing stage in each of the factories was performed by a team of highly-trained chemists. Inside the laboratories, men and women in freshly starched overalls and disposable medical booties busied themselves at their respective stations. In the packing sheds outside, thousands of brick-sized parcels were inserted in all manner of conveyances—ingenious disguises intended to fool their way past an army of customs officials at the world's busiest ports.

"Hey Vlad, catch." Brutus lobbed a sealed packet of cocaine at Morozov. "That's for you. It's a gift from the cartel."

Briefly weighing it in his hand, Morozov tossed it back at the Colombian. "No thanks. I don't do drugs."

Brutus walked up to the Russian and patted him on the back. "You have just passed the final interview. Welcome to my team."

Driving back to their villa on the outskirts of Medellín, Brutus eventually broke the silence. "Vlad, you don't need to tell me what it is that takes you to America, but if there's anything we can do to help, please let me know."

As Santiago negotiated the potholed roads, Morozov considered his options. He had quickly developed a rapport with this man who went by the name of Brutus. He sensed they were cut from the same cloth. Over a period of only a few days, the Colombian had welcomed this stranger and introduced him as an equal. It was apparent that employees up-and-down the chain respected Santiago. By extension, Morozov had been afforded similar eminence. He had a powerful sense that this was his new family … in fact, his only family. As the Land Cruiser jostled down the road, the Russian reached an important decision. He wanted to share his story.

Morozov started off by revealing his true identity to the Colombian. He then proceeded to tell him the story about Dax Hunter. He knew Brutus would understand.

As Morozov finished telling his story, Brutus found some shade under a Magnolia tree and killed the engine. "Vlad, you have already got an idea of the size and diversity of our organization. We have tentacles that reach into every facet of government. Not only here in Colombia, but also in neighboring countries and even overseas. There are at least fifty men on our payroll who have influence in America: highly-placed members of the Drug Enforcement Administration; United States Marshals; Bureau of Alcohol, Tobacco and Firearms; US Border Patrol and CIA. Before you go blindly in search of this guy Hunter, let me tap into some of our associates and find out more. I swear to you, when we have located him, I will let you go and finish your business. Right now, all you have is a forwarding address. For all you know, it could be weeks before he comes to collect his mail."

40

JAMBALAYA

After landing in New York, Dax and Apple took a short connecting flight to Dulles outside Washington. As a boy from Africa, Dax had no idea how to dress for northern hemisphere winters. She punched him on the shoulder as they waited outside for the next cab. "We're definitely going to buy you a proper jacket tomorrow," she chided playfully.

Apple's aunt stayed about twelve miles from the CIA's headquarters in Langley. Widowed ten years earlier, and with her kids now living on the other side of the country, she was more than happy to have Apple lodge with her in her rambling home on the Potomac.

Apple had called her aunt a few days prior to leaving Durban and asked whether her friend—a male friend!—could come and stay for a short while. "Honey child, you know I love having guests drop in anytime. You want me to make up the spare bedroom for him?" Apple smiled at her aunt's ill-disguised innuendo.

Barely through the front door, an elated Aunt Jinny threw her arms around her favorite niece. Untangling herself from the hug, Apple pulled Dax into the room and introduced him to her aunt. Dax could sense her genuineness through the warm embrace. "You two bring your appetites, I hope?" said Jinny in her distinctive delta accent. She hustled them through to the dining room. Both were done with airline fare. Being an athlete, Dax had a voracious appetite. It was only due to his good sense of decorum that he politely declined a third helping of her famous jambalaya.

Even though it was Saturday, Apple needed to talk to Sneddon about the next step in enrolling Dax onto the CIA's Nicaragua program. She couldn't risk calling him on her aunt's unsecured phone line. She slipped a note under Dax's door and tiptoed downstairs. Jinny was feeding her pampered calico cat. "He a fine boy, child," said Jinny. "You two going anywhere with this?"

"I'll tell you in a year," Apple answered enigmatically, kissing her aunt on the forehead. "You okay making him some eggs and grits when he wakes up? I gotta run to the office for about an hour."

Sneddon picked up the phone on the second ring. "Morning boss, it's Apple."

"Apple, welcome back." Sneddon, as ever, was plainspoken. After a brief exchange of pleasantries, he got straight to the point. "What's on your mind?"

"Boss, how do you want me to proceed with Hunter? Get him to our base in Costa Rica as soon as possible?"

"Well, we've just recruited four other foreign nationals onto this program. I've hired an old friend—the owner of Aero Contractors—to train these guys before they head off to the jungles of Nicaragua. He's an old CIA stalwart, a true patriot and one of the finest aviators around. He's going to train Dax and the other four at an airfield outside Van Horn in Texas. But he's taking a much-needed break right now and plans on spending a quiet Christmas with his family. He's only available to start training in early January. Our Central America desk is pretty quiet at the moment so why don't you take a bit of time off over the holiday season and report back to me on January 2nd? Same goes for our new guy Hunter."

As she drove back to Jinny's place, Apple's mind wandered to thoughts of Dax. In the days that followed their meeting in the Elangeni hotel, the two of them had been awkwardly businesslike. While Elroy and Cathy had been in attendance at a few of those meetings, Apple and Dax had mainly worked alone. They'd ploughed through a mountain of paperwork that covered aspects of the CIA's front companies, integration programs for foreign employees, political history of the Central American region, and finally a series of geography lessons on the entire isthmus.

Apple smiled to herself as she recalled their initial discomfiture. As their departure date had drawn near, they had to consider where Dax would stay in the days before his departure for Central America. Without a thought for the implication, she had suggested that he could stay with her—or rather at her aunt's place, she'd added hastily. On the night before their departure, Dax had invited her to join him and a few friends for a farewell drink on the city's Golden Mile.

As they walked down the Marine Parade later that evening, Dax's fingers gently interlaced with hers. Apple didn't discourage him, but she did turn to look searchingly into his eyes. She had told him that however their relationship developed, it would have to be kept a closely-guarded secret. Given his new line of work, they both knew it was as much for his own safety as it was for the safeguarding of her career.

Dax wrapped her in a reassuring embrace. Closing her eyes, Apple had tilted her chin toward his face. With dreamy reflection, Apple recalled how his mouth had explored her throat and lips.

Just the memory of that night made Apple's head spin with lustful thoughts. She drove home with a little more urgency. She could feel the powerful flush of arousal as her essence began to seep through.

Aunt Jinny had left a note on the kitchen table.

Your man might be dead! He hasn't woken up yet. I've gone to

meet the choir ladies for coffee. Home by 11. Love, AJ.
PS. Can I tell them about your new boyfriend?

Apple smiled. She knew her aunt was going to tell them anyway. She checked her watch.

Apple quietly let herself into Dax's room. She could hear the rhythm of his breathing. Undoing the sash of her bathrobe, she let the soft garment cascade to the floor. She gently lifted the corner of the duvet and slid beneath the cover. Edging closer to Dax, she pressed herself against his warm torso. He stirred then lifted his head off the pillow. "Well good morning to you, Miss Lacroix," he said sleepily. He turned to face her and drew her close. "To what do I owe the pleasure?"

"Well, it was either a bucket of cold water … or this," she purred, guiding his hand toward her breast. With the duvet slipping off his shoulders, Dax rose up on his knees and admired Apple's lissome body. She too had a perfect view as she gazed up at him. He was already getting aroused. "Oh my word! My Adonis," she breathed hotly. He bent forward and started nuzzling the crease in her neck. Dax flicked his tongue lightly down the centre of her throat, lingering for a while at the small indentation between her collarbones. Using his free hand, he drew his finger lightly around her tight nipples. Apple arched her back to meet his touch and moaned ever so softly. She reached down between them and started to caress him. He was fully ready.

Moistening his lips, Dax started brushing and blowing gently on Apple's olive skin. She shivered involuntarily as her skin puckered into a field of ticklish goosebumps. Slowly, downwards, he followed the crescent of her breast toward the erotic fold of her navel. As he did so, his fingers found the secret contours of her inner thigh. Under the spell of his conjuring touch, Apple raised her derrière to meet his inquisitive fingers. Unable to contain her passion any further, she pulled Dax down and guided him to her.

41

MOROZOV DISAPPEARS

Apple's parents had been thrilled when they heard she'd be coming home for Christmas. Of course they'd heard all about Dax by that stage, both from Apple as well as Jinny.

Jeremiah Lacroix was Jinny's younger brother. In the two weeks since Apple's return to the States, he'd called his sister at least four times to interrogate her about Dax. Despite Jinny's assurances, Jeremiah had decided he'd reserve judgment until after meeting the boy—he figured it was a father's prerogative.

Christmas lunch at the Lacroix's house was a noisy affair. After introductions, Dax managed to remember the names of all twenty members of the extended family. That small courtesy hadn't gone unnoticed—nor had his sharp wit and infectious personality. Apple told everyone about the genesis of Dax's Joke of the Week, then proceeded to put him on the spot by insisting he tell his latest story. Jeremiah was certainly warming toward the young man.

While Apple's granny was serving her famous eggnog, the phone in the hallway jangled loudly. "I don't care which one of my boyfriends that is, just tell them I'm busy right now," called out Momma Lacroix. The table erupted in laughter.

Jeremiah got up to answer the phone. His voice boomed down the passageway a few moments later. "Apple, it's your boss Elroy, he wants to wish you happy Christmas, but hurry, he's calling you from Africa."

Odd of him to call now ... must be important. Apple pulled the cord into the kitchen to get a bit more privacy. "Hi Elroy. Merry Christmas. Must be nearly midnight there? How are you?"

"Hey, Apple. Yeah, doin' okay. Busy as all hell here." Elroy knew she was celebrating Christmas with her family in Louisiana. He also knew that it was foolhardy to share sensitive information over an unsecured line. "Hey, I'll be quick, okay. We've had some interesting developments. How soon can you get to the regional office? Is tomorrow good for you?"

"Yeah, I can go in to the office tomorrow. How about 6 PM Central African Time?"

"Perfect. Chat tomorrow," said Elroy. "Say hi to Dax for me," he added, just before hanging up.

The CIA office in Lafayette was operating on a skeleton staff. Since Dax had already received his CIA clearance, Apple was able to take him into the office with her. They were directed to a booth with a telephone in the middle of the table. Elroy picked up immediately. "Hi Elroy. I've got Dax on speaker phone here with me."

"Good morning to you both," said Elroy. "Thanks for coming in to make this call. Got some stuff I need to share with you both. Let me get straight to the point. In the past couple of days we've received intel from two independent sources. We're able to confirm that Morozov has been declared a rogue agent by the KGB. It's official: he's now operating off-reservation. It appears as if he received a summons from Moscow. He'd been ordered to attend a military enquiry on Dec 14. By sheer coincidence, he was due to take a week's leave at the same time as the hearing. Ignoring the summons, he gave them the middle finger and decided he'd rather take his holiday instead of appearing before the board. If you'll excuse the pun, the red flag was raised when he failed to turn up for his hearing. Every foreign-based KGB agent has now been put on alert and instructed to be on the lookout for him."

"Just what I needed to hear," said Dax, leaning back in his

chair. "Got any idea what this military hearing was about?"

"We don't know. But I surmise that he must've gotten on the wrong side of his military colleagues somewhere along the line. If he was merely a third-party witness to a case, they'd have just requested his written statement, or maybe sent someone to take his affidavit. But to summon him to appear in person ... that's a different ball game altogether. For him to skip the hearing entirely suggests to me that he knew it'd be a bad outcome for him. Remember, if he is a psychopath as we suspect, he'll have no remorse giving-up on his career like this. His sole focus is on you, Dax, and will remain so until he gets closure ... sorry man, I didn't mean it to come out like that—until *we* get closure."

"Do they have any idea where he is?" asked Apple.

"They issued him with three false passports a number of years ago. In order to help them narrow their search, the KGB has divulged those three names to their own field agents. They've been told to use all means possible to track him down. Our mole is trying to get access to those three identities for us ... but I already know one of them," said Elroy triumphantly.

"How the heck did you discover that?" asked Apple.

"I ordered a filter search on every passenger leaving Seychelles from the day before he was due to go on leave, to a few days after. We know he's coming after Dax so I narrowed my search to single males traveling to South Africa. I also managed to squeeze a favor from a South African colleague: he delivered a bunch of airport surveillance videos to me spanning the days in question. Heck, with *that* scar, even a blind man could pick out Morozov in a police line-up."

"That's why you're our boss, Elroy," teased Apple.

"Here's what we eventually found," continued Elroy. "He left Seychelles on December 10 and traveled to South Africa on a Kenyan passport under the assumed name of Vladimir Chenkov. He arrived in Johannesburg on the same day. He was processed by an immigration official at 20:12 local. I personally eyeballed the surveillance footage lifted from around that time. It took me less than ten minutes to ID our man and link it back to a name."

"Great news, well done Elroy," applauded Apple.

"Knowing his new alias, we were able to track him quite easily after that. He resurfaced early the next day in Durban," continued Elroy. "Now to me, that's telling. In my book, it strongly suggests that he must've pinpointed Dax's exact location beforehand. No dithering, just bam! Straight to Durban. This guy's crafty. But here's where it gets really interesting … and, I'm afraid, a little worrying."

"What's that supposed to mean?" asked Dax.

"Well, he flew out of Durban the very next day bound for New York, via Buenos Aires. But consider this. Remember, at that point, he still wasn't officially regarded as a rogue agent by the KGB. He knew that he was only likely to invite the wrath of the Soviet apparatus a day or two *after* his no-show. Morozov wasn't high-tailing it out of Durban because the KGB was after him. No, I think his departure suggests something even more concerning."

"So why do you think he left?" pressed Dax, already sensing Elroy's answer.

"Well, as we know, this guy's not going to relent until he finds you. Now that he's got the scent of blood in his nostrils, he's coming after you. Dax, I reckon that he somehow figured out that you not only left South Africa, but that you left for the States. Why else would he book a ticket to New York at such short notice? As if that's not worrying enough, it gets even freakier."

"Oh shit. What now?" Dax sounded unenthusiastic.

"After landing in Buenos Aires, he had three hours to kill while waiting for his New York connection." Elroy paused to take a sip of water. They heard the faint tinkle of ice in his glass. "But he never took that flight." Elroy gave them a moment to process the implication.

"What? Why didn't he continue to the States?" asked Dax.

"Hang on, there's more," said Elroy. "I alerted a colleague in the Buenos Aires office and asked her to dig around a bit. She did a great job in tracing his movements from there. For some inexplicable reason, Morozov went and changed his ticket for Bogotá. Why? We don't know. It's mystifying. At least we were able to confirm that he actually boarded *that* flight. I've alerted another colleague in Colombia to be on high alert for any news on Morozov. I'm afraid our guy, aka Vladimir Chenkov, has evaporated. That's why we're pressing our sources to try and furnish us with his other two aliases. Perhaps he changed identities in Bogotá and is already in the States under one of those two names."

"Is it possible that he might've diverted to Bogotá to throw us off?" Apple enquired.

"Yes it is. If that was his plan all along, then I admire his style. Where better to change passports than in a city where your pursuers are least likely to expect you to be? It's like a double dupe," said Elroy.

"But who are his pursuers? Us? The KGB? Or is he just being super cautious?" asked Apple.

"Let's just hope like hell that he hasn't somehow figured out that we're after him as well," said Elroy.

42

TRACING HUNTER

The hacienda where Morozov stayed was actually one of five separate residences scattered across a sprawling ranch. Although each one housed several senior members of the cartel, their accommodations were discreet enough to ensure their privacy.

Although he had never experienced such opulent living, Morozov was incapable of deriving any delight from his newfound circumstances. Unaware of the subnormal functioning of his limbic lobe, he was simply oblivious to his indifference. Each morning, Morozov woke to a lusty combination of fragrant bougainvillea and horse shit. *These Colombians love their fucking horses.*

It was Sunday morning, two days after Christmas. The villa was deserted; everyone was back at church. *Fucking horses AND church*, he added to his list.

Sitting on the wide verandah eating breakfast, Morozov noticed a vehicle approaching from a distance. As it turned-off and headed up the long driveway, he recognized Brutus' Land Cruiser.

Parking-up around the back of the villa, Morozov heard the car door slam shut. He shouted out to Brutus to come around to the verandah. "Good morning Vlad." Both Brutus and Morozov were relieved that they'd moved beyond the pretense of shaking hands.

"Good morning Brutus. You must be the only Catholic in South America not attending mass this morning."

Brutus smiled. "My Savior understands that my work is a full-time job. My priest? Hmm. Not so much."

"What brings you over to spoil my perfectly good Sunday?" In just under a fortnight, Brutus had taught Morozov the concept of sarcasm.

"We have made a very interesting discovery," said Brutus, pulling up a chair. "I got one of my accountants to do some digging." There were only three categories of employment in the Medellín Cartel: producers, accountants, and enforcers. Anyone in the cartel employed in an administrative role was referred to as an accountant.

"And what did he find?" enquired Morozov.

"He contacted a few of our American associates, you know, the guys in law and order who I told you about?" Morozov nodded. "One of them provided us with some interesting information." Brutus stopped talking as one of the servants came out bearing a pot of coffee.

"*Café señor?*"

"*Sí, gracias* María," said Brutus. He waited until she was out of earshot. "Our insider has advised us that your guy Hunter has been recruited to work for the CIA."

"You are making a joke, right?" said Morozov flatly.

"No. I am being deadly serious. He's joined a CIA dummy company that is giving assistance to the Contras in Nicaragua."

Morozov sat forward. "Go on."

"As soon as he has undergone some specialized training in USA, he'll transfer out to Costa Rica in the middle of January." Brutus took a sip from his cup. "Vlad, you see what I mean now? Our cartel has powerful connections. Soon, Hunter will be operating on *our* turf. It means you can engage him on *your* terms."

"This news makes me very happy," said Morozov without a trace of emotion.

43

RECRUITING ELROY

In order to be accepted by the ancient guilds, medieval journeymen were obliged to spend time under the watchful eye of a master craftsman. A similar philosophy was applied to the enthusiastic new agents of the CIA.

With their arduous training program behind them, and an exciting career ahead, freshly-minted recruits from the CIA academy eagerly awaited details of their first real assignments. The idea of letting the recruits get their feet wet in this manner contributed to their development as junior agents.

When the Seychelles job first appeared on the CIA's radar, Sneddon had approached Elroy to act as Apple's mentor. Eager to give his protégé some meaningful exposure, Sneddon was confident that Elroy was up to the task. As a right-of-passage, every mid-level agent knew that one day they'd be called upon to take just such a novice under their wing.

Elroy's time had come. While he didn't report directly to Sneddon, he *was* obliged to liaise with him on Apple's progress.

With both men having a vested interest in her development, they had collaborated freely throughout her assignment. But with Apple having returned to his team on the Central America Desk, Sneddon's need for Elroy's updates had all but evaporated.

It therefore came as a surprise to Elroy when he took a call from Sneddon just after Christmas. "Elroy, a belated merry

Christmas to you. How are you?" Elroy recognized Sneddon's voice immediately.

"I am very well thanks Sneddon. And a merry Christmas to you too. To what do I owe the pleasure?" Sneddon had insisted from the beginning that Elroy call him by his surname.

"Elroy, I know I have thanked you already for the role you played as Apple's mentor, but it would be remiss of me not to remind you again of how grateful I am."

"Aw, thank you sir. You're making a black dude blush here. She'll be a great agent."

"Elroy. Let me ask you a question outright. You've been in Africa now for what, five years?" He didn't wait for a response. "I know you like it over there but how willing would you be to consider moving back stateside?"

There was a long pause as Elroy considered his response. "Wow. Crazy question. Yeah, I do like it over here, no doubt. But I will admit I *have* been checking the bulletin board lately for suitable positions back in the US of A. Why? You know of something back home that might be of interest to me?"

"Matter of fact I do Elroy. How about you come over here and join me on the Central America Desk? God knows this region is heating-up. Reagan has practically given us the keys to Fort Knox to rid Nicaragua of the Sandinistas. We've got our hands full with the drug cartels up-and-down Central America, Cuba's still Cuba, and El Salvador, Guatemala and Honduras are all precariously balanced at the moment."

"I, I can't think of what to say," Elroy stammered uncharacteristically. "That's very humbling. Thank you Sneddon."

44

REUNION

Shortly after New Year, Dax received orders from Sneddon to report to hangar 12 at Tipton airfield. He was due there the following day. Apple knew the location; it was across the main road from Fort Mead. Bidding Aunt Jinny farewell, they left after breakfast and headed for the outskirts of Baltimore, just over an hour away.

Parking outside the hangar, Dax and Apple had just exited their car when a man nearby called out. "You must be Dax Hunter."

"Yes, sir," answered Dax. The stranger looked to be in his late forties.

"I'm Jim Rhyne, your instructor for the next two weeks. Welcome."

"Sir, pleased to meet you. This is my ... colleague, Apple Lacroix." Dax nearly blew it. He was already becoming accustomed to the idea of calling her his girlfriend.

"Mr. Rhyne. It's a pleasure to meet you," said Apple.

"The pleasure's mine Apple. Please, call me Jim. Come. Let's get out of this cold." He turned and headed toward the building.

A small crease had appeared across Apple's brow; she knew she'd heard the name somewhere before. Like a whirring rolodex, she hunted through her memory for a cross-reference. It came to her after a few moments. "Jim, forgive me for prying. Weren't you the pilot who flew a small team of engineers into Iran last year to prepare a landing strip for the Delta Force hostage rescue team?"

"I don't know if I should be worried that you know about that," said Jim casually. "Where on earth did you find out about that?"

"I was a rookie on the CIA Professional Trainee Program in April last year. The US Embassy hostage drama in Tehran was reaching a climax. I just remembered one of our lecturers mentioned your name in connection with a possible rescue mission."

"Well Apple, you sure have a head for detail ... and names, I must add." He paused then switched topics. "So Dax, I see from your file that you're an ex-Rhodesian Air Force pilot."

"That's right sir."

"Well, you're going to love the surprise I have in store for you," said Rhyne, his eyes twinkling. Following him inside, they entered into a small lounge area where passengers could relax before boarding their flights. Four lean young men were lounging casually in their chairs and chatting amongst themselves. They all rose as Rhyne led Dax and Apple into the room.

"No ways!" called out one of the men.

Dax recognized the voice in an instant. He turned toward the source.

"Holy crap! Phil ... what the hell?" exclaimed Dax.

"Dax, you beauty. It's been a while," responded Phil enthusiastically. They embraced like brothers. They practically were: as schoolboy rivals they'd played rugby against each other for several years. After leaving high school, both were selected onto the same Pilot Training Course. It was in that cauldron that Dax, Phil and the other cadets had started forging lifelong friendships.

Whereas Dax had stayed on in the Air Force of Zimbabwe, Phil had left Rhodesia straight after independence. He'd headed south to join the South African Air Force. He'd flown for them for almost two years before accepting the CIA's offer to fly sorties into Nicaragua.

"Hey, you two," interrupted Jim. "Break it up," he said, smiling. "Let me introduce y'all. So Dax, I guess you know Phil?" They all laughed. One-by-one, Jim introduced everyone around the circle. "And this is Sonny Janeke, ex-South African Air Force; this is Ingo Konrad, ex-Luftwaffe; and this is Mark Rowland, also an ex-SAAF pilot. Guys, meet Dax, ex-Rhodesian Air Force. And finally, his beautiful … colleague, Apple Lacroix." Dax smiled to himself: he knew the joke was on him. He liked Jim already. Everyone shook hands.

Standing outside next to the car, Dax hugged Apple goodbye. "You be safe now, hear?" said Apple, clutching onto the lapels of his new fleece jacket.

"Hey, I'm only gone for two weeks. I'll see you when we're done in Texas. I'm sure we'll have a few days together before I fly out to Costa Rica." They kissed passionately. Apple eventually broke from the embrace and pushed Dax lightly toward the building.

"I'll miss you," she whispered.

"I'll miss you too. I'll call as soon as I get a chance, okay?" With that, Dax turned and walked back to the building.

45

PANAMA CANAL

Toward the end of the previous week, Sneddon had told Sergio, Lynn and Styles that there was to be a Tagma Group meeting the following Monday. As was often the case, he gave them no indication as to what it was about.

Half-an-hour before their arrival, the ever-cautious Sneddon had swept the office for listening devices. On the hour, the other three members of the team filed in quietly and took their seats. "Torrijos may be gone, but his legacy lives on in the Torrijos-Carter Treaty." Sneddon wasted no time with pleasantries.

"As you are aware, this treaty will place eventual control of the canal in the hands of the Panamanians. In the meantime, staggered over the next nineteen years, the nation who built and controlled the canal will incrementally lose more-and-more authority over this valuable asset.

"Just how important is this canal to us?" Sneddon looked at each member individually; they knew it was a rhetorical question. "Let me tell you. There is something called the PANAMAX. It describes the maximum dimensions and deadweight of the largest vessel capable of traversing the Panama Canal. Since the canal was opened in 1914, American naval architects have been forced to design the majority of our battleships in accordance with PANAMAX. With a moral obligation to defend the free world, America is forced to design its fighting fleet around the width of a goddamn lock in

333

the middle of a country that we have no control over." Sneddon slapped the tabletop with an open palm. "It's goddamn farcical." The irony wasn't lost on the group.

"Fortunately for us, our team of negotiators inserted a clause in that treaty which allows America the right to use whatever means necessary to safeguard the access and integrity of the canal," Sneddon paused to rub his jowls. "Any disruption to the flow of ships would constitute a legitimate reason for us to go in and fix the problem. So, my fellow tagmata, with Torrijos gone and too many heirs-apparent trying to jockey into position, I believe the time is right for us to restore some sanity in Panama and remind these pretenders who's really in charge here." The other three nodded. "Right now it would be premature for us to usher Noriega into power. While that agenda is still on-track, the timing is not quite right for his ascension. When it is, we will sponsor his quest for glory."

"What are you suggesting we do?" asked Lynn.

"I believe our best option is to arrange for an untoward incident in the canal. But nothing major. We need an event— an incident—that will cause a disruption to maritime continuity. It must be of sufficient magnitude to attract attention ... and trigger our intervention. Such an incident would give our president the legal right to intervene and restore the operability of the canal. There's a secondary benefit attached to our presence: exerting our rights in the canal would also project our influence across the country. Granted, it's only temporary, but it'll remind the Panamanians that we are still the overlords of the canal ... at least until Dec 31, 1999."

"I think you're right," agreed Styles. "It'd be a clever way of exploiting the canal agreement to realign the thinking of a growing band of political firebrands and treaty dissenters." Sneddon nodded in response to Styles' endorsement.

"Yes," continued Sneddon. "These dissenters appear to have come crawling out of the woodwork since Torrijos' untimely death." Considering the way he'd phrased his last statement, the three tagmata wondered if Sneddon had forgotten that it was he who had ordered Torrijos' liquidation a little over five months before.

The members of the Tagma Group were well aware that Sneddon mixed with influential people on Capitol Hill. There'd been two occasions when members of Tagma had challenged Sneddon's mandate, only to discover that he actually *did* have authority from higher-up the chain of command. Such challenges to his authority could severely curtail one's career aspirations.

Careful not to be labeled as an obstructionist, it was sometimes prudent to trust that Sneddon was *indeed* working within the bounds of a higher privy. On this occasion, it appeared as if he was paraphrasing the private musings of their own president.

"My fellow tagmata, need I remind you that tagma in Greek means 'to set in order.' It encapsulates our raison d'être and is precisely why we formed this group. Can I take it then that we are in agreement that the Panamanian situation needs to be set in order?" Sneddon's question elicited three nods.

"Excellent. I'll need some input from each of you. Lynn, would you give us a psychologist's perspective of the current and collective mood on Capitol Hill. We know where Reagan stands on matters concerning Central America, but we need to know what sort of resistance he'll encounter, especially from the Democrats. Who are likely to be the biggest dissenters and what sort of opposition support are they capable of lobbying? We're already starting to hear rumblings from DC about our interference in Central American politics. Forewarned is forearmed. Let's give the president everything he'll need to counteract negative sentiment on the Hill." Lynn nodded as she jotted down some notes.

"Styles, I need you to give us an assessment of the wider political ramifications within the Panamanian party elite. You've spent as much time in Central America as I have … you know the lay of the political landscape. There will be political fallout if we muscle-in to restore the functionality of the canal. Let's be prepared with a few scenario analyses of how it might play out internally down there."

"Sure," answered Styles.

"Sergio, I need you to compile the action proposal for us. I need three workable scenarios for the incident. Although I want you to be creative, I don't want you blocking the canal for days; don't propose anything that involves damaging the locks, okay?"

"No problem," answered Sergio.

"And there's one other constraint I want to impose. Your three options must be prepared on the basis that each one is capable of being executed by a maximum of two highly-skilled special force operators. Regardless of which option we choose, the outcome must look exactly like what it is—a deliberate act of sabotage. If the incident appears to be nothing more than an unfortunate accident, we won't have a legitimate excuse to roll in with our cavalry."

"I understand," said Sergio.

"Sergio, when you get Lynn and Styles' contributions, I want you to collate the document. Tagmata … one copy only. No carbon paper, no electronic storage. I need it by no later than midday, Tuesday 12. For our eyes only."

46

SERPICO

By the early 1980s, Pablo Escobar's burgeoning drug empire had successfully cornered the lion's share of the world's cocaine market. In six short years he'd forged a world-wide network of customers, collaborators, insiders, informants and loyal servants. His apparent impunity had not only frustrated the efforts of law enforcement agencies in Colombia, but also in the United States. Within the ranks of the country's lower strata, many Colombians unashamedly revered the man. As his folkloric status grew, he was soon anointed as their *patrón*. On the opposite side of the social spectrum, the man was reviled by the elite and the educated middle class. Escobar had created a schism that divided the nation.

Escobar's success could be attributed to many factors, but his high-level connections probably represented his biggest advantage. With a slew of influential people in his pocket—and the promise of unimaginable riches—he managed to inveigle his way into the corridors of power, both political *and* jurisdictional. His sinister influence was not limited to Colombia alone. Regardless of their mandate, no authority was immune to his sway. Not even the CIA.

Whether they were local or foreign, politician or law enforcer, Escobar understood the value of his network of informants, patsies and puppets. Even more than this, he understood the wisdom of protecting their identities. He took great pride in personally assigning code-names to each of his higher-placed snitches.

One of Escobar's favorite movies was the 1973 blockbuster, *Serpico*. Al Pacino plays the part of Serpico—a principled cop who stands firm against the corruptible actions of his fellow NYPD officers.

Within a few months of proving his worth to Escobar's operation, the drug baron had rewarded one of his more fruitful CIA moles with a new alias: Serpico. That had been over four years before. Serpico often wondered if Escobar was being intentionally ironic with his choice of cryptonym.

The satellite phone on Escobar's desk trilled loudly. Since there weren't that many people who knew the number, he knew it was likely to be important. Two men were sitting playing cards on the far side of the room. One of them stood up, walked over to the desk and lifted the phone to his ear. "Hello." He listened for a few seconds. "Boss, do you want me to take a message?" he called from across the room.

"Who is it?" demanded Escobar.

"He says his name's Serpico."

"Fuck! I'll take it. Tell him to wait." Escobar shoved the topless woman off his lap and cursed a second time as he rose from the chair. He checked his hair as he passed in front of a large mirror. "Serpico, I presume there's a good reason for this call?" Escobar had switched to English. Both caller and recipient knew the connection was secure.

Serpico knew not to waste Escobar's time with idle gossip. "*El patrón*, a few weeks ago I provided some critical information for your man Brutus. I am hoping your organization can repay that good deed with a small favor."

Escobar was blessed with a keen intellect. He certainly would've remembered if he'd instructed Brutus to reach out to Serpico. He disguised his uneasiness. "Yes, yes, but you'll have to remind me of the details," said Escobar disarmingly.

"Your new man Morozov … the former KGB agent," said Serpico. Escobar knew of Brutus' new recruit but hadn't met him yet. He remembered being impressed by Brutus' description of the Russian.

"Yes, yes. The details are hazy. Go on. Remind me again," Escobar lied.

"I provided the name and whereabouts of the ex-Rhodesian pilot that your new Russian enforcer is trying to locate."

"Yes, yes, of course. So what is the favor you are asking for?" said Escobar.

"My agency has instructed me to create a small diversion in the Panama Canal. It ties in with our larger agenda. By its very nature, the diversion I speak of needs to be executed by someone with a military background. More importantly, that person must be able to guarantee us plausible deniability if they were to be compromised in any way. Would you be prepared to let me use your Russian for this important job? If he succeeds, I will give him the pilot he so desperately seeks."

"Let me speak to Brutus. Phone me back in twenty four hours." Escobar turned off the phone. His face was already reddening with rage. "Tell that fucking Brutus I want to see him ... now!"

With his phone pressed against his ear, Brutus strained to hear his fellow *sicario's* whispered instructions. "Brutus, it's Blackie. The boss is enraged. I don't know what's happened but he wants you here *now!*" Brutus made the forty-five minute journey to Escobar's hacienda in under half-an-hour.

As Brutus entered the office, Escobar waved the others out. They had barely closed the door behind them when they heard their boss explode. "What in Saint Dimas' name were you thinking Brutus? Are you fucking mad?" roared Escobar. Brutus looked dumbly at his boss. "You fucking used one of our most valuable assets in the CIA to run some lost-and-found advert for your new Russian friend." Escobar's arms windmilled wildly. "You know damn well that we only reach out to our insiders when it is for legitimate business. Cartel business. We use these assets selectively ... you should know this Brutus." Brutus looked contrite but Escobar hadn't finished berating him. "What the fuck were you thinking, showing-off to your Russian friend like that? 'Look at me Morozov, look how well-connected I am,'" mimed Escobar in a strained falsetto. "Are you his bitch, Brutus?" Escobar knew the comment would cut to the core of Brutus' masculinity.

Striding about the room, the head of the cartel tried to rein-in his anger. Brutus remained mute. When Escobar next spoke, his voice was tight with intent. "As is customary in such circumstances, I am now obliged to offer something in return. It is how these mutually-beneficial relationships survive, Brutus. Serpico wants to use your man Morozov to carry out an event … an incident, in the Panama Canal. It has the CIA's full backing but they need plausible deniability. There can be no links between the incident and the Americans. You are to be here at 2:30 tomorrow afternoon to talk to Serpico, you hear me? Get the fucking job done, then get your Russian friend to start earning his keep around here, you understand?" Escobar's order was laced with menace.

"Yes boss, I understand," said Brutus meekly.

"One last thing," said Escobar, as Brutus was turning to leave.

"Yes boss?"

"Serpico said something about handing-over a pilot if your Russian friend succeeds in his mission. I want you to use that as *our* incentive to Morozov, not Serpico's. If he succeeds, I want him coming back to *us* to collect his reward. That way, I can secure his loyalty. If he can pull-off whatever hare-brained mission the CIA has in mind, he'll have proved to me that he's worthy of a place on our team."

Brutus was alone in Escobar's office when Serpico called at the agreed time. After concluding their discussion, he drove straight to the ranch where Morozov was training a phalanx of new recruits. Parking his Land Cruiser at the back of the shooting range, he hooted for Morozov's attention. The Russian instructed the recruits to make their weapons safe. He then walked toward Brutus.

"Vlad. Come with me, let's talk." Morozov fell in step alongside the Colombian. Brutus knew it was probably best to be selective with the truth: he didn't want to reveal that he'd been chastised by Escobar for his careless use of the cartel's assets. "I have just come from a meeting with Escobar," he lied. Brutus' intention was to add credence to his proposal. "Our boss has been approached by our CIA mole ... you remember, the one who gave us the details of Hunter's whereabouts?"

"Yes, I remember," said Morozov.

"Well, in the spirit of co-operation with our CIA informant, Escobar has agreed to send you on an important mission."

"A mission? This is good. Tell me more."

"We are sending you on a special assignment to the Panama Canal. The objective is to create an incident in the canal that bears the trademark of a deliberate terrorist attack. Since subterfuge is their specialty, and secrecy their watchword, we did not ask our CIA mole to explain why they want to do this."

"No need. I know how they think," Morozov reminded Brutus.

"Despite their fondness for ambiguity, the CIA specifically requested that *you* be assigned to the task. Not only are they fully aware of your capabilities, but they made no secret of the fact that your incentive to complete the job will guarantee mission success."

"And what is this incentive they speak of?" asked Morozov.

"Your man Dax Hunter."

"If they can guarantee that they will give me Dax Hunter after the mission, I will do it."

"Yes, this they have promised."

"When do I go?"

"It looks like it will happen next week," said Brutus. "Our informant will send me the name of your contact in Panama. He will provide you with the weapons and explosives you need for the mission." They walked on in silence for a few more paces. "So Vlad, you eventually get your man, huh?"

47

SYSTEM DATA ENTRY

Elroy started his new job the day after he returned to the States. On his first day, barely fifteen minutes after arriving at the CIA Headquarters, Sneddon apprehended him in the corridor. "Come Elroy, let me take you around the office to meet your new colleagues."

After attending to the formalities, Sneddon led Elroy to his office. "Elroy, your new recruit, Dax Hunter, has apparently acquitted himself well under the watchful eye of Jim Rhyne. In fact Jim has been very impressed with all of their flying skills. But he did make an interesting comment. He said that Konrad the German, although technically precise, was at a disadvantage because he lacks any real aerial battle experience. While he's got the hours, plus a few NATO exercises in his logbook, he hasn't ever flown into a proper scrap. Just keep that in mind when he starts flying operationally."

"Duly noted," responded Elroy.

"This leads me to the next point. Day after tomorrow—that's Friday 15—I want you to fly to our ranch outside Van Horn to meet your five pilots. Jim aims to wrap-up their training by Saturday. He's already planned your two-day ferry route to Costa Rica. You'll be leaving on Sunday. I want you to fly with them and get them settled into their new home. I expect you'll need to be there for at least a week, getting them properly integrated into the program."

"No problem sir, but wasn't Apple meant to be the pilots'

assigned liaison?"

"She was … she still is, but I need someone a little more senior … someone like you, to settle the guys into their new role," answered Sneddon. "Besides, I need to take her to Panama soon and introduce her to her colleagues at the regional hub."

"Yes sir," said Elroy. "I'm on it."

After ushering Elroy out of his office, Sneddon took the elevator downstairs. He bustled over to Apple's desk. "Apple, I'm sending Elroy to pick up our five pilots in Van Horn at the end of the week. I know you were meant to go, but I've got something far more important for you."

"Okay, boss. What you got?" Apple was gutted; she fought hard to disguise her disappointment. *Now I won't see Dax.*

"You, me and Sergio are going to Panama tomorrow for a few days. I need to get down to our hub office and I thought it'd be a good time to introduce you to the team down in Panama City. Besides, I've got you earmarked for greater responsibilities on the Central America Desk, and you can't do that blindly from an office."

"What time we leaving?" asked Apple.

"5 AM from our hangar," said Sneddon, turning to leave.

After advising Apple of their trip, Sneddon went to Sergio's office and closed the door behind him. "Sergio, that document I requested last week. It's ready?"

"Yes, the other two submitted their sections on schedule. I collated the report and had it ready yesterday, as you requested," replied Sergio.

"Excellent. Hang on to it for the time being. Listen, I need you to join me and Apple on a short visit to Panama tomorrow. Apple and I are only staying two days. You'll probably need to stay a few more days. I want you to go and eyeball the locations you've chosen for your three scenarios. If your site inspection reveals any unforeseen snags, it'll give you an opportunity to revise our planning document accordingly.

You can have the final copy ready for me by Tuesday 19."

"Great, that'll help if I need to fine-tune the plans," answered Sergio. "What time are we leaving tomorrow?"

Sneddon had already stood to leave. "We depart at 5 AM." He paused in the doorway. "Wait, on second thoughts. I want you to bring our document with you tomorrow. It'll give me the chance to read your first draft on the plane."

For most of the day, Elroy was kept busy by a fastidious member of the personnel department. In order to process onto the payroll, he had to endure the best of the agency's myriad requirements. By the end of the day he was exhausted; the jetlag was starting to set-in.

Returning to his desk, he sat down and logged onto the system. Since accepting Sneddon's offer, Elroy had been running helter-skelter to finalize his move back to the States. He'd had very little opportunity to attend to some of his more pressing admin jobs. One of his priorities was to update Morozov's file with the details of his arrival in South Africa, departure for Buenos Aires, and unscheduled diversion to Bogotá.

Elroy waited as his screen warmed up. He logged in and navigated to the *Persons of Interest* archive. The familiar-looking personnel file blinked onto the screen.

Elroy's brow furrowed. He leaned forward in his chair. The data entries on Morozov—much of which he'd inputted himself—had grown by several lines of text. The latest submission had been entered anonymously.

> *Subject failed to appear at a military hearing in Moscow on 12/14/81: declared 'rogue' by KGB. Subject went on leave on 12/10/81. Destination, South Africa: speculated that he is on a personal vendetta to liquidate Hunter, Dax. (See above). He left South Africa next day for JFK, NY, NY via Buenos Aires. Subject inexplicably changed flight in Buenos Aires to Bogotá, Colombia. His mission objective is unknown. He's known to be traveling on a false passport.*

It wasn't so much that there was a new entry in Morozov's file—entries were expected to be filed by all active-duty agents—but rather that this latest update didn't give the originator's name. It wasn't just a careless omission either: the system had to be deliberately overridden in order to conceal the identity of the author. Besides that, one other thing troubled Elroy. *His mission objective is unknown.*

Elroy's initial thought was that it must've been entered by one of his two colleagues; Tawana in Buenos Aires, or perhaps Joe in Bogotá. The former had helped him trace the elusive Morozov after he failed to catch his JFK flight, the latter had promised to keep an eye out for the Russian around Bogotá.

After separate conversations with Tawana and Joe, Elroy was satisfied—but no less confused—that neither of them had any idea what he was talking about.

Elroy sat back in his chair and pondered. *Apple would never have willfully overridden the system and left her name off the entry. Heck, I don't even think she knows that it's possible. Why did the writer say that Morozov's mission objective is unknown? We know damn-well what his objective is. The only other people who are privy to the Morozov narrative are the staffers on Sneddon's team. Why would any of them want to make an entry in Morozov's file?*

48

LUNCH WITH NORIEGA

Before leaving the office on Wednesday night, Apple had checked the weather report for Panama City. As forecast, it was a balmy 81°F as they stepped off the plane the following day. She was glad to have dressed accordingly. "Here's our ride," said Sneddon, pointing at a gleaming black limousine sweeping up alongside their private jet.

"Wow! Traveling in style," said Apple. "You sure the accountants are going to let you put that on your expense account?"

Sneddon laughed. "No, I have a surprise for you. It's our host's limo." The three of them settled back into the sleek Lincoln.

As they approached the impressive iron gates, Apple couldn't help notice the armed sentries perched atop the perimeter wall; there was one at each corner. "Who the hell are we coming to visit? The President of Panama?" enquired Apple.

"Almost," answered Sneddon vaguely.

Their limo glided up to the main entrance. "*Señores, señora, bienvenido*," said the footman as he opened the car door for them. "*Por favor sígame.*" The three CIA agents followed the servant into a domed reception area.

Apple was immediately put-off by the décor; it was ostentatious, if not gauche. After offering each of them a glass of freshly-squeezed juice, the footman moved off to the side of the atrium and knocked discreetly on a pair of oversized, carved mahogany doors.

"*Sí* Alejandro, *gracias,*" they heard the stifled response from beyond the closed doors. Moments later the doors flew open dramatically.

"Ah, Sneddon, it is good to see you again," said Manuel Noriega, parading into the room. He walked over to Sneddon and embraced him in the Latin manner. "Welcome to my humble home."

"Manuel, you are looking exceptionally well, as usual. Please. Let me introduce you. Sergio, my associate, you've met before. And this is the latest addition to our team, Miss Apple Lacroix." Sneddon's sycophancy was calculated to impress.

From the moment they shook hands, Apple detected something unsettling in Noriega's eyes. He was shorter than she'd imagined. For a man of forty eight, his skin still bore testament to the ravaging effects of puberty. From any other man, the greeting might have been charming, but Apple sensed the raw innuendo behind Noriega's forced flattery. Apple knew to trust her instincts; she hid the prickle of discomfort.

"Please follow me. We will have lunch out on the verandah." Noriega turned and led them to an ornately-laid table. They were shaded from the equatorial sun by the spreading canopy of a giant kapok. Colorful songbirds flirted in the branches above their heads.

"Let's talk business, shall we?" said Noriega after desserts had been served.

"Yes, indeed," said Sneddon. "Manuel, the first order of business is to assure you that the CIA continues to regard you as one of our most valued intelligence sources. It seems that while *your* country benefits from having a stable and responsible government, the same cannot be said for many of your neighbors in Central America."

Noriega nodded vaguely while Sneddon continued. "I extend an assurance that the USA will continue to play its part in bringing stability to the region. We will carry on funding and supporting those regimes and organizations which have demonstrated a willingness to push back against the communist tide. The CIA will continue to supply these counter-insurgency forces with the weapons, military equipment and cash that they need to fight their wars against communism. As has been our long-standing arrangement, you personally will remain responsible for acting as our main conduit to these counter-insurgency groups."

Hours earlier, thousands of feet above the Caribbean, Apple had listened transfixed while Sneddon described how the CIA *actually* functioned in the real world. She listened dismayed as she learned about her organization's subterfuge and large-scale shadowy maneuvers. But Sneddon wasn't finished with his surprises. Apple was left aghast when he told her how much Noriega actually earned from his extortionate commissions as a middleman. She was appalled to think that much of it was funded by the American tax dollar.

"So in conclusion Manuel, in return for our support, can I count on you to continue providing us with your valuable intelligence updates from across Central America?" asked Sneddon.

"Yes, most certainly, I give you my assurance," Noriega gushed. Apple winced as he shot her another lascivious glance.

"Just to confirm my understanding, you are also able to give me your personal assurance that Panama will continue to block shipments of Colombian cocaine destined for the US market?"

"Sneddon, my friend, come now." Noriega raised his hands in mock indignation. "You have known me since our days together at the Chorrillos Military School in Peru, yes? My word has always been my bond. No drugs from Colombia will pass through my country. I assure you."

49

MISS DAVIS

Elroy took the stairs three at a time. He was still curious about the anonymous entry he'd discovered in Morozov's file the day before. He was hoping Sneddon knew something about it. *There must be a simple explanation.* It was early Thursday morning and the office was just coming to life. As Elroy approached Sneddon's glass partitioned office he could see the door was closed and the office empty. He'd met Sneddon's PA the day before. He approached her desk. "Miss Davis, good morning to you."

"Good morning Mr. Matthews, and how are you this morning," she asked brightly.

"Very well thanks. Tell me, is Sneddon around?"

"He flew to Panama early this morning. He went with Sergio Teves and Apple Lacroix."

"Wow! He told me yesterday he was leaving soon ... I just didn't realize he meant *that* soon," Elroy chuckled. *I guess I'll have to wait until he's back.* "Do you perhaps know when he's returning?"

"Yes, they're expecting to be back around 5 PM on Friday 15. They're only gone for two days."

"Thank you Miss Davis, have a good day."

50

VAN HORN

Just shy of fifty, Jim Rhyne was already regarded as a living legend in flying circles. After an early start with the USAF and Air National Guard, he eventually joined the CIA's covert dummy corporation, Air America. One day, after completing yet another clandestine operation for the CIA, Jim's daring skills were forever lionized when a grateful agent described him as 'the greatest pilot we never saw.'

Fast approaching twenty thousand hours aloft, Jim's exploits had become the stuff of legend. A few of his allegiants swore he was capable of flying a sewing machine—all it needed was wings. Under clear Texan skies, Dax and the other four foreign pilots quickly discovered that there was substance to that claim.

During the course of the preceding two weeks, the five new CIA pilots watched and learned as Jim imparted his immense knowledge. The pilots also came to appreciate the capabilities of their CASA C-212 twin turboprops. Flying nap-of-the-earth exercises on moonless nights, they quickly came to trust their newfangled night vision goggles. In just under a fortnight, Jim had gotten them to master the tricky skill of low-level, night-time pallet drops over ill-defined clearings. It would be measurably harder over hostile jungle while being fired upon by the enemy: the CIA's jargon for such situations was referred to as *sporty*.

In preparation for their new jungle role, the CIA had ordered its technicians to make several changes to the CASAs. One of the more interesting modifications was the removal of each and every serial number off every one of the aircraft's components. If they were unlucky enough to get shot down, the CIA didn't want any part of the wreckage to be traced back to the USA. After that small revelation, it became obvious to the five pilots why the CIA had selected foreigners instead of Americans.

Dax and the other four were as ready as they'd ever be. They were scheduled to fly their small armada of CASAs to Costa Rica on Sunday 17, just two days hence. Jim had arranged a stopover on Sunday night at an undisclosed destination in the south of Mexico. The plan was to push on southwards to Costa Rica the following day.

It was Friday afternoon and Dax had been well pleased with his day's training sortie. He missed flying helicopters, but loved being aloft, regardless. Each pilot faced one final check ride with Jim the following morning.

When the pilots weren't flying, they busied themselves around the hangar. They assisted the mechanics and parachute packers where they could. Dax's mind wandered back to his conversation with Elroy earlier in the week. He had been caught completely off-guard when Elroy advised him that Sneddon had swapped out Apple for Elroy on the ferry flight down to Costa Rica. Even now, recalling that conversation, Dax fought to control his disappointment. As he helped fold a heavy cargo parachute, he heard the distinctive drone of a twin-engine turboprop as it adjusted its propellers for landing.

Along with two other CIA agents, Elroy had boarded one of the agency's King Airs just before daybreak that Friday morning. The aircraft had made two stops; one in Atlanta to drop off the first agent, then Houston to drop the other. While the seats weren't uncomfortable, it was almost impossible for a 6'7" man to move around the cabin and stretch his legs. Apart from that, Elroy's flight to Van Horn in Texas had been uneventful.

After touching down lightly on the grass strip, the aircraft taxied toward a line of low buildings. Peering through his porthole window, Elroy saw Jim Rhyne coming out of the hangar to greet them. After shutting down the engines, the co-pilot came forward to open the door and lower the ladder. Elroy's legs almost betrayed him as he alighted.

"Jim, it's good to see you. It's certainly been a while," said Elroy, trying to shake the feeling back into his stiff legs.

The two men shook hands warmly. "Elroy, I've got just the thing for you. Come meet your boys over a beer. Same goes for you two greenhorns," said Jim, calling out to the crew of the King Air.

"If we're greenhorns then who better to blame than our instructor?" said the pilot, laughing. Somewhere along their career paths, almost every CIA pilot had received instruction from Jim Rhyne. Everyone knew Gentleman Jim.

Up at the ranch house it was apparent that no expense had been spared in the construction of the traditional saloon bar. An equally impressive collection of liquor lined the shelves. With everyone having been formally introduced, Konrad took up position behind the bar and served the first round of beers. In his Germanic monotone, he raised his bottle and toasted the gathering. "Gentlemen, a true pilot never smokes within twelve hours of flying, nor does he drink within ten yards of his plane." It took the group a moment to realize that he'd intentionally muddled the old aviators' mantra. It elicited a round of lighthearted heckling. The unmusical clinking of nine bottles was drowned-out by a hearty chorus of 'cheers.'

The five pilots under Jim's care were due to commence their final check rides after breakfast the following day. As was customary, Jim called the last round of drinks at 7:30 PM. Elroy couldn't help notice that none of the pilots took him up on his offer.

51

KIDNAPPED

After their lunch with Noriega, Apple and Sneddon had gone to the CIA's regional nerve-center on the outskirts of Panama City. Excusing himself from this meeting, Sergio had gone off to attend to company matters.

With a few exceptions, most of Sneddon's Central America team members were in the office that afternoon. Sneddon introduced Apple to her new co-workers. It was good to eventually put faces to the names.

Early the following morning, Sergio, Apple and Sneddon headed out to the US Army's School of the Americas. Located within the perimeter of the US-administered Panama Canal Zone, the SOA was close to the city of Colón. Heading northwest from Panama City, the drive took them almost an hour. Sneddon had advised Apple to dress casually; they could expect to do a fair bit of walking on their tour of the facility.

Under the terms of the Torrijos-Carter Treaty, Apple knew that the SOA was destined to be expelled from Panama in September 1984. Although its focus had shifted to the training of anti-communist combatants during Kennedy's administration, it had since earned an unsavory reputation as a breeding-ground for political bullies. It was an open secret that it operated under the aegis of the CIA.

Along with a handful of CIA advisors, Apple met several senior army officers during the tour of the SOA facility.

Soon after the tour commenced, Sneddon and Sergio excused themselves from the group. Offering their apologies, they left Apple in the capable hands of Kowalczyk, a charming major who hailed from Arkansas. She'd read his name off his shirt badge but hadn't attempted to pronounce it.

Sergio rejoined the group a few hours later. Apple gave him a quizzical look as he fell back into the small touring party. *Where's Sneddon?* She hoped he understood her nonverbal communication. Sergio smiled back reassuringly. She went over to him at the first available opportunity. "Hey Sergio, is everything all right? Sneddon's not with you," said Apple.

"Everything's fine. Sneddon asked me to give you a message. Something's come up and we're going to have to stay over in Panama for a few more days. The Duty NCO at the guard house will arrange a cab to take you back to the hotel. You can tell the driver to wait downstairs while you collect your luggage. He can then take you to the airport. Sneddon has already told our pilot that you'll be traveling home alone tonight."

Although Apple's Spanish was passable, the cab driver insisted on speaking English. After a few minutes she asked him how he'd come to learn the language so well. "My parents were Catholic *señorita*, they sent me to the Holy Jesuit mission school."

After driving a few more miles Apple started to notice that her surrounds were becoming less familiar. While she might've struggled to identify the exact route they'd taken earlier that day, she couldn't help notice that they'd moved off the wider road that connected the two cities. "Enrique, where are we going? This road doesn't look familiar," said Apple, trying to disguise her concern.

"Ah, *señorita*, it is Friday market and the normal route back to Panama City gets very busy. The streets are crowded with traders and customers. I am taking a short-cut."

Soon, even the passable roads began to give way to crumbling potholes and piles of decaying trash. Gaudily-colored shacks crowded against the narrow road. Easing the cab between the obstacles, the driver made a sudden turn into a side alley. By this stage, Apple was close to panicking. She started to remonstrate with her driver. "Enrique, this is not right. Where are you taking me?" she demanded. Enrique remained silent. "Enrique ..."

Out on the edge of her peripheral vision, Apple sensed a shadow passing by her right side. She instinctively looked in the direction of the movement. A man had walked past the cab and was disappearing down the narrow alleyway. She relaxed slightly.

Bang!

Apple screamed. She heard her window explode. With her attention diverted by the man on her right, she hadn't seen his accomplice approaching from the left. With a half-brick clutched in his fist, he'd smashed the side window of the cab. A shower of glass shards sprayed over the back seat. Apple was frantic. She fumbled with the handle, desperate to try and escape out the right-hand door. Her fingers simply wouldn't obey her intentions. "Enrique ... Enrique, help me," she screamed.

Reaching casually through the broken window, the attacker found the handle and opened the door from the inside. Apple was completely cornered. Time seemed to distort and her own frantic cries echoed mutely in her ears. She was in imminent danger. Apple continued to fumble with her own door handle. *It won't open.* Flinging the left door open, the burly attacker stooped down and reached into the cab. Apple fought off his prying hand but he was built like a wrestler. Bracing herself against her closed door, she pulled both legs up to her chest and unleashed a double kick toward the man's body. She grunted from the exertion. Her right heel connected squarely with the attacker's jaw. He blinked his eyes, shook his head and growled in anger. With his face etched with menace, he reached into the cab a second time.

Apple felt herself falling.

Returning to the same side he'd walked past moments earlier, the first accessory yanked open Apple's door. With all her body weight pressed against the door, she tumbled back into the void as her support was snatched away from her. Her head hit the road. A cascade of bright lights burst behind her eyeballs. Her vision dimmed as she faded from consciousness.

With their unconscious hostage bound and gagged in the trunk of their car, the two hijackers paid-off the cab driver. They reluctantly added a further thirty dollars after he quibbled over his broken window. After negotiating the alleyways of Colón's barrio, the thugs turned onto Expressway 9 and headed toward Panama City. "She's a fighter, that one," said the driver, rubbing his swollen jaw.

"She's crazy," agreed the other man. "Do you think the boss will want to play with one as *loco* as this?"

"Of course he will. *El Man* will be well pleased with her feistiness."

52

HURRICANE

Someone was pounding on Dax's door. He'd been in a deep sleep. He opened his eyes and shook his head. Dax was fully alert within seconds; a survival instinct he'd developed during the Bush War. He recognized Jim's voice. "Dax, you awake?"

"Yes Jim, what's up?" It was still dark outside. The pilots normally came down for breakfast at 7 AM.

"Get yourself down to breakfast at 6 AM sharp. There's been a change of plans."

"Roger that." Dax checked his watch. It was 5:30.

Whatever Jim had to say, it must've been important. Even Elroy had been woken. "Gentlemen, my apologies for interrupting your beauty sleep. About two months ago, November 6, 1981 to be exact, a devastating hurricane ripped across the Caribbean. A few days ago our meteorologists advised us that they've detected another unseasonal tropical weather system developing out over the Atlantic. I checked in with them a few hours ago and they've advised me that the cyclone has now veered westwards from its anticipated path. It looks like it's now making its way directly toward Cuba and the Mexican coast. If it maintains this track, it'll intersect our intended flight path. If we leave on Sunday, as scheduled, we'll be flying right through the belly of the beast." None of the foreign pilots, not even Konrad the German, had ever experienced such potentially ferocious weather systems.

"If we wait it out, we could be delayed by four or five days, maybe more," said Elroy.

"So gentlemen, after breakfast I want you to get your gear packed into your aircraft. We're leaving for Costa Rica in two hours," said Jim.

"Are we going to push through all the way?" asked Phil.

"No. We'll still be breaking our journey at our location in the south of Mexico tonight. If it follows its new course, we'll be beyond the eye by the time it makes landfall sometime on Saturday night. Sunday's last leg down to El Rótulo in Costa Rica should be uneventful," predicted Jim.

53

C-4

It made perfect sense that the Medellín airport was so quiet. It was Sunday morning and the faithful had been called to their knees. Brutus double-parked outside the main terminal and kept the car running. "So Vlad, here is the phone number of your contact in Panama. He will be expecting your call from sometime after 2 PM today." Brutus handed Morozov a piece of folded paper.

"What about money?" asked Morozov.

"There's ten thousand dollars." He indicated toward the briefcase lying on the back seat. "It's in the hidden compartment. Your contact's fee is four thousand, including the hardware. The rest will cover any other expenses. Remember, you are to time your attack for no later than 6 PM tomorrow. And don't forget ... make sure your collateral damage doesn't affect the locks. Serpico doesn't want to block the canal; he just wants a big fireworks display."

"Stop patronizing me Brutus. You've told me this three times already. I know how to handle this." With that, the Russian let himself out the car. Reaching into the back, he took the briefcase, along with his small carry-on bag. "Will that be all, Brutus?" he offered a mock salute as he slammed the door and strode toward the entrance.

It wasn't exactly an AK-47, but then again it was designed with an entirely different purpose in mind. From time spent in

Angola, Morozov was already familiar with the Uzi submachine gun. He released the magazine from the grip, cocked the mechanism and inspected the receiver and moving parts. Although not brand new, the weapon appeared to have been well-maintained. He noticed that the serial numbers had been filed off.

"How many rounds are you giving me?" asked Morozov.

"Two hundred and fifty," said the Panamanian. Morozov shrugged his shoulders. Carrying more ammunition would only weigh him down. Besides, this Uzi fired the ubiquitous 9mm NATO round: a shrewd soldier knew that the battlefield was a good place to scavenge extra ammunition.

"Show me the explosives." The Panamanian reached down and lifted a duffel bag onto the countertop. He unzipping one of the bag's three compartments and held it open for Morozov to peer inside. Even though tightly sealed in clear cellophane, the three blocks of C-4 explosives emitted the distinct aroma of engine oil. Weighing one-and-a-quarter pounds each, Morozov knew there was enough explosive to achieve his objective. Besides, he also knew that by shaping the charges he could effectively amplify the detonation. "Where are the fuses and the blasting caps?" asked Morozov.

"Just as you requested," said the Panamanian, unzipping the bag's second compartment. "Three rolls of fifty feet each. And over on this side here, the eight pyrotechnic blasting caps." Morozov's contact unzipped the final compartment to show him the goods.

54

PRISONER

Apple's head was throbbing. She tried to blink. Rheum had dried over her eyelids and was making it difficult to focus. A thin shaft of sunlight pierced through a chink in the curtains. She lifted her head. Her vision swam. She saw she was lying on a narrow bed.

Apple needed water. Just sitting up made her dizzy. Fighting both the pain and the waves of nausea, she surveyed her surrounds. Looking down, she realized why the movement had required so much effort. Her wrists had been bound by a thick cable tie. As she suspected, so were her ankles. A length of chain had been padlocked around her waist. Two loops of rope, anchored on opposite sides of the room, had been fed through the chain alongside each of her hips. Each loop of rope provided enough slack for her to reach a nearby table, but not enough to reach either anchor point. She was tethered like a goat. A pitcher of water beckoned from the table. She guessed it was just within her reach.

She hopped over toward the water. The pain in her head was blinding. Careful not to let the jug slip from her clumsy grip, she poured herself a cup of water. She noticed that both vessels were made from plastic. After gulping down a cupful, she quickly poured herself a second.

Hopping backwards toward her bed, Apple's foot brushed against a large plastic bucket. In the pale light she noticed a few sheets of paper lying in the bottom of the container. *Bastards thought of everything, didn't they?* Apple looked down at her bound wrists. They'd taken her watch. Raising her hands above her head, she was able to rub her forearm over the bump on the back of her skull. A stabbing pain made her gag. Apple thought she detected matted blood in her hair. She turned and checked the thin pillow. *Just as I thought.* She collapsed resignedly back onto the bed. The pain was just too intense for her to concentrate.

When she next awoke, Apple noticed a plate of fruit and bread on the table. The jug had also been refilled. Perched on a cabinet on the far side of the room, a bulb glowed feebly from a cheap lamp. She spotted her wristwatch lying under the lamp. She knew the tether around her waist wouldn't let her reach that far. *The glass from my watch sure would've been useful.*

Apple was completely disorientated; she knew neither the day, nor the time. Despite her predicament, she was grateful for one thing: the crippling pain in her head and neck had begun to ease. "Is anyone there?" she called out. There was no response. She looked around the room. Although it was sparsely furnished, the interior finishes suggested it was part of a lavishly-built structure: polished wooden floors and an AC vent recessed into the ceiling.

She shouted a little louder but still nobody came. *Think Apple, think!*

55

M.V. ODESSA

With Brutus acting as middleman, Serpico had given a specific set of orders regarding the execution of the canal incident. But there was one obvious flaw to his plan: the success of the operation hinged on an unbalanced man's single-minded obsession with a Rhodesian pilot. All things considered, Serpico knew it was a gamble. But given the incentive—offering Hunter's head on a platter—Serpico had to trust that Morozov would do his bidding.

What he didn't know was that Morozov was his own man. He seldom listened to his own superiors, let alone a traitorous American. He would do Serpico's bidding—of that there was no doubt—but he'd already decided that he would be doing it *his* way.

As for Hunter, Morozov didn't need the American to hand him over like a trussed turkey: the CIA mole had already revealed Hunter's whereabouts in December. Morozov was arrogant enough to know that he was capable of tracking-down Hunter himself in the jungles of Central America.

With Escobar's cocaine business booming in Florida, his drug mules were flying between Miami and Medellín on a daily basis. As if they didn't already earn enough money, the pilots flew luxury American goods back to Colombia, regularly fulfilling private orders for their fellow *narcos*. But it was Brutus' new guy—the Russian—who most puzzled Escobar's pilots: no

TVs; no high-end stereos; no liquor; no kinky porn videos for him … just English newspapers.

A few weeks earlier, a newspaper article had attracted Morozov's attention. It appeared in the travel section of the Miami Herald in late December, 1981. A familiar name in the heading caught his eye.

> *The Russian registered cruise ship, the M.V. Odessa, is due to dock in Miami on New Year's Eve. Those disembarking in The Magic City will be making way for hundreds more American travelers. The ship is due to set sail for the Caribbean, whereafter it will be making its way to the Pacific through the Panama Canal.*

Morozov was amazed. *Russian ships still calling in American ports? In the height of the Cold War?* Beyond that, he didn't give it much thought. Until a few weeks later.

After hearing of Serpico's offer—Dax's head in exchange for committing a supposed terrorist attack in the canal—Morozov had started to weigh his options. *My beloved Russia—the Motherland—has abandoned me. In exchange for Hunter, this American capitalist traitor pig wants me to blow a hole in the hull of a small merchant ship. For what? Blame it on Russia? Blame it on the Palestinians? Fuck him. Yes, I will blow up a ship … but it will be the ship that carries the flag of the country that has betrayed me. And it will be full of fucking Americans. As for Hunter, he cannot hide from me. Anywhere. I don't need this American fucker Serpico to do my work.*

56

EL RÓTULO

The weather system that had prompted the pilots' early departure from Van Horn had indeed maintained its westerly track. Fortunately for them, it had largely petered-out by the time it reached the Mexican coast. Apart from some wild buffeting in the first half hour of their second leg, their journey was unremarkable.

After landing their aircraft and shutting down, the group clambered aboard a small convoy of jeeps. Like the airfield and the main camp, the short road that connected the two had also been hewn out of the dense Costa Rican forests.

Dax had endured some pretty rudimentary accommodations during his time as a pilot in the Bush War. Thankfully, their CIA training camp near El Rótulo appeared to be better appointed than he'd anticipated.

The Contra contingent was housed in a series of large barracks and the entire camp could accommodate a maximum of a hundred and eighty recruits at a time. All the CIA staffers—including the foreign pilots—were accommodated in neat, pre-fabricated units on the far side of the camp. The pilots were impressed with their new home: Dax even noticed a hot-water boiler perched on the roof of their ablution facilities. As Jim concluded their tour, a tempting aroma wafted over from the DEFAC; it reminded the pilots that it was lunchtime.

After their meal, Dax cornered Elroy. "Hey Elroy, this is awkward man. I don't know how to say this."

"Don't be getting all soft on me now Hunter, you hear? What is it, man? You got girlfriend problems?" Elroy's eyes sparkled mischievously.

"Well, I … ah, I …" Placing his massive hand on Dax's shoulder, Elroy prevented Dax from embarrassing himself any further.

"Listen man. I'm kidding with you. I know about you and Apple."

"What … how?" stammered Dax.

"She's told me already. In confidence. And it's safe with me. But I'm gonna give you the same advice I gave her. Keep it on the down low, man. The company doesn't look favorably on inter-departmental fraternizations. You hear what I'm saying?" Elroy's hand was still resting on Dax's shoulder. "When she comes out here as the pilots' CIA liaison officer, you can't be flying paper airplanes at her with love notes scrawled in them, hear?" They both smiled at the imagery.

"Thanks Elroy. Thank you man." Dax paused for a moment. "Can I use your satellite phone to place a call to her?"

"Sure man. Just get out of earshot, okay?"

It was Elroy's turn to take Dax to one side. It had been a few hours since their last conversation and the big American had noticed that Dax's mood had turned.

"What is it man? You've been looking pensive all afternoon."

Dax shook his head, trying to convince himself he was over-reacting. "I called Jinny … that's Apple's aunt."

"I know Aunt Jinny. Go on."

"She says Apple was due back home on Friday night. She never came home. Jinny didn't think anything of it … work demands, you know. She said it's happened before. But it's now Sunday afternoon and there's still no sign of her. Jinny's beyond anxious. She's now even more concerned because I've just called her and I don't know her whereabouts either."

"Hey Dax, I'm sure there's a logical explanation. I know she went to Panama on Thursday morning with Sneddon and Sergio. It's not uncommon for trips like these to get extended. Let me make a few calls, okay?"

57

REAGAN

Early on Monday morning, just ten hours before the planned attack, Morozov put a call through to the Soviet Embassy in Havana, Cuba. "*Buenos días, ¿cómo puedo ayudarte?* Good morning, how may I help you?" answered the Soviet receptionist cheerfully.

"Good morning," answered Morozov in English. "Can I speak Russian please?"

"Certainly comrade, how may I help you?" asked the assistant.

"Yes, my cousin Dimitri is an engineer on the *M.V. Odessa*. The last time he wrote to me he said he was passing through the Panama Canal sometime in January. I believe it might even be later today … the 18th, yes? They have a day's shore leave in Panama City and I'd very much like to see him again. I'd like to confirm that this ship is still on schedule."

The woman on the other end of the line didn't hesitate. "Ah, comrade. I am sorry to bring you bad news. These Americans, they are full of shit," she said disdainfully. "Just two weeks ago, President Reagan placed very tight restrictions on much of the Soviets' commercial and passenger fleet. Apparently the capitalist imperialists don't like the way we are interfering in Poland's affairs. On the 2nd of January the *M.V. Odessa* was forced to divert to New Orleans to drop-off over three hundred American passengers. Their government ordered them off. The *M.V. Odessa* was sent home to the

Motherland. I am sorry comrade. I hope you see your cousin soon. Is there anything else?"

"Thank you comrade, that is all." He cradled the phone. *Then I will just have to fucking sink another passenger ship.*

58

ESCAPE

Lying back on her bed, Apple performed a series of quick mental tests. Despite the blow to her head, she was satisfied that her faculties appeared to be functioning normally. She sat up to assess her situation. While looking down at the cable-tie around her ankles, she noticed her sneakers were still on. *Remember to thank Sneddon for suggesting I dress casual on ... what day was it? Friday. Yes Friday.*

Drawing her feet up onto the bed, Apple fumbled with the laces. Her dexterity was hampered by the fact that her hands were bound. She was able to unlace each shoe to about halfway. Groping clumsily, she eventually managed to tie a large knot in the one end of the shoelace on her left foot. Working between the eyelets, she fed this lace all the way through until the large knot anchored on the eyelet midway down the shoe. She drew the shoelace taut and made sure the shoe was firmly cinched to her foot. She repeated the process with her other shoe. Apple then threaded one lace through the loop of the cable tie that bound her wrist and tied it firmly to the free end of the other lace. The irony wasn't lost on her: she'd now rendered herself virtually immobile.

Swinging her legs back over the bed, Apple prayed that her strict exercise routine would now pay dividends. Although her ankles were bound, the loop of the cable tie had only been tightened to the point where it prevented her from slipping her slender ankle through the restraint.

With her buttocks planted on the edge of the bed, and her legs protruding off the side, she started to perform alternate miniature leg thrusts. Pulling back gently on her wrists, Apple was able to regulate the tension in the loop of her makeshift bow saw. In effect, the shoelace had replaced the function of a blade. She could feel the lactic acid building up in her legs but she was determined to keep them pumping.

Apple knew the physics. Apply enough pressure, combine it with motion, and you generate heat. She didn't need a knife, but she knew that the principle was exactly the same. *It's the heat that interferes with the integrity of the molecules and causes them to forfeit their microscopic bonds.*

The cable tie burst open. After flicking the life back into her wrists, Apple massaged them vigorously. After sensation had been sufficiently restored, she removed the laces from each shoe. She then reworked them so that both were bound by a single knot. After threading one end through the cable tie around her ankle, she took up sufficient slack in each hand and wound the ends around her wrists for a better grip. Applying the same reciprocating motion, she was able to saw her way through the cable tie around her ankles. Now able to use longer strokes, Apple managed to sever the cable-tie in a fraction of the time.

Although her limbs were free, Apple was still tethered by the rope. She realized the same technique wouldn't work on *that* restraint. Both shoelaces were starting to fray and weren't likely to survive much more heat and friction. She needed another solution. *The globe in the lamp.*

Weak light was beginning to filter through the chinks in the curtain. *C'mon Apple … Move girl.*

Grabbing her pillow, Apple moved toward the lamp. With the ropes straining against her waist, she was still over a yard short of the cabinet. *Make this count.* She lobbed the pillow toward the lamp. If she hit it too hard it would fall off the side of the cabinet, knocking it even further from her reach. Ideally, she wanted it to topple forward.

Teetering unsteadily, the lamp rocked on its base. Apple

held her breath. Like a tree about to yield to a woodsman's axe, it slowly toppled forward. Although it fell, it didn't reach the floor: it got snagged on its own lead. Still swinging from its cord, it dangled enticingly beyond her reach. "Fuck!" She cursed under her breath. During its last pendulumlike swing, the glow of the bulb reflected momentarily off Apple's watch: it too had been knocked off the cabinet and lay a short distance off to the side. *Thank you Jesus … sorry I swore.*

Squirming around within the confines of her chain belt, Apple turned to face the bed. She then lay down on the floor. She inched herself backwards until the ropes were again taut. Sweeping with her foot, and using her toes as probes, she gently caressed the floor in search of her watch. *There it is.* It seemed to taunt her at the very edge of her reach. Using her hands to push back against the floor, she squeezed a further half inch of reach out of her restraints. The chain bit painfully into her waist. She managed to get a toenail—nothing more—onto the strap. Fighting her impatience, she edged it delicately toward her. *Got you!* With a flick of her ankle, she scooped it forward along the smooth wooden floorboards.

Apple intended breaking the window on her watch and using a shard to saw through the rope. The problem was that it was a small piece of glass. Breaking it would simply crush it into unusable sizes. A thought occurred to her. Looking down at the padlock that fastened the two ends of the chain, Apple identified it as a cheap Asian variety. She inspected the base of the lock. To her immense relief, she noticed a small hole adjacent to the key plug. As a kid she remembered watching in awe as her father opened the padlock on their garden shed by inserting a thin nail into just such a hole. All she needed was a nail.

My watch!

Apple studied the buckle tongue on the end of her watchstrap. *I hope it's long enough.* Squinting in the poor light, she inserted it into the hole in the base of the lock. *Click.* Nothing could've sounded more satisfying. The steel shackle popped open.

Apple moved quickly through the room. She couldn't see anything that resembled a weapon. She needed to be able to defend herself when her guard next paid a visit. Moving over to the window, she peered carefully through the curtains. In the pastel light of dawn she could see a mansion up at the top of a manicured garden. Towering above the impressive verandah, a grand old kapok tree stood sentry over the garden's lesser denizens. The same one she'd sat under during lunch with Noriega on Thursday afternoon. *Bastard!*

She detected movement. Emerging from the gloom, a man appeared on the path leading down to Apple's building. Although she'd only seen him fleetingly, she immediately recognized him as one of the kidnappers from the barrio. Her nerves jangled. *Shit! I need a weapon.*

Her eyes fell on the length of chain lying on the floor. She estimated it was slightly longer than a yard. Apple knew she could increase its potential force by drawing the two ends together and halving its length. She heard a key rattle in the door lock. She could hear her pulse drumming in her ears.

A curious thought flashed through her mind. Back in her academy days, her old self-defense instructor had once told the class that a fight was mostly about attitude. While skill and speed were both important, your mind-set was invariably your best weapon. *Imagine you're the third gorilla to arrive at Noah's Ark. There's only space for two of you on board. Fight like that gorilla.* His words had stuck with her ever since. *Apple, you are gorilla.* She knew what she had to do.

Stepping casually into the room, the man immediately paused. He was clearly confused by the empty bed. He never saw the chain arcing down onto his head. He reeled from the blow. With devastating effect, the swinging links wrapped over the top of his skull. He started to bring his arms up to defend his face but it was already too late. Apple was about to deliver a second, even more powerful blow. The second swing took him across the bridge of his nose. It fountained like a ghoulish wellspring. As the tip of the chain hurtled toward him on the third swing, it found a small opening between his raised arms. It accelerated into his mouth, pulverizing his teeth with a nauseating eruption. The dazed man cried out in pain. Tears stung his eyes. Judging her distance to perfection, she unleashed a backhanded flick toward his unprotected groin. Again, he didn't see it coming. Apple felt the chain connect with his testicles. His hands dropped to his ruptured scrotum. The man doubled over in agony.

Apple quickly loosened her grip and removed one end of the folded chain. She needed its full length. Wrapping the two ends several times around each wrist, she made sure she had a firm grip. Shifting behind him, she slammed her instep into the back of his calf. He dropped to his knees. She looped the chain over his head and pulled both ends toward her. It bit viciously into his throat. A mixture of blood and saliva gargled in his broken mouth.

Apple was only vaguely aware of her participation in the deadly attack: somehow her violent deeds were being mercifully filtered from her sensorium. It felt more like an out-of-body experience. She felt no hatred, nor anger; just the overpowering urge to survive.

Drawing up her right knee, she placed it firmly in the center of his back. She drove it into his spine and forced him to arch his back, further exposing his neck. At first she could hear his frantic gasps, but as the pressure increased, she cut the airflow over his vocal chords.

His fingers clawed at the chain. Like a defeated boxer, his arms eventually flopped down to his side. His head lolled. All resistance melted. But Apple knew she couldn't take any chances. Despite the temptation to let go, she held the choke for a further minute.

Apple retched over the toilet bowl, but she knew she couldn't linger. Clearly her guard had come to fetch her. Suspicions would be raised if she and the guard didn't appear anytime soon. All she wanted to do was stand under a blast of scalding water and scrub the vileness from her skin. *Get a grip Apple.*

This isn't over yet … not by a long shot. She washed her hands and forearms and removed most of the splatter.

Patting his pockets, Apple found the man's pistol. She released the magazine and checked she had a full house. Slapping it back into position, she cocked the weapon and slid the catch to the safe position.

Using the garden's dense foliage as cover, Apple approached the mansion. An earlier inspection of the perimeter wall had confirmed her suspicions: her only escape option was going to be through the front gates. She was just about to move around the side of the mansion when she heard a familiar voice coming from above. She peered through the fronds of a large cycad. *Noriega!* He was standing on the verandah and talking on his satellite phone. He was facing away from her.

"*Si*, Don Pablo," said Noriega. "Our CIA man Sergio was here on Thursday. We had lunch at my house."

Five yards below, concealed in the shrubbery, Apple strained to hear Noriega's conversation. *What! Our CIA man Sergio? He's a mole? So it was him who set me up? Bastard.* Although five minutes had passed since she'd released the chain from Sanchez's throat, the adrenaline was still coursing through her veins. She knew she had to try and control its inhibiting affect. *And Don Pablo … that can only be Pablo Escobar.*

"Don Pablo, please, wait. I don't understand," continued Noriega. "Our mole is planning to blow up a ship in *my* canal? Today? And he's getting a crazy Russian called Morozov to do his dirty work?"

Apple was dumbfounded. *Morozov? Here? What the hell is going on? Am I dreaming?* In case Apple thought she might be hearing things—that her grasp of Spanish might be letting her down—Noriega's next comment dispelled any lingering doubts.

"And you say the only way I can identify this Russian is from a vicious scar on his left cheekbone? You have nothing more for me to go on?" There was a brief pause as Noriega listened to Escobar's response. "Do you know what time this attack is scheduled?" There was another pause. "Yes, I got that … 6 PM today, close to the Bridge of the Americas" confirmed Noriega.

Apple was finding it hard to comprehend the lunacy of it all. *Why in God's name would Sergio want to blow up a ship in the canal? And how the hell did he manage to get Morozov to do his bidding? He must be working for the KGB as well.*

"Don Pablo, I am extremely grateful for this information. But I am perplexed by our informant's behavior … an attack like this is not only against my country, it is against me. I have always considered him to be a dependable ally. But there is one other thing that intrigues me, Don Pablo. He has also been one of your most reliable moles for nearly four years now. Why is he now biting the hand that feeds him?"

Crouched in the shadows below Noriega's verandah, Apple wished she could've heard Escobar's response to that question.

In his secret hacienda in Medellín, just over three hundred miles away, Escobar's voice grew menacing. "I'll tell you why, Manuel. It's because that fucking American had the audacity to call me, Don Pablo Escobar, the savior patron of Colombia, and ask *me* to provide one of *my* men to do *his* dirty work. If something happens, it happens because *I* order it. Don Pablo Escobar only *gives* orders … he never fucking *takes* them."

After concluding his call, Noriega turned toward the guest house at the bottom of his garden. "Sanchez!" He yelled. "Hurry. Bring me my little American *novia.*"

Upon hearing that, Apple was under no illusion as to Noriega's intentions. *Fucking sleaze ball.*

The Panamanian strongman must've sensed all was not well down in the guest house. He descended the steps. With her pistol at the ready, Apple remained undetected as he passed within three yards of her. Suppressing the urge to fill him with lead, she waited for him to pass. She then crept stealthily up the side of the mansion toward the driveway. *I've got to get out of here … fast.*

Parked in front of the mansion—with a driver behind the

wheel—Apple spotted her opportunity. The driver's head was tilted far back; his chauffer's cap far forward. Before opening the passenger door behind the driver, she checked to see that the central locking button was in the up position. *Good.* Dashing from her cover behind some shrubs, she quickly opened the door, slid inside, and then closed it.

The driver woke with a start. In his haste to sit up, he knocked his cap off his head. "*El Man, lo siento. Me dormí,*" pleaded the driver. *Boss, I'm sorry, I dozed off.*

Apple responded in Spanish. "Listen carefully. I have a gun pointed at the back of your head." She tapped him twice on the skull to reinforce her statement. "I'm not afraid to use it. Just ask Sanchez," she said ominously. "Let's drive right out of here, nice and slow. No silly mistakes, you understand?"

"*Sí señora, sin errores.*" He started the car and eased toward the large iron gates. From behind his thick sheet of bulletproof glass, the gatekeeper pushed the button that opened the monstrous barricade. The heavy structure trundled open and the car passed through without incident. "Where to?" he asked.

"American Embassy."

59

EMBASSY

Although the CIA's main office was at a secret location across town, they did have a handful of senior liaison officers and attachés assigned to the US Embassy in Panama City. Bill Dollar, the most senior of those attachés, was sitting at his desk when the Marine sergeant at the gatehouse called him on his phone. "Sir, I have a Miss Apple Lacroix here. She says she's with your agency?"

"Escort her up immediately," barked Dollar.

Striding down the corridor to meet them, Dollar was taken aback when Apple appeared around the corner. "Thank you Sergeant Joel, I've got this." Apple was disheveled. Her hair was matted and her arms still bore evidence of Sanchez's blood. Dollar led her back to his office. "My God, Apple. Are you alright? We've been searching frantically all over Panama for you. Come, let's get you sorted out."

"Thank you sir, but I can clean up later. Right now we have a major crisis looming. I need to debrief you on what I've discovered."

"Certainly Apple," he said, ushering her to a seat at a small conference table. "I need to let Sneddon know you're safe. He's been blowing up my phone since you went missing on Friday. He's been worried sick about you." Dollar dialed Sneddon's number. He let it ring for almost thirty seconds. "No answer. I'll try him again later."

An enticing aroma permeated Dollar's office. "Can I have a cup, please sir?" Apple indicated toward the fresh pot of coffee on his desk.

"Oh, I'm sorry … sure." He poured each of them a cup. "I guess you need this, right?" He didn't wait for a response. "So, from the top, tell me what happened." He couldn't help notice a small tremble in Apple's hand.

Starting with the cab ride outside the School of the Americas, Apple described the sequence of events up to her arrival at the embassy. After summarizing her ordeal, Dollar was about to say something, but Apple interrupted. "Please sir, since we can't inform Sneddon right now of my status, do you mind if I call my supervisor, Elroy Matthews, in Costa Rica?"

Dollar had graduated one class behind Elroy a number of years before and counted him amongst his good friends. "Big Elroy? Sure Apple, of course," he said, handing her his satellite phone. "I wasn't aware he was back from Africa."

Stepping out of the prefabricated meeting room deep in the Costa Rican jungle, Elroy unclipped the bulky phone from his belt and flipped the aerial. "This is Elroy." Although Apple's reason for calling appeared to be out of a sense of duty, her true motive was to get word to Dax that she was alright.

"Elroy, it's me. I'm safe."

She yanked the phone away from her ear as he roared into the mouthpiece. "Dax! Get over here. Apple's safe." Stifling a smile, she pressed the phone back to her ear. "What on earth happened to you?" Dax sprinted outside and crowded against Elroy to listen in.

"I'll fill you in on all the details later, but I was kidnapped by Noriega's henchmen. Right now, I'm with your old friend Bill Dollar at the embassy. But there's something vital I need to tell you. It's Sergio … he's a mole."

Elroy immediately connected Apple's revelation with the curious, un-authored entry in Morozov's file. *Damn you, Sergio.*

"It appears as if he's working for Noriega *and* Escobar,"

continued Apple. "But something must've gone bad, because I've just discovered that he's planning an attack in the canal today. Don't ask me why. But here's where it gets really crazy. He's somehow managed to get Morozov to enact the deed."

"Say what?" Elroy was thunderstruck. He looked at Dax, pointed silently at the phone and pulled an enquiring face. *Did you just hear that?* Dax nodded disbelievingly.

"You heard right ... Morozov. He's in Panama City to conduct the attack. Apparently it's going to be near the Bridge of the Americas around 6 PM. In all probability it's going to be aimed at a vessel. I have no other detail."

"Jesus H Christ," said Elroy softly. "How does Sneddon think we should proceed?"

"We've tried calling him. He's not answering his phone."

The enormity of the situation demanded an on-the-spot executive decision. "Apple, you wait there with Dollar. We're leaving now. Dax, give me an estimate. How long will it take to fly the CASA to Panama City?"

Dax's uncanny navigational skills immediately came to the fore. He visualized a map of the isthmus, dead reckoned the position of Panama City relative to their base in El Rótulo, then calculated an approximate distance. "It's around three hundred miles as the crow flies ... which means flying a fair bit over the Caribbean. If the winds are favorable, that's just under two hours' flying time."

"Did you hear that Apple? Sit tight at the embassy. We're leaving in ... ten minutes?" Elroy looked at Dax for confirmation. He nodded. "Yep, ten minutes." One thing Dax knew for certain was that all their aircraft were kept in a high state of readiness. "We'll call you when we get airborne, okay?"

"Thanks, yes ..." Apple desperately wanted to talk to Dax, but bit her tongue. What she had to say was too personal in front of Dollar. On cue, she heard her boyfriend's slightly muted voice through the phone.

"Wait, Elroy. I have an idea," said Dax. "Let's take Phil. We have no idea what kind of delays to expect over the airport in Panama City. We'll be airborne for two hours and we'll have contact with Apple throughout that time. Things can develop quickly in two hours. If I have to, I can parachute in. Phil can then fly you onwards to the airport. It's good insurance against unforeseen situations."

"I like it," said Elroy without hesitation. "Phil!" His voice boomed around their jungle clearing. For the second time in as many minutes, Apple was forced to haul the phone away from her ear.

With the azure waters of the Caribbean stretching away to their left, Phil kept the nose up as he nudged the CASA through nine thousand feet.

Elroy was trying to raise Sneddon on the satellite phone. It was his third attempt. He eventually got through. "This is Sneddon."

"Boss. It's Elroy. Can you hear me okay?"

"Elroy, are you in a washing machine? You're going to have to shout. What's up?"

"Apple is okay. She was kidnapped by Noriega but she managed to escape. We've been trying to raise you for the last forty minutes or so to tell you. She's at the embassy now."

"Thank heavens. Was she harmed?"

"No, I don't think so. But she managed to discover some unsettling news." Elroy had to shout in order to out-compete the noisy CASA.

"What news?"

"Sergio is a double agent. He's a mole for Noriega and Escobar."

"What? Say that again. Did you say Sergio?" Sneddon was incredulous.

"That's right. She overheard a phone conversation between Noriega and Escobar."

"Sergio? My God!"

"Yeah, crazy, isn't it? But that's not all. He's apparently attempting to pull off an attack in the canal this afternoon around 6 PM. But here's the kicker. He's somehow managed to get Morozov to do the dirty work."

"You're fucking kidding me?"

"Yeah, Morozov," said Elroy.

"Where are you now?" asked Sneddon.

"We're flying to Panama."

Sneddon paused for a moment. "I'll have a car pick you up at the airport. When will you land?"

"Around 10 AM," shouted Elroy.

"I'll get one of my guys to take you to the embassy. I'll meet you there." Sneddon broke the connection.

60

MAXIMUM DAMAGE

High over the shimmering Caribbean, the three men had been lost in their own thoughts. Dax eventually broke the silence. "So Morozov is expected to pull the trigger at 6 PM? And he's planning on doing it under the Bridge of the Americas?"

"Yeah," replied Elroy.

"Given everything you've told me about this psycho, do you really believe that he's going to stick to the program?" asked Phil. As a trusted friend, Dax had told Phil all about his history with the Russian.

"Who knows?" answered Elroy blandly. He was still trying to make sense of Sergio's betrayal.

"But if he does try to pull off the attack under the Bridge of the Americas at 6 PM, it's a given that the Panamanian SWAT team—or some special forces equivalent—will be in position waiting to neutralize him, right?" asked Dax.

"Where you going with this Dax?" asked Elroy.

"My point is this. Morozov has proven time-and-again that he has a predilection for doing his own thing. The hottest lead we have is that it's happening at 6 PM under the bridge. Why not let the Panamanian SWAT team deal with that baby? Seriously guys, what difference can we make in an unarmed CASA? We'll just be getting in their way."

"You make a good point Dax. But it's unlike you to suggest we do nothing," said Phil.

"On the contrary. I'm suggesting that while the canal might

still be his primary target, in all probability he's shifted the time and location to suit his own agenda. I believe we must search for him elsewhere."

"So where would we start?" asked Elroy.

"Well, start off by putting yourself in Morozov's shoes. What would give this lunatic the greatest satisfaction?"

"He'd probably be seeking the maximum amount of collateral damage," offered Phil.

"Exactly," answered Dax. "Which means what?"

"That he's likely to direct the explosion at the locks. Wreak maximum damage. He'd also be close to a network of roads and built-up areas ... make for a good escape," said Elroy. He was starting to warm to the exercise.

"Precisely. So here's my suggestion," said Dax, twisting against his harness to get a better look at Elroy. "We start at the first lock on the Pacific side and work our way inland. Phil can slow us down to just above stall speed, and you and I can get the binoculars on anything that looks suspicious down on the water."

"How far out are we?" asked Elroy.

"About thirty minutes from Panama City," said Phil.

"Okay. But let me suggest a minor modification to the plan. Phil, you get me down on the ground first. I'll be more useful down there than up here. Sneddon's got a car at the airport waiting to take me to the embassy. Once you've dropped me, get airborne right away and fly over the canal, Dax can be the spotter. I'll call my buddy Dollar and get him to clear this with air traffic control. Phil, can you give us a quiet radio frequency that you, me and Dollar can communicate on? I know it won't be secure, but at least we'll limit the number of potential eavesdroppers."

Phil toggled a random frequency into his second radio and made a dummy transmission. There was no response. "Here Elroy, this one seems to be quiet."

Elroy was already dialing Dollar's number. "Dollar, this is Elroy. My boys are going to use the following frequency to communicate with you. You got a pen?"

61

SAN ISIDRO

Apart from the disabling of a ship in the canal, Morozov's own plan bore no resemblance to Serpico's. He'd already discarded the idea of committing the act close to the Bridge of the Americas. *Why lessen the effect of the blast in wide-open waters?* Besides, Morozov knew that his escape options would be limited out on the open expanse of water. He was also naturally mistrustful; he had no idea of knowing whether he was being set-up or not. *Fuck you Serpico. Not only will I set off the explosion in a different place, but I'll also do it at a different time.*

When Brutus had originally arranged a false Chilean passport for Morozov, the intention was that he'd use it to gain entry into the USA as a trade representative for a Chilean copper company. Traveling under the pretext of being a high-level salesman, Morozov's real motive was to track down Dax in the USA. But since Serpico's somewhat unorthodox offer appeared to be far simpler, there was no need for Morozov to bring his Chilean ruse into play. But while developing this original cover, Morozov had spent many days memorizing details about the global copper industry. One of the things he'd discovered during his research was that a Texan chemical manufacturer had cornered the market for explosives in the Chilean mining industry. They were also one of the primary suppliers of cyanide, sulfuric and nitric acid to the country's gold mining industry. It had been simple enough for Morozov to find out when the next shipment from Galveston was due to pass through the Panama Canal.

The Russian had already checked the men's toilets. They were empty. *Perfect.* He took up position a short distance away and waited. A hundred yards away, a large container ship was bobbing in one of the Pedro Miguel locks.

From his control room high above, the operator started draining the lock. Inch-by-inch, Morozov watched as the ship started sinking from view. The Russian adjusted his gaze. Beyond the giant water gates, the next vessel was waiting its turn to enter the lock. It was the *San Isidro* out of Galveston … and Morozov was well-aware of what appeared on her cargo manifest.

The Russian didn't have to wait long. Dressed in light overalls and wearing a blue safety helmet, a swarthy looking longshoreman approached the men's toilets. Morozov spied an ID badge dangling from his neck.

Leaning casually against a far wall, his backpack resting at his feet, Morozov waited for the stevedore to enter the men's room. After inserting a cigarette in his mouth, Morozov quickly checked to see if anyone else was around. He followed the man inside. "Friend, have you got a lighter for me?" asked Morozov in broken Spanish.

"Can't a man take a crap in peace anymore?" The Russian caught the gist of his comment and shrugged apologetically. As the man dug in his pocket, Morozov struck. After jabbing the fingers of his right hand into the man's eyes, he used the back of his left hand to flick the man's groin. The dock worker let out a startled yell. Driving the instep of his shoe down the length of the man's shin, Morozov delivered a crushing blow to the small bones of his victim's foot. Before the man could fully react, or even attempt to defend himself, his attacker placed the blade of his forearm across his jaw and shunted him backward into one of the stalls. In one fluid movement, Morozov used his free hand to draw a knife from his pocket. Not wanting any arterial splatter over his face, he decided not to shunt the blade into his victim's throat. Instead, he drove it deep into the man's femoral artery, just at the point where the leg meets the torso. Morozov pushed him down onto the toilet seat, clasped a hand over the docker's mouth and quickly withdrew his blade. Blinded by pain and already in shock, the man struggled feebly. Using the same hand that held the knife, Morozov unfurled a yard of paper from the roll, twisted it around the blade and plunged it into the man's throat. The victim wheezed like an asbestos miner. Morozov removed his knife, as well as the man's ID badge from around his neck.

Outside the stall, Morozov used a coin to twist the door mechanism into the locked position.

Standing in front of the mirror, his bag slung over his shoulder, the Russian rinsed the blood off his hands, pulled the ID badge over his ears and popped the safety helmet on his head. "*Buenos días,*" said Morozov breezily, greeting the reflection that had just appeared over his shoulder.

"*Buenos días, amigo,*" the newcomer responded politely.

With a badge hanging from his neck and a worker's helmet on his head, Morozov blended-in with the other workers. He welcomed the orderly confusion as each man appeared to bark a contradictory order from the one just given.

Alongside the *San Isidro's* gunwales, the mechanical guide mules were busy maneuvering into position. As the process was wholly automated, only two of *San Isidro's* sailors were on deck. They watched disinterestedly as their vessel was bumped into position.

High up in his observation post, satisfied that the ship was in position, the operator started closing the double-leaf gates behind the *San Isidro's* stern. With the massive tank closed-off both front and back, he shifted the controls and set in motion a process that would drain over twenty six million gallons of water from the chamber.

Like an impressive science experiment, a miniature replica of the locks was laid-out on a vast table in front of the operator. For every input he made, the scale model simulated the process in real time. By studying the mechanical model, the operator was able to precisely monitor what was taking place outside.

As the water drained, so the *San Isidro* began to drop lower-and-lower into the chamber.

In comparison with the last ship that had just passed through, the *San Isidro* was relatively small. At about forty yards in length and nine yards across the beam, Morozov estimated her capacity at between two and three hundred deadweight tons. Inching steadily downwards, the vessel eventually drew level with the side of the lock chamber. Morozov checked to see if anyone was watching. It took nothing more than a small hop for him to clear the gap between the chamber wall and the ship's railing.

The two crewmen had since moved up to the bow and were blissfully unaware of the presence of their stowaway. By stepping quickly behind a lifeboat, the Russian was able to shield himself from any observers up in the ship's bridge. Morozov hoped that by pretending to batten the lifeboat's ropes and rigging, he'd fool a land-based observer into thinking that he was just one of the ship's sailors going about his duties.

No one raised the alarm.

62

UTOA

Colonel Matías López brooked no shit. He'd been handed the reins of the military's crack UTOA unit a year before. Along with a handful of other specialized counter-terrorism and counter-narcotic units, the UTOA team competed unofficially for the accolade of being Panama's best-of-the-best. The bragging rights were good for morale and maintained high standards throughout.

When he'd addressed his men on the first day of his appointment, López's speech had the effect of forever changing how the unit operated—and how its men saw themselves. "When you reach the point when you think you are the best, you are merely at the start of a slippery descent." López had abandoned his podium and was walking between the ranks of his unit. "From that moment, your performance is guaranteed to go into decline. Your mind will trick you into believing you no longer need to improve. And you will start to make mistakes. Such mistakes will cost lives: yours ... and your fellow soldiers. From now on, this unit will stop obsessing about being the best. But what we *will* do from this day forward is continually strive to be better. Each-and-every one of you currently carries a master proficiency in at least one skill: underwater demolitions; ship-borne special weapons and tactics; combat medicine; freefall and HALO; sniping ... our list is long. Starting tomorrow, each of you has six months to master one more, and within a year, a third specialized skill.

Each of us will become a complete fighting unit, but our success will be forged in our unity. We are a brotherhood, here to serve our beloved Panama."

On the third floor of the US Embassy, somebody knocked quietly on Dollar's door. "Come in," he said.

"Good morning sir … ma'am." A smartly-dressed CIA orderly entered the office with a manila folder under her arm.

"What have you got for me Vasquez?" asked Dollar. Vasquez hesitated, shooting a glance in Apple's direction. "Don't mind her, she's also CIA," reassured Dollar.

"Sir. This just in. It's from our Medellín office." She handed Dollar the folder. "Earlier this morning our guys intercepted a conversation between Escobar and an unknown contact here in Panama. This is the transcript of that conversation. It sounds like something big is brewing here in the city today."

"Thank you Vasquez. We already know about it. Apple here managed to eavesdrop on the other half of that conversation. Escobar was talking to none-other than Noriega. I already alerted the Public Security Minister this morning, right after Apple broke the news to me. He too had already heard about it from Noriega. The minister told me he'll be assigning the task to the crack UTOA team. They're the country's tactical amphibious operations unit. UTOA stands for *Unidad Táctica de Operaciones Anfibias*. Right now we're in full co-operation mode with the Panamanians."

"Will there be anything else sir?"

"That's all, thank you Vasquez." As the orderly closed the door behind her, Dollar slid the folder across the desk to Apple. "You might as well have a read. It'll fill in the other half of the conversation you missed."

Apple flipped the folder open and started reading. The color drained from her face. She sat back in her chair and raised her face to the ceiling. "Oh my God."

Dollar looked up from his desk. Apple looked ashen. "What is it?"

"Mr. Dollar, I need to call Elroy. Urgently."

63

THE CANAL

Setting up his approach to the airport's main runway, Phil was making fine adjustments to the CASA's throttles when he heard his call-sign over the radio. "Papa Mike Hotel-Thirty Four, this is Panama Control, you are to ..." Suddenly, from the back seat, Elroy's satellite phone started buzzing.

With its powerful circuitry activated by the incoming call, the phone immediately polluted the tower's inbound signal. All Phil heard was a medley of electronic hisses, pops and frequency whines. "Quick Elroy, switch it off," admonished Phil.

Elroy fumbled with his satellite phone and managed to turn it off. "I'm sorry."

"Panama Tower, you were blocked, say again for Papa Mike Hotel-Thirty Four."

At that moment, six miles away, Apple tried calling Elroy's number a second time. But his line was dead.

Colonel López didn't have the luxury of a thorough operational plan. With barely any details himself, the Public Security Minister's action-brief was wooly and ill-defined. Of one thing Colonel López was certain: their highly-trained adversary would not be playing by the rules.

With six hastily-assembled Quick Reaction Teams standing before him, the first thing López told them was that they should ignore the supposed 6 PM deadline.

Morozov noticed a hatch a short distance from where he hid behind the lifeboat. Staying low, he moved to the hatch, spun the locking mechanism and then heaved on the solid door. The hinges protested noisily. Careful not to let the hatch bang down, he peered inside the gloomy hold. A ladder descended into the cavernous hold. Pulling the hatch closed over his head, he climbed down into the cargo hold.

The vast storage area was full of different colored drums. Amongst the mixed cargo, Morozov ignored those that contained acid: cyanuric acid; sulfuric acid; and nitric acid. While *ANFO* didn't mean much to him, he knew from the international symbol for explosives—stenciled alongside—that he'd discovered what he was after.

The *San Isidro* was almost at the bottom of its descent inside the Pedro Miguel lock. Once the double-leaf gates were opened, the ship would enter the canal's short Miraflores Lake section.

Unzipping his bag, Morozov removed the C-4 bricks, the three rolls of visco fuse and the packet of pyrotechnic blasting caps. Working quickly, he molded a number of explosive charges, primed and crimped the fuses into the back of the blasting caps and then pressed them deep into the clay-like C-4 explosive. With three separate charges, and three separate fuses, Morozov knew that it'd take only one successful detonation to destroy the ship. He liked having some redundancy insurance. He then ran his three separate fuses back toward the hatch where he'd first entered the hold.

Once everything was set-up, he turned his attention to the last items in his carry bag: his Uzi submachine gun. Morozov also pulled out two full magazines. *Just for insurance.* He stashed the empty bag, slung his Uzi, drew his knife, and went in search of his first victim.

In accordance with Elroy's request, Dollar had been able to convince the Panama tower controller to let the CASA land and take-off hastily. After a fast taxi to a nondescript building on the side of the main airport complex, Elroy hurriedly climbed out of the aircraft. With the controller's cooperation, Phil and Dax were hastened to the front of the queue where they were able to get airborne almost immediately.

They were still in the climb when Phil's second radio hissed into life. Mindful that it was an open channel, the caller remained deliberately vague. "Two Zimbabweans, two Zimbabweans, do you read, over?" Dax smiled as he recognized his girlfriend's voice. Back at the embassy, Dollar had arranged for a radio set to be brought up to his office.

"This is Two Zimbos, we read you strength five," answered Phil.

"I'll be keeping a listening watch if you find anything, over," said Apple.

"Copy that," said Phil.

Swinging in from the southeast, Phil flew low over the Bridge of the Americas and aimed the CASA for the Miraflores Locks. "First set of locks coming up. You got your binoculars ready?" asked Phil.

"Sure do," said Dax. In order to improve Dax's overall view of the canal below, Phil had lowered the CASA's rear hatch. Setting his flaps to approach angle, he reduced his speed to 120 knots, adjusted his throttles to maintain level flight and nudged the nose up a little higher. Already strapped into his parachute, Dax tethered himself to an overhead anchor-point, leant out and started searching the waters below.

Elroy wasn't hard to miss. Sneddon's driver spotted him standing outside the airport concourse and aimed his car toward him. He pulled up alongside, wound down his window and called across to the tall man. "Sir, are you Elroy?"

"I sure am," he responded, approaching the passenger door.

"Sir, mind if I just confirm it's the right Elroy?" he asked sheepishly. Elroy could see the kid was barely out of the academy; he was still doing his job by the numbers.

"Sure."

"What's the name of the person I'm taking you to see?"

"Sneddon."

"Thank you sir. I'm Harrison. Hop on in." As they pulled away from the curb, the youngster spoke. "Sir, Mr. Sneddon directed me to tell you that I'm to drop you off at his motel. He says to tell you he has information on Sergio Teves."

"Thank you Harrison."

Although Elroy wasn't to know it, Apple's frustration was growing: she'd tried several times to raise him on his phone.

With hellborn intemperance the volatile Russian dispatched each of his victims in under eight minutes. He left the bodies of nine crew members scattered around the ship: a trail of carnage that spread from the engine room, to the galley, to the decks and finally the bridge of the *San Isidro*. The ship was now his. *I am the feral reaper.*

Although still just over a mile away from the Miraflores locks, the *San Isidro* was more-or-less lined up on the lock's approach walls. As there were still two vessels queued ahead of her, the captain's last speed setting was 2 knots—*Dead Slow*.

Not as ritzy as a hotel, not as economical as a motel, Sneddon was regarded as a satisfied regular at the *Amistoso Cabañas* on the outskirts of Panama City.

Elroy had just been dropped-off by Harrison. He was walking toward the *Cabañas'* front desk when he remembered his phone was still turned off. He stopped, switched it on, and continued walking toward the receptionist. "*Buenos días*, good morning. How may I help you sir?"

"Good morning. Yes. I'm looking for Mr. Sneddon please."

"Ah *sí*, Mr. Sneddon. Of course, sir. He's in room 18. Through there, down the corridor, it's to your right."

Up ahead, barely moments after turning into the corridor, Elroy heard a commotion. Sneddon had just staggered back out of one of the *cabañas*. *Sneddon?* Even at that distance, Elroy could see he was a little wild-eyed. To no one in particular, Sneddon cried out. "Please, quick! Somebody help me."

Sprinting toward his boss, Elroy noticed a silenced pistol hanging loosely in Sneddon's hand.

Elroy placed his hand on his boss's shoulder and shook him gently. "Sneddon! It's me, Elroy. What the hell's going on?" The big man drew his own revolver. It was obvious that Sneddon was in a state of shock. He had a large gash high over his left eye. "Boss, talk to me. What happened?" Sneddon turned and stared blankly at Elroy. "What happened?" repeated Elroy.

"Sergio … it's Sergio," intoned Sneddon. "He attacked me. I accused him of being a spy. I think he's dead Elroy. I'm sure he's dead."

With his weapon at the ready, Elroy entered cautiously. "Come in and close the door behind me," instructed Elroy. *This is company business … no point in getting outsiders involved unnecessarily.*

"Check his pulse Elroy. Is he breathing?" Sergio was sprawled across the bed. He was laying face-down across a half-packed suitcase. Perched on a side table, an electric fan was blowing at full speed. Alongside Sergio's head, the pages of a bound document rustled in the draft.

Elroy kept his weapon at the ready. Probing with his fingertips, he felt Sergio's neck. "He's got a pulse! It's weak though. Call an ambulance."

"Elroy, just look at that document. The crazy bastard had this whole sabotage planned down to the last damn detail."

"Call a goddamn ambulance," shouted Elroy, holstering his revolver. He preferred to carry his piece in the small of his back.

"He's a traitor Elroy. Just read the fucking document he prepared. It's all there."

Elroy was about to flip Sergio onto his back when he heard a small moan. "Sergio. Sergio! Hang in there dude, we're getting you an ambulance."

"El … Elroy," whispered Sergio.

"Stay with me dude … Sneddon, for Chrissake, call an ambulance."

Weak from blood loss, and barely able to move, Sergio beckoned with his index finger. Elroy leaned in close to listen. "I'm … I'm not Serpico," he whispered.

From somewhere behind him, Elroy heard Sneddon speak. "It's true Elroy. Apple heard wrong. Noriega said 'Serpico' … not 'Sergio.'" Elroy turned, confused by the transformation in Sneddon's tone. His boss's earlier bewilderment had been replaced with an edge of menace.

Sneddon's weapon was pointed directly at Elroy's chest.

Raising the captain's binoculars, Morozov focused on the locks ahead. A mirthless smile creased the corners of his mouth. *Now that is a good sight.* Somewhat fortuitously, a passenger ship had just entered the Miraflores Lake from the opposite direction. Revising his objective, he calculated the best maneuver that would position his deadly ship between the cruise liner and the far-off lock. All he needed to do was coordinate the *San Isidro's* speed with the time-delay on his visco fuses.

Swiveling his binoculars to the left bank, he saw that the terrain beyond the shore was thickly forested. *A perfect place to disappear for a while.*

Morozov bent down and unbuckled the captain's belt. Making a fine adjustment to the ship's wheel, he used the belt to fasten it in position. He then slid the throttle forward from *Dead Slow* to *Slow Ahead.* Morozov estimated his cargo would detonate in thirteen minutes.

Time was of the essence: the Russian sprinted off the bridge and headed toward the forward hatch where he'd initially gained access to the hold. He yanked the lid open and climbed down the ladder. Removing a lighter from his pocket, he thumbed the roller and touched the yellow flame to the end of the first fuse. Hissing like an angry adder, it started its inexorable journey toward obliteration. He lit the ends of the two remaining fuses.

Grabbing his carry bag, Morozov climbed to the deck. He quickly stripped off his shirt, shoes and socks and stuffed them into the bag. *Fuck it! No time to go back to the bridge for my Uzi.* He patted his pocket to check he still had his knife.

Shouldering the bag, Morozov leapt feet-first off the side of the ship. *Twelve minutes … I still have plenty of time.*

Flying only four hundred feet above the canal, something caught Dax's attention. He raised his binoculars and focused on the water below. *Holy crap, I was right!* A swimmer was striking out for the opposite bank. Judging by his distance from the ship—as well as his easy stroke—Dax reckoned the swimmer had probably been in the water for about a minute. He shouted into his microphone. "Phil … quickly, go around. Directly below us … there's something not right." As Phil banked hard to the left, Dax unclipped his harness and moved up to the front. "There it is," Dax tapped Phil's shoulder and pointed. "Go lower." He raised his binoculars. "This is bad news buddy. I can't see anyone at the bridge … wait! Shit Phil, there's a body lying on the deck. This is it! Alert Apple. And get me over that far bank. That's gotta be Morozov in the water."

"We're too low for you to jump Dax. I need to give you at least another two hundred feet," yelled Phil. As he applied power, Phil called Apple on their open frequency. They didn't have the luxury of trying to encode *this* message.

Eight hundred feet above the Bridge of the Americas, Colonel López was circling in his command chopper when his radio squawked into life. Repeating Phil's message almost word-for-word, Apple gave the colonel a concise description of both the *San Isidro,* as well as Dax's assessment of the situation. The colonel slapped his pilot's shoulder and pointed him toward the canal. The pilot lowered the Huey's nose and headed in the direction of the Miraflores Lake. López estimated they were four minutes away from their target.

Although Elroy's left hand was partially obscured from Sneddon's view, he knew it would be foolhardy to try and reach for his revolver. Instead, he stealthily fingered his phone and pressed the call-back button. It would automatically dial the last active number. In the US Embassy, just a few miles across town, Dollar's satellite phone began to ring. "What are you saying Sneddon? Are *you* Serpico?" Elroy's fate depended on someone hearing this conversation.

"I am."

Dollar answered the call.

"But why?" implored Elroy.

"When I saw the fortune Noriega and Escobar were making from trafficking, I thought I'd offer them some assistance in exchange for a slice of the action."

Dollar's face creased in a look of puzzlement. He suddenly grasped the enormity of what he was hearing. He waved frantically for Apple to come and listen.

"So you sold out your country for a few hundred thousand?" asked Elroy contemptuously.

"Millions, Elroy … millions." Sneddon held his aim on Elroy's chest.

A few minutes earlier, having just read the CIA's intercepted telephone transcript, Apple realized that she must've misheard the name 'Sergio' while hiding under Noriega's verandah. Desperate to warn Elroy, she must've tried his phone eight times already. She needed to warn him that 'Serpico' was clearly Escobar's code-name for Sneddon. As each frantic phone call went unanswered, Apple's anger at Sneddon multiplied. But the thought of his treachery paled against the looming realization that Elroy was in imminent danger.

Apple's sense of helplessness was making her frantic. She whispered to Dollar. "Keep listening. I've got to try and do something for Elroy." Dollar nodded. He was already pulling his cassette recorder from his top drawer.

Dax looked down; the swimmer was about fifty yards from the bank. It was obvious that Morozov intended using the heavily-wooded hillside to cover his escape. Dax glanced back at the altimeter. *Four hundred and fifty feet … it'll have to do.* With his hand on the ripcord, he launched himself out of the back of the CASA.

As the *San Isidro* came into view, López was confident that it fit the description given to him by the female CIA agent. Just then, on the upper limit of his peripheral vision, something caught the colonel's eye. Beneath the American spotter plane, a drab-green parachute had just popped open. His only thought was that he hoped it wasn't the pilot.

Seven minutes had elapsed since Morozov had lit the first fuse. Unaware of the pending calamity, López indicated to his pilot to hover above the deck. Using hand signals only, he prepared his six-man assault team for a fast-rope descent onto the deck. While López and three others descended, the men aboard the chopper provided them with cover. As soon as the first four were down safely, the three remaining soldiers descended to the deck. Just as they boarded the *San Isidro*, the captain of the approaching cruise liner blew a deafening warning on his foghorn. He'd just noticed that the cargo vessel was maintaining a dangerous line across his bow.

Operating in two-man teams, the soldiers split up and started a systematic search of the ship. López assigned himself to the team responsible for the bridge. After executing a precise entry onto the bridge, the colonel and his two men surveyed the carnage. The master and his chief mate lay in a puddle of dark blood. López noticed the belt around the wheel. "Corporal, take control of this vessel and get us out of the way of that fucking ship." The cruise liner blew its foghorn for the second time.

Right at that moment, the colonel was gripped by a devastating thought.

Running down the corridor of the embassy, Apple was fighting to control her panic. Elroy was in mortal danger. *Think Apple, think.* An idea came to her. *Surely there's a valet down in the basement car park.* She bounded down the stairs.

Turning the last corner, she almost collided into the back of a man going in the same direction. He turned to see who was in such a hurry. "Miss Apple, is everything alright?" It was Sergeant Joel, the Marine who'd escorted her up to Dollar's office a few hours earlier. He'd changed out of his uniform.

"Sergeant Joel. Thank God! Please. I need your help. My boss is in mortal danger. Do you know where the *Amistoso Cabañas* are?"

"I do, Miss Apple. It's a favorite amongst your CIA colleagues."

"Can you take me there?"

Morozov knew he was close: he'd just scooped-up a handful of oily sediment from the bed of the canal. Looking up, he saw he was about fifteen yards from the bank. Staying low in the water, he waded awkwardly through the sticky morass.

Whump, whump, whump.

Behind him, the Huey's distinctive throb made him turn. *Cyka, blyat!* Morozov spat in anger and watched as four armed soldiers roped down onto the deck of the *San Isidro*. They were quickly followed by three others. He checked his watch. *Six minutes before detonation. Fuck! Maybe they won't find the explosives in time.*

Once out of the water, Morozov slipped across the small service road that paralleled the canal. Hiding behind a large tree, he removed the clothing from his bag and swiftly wrung-out his wet socks and shirt. It was now obvious: *You're a hunted man, Vladimir Morozov. You need to disappear for a few days.* In that moment he realized that the densely-forested hills behind him were his only source of refuge.

A short distance ahead, just beyond the rise, a lone parachutist descended into a clearing. No one saw him land.

Elroy had no way of knowing whether Dollar had answered his phone, let alone hear the conversation between Sneddon and himself. If there was any way of surviving this predicament, it lay in the hands of whoever was listening.

Straight after Apple left his office, Dollar had called a junior colleague at the CIA's offices in Panama City. He'd quickly described Sneddon's deception. Since the man was one of Sneddon's subordinates, it had taken some convincing to get him to agree to go to the *Amistoso Cabañas* to apprehend his boss.

Like two humanoids, the electronic devices sitting on Dollar's desk appeared to be engaged in an earnest conversation: the cassette recorder was listening intently to the satellite phone.

"But why the canal? Why a bomb?" asked Elroy. He knew he had to try and keep Sneddon talking.

"Because Elroy, I am the puppet-master. I engineer situations that sow the seeds of fear and confusion ... they offer opportunities. What better way for America to be able to come into Panama and assert its authority?"

"But why did you get Morozov to do your dirty work?"

"He's an expendable accessory ... he'll be seen as nothing more than a known rogue agent who committed a vile act in an attempt to earn redemption from his KGB paymasters. Besides, he was more than willing to do my bidding in exchange for Dax's whereabouts."

"Oh. So he's expendable too?"

"Of course he is Elroy. Just like you."

"You're going to need more evidence than just that document, and your word, to make this accusation of treachery stick against Sergio."

"C'mon Elroy, you're smarter than that. I've got two weapons here, one of which I'll plant in Sergio's hand; we've got a lunatic Russian willing to do his bidding, his psychoses are even documented in our own files; I've got Apple's word that she overheard Noriega mention Sergio's name this morning; I've got Sergio's document over there, and finally, I've got a great big self-inflicted gash on my forehead. I've got all the loose ends tied up."

"Except ... me?"

"Yes, except you. But, as I'll explain to the Board of Enquiry, you and I confronted Sergio over his treachery, he pulled his gun and shot you, I then managed to draw my own weapon and shoot him. I'll then simply stage this crime scene accordingly. Tragic that an innocent man had to die in the line of duty, but at least the CIA found their dirty mole before he could offer his services to the Soviets as well. Heck, I might even receive that promotion," Sneddon gloated.

"Why the fuck did you bring me back from Africa, Sneddon?"

"You want to know why? Because I still have a good future ahead of me in the CIA. Heck, maybe even in government one day. As any good manager will tell you Elroy, you gotta have a succession plan. I was going to groom you for my position."

Intuiting the madman's motive, it had just occurred to Colonel López that Morozov wouldn't be satisfied with a mere collision in the canal. *No! Fuck it! The cargo hold.*

Careful not to slip on the bloody floor, the colonel rushed off the bridge, descended the stairs and sprinted across the deck. Approaching the manhole hatch, he could see that it was open. There was no time to bring the chopper in to airlift his men out of harm's way. "Abandon ship. Now! She's going to blow," he yelled at his second-in-command. "Everyone off," he ordered. "Swim for your lives!"

Sliding down the ladder, López disappeared from view. Moving from the bright sunshine to the dimly-lit hold, it took a few moments before his eyes adjusted. Even if he'd looked down, he might not have seen the telltale trail of ash left by the burning fuses.

The moment he saw it, López's worst fears were confirmed: he'd just spotted the first drum of ANFO—high explosive ammonium nitrate fuel oil. *At least I won't suffer when it blows.* In the stale confines of the cargo hold, López detected a familiar whiff: the acrid tinge of burning cordite. His eyes immediately fell to the floor. *The ash trail. I must find the ash trail.*

Fighting his every instinct, López forced himself to focus. Moving hastily between the rows of drums, he spotted the evidence he so desperately sought. "Fucking hell! There are three," he yelled out in frustration. He chose one at random and followed it. It took him almost twenty seconds to locate the charge. He pulled the blasting cap out of the C-4. It was a hollow victory. He couldn't help notice that there wasn't much more than sixty seconds left on the fuse. He also knew it was foolhardy to believe that each fuse was the same length, had been lit simultaneously, and burnt at exactly the same speed. *Too many fucking variables.* He rushed back to trace the second line of ash. Although López's heart rate was hammering above 140, he forced himself to concentrate. He found the second charge. The end of the burning fuse was barely inches away from the C-4.

López's neck and shoulder muscles were rigid with dread. He braced himself for the inevitable fireball.

Sergeant Joel's tires shrieked as he veered into the driveway of the *Amistoso Cabañas.* Even before the car had come to a complete stop, Apple flung her door wide open. On the far side of the guests' car park, a slightly overweight, balding male Caucasian was climbing into his rental. "Sneddon!" Apple shouted. He looked up, startled, then threw himself behind the wheel.

Because Apple was CIA, she hadn't been subjected to the mandatory search at the embassy earlier that morning. She still had Sanchez's semi-automatic.

With his tires spinning angrily, Sneddon gunned the motor and pointed his car at the exit. Apple was standing directly in his path. With the car fishtailing toward her, she drew the weapon, thumbed the safety and took aim. For the second time in five hours, the words of one of her instructors echoed through her mind. *Aim low at the windshield. The rounds deflect upwards as they penetrate the glass.*

Apple waited until he was within eighteen yards. "Sneddon, stop!" Against her instinct, she aimed at the wiper blades. The car was accelerating.

Fifteen yards.

"Apple, get out the way!" But her body's physiological

response to stress had muted Sergeant Joel's desperate appeal.

Twelve yards.

In quick succession, Apple fired four rounds. The car maintained its headlong rush. "Apple!" yelled Joel.

She dived headlong into the flower bed. Her only hope was that her aim was true. The car thundered past the point where she'd been standing less than a second before. On the far side of the motel's drop-off area, the runaway car slammed into the back of a stationary delivery vehicle.

Approaching on a wide arc, her weapon at the ready, Apple moved toward the driver's door. Steam was hissing from beneath the crumpled hood. Sneddon was slumped forward in his seat. Cautiously opening the driver's door, she used her free hand to pull him off the steering wheel. He flopped back into his seat. She counted three holes in his neck and head.

"Elroy!" she shouted.

López felt lightheaded; it was as if he'd crossed-over into an altered state. Time seemed to have warped and folded. Although he felt a strange detachment, every fiber of his existence tingled with an ageless wisdom. He felt neither vulnerable nor invincible, yet was wholly attuned to his corporeal surrounds. He followed the third ash trail as if buoyed on a cushion of helium. It led him right to the charge. With detached curiosity, he noticed that the fuse had less than half-an-inch to burn. With deliberate dexterity—but somehow disconnected from his senses—he reached for the pyrotechnic blasting cap. He pulled the device from the C-4 like a lover might pluck a petal.

Barely inches away from its deadly host, the blasting cap detonated in López's grip. He didn't even feel it amputate the tip of his index finger.

As he climbed back up the ladder, a dark shadow appeared overhead. López looked up, startled. A hand reached down to him. "Colonel, let me help you up." It was his second-in-command. The other five members of his assault team were standing close behind.

64

THE TITANS

Suspended beneath the vast nylon canopy, Dax floated gently toward the earth. Twisting about in his harness, he frantically scanned the forest below for a sign of the Russian. In the last few moments before descending below the tree line, he caught a brief glimpse of him near the edge of the canal. He was crouching behind a large tree no more than a hundred-and-fifty yards from where Dax was about to land. It was obvious that Morozov was trying to conceal himself from casual observation. It appeared as if he was tying his bootlaces.

The ground was fast approaching. Tucking and rolling, Dax executed a text-book landing. He stood up, unfastened his buckles and stepped out of the harness. Working quickly, he bundled the billowing parachute, moved to the edge of the clearing and stashed his rig under a bush.

With thick foliage all around, Dax's only means of orientation was the slope of the ground. Moving stealthily, he headed down the hill in the general direction of where he'd last seen Morozov. With much of the hillside covered by equatorial vegetation, a carpet of decaying leaf matter made it treacherous underfoot.

Dax regretted not having a firearm. He felt for the knife in his pocket. He pulled it out and flipped the blade. A familiar tightness gripped the pit of his stomach: the same raw, visceral sensation he experienced whenever he flew his gunship into battle. His every nerve, his every fiber, was strung like a circus high wire.

Eager to put distance between himself and the *San Isidro*, Morozov started moving cautiously up the hill. Erring on the side of caution, he too held his knife at the ready.

Dax was barely twenty paces into the forest when he noticed that it had closed-in around him. It was rank with the odor of decaying vegetation. Like ghostly prisms, only the most tenacious shafts of sunlight were capable of piercing the dense canopy. An eerie stillness hung between the audience of ancient trees. Ahead of him, Dax heard a twig snap. He froze. Moving only his eyeballs, he scanned his surrounds.

Like an old photographer's image slowly morphing from within its bath of chemicals, so a vaporous shape began to emerge from its tangled background. Dax could see how Morozov's coating of dried silt had helped camouflage his presence. Although Dax remained unseen, Morozov's feral instincts were crackling with expectation. He too was somehow aware of an imminent threat. With knife in hand, he stood poised.

This moment had been fated. Dax knew that he and Morozov had now reached their time of reckoning. He stepped into plain view.

Morozov looked unstartled. "Dax Hunter. I've waited three years for this day."

Like two mythical titans, the men began to circle. Both were certain of two things: there was only space on the podium for one victor; the fate of the vanquished had already been ordained by the gods. From a safe distance, Morozov tore off his shirt. With eyes fixed on his opponent, he slowly wrapped the garment around his left forearm and wrist.

From his stance alone, Dax could tell that Morozov was a boxer; an orthodox right-hander. With both hands raised to protect his torso, neck and face, Morozov held his knife in his right hand. The blade protruded from the underside of his grip.

Nimrod had been one of Dax's father's trusty foremen. With an insatiable libido, he was forever incurring the wrath of some-or-other jealous boyfriend in their farming district. For the sake of his own survival, he'd had to learn how to defend himself. A knife, he professed, was his weapon of choice. He'd offered to show young Dax a few of his techniques. Back then, it was just good clean fun.

It was now a matter of life and death.

Nimrod's first lesson was that it was pointless keeping the knife in your right hand if you were going to negate your reach by adopting an orthodox stance. Adopting a southpaw stance, with the knife in his right hand, Nimrod had demonstrated how easy it was to gain a few extra inches of reach. *Lesson Number One.*

Checking Morozov's grip, Dax was reminded of Nimrod's next bit of knife-fighting advice. *Never hold the weapon in an underside grip. You want to hold it so that you bring the tip of the blade as close to your opponent as possible. Stance and grip ... stance and grip.*

Morozov lunged at Dax. Leading with the right hand, he made as if to punch his opponent on the jaw. Just at the point of furthest reach, he flicked his wrist up to bring the blade into play. Dax swayed back. Scything upwards, the tip of Morozov's blade nicked Dax's chin.

In the quarter-second it took Morozov to bring his arm back into a defensive position, Dax struck at his retreating hand. Steel thrilled as the two blades connected. "Come on Hunter, at least make this a challenge for me," goaded the Russian. They continued to circle, each waiting for an opportunity to strike. Dax's foot snagged a protruding root. Although he barely stumbled, Morozov struck like a cobra. With his left arm bound-up in the shirt and his right arm raised above his head, he rushed at Dax.

Crossing his wrists to form a V, Dax raised his arms to meet the blade's descending arc. As they made contact, he swiveled his left hand inwards and used his fingers to lock Morozov's wrist within the wedge. Instead of trying to match him with an immovable force, Hunter used his attacker's momentum to his own advantage. While being driven backwards, he bent his knees and started pulling Morozov downwards on top of himself. Just before his buttocks hit the ground, Dax raised his right leg and placed his boot in his opponent's solar plexus. With leg bent and spine curled, he dropped to the ground. By harnessing the Russian's impetus, he was able to maintain their combined rotational movement. With explosive force, Dax straightened his leg at the top of the arc. Morozov flailed as he was launched into the air. Beyond Dax's head, the Russian landed hard on his back. Not only was he surprised by the speed and agility of his opponent, but he was winded too. They both scrambled to their feet.

With his weapon firmly gripped in his right hand, Dax instinctively raised his arms to protect his head and throat. Upon adopting his defensive pose, he immediately noticed that Morozov's knife had opened a neat slice on his forearm. It was already starting to bleed.

At that moment, Nimrod's third lesson sprung to mind. *Don't obsess over trying to deliver the killer thrust. Be patient. Work inwards from the extremities. Your opponent won't like seeing their own blood dripping from their hands and arms.* Dax had to subdue a worrying thought: the Russian had already struck twice.

In the steamy confines of their gladiatorial ring, the humid air was making both of them sweat. Bringing his swaddled arm up to his face, Morozov wiped away his perspiration. As he mopped the mud and sweat, he exposed the angry cicatrix that fouled the left side of his face. With uncanny intellection, he read Dax's thoughts. "Yes Hunter. This was caused by you." They continued to circle warily. "On the banks of the Zambezi River, before I shot you down … you did this to me. And today … today, Hunter, you will pay."

Like a parable from beyond the grave, Dax recalled Nimrod's fourth maxim. *Let your opponent do all the talking. Keep quiet. Focus on staying alive.*

Ignoring the ominous warning, Dax lunged at the Russian. Starting high to the right, he slashed diagonally downwards.

Advancing aggressively into Morozov's defensive space, he forced him onto his back foot. While streaking downward, Dax sensed that the tip of his blade had encountered some resistance; he hoped he'd sliced through the swaddling on Morozov's arm. Dax's lunge had forced the Russian to retreat a step. Recovering at the bottom of his arc, he flipped his wrist and slashed upward in a reverse fashion. In under a second, he'd inflicted two cuts on Morozov's forearm. *Get in, get out!* It was as if Nimrod was coaching him from ringside. Dax parried before Morozov could retaliate.

Taking-up a defensive stance, the Russian raised his arms to the side of his head. Whether he was aware of it or not, Morozov appeared to ignore the blood that had started to soak through his protective wrap. Emitting a wild snarl, he launched a counterstrike at Dax.

Slashing horizontally, he tried to eviscerate his foe. Dax stepped back instinctively. His heel connected with the base of a tree. He knew what would happen if he allowed himself to get pinned. Without his balance, it would be impossible to meet Morozov's onslaught with an effective counterattack. With his opponent still hacking wildly, Dax had only one option: if he could shift position at the precise moment that the Russian completed one swipe, he might be able to escape the lethal reverse slash. Morozov was close to breaking through the arc of Dax's defensive sweep. The Rhodesian had to make his move: if not, his belly would be sliced open.

Swiveling to the side, Dax barely eluded the mortal stroke. Had he connected, Morozov would have spilled Dax's glistening innards onto the forest floor. But as he spun around the side of the tree, Dax felt the cold tug of tempered steel as it sliced into his hip.

It wasn't painful … yet. But he knew it was deep.

Unbalanced by the evasive maneuver, Dax stumbled and fell to the ground. Just before rolling back to his feet, he scooped-up a handful of dirt in his left hand. Morozov hadn't noticed.

"I'm tired of playing now, Hunter." There was no

disguising his intent.

Although Dax knew there was no artery in the vicinity of his cut, he still had to fight the urge to look down. *Stay focused, Hunter.* He could feel the warm blood oozing into his trousers. The gash was starting to sting.

"I'm going to carve you into small pieces Hunter. But I'll make sure you're still alive when I push your testicles into your eye sockets." Morozov was already starting to savor his prize. As he circled around the tree, the Russian began to toss his knife from one hand to the other.

Never become cocky during a fight. Nimrod's Lesson Number Five.

Dax launched himself at his foe. As he did so, he flung the handful of dirt at Morozov's face: it was a perfect distraction.

The Russian was a natural right-hander; not only was he momentarily blinded, but he found himself with his knife in his left hand. Blinking the dirt from his eyes, Morozov was unaware that Dax had nimbly stepped to his unprotected side. Just as Morozov recovered his situational awareness, a fist crashed into his right temple.

Dax was a rugby player. It's a hard game. If called upon, he could give as good as he got. He knew that a lesser man would've buckled under that blow. Bellowing with rage, the Russian shook himself like a wet mastiff. He then launched himself at Dax. There was no time to land a second shot. In that moment it was apparent that Morozov was intent on taking him to ground. He clearly fancied his chances in a grapple.

The Prince Edward First XV had a reputation of being a formidable schoolboy rugby side. Throughout his high school years, Dax had benefitted from a string of fine coaches. There was one skill he'd never forgotten: how to tackle a ball carrier, bring him to ground in a favorable position, and present one's teammates with the opportunity to plunder the ball from his grip. It all depended on how you twisted him in mid-air.

Dax wasn't after a ball. And neither did he have any teammates to help him. But what he did want was to tackle Morozov and drop him onto his left side: the side that was holding the knife.

Anticipating the impact, Dax rolled smoothly into the Russian's headlong charge. With his arms wrapped around his enemy's upper body, he twisted aggressively and altered the plane of Morozov's trajectory. To avoid having his own arm pinned beneath the heavyset man, Dax was already withdrawing it before they crashed to the ground.

As he stood up from the tackle, Dax unleashed a powerful right into Morozov's exposed jaw. It was only then that he realized that his knife had become dislodged in the mêlée. *No, fuck!*

Lying on the ground, Morozov was acutely aware of the danger of leaving his face and jaw exposed. But in that instant, he also realized that Hunter must've lost his knife … why else would he have unleashed a vicious right instead of stabbing him in the throat?

Rather than protect himself with his free arm, Morozov chose instead to hunch his shoulders to limit the size of target. At that moment, he also realized that his right hand could serve a far better purpose—seek out and retrieve the knife that was still pinned in his left hand.

As he'd expected, Dax's fist smacked down onto his exposed cheekbone. The Russian felt the bone disintegrate beneath the blow. But it was a small sacrifice to make in order to reclaim his weapon. Unbeknownst to Dax, Morozov had managed to reach around with his free hand to retrieve his knife.

The Russian lunged. He dug his blade into Dax's calf muscle and viciously pulled him to the ground. A white-hot bolt of pain detonated in Dax's head. He screamed out in agony. Without releasing his grip, the Russian sprung to his feet. Dropping down on Dax's chest, he pinned him to the wet earth. While Morozov's left hand groped for his opponent's throat, he tried to wriggle the knife free from Dax's calf. But it wouldn't slide out; the blade appeared to be anchored. The serrations across the top of Morozov's blade had bitten into the bone. Grunting in frustration, he pulled even harder on the handle. Despite his efforts, he couldn't dislodge the knife.

The pain was intolerable. Dax could feel Morozov's fingers closing around his windpipe. It was only a matter of time. He was certain he was about to lose consciousness. *So is this how it all ends, Dax?*

The pilot knew he was slipping. A translucent veil started swirling across his vision. Soothing voices beckoned. They'd come to fetch him; to rescue him from his nightmare. He sensed they were close. His vision began to swim. Dax's fingers clawed feebly as he tried to reach toward his calf. *Stop it, please.* Morozov was still hacking on his knife handle. The torment was unbearable.

This is not how it ends son. Somewhere beyond the throes of misery, Dax heard his mother's voice.

As he gasped and spluttered for air, a strange euphoria descended: the pain began to fracture and dissolve. Out on the edge of his fading reality, Dax was beginning to ebb.

What is this? His hand had just brushed against something hard.

Take it Dax, take it.

His fingers scrabbled frantically through the leaf litter.

Suspended in a place without dimension, Dax slowly began to recalibrate. *It's the knife.*

Yes, it's the knife.

He fumbled for the weapon. The handle was slick from the decaying leaf matter. Making sure he had a firm grip, he anchored his thumb over the back of the handle.

Summoning his very last reserve, Dax thrust the blade into Morozov's torso. The Russian grunted as the tip sliced between his ribs. Mustering one last effort, he plunged it all the way to the hilt.

Dax was spent. He rolled the Russian off his chest. Even the fetid jungle air tasted sweet as he filled his exhausted lungs. Several minutes passed before Dax attempted to stand. Although the knife still protruded from his lower leg, the signals to his brain appeared to have been hijacked. He'd lost all sensation. He looked down dispassionately at Morozov. Not even the malevolent Russian could trigger any hatred.

From nowhere, a hand clasped Dax's shoulder. It was as if he'd been woken from a dreadful nightmare. Recoiling in fear, he let out an anguished cry. "Easy my friend, easy," said a calming voice.

Dax turned and looked blankly at the soldier. His eyes dropped to the badge sewn on the man's chest. *López.*

Spread-eagled on the ground, Morozov tried to shift his left arm. He grimaced from the pain. Slowly, agonizingly, he reached down. An explosion of light seared the back of his eyeballs. *What is happening? What is this jutting from my chest?* As his fingers brushed against the hard object, Morozov could feel the slickness of his own warm blood. His face contorted.

Even in the gray space between life and death, Morozov knew he had to fight the gathering darkness. He raised his head feebly and tried to identify the cause of his crushing pain. Just beneath his left nipple, he saw the handle of a knife protruding from his ribs. The Russian's vision was starting to dissolve; he had to force himself to concentrate.

A single shaft of light pierced through the overhead foliage. With a celestial glow illuminating the forest floor, Morozov noticed a neatly-etched inscription in the handle of the knife. Four letters drifted slowly into focus: *V I U M.*

The Russian inhaled sharply. The effort made him wince. "It's my own fucking knife," he whispered disbelievingly. His head collapsed onto the dirt.

Everything faded.

To be continued …

TRIBUTE

ANZAC Day Prayer
25th April, 2017

While fighting against the Ottoman Empire during World War I, thousands of ANZAC (Australian and New Zealand Army Corps) soldiers gave their lives in the Gallipoli Campaign. In remembrance of all those who have served, ANZAC Day is observed in both Australia and New Zealand on the 25th April each year.

A significant number of ex-Rhodesian servicemen and women have adopted Australia and New Zealand as their new homes. In commemoration of fallen comrades, Dave Hodgson read the following prayer at the ANZAC Day parade in Brisbane, Australia on 25th April 2017. He is a veteran of the Rhodesian Bush War.

Our Heavenly Father

We are assembled here before You today as Veterans of the Rhodesian Armed Forces: that is the Rhodesian Light Infantry, C Squadron Rhodesian SAS, the Selous Scouts, The Grey Scouts, The Rhodesia Regiment, Rhodesian African Rifles, The Rhodesian Air Force, BSAP, PATU, INTAF, and other units, along with our families and loved ones.

We are here to remember those of our comrades, the manne, *the* ouens, *the* shamwaris, *our* chinas, *(†) both men and women, who were killed in the Rhodesian war, and also those members who have since died directly or indirectly from the traumas of that war.*

We also remember the wives, fiancés, girlfriends, children, families and friends of those who were killed in action. We empathize with their pain and their anguish, even after all these years, and decades. And even after the century rolled over, and on into a new millennium, we still remember all of them.

As we look back now from a different vantage point, we recognize that despite the macro-politics of self-centered world powers that forced Rhodesia into submission, these lives were not lost in vain, but were sacrificed in the pursuit of what we still hold dear—that is freedom, righteousness, and prosperity for all. A 'fair-go' as it is called here.

And although these incredible military units are long disbanded, and Rhodesia the country is fading into history, that same battle continues on today in a Zimbabwe ravaged by despotic dictatorship, overt corruption, rampant incompetence, desperate poverty, starvation, and human misery.

Despite world opinion on the day, it is this corruption and human misery that we fought against and fought to prevent, under the proud ensigns of the Rhodesian Armed Forces.

We have now adopted new countries and many of us have become citizens and sworn to defend these nations. Therefore, this means the battle for freedom, righteousness, and universal prosperity continues on in our adopted lands, but in a different format.

Lord in Heaven, let us not be deceived as the corruption and unrighteousness prevails here in these adopted lands, albeit more sophisticated and covert. There is homelessness, sex slavery, domestic violence, substance abuse, massive suicide—the biggest killer of men aged 17 to 45 in Australia today, and all manner of human misery which will trash this land just as thoroughly as Zimbabwe has been trashed, if we do not continue the battle.

Therefore Lord, in memory of those members killed, we still uphold the same values that we fought and died for in Rhodesia.

As the memory of Rhodesia the Country fades with aging and passing of Rhodesians themselves, the legacy of the Rhodesian Armed Forces lives on and continues to gather legendary status in the magazines, journals, and annuls of the military around the whole world. The formidable task of defending a nation against insuperable odds, of fighting a war day after day which was nearly 3 times as long as World War II, and of physically winning this war on the ground, has set a standard in military excellence.

Almighty God, we are not here to glorify war, but to honor the lives and the achievements of those who died defending the standards and principles that are Your will in the Earth, and doing so with innovation, excellence, devotion and courage, and against all odds.

And today, 37 years later, we stand together and we acknowledge that WE WILL NEVER FORGET THEM.

Sir Francis Drake, was the son of an ex-mariner & poor Protestant lay preacher. He became the greatest mariner of his day, a Vice Admiral in the English Navy, and the first man to captain a circumnavigation of the globe. Evidently he also had a real faith which he expressed in a powerful poetic prayer to challenge us all here today.

Disturb us, O Lord,
when we are too well pleased with ourselves;
when our dreams have become true because we have dreamed too little,
when we arrived safely because we sailed too close to the shore.

Disturb us, O Lord,
when with the abundance of things we possess, we have lost our thirst

for the Waters of Life;
and having fallen in love with life, we have ceased to dream of eternity;
and in our efforts to build a new earth, we have allowed our vision of the new heaven to dim.

Disturb us, O Lord
to dare more boldly, to venture on wider seas, where storms will show Your mastery; where losing sight of land, we shall find stars.

We ask you to push back the horizon of our hopes, and to push us into the future with strength, courage, hope and love.

Amen

Dave Hodgson served with C Sqn. Rhodesian SAS and the Selous Scouts

(†) Manne, ouens, shamwaris and chinas: In the colorful lexicon of Rhodesian slang, they are used interchangeably to refer to either friends or brothers-in-arms.

ACKNOWLEDGMENTS

Several years ago my best friend and I were locked in a manly version of a playground squabble. And what caused this little contretemps? It was an argument over which author had created the best name for a fictional hero. Fleming's James Bond; Child's Jack Reacher; Hemmingway's Santiago in *The Old Man and the Sea*—from classic to contemporary, and everything between—the debate raged. But we reached a stalemate. To break the impasse he suggested we each create our own hero's name, the best of which would settle the dispute. Ian Trethowan, thank you for letting me use your undisputed winner—Dax Hunter—as the book's central character.

Several friends make cameos throughout the book: in some instances their eponymously-named characters bear uncanny resemblances to their real-life exploits. In no particular order, my thanks to Phil Holloway, Nick Fergus, Max McLean, Beaver Shaw, Barry Roberts, Bruce Spargo, John Kidson, Craig Bone, Tomi Poikolainen, Fedor Scholvinck, Paul McIlroy and the Blarney Brothers, Sonny Janeke, Mark Rowland, Rhett Thompson, Steve Gray, Ash Flinders, Greg Vogt, James Denton, Ian Harries, Nova Nicolson, Fiona Swart, Ian Durand, Joel Hinz, Allan Johnston, Greg Harrison, Rynier Keet and Mike Ortiz.

In an earlier cooperative venture, renowned artist Craig Bone once lamented that all it took from me was a snap of the finger to get him scurrying to his easel. While I might attempt to defend myself against his exaggerations, I am left wondering whether our latest collaboration might just add a bit of credence to his lament. With typical generosity, he not only agreed to let me use one of his fine paintings for the cover of this book, but also corralled the assistance of his daughter, Maxine Killian, to assist with the design. My thanks go to you both.

I recall with fondness the no-nonsense approach of my childhood swimming instructor, Frank Parrington. As a young man he'd coached his future wife, Lillian, to two Olympic Games. Following in their footsteps, son Dave went on to become an Olympian himself when he represented Zimbabwe at diving in the 1980 Games in Moscow. He has gone on to coach a multitude of divers at the highest level. Dave, you're a true Olympian. Thank you for sharing some of your insights to Zimbabwe's participation in the Moscow Games.

To Phil Holloway, Bruce Spargo and Nick Fergus, my thanks for all your advice and feedback, especially on matters technical.

My thanks to Dave Hodgson for allowing me to include the prayer he delivered at the ANZAC day memorial on 25th April 2017 in Brisbane, Australia.

Whether it was her suggestions, critiques, ideas or support, my wife Cathy was an invaluable collaborator throughout this project. I am truly grateful for your unwavering help and encouragement.

GA
California, USA
September 2017

ABOUT THE AUTHOR

Gary Albyn has authored and ghost-written a number of books. He also puts his engineering background to good use as a professional technical writer. Originally from Rhodesia—Zimbabwe today—Albyn is an avid traveler and adventurer whose life has encompassed many divergent interests, careers and experiences. His life-long passion for aviation started as a trainee pilot with the Rhodesian Air Force in the late 70s. Besides delighting in rotary flight, Albyn has held board-level positions in the corporate arena; worked as a civilian coalition contractor in the Second Gulf War; consulted with TV documentary crews on two continents; presented internationally on conservation matters; and spent over three years as the senior instructor at one of the world's foremost bodyguard academies in Cape Town, South Africa. As evidenced in *Manzovo*—his first acclaimed title—Albyn is also passionate about wildlife conservation. He lives with his wife Cathy in California, USA.

12564361R00252

Printed in Great Britain
by Amazon